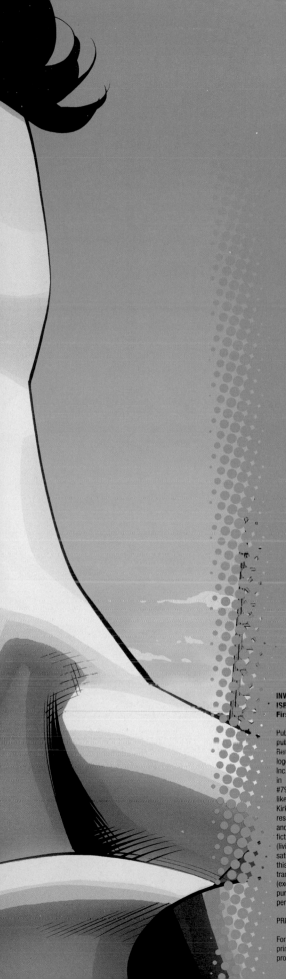

writer
ROB N

D1086394

RYAN OTTLEY

inker
CLIFF RATHBURN
RYAN OTTLEY
(chapter 5, pgs 1-7)

colorist
NIKOS KOUTSIS
(chapters 1-3)
JOHN RAUCH
(chapters 4-6)

color assistant
MIKE TORIS (chapters 1-3)

letterer
RUS WOOTON

editor
SINA GRACE

cover
RYAN OTTLEY
& JOHN RAUCH

INVINCIBLE, VOL. 15: GET SMART
ISBN: 978-1-60706-367-4
First Printing

Published by Image Comics, Inc. Office of publication: 2134 Allston Way, 2nd Floor, Berkeley, California 94704.

PRINTED IN U.S.A.

For information regarding the CPSIA on this printed material call: 203-595-3636 and provide reference # EAST – 420267

SKYBOUND ENTERTAINMENT
www.skybound.com

Robert Kirkman - *CEO*
J.J. Didde - *President*
Sina Grace - *Editorial Director*
Shawn Kirkham - *Director of Business Development*
Tim Daniel - *Digital Content Manager*
Chad Manion - *Assistant to Mr. Grace*
Sydney Pennington - *Assistant to Mr. Kirkham*
Feldman Public Relations LA - *Public Relations*

For international rights inquiries, please contact: sk@skybound.com

IMAGE COMICS, INC.
www.imagecomics.com

Robert Kirkman - *Chief Operating Officer*
Erik Larsen - *Chief Financial Officer*
Todd McFarlane - *President*
Marc Silvestri - *CEO*
Jim Valentino - *Vice-President*

Eric Stephenson - *Publisher*
Todd Martinez - *Sales & Licensing Coordinator*
Sarah deLaine - *PR & Marketing Coordinator*
Branwyn Bigglestone - *Accounts Manager*
Emily Miller - *Administrative Assistant*
Jamie Parreno - *Marketing Assistant*
Kevin Yuen - *Digital Rights Coordinator*
Tyler Shainline - *Traffic Manager*
Drew Gill - *Art Director*
Jonathan Chan - *Senior Production Artist*
Monica Howard - *Production Artist*
Vincent Kukua - *Production Artist*
Jana Cook - *Production Artist*

CHAPTER ONE

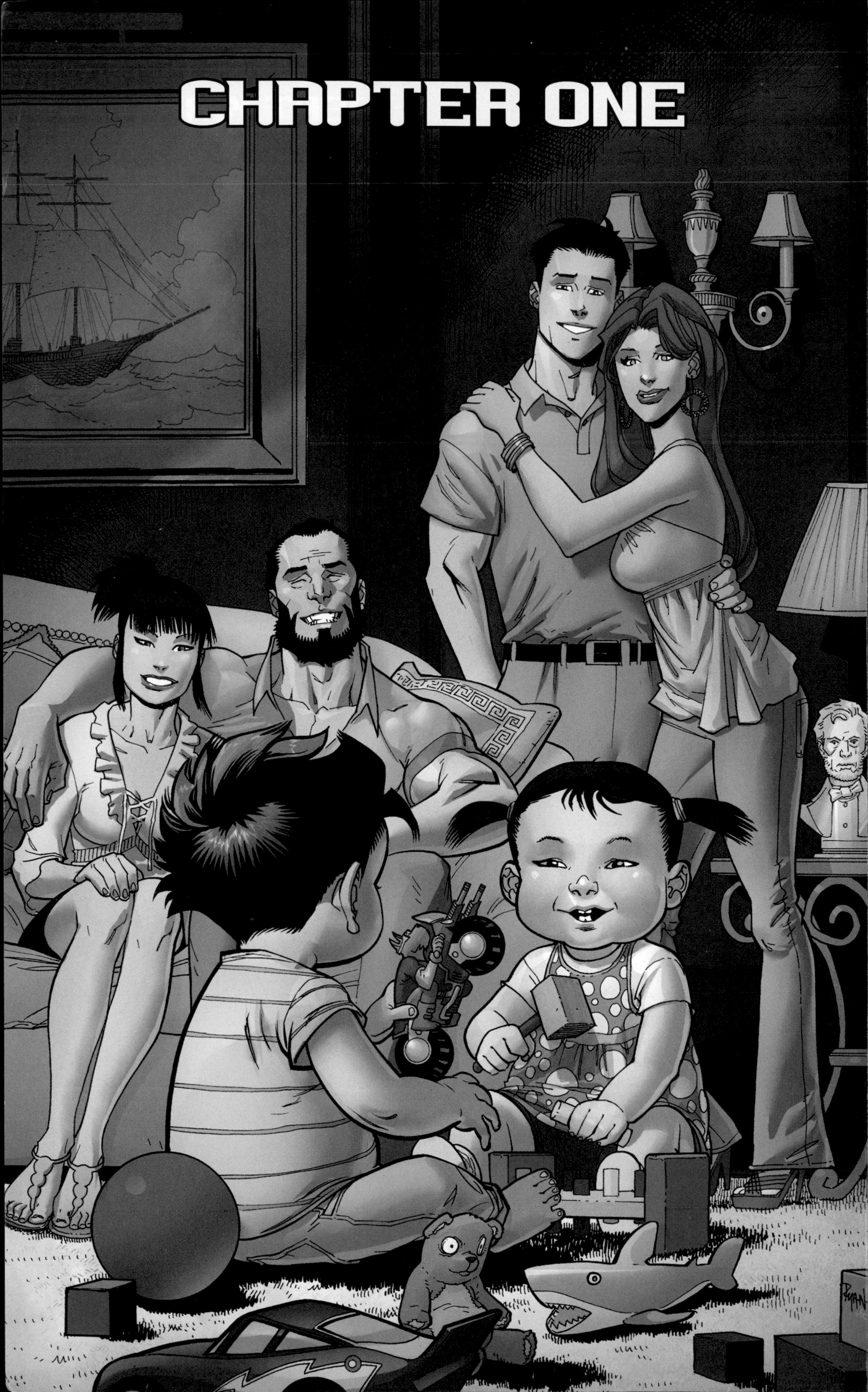

image® COMICS PRESENTS

INVINCIBLE ™

GET SMART

CREATED BY

ROBERT KIRKMAN
& CORY WALKER

image®

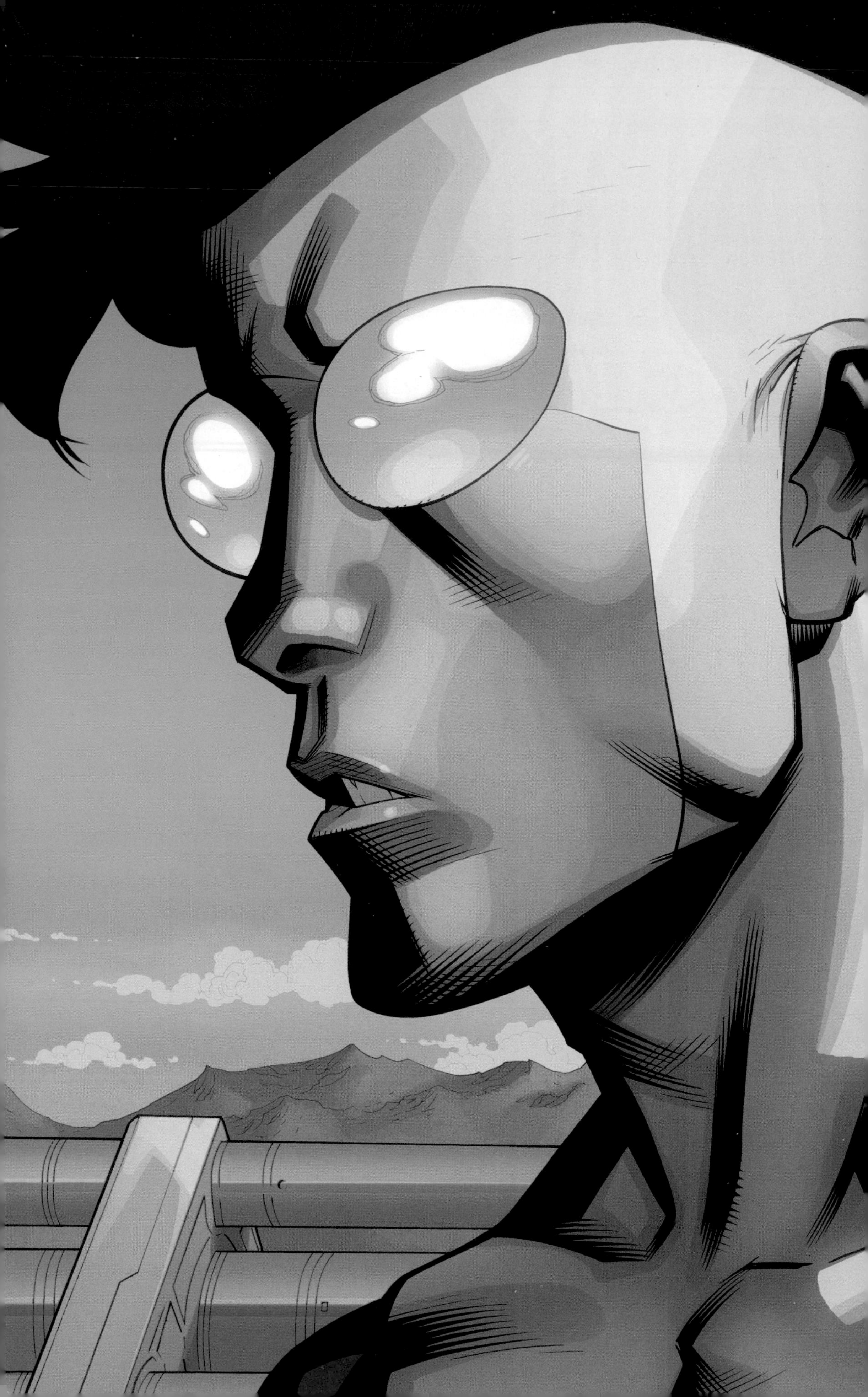

MARK! YOU'RE BACK!

YEP. SURE AM.

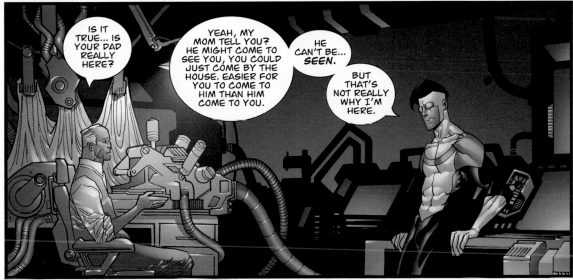

IS IT TRUE... IS YOUR DAD REALLY HERE?

YEAH, MY MOM TELL YOU? HE MIGHT COME TO SEE YOU, YOU COULD JUST COME BY THE HOUSE. EASIER FOR YOU TO COME TO HIM THAN HIM COME TO YOU.

HE CAN'T BE... SEEN.

BUT THAT'S NOT REALLY WHY I'M HERE.

OH, SURE... UH... WHAT CAN I DO FOR YOU?

I KNOW YOU'RE CREATIVE... AND YOU LIKE TO TWEAK THINGS, AND I APPRECIATE THAT. IT'S COOL, REALLY...

...AND I DON'T WANT TO OFFEND YOU...

C'MON, MARK. JUST SPIT IT OUT.

IT'S JUST NOT WORKING FOR ME...

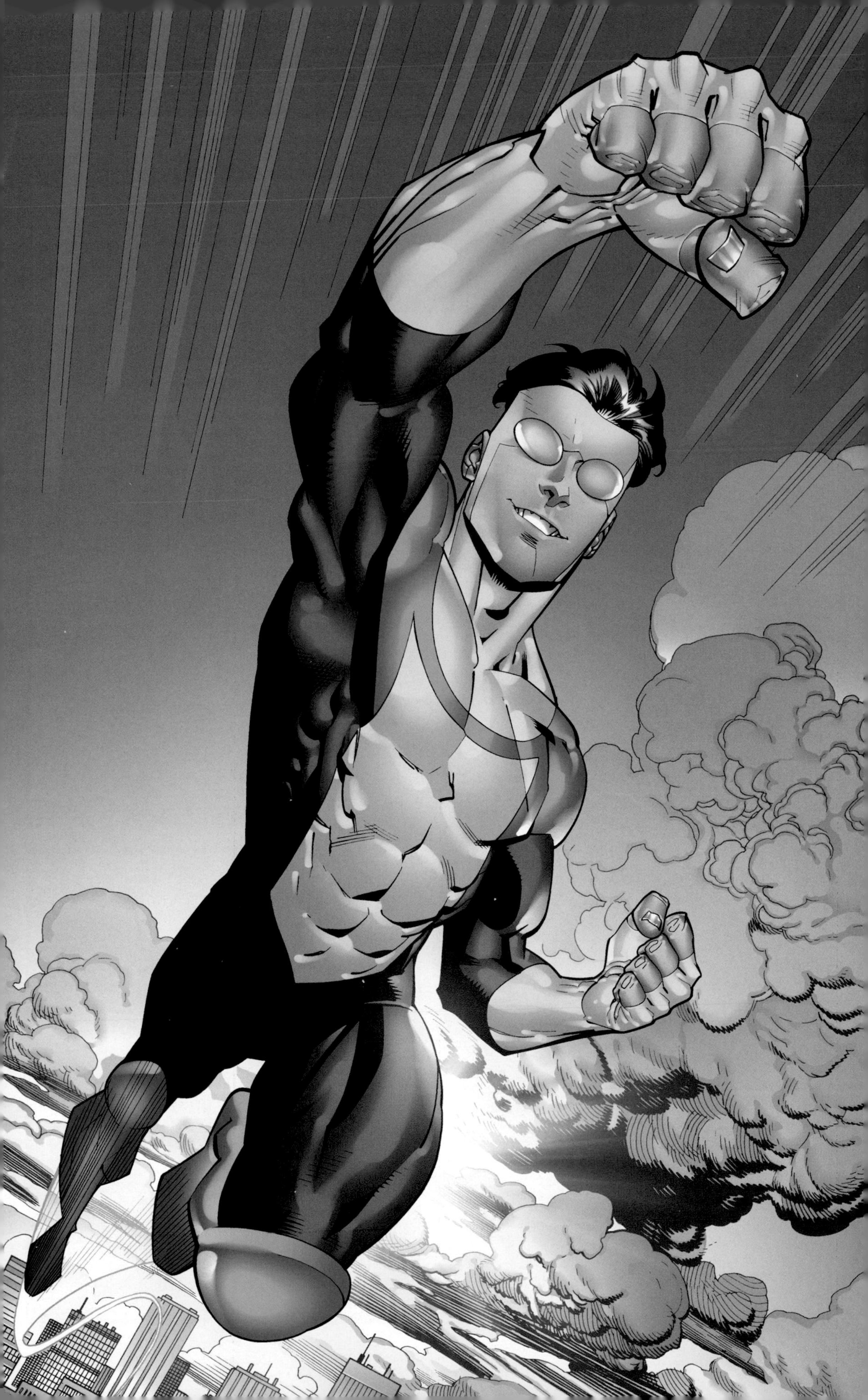

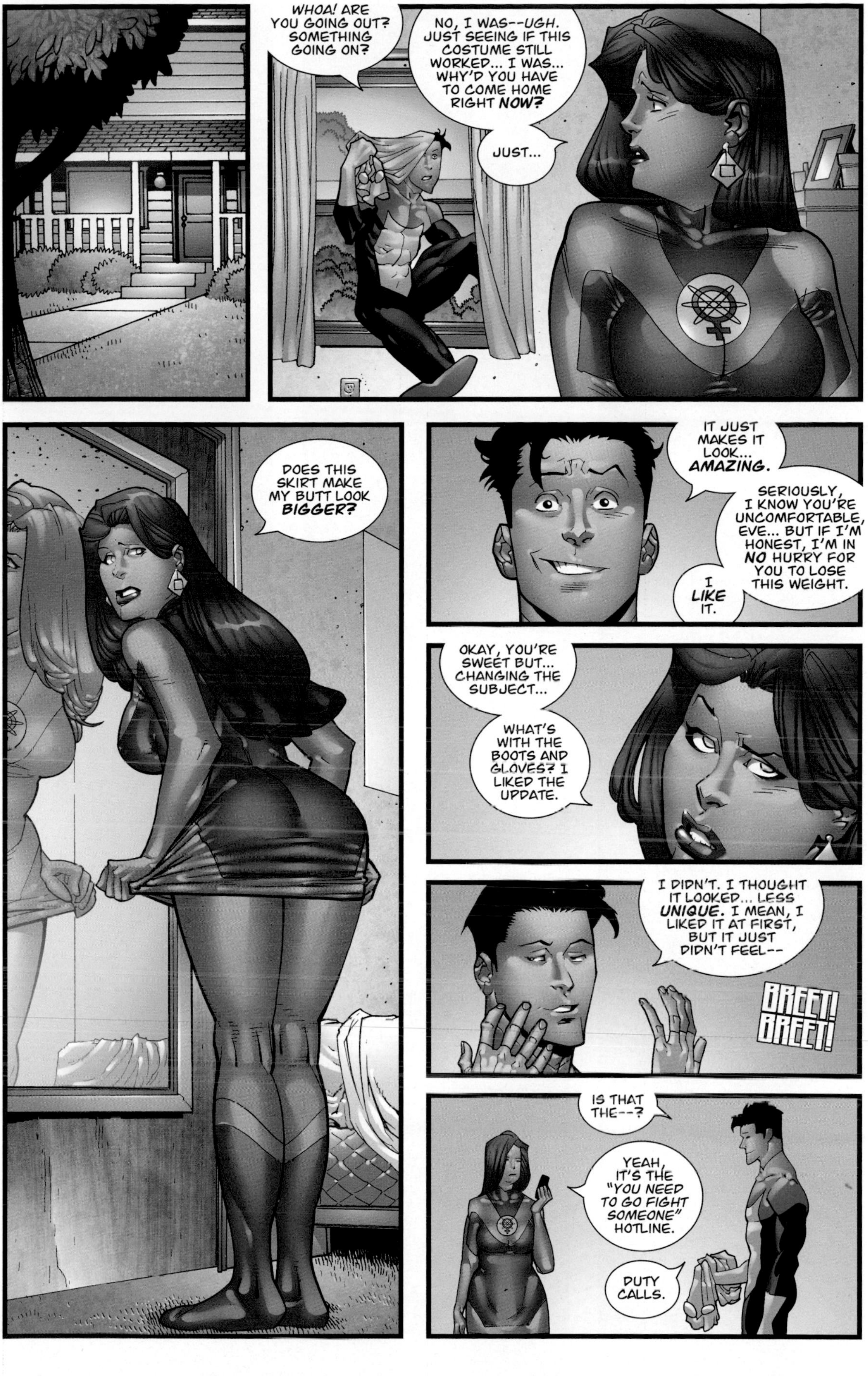
WHOA! ARE YOU GOING OUT? SOMETHING GOING ON?
NO, I WAS--UGH. JUST SEEING IF THIS COSTUME STILL WORKED... I WAS... WHY'D YOU HAVE TO COME HOME RIGHT NOW?
JUST...
DOES THIS SKIRT MAKE MY BUTT LOOK BIGGER?
IT JUST MAKES IT LOOK... AMAZING.
SERIOUSLY, I KNOW YOU'RE UNCOMFORTABLE, EVE... BUT IF I'M HONEST, I'M IN NO HURRY FOR YOU TO LOSE THIS WEIGHT.
I LIKE IT.
OKAY, YOU'RE SWEET BUT... CHANGING THE SUBJECT...
WHAT'S WITH THE BOOTS AND GLOVES? I LIKED THE UPDATE.
I DIDN'T. I THOUGHT IT LOOKED... LESS UNIQUE. I MEAN, I LIKED IT AT FIRST, BUT IT JUST DIDN'T FEEL--
BREET! BREET!
IS THAT THE--?
YEAH, IT'S THE "YOU NEED TO GO FIGHT SOMEONE" HOTLINE.
DUTY CALLS.

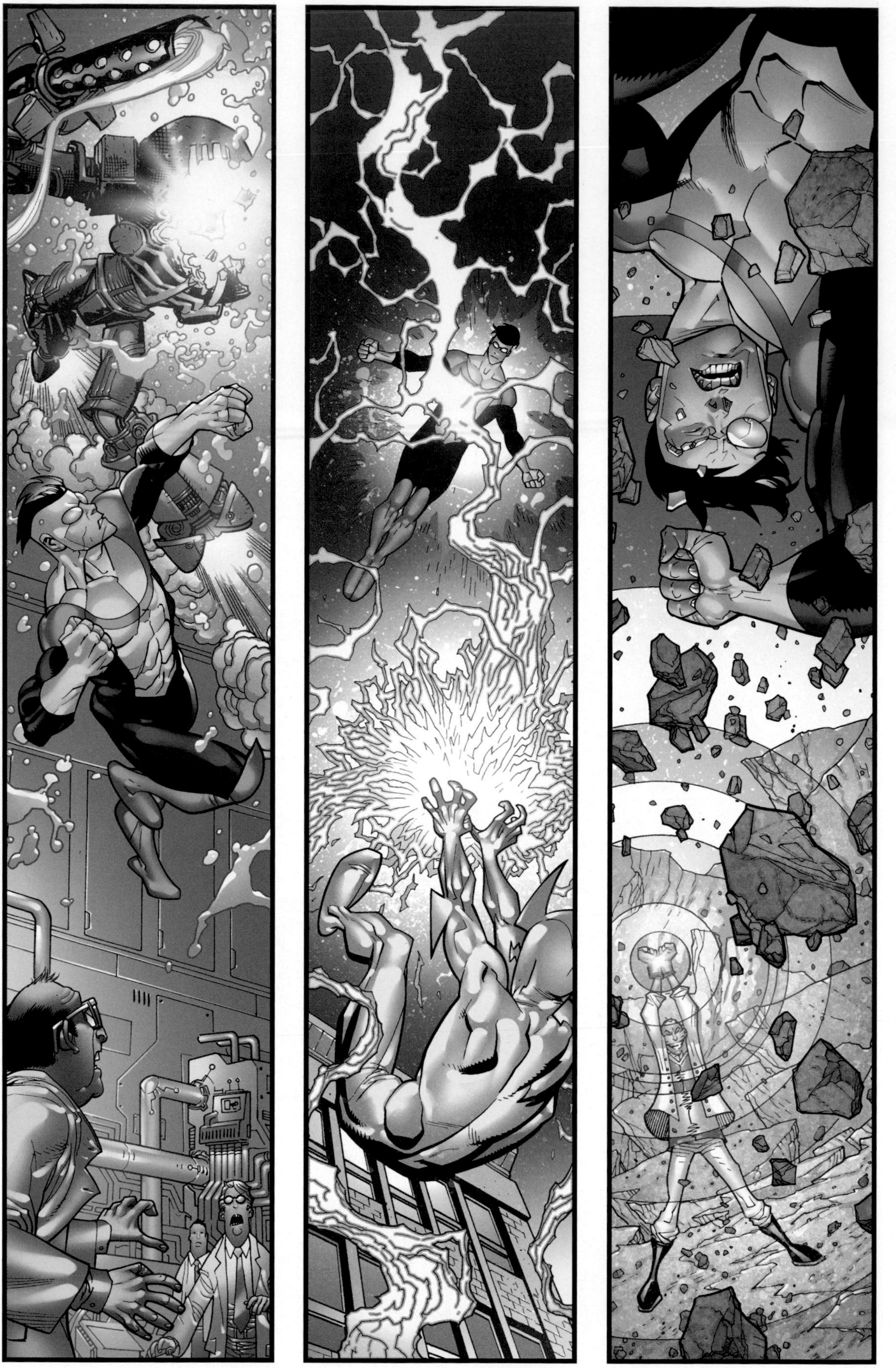

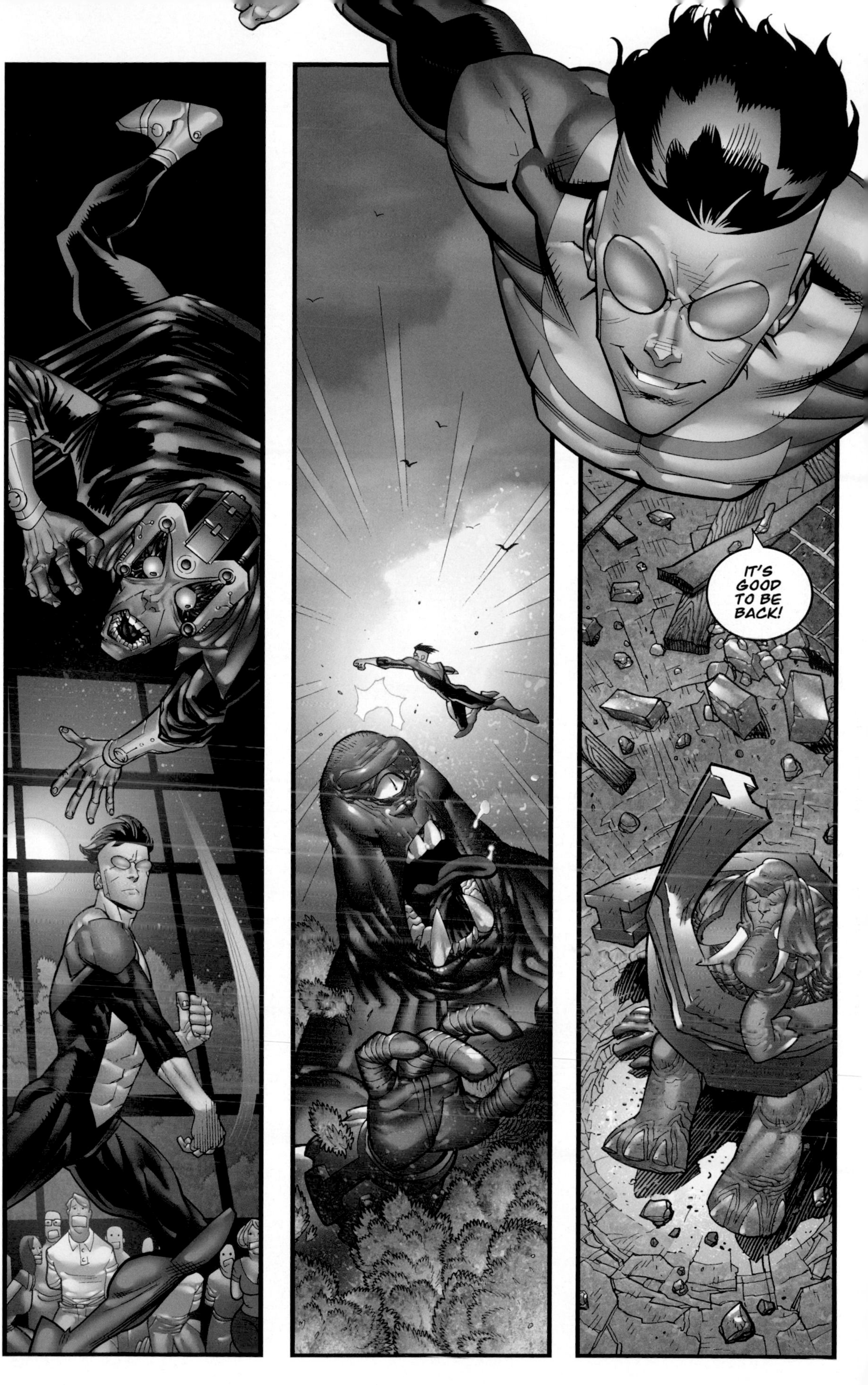
IT'S GOOD TO BE BACK!

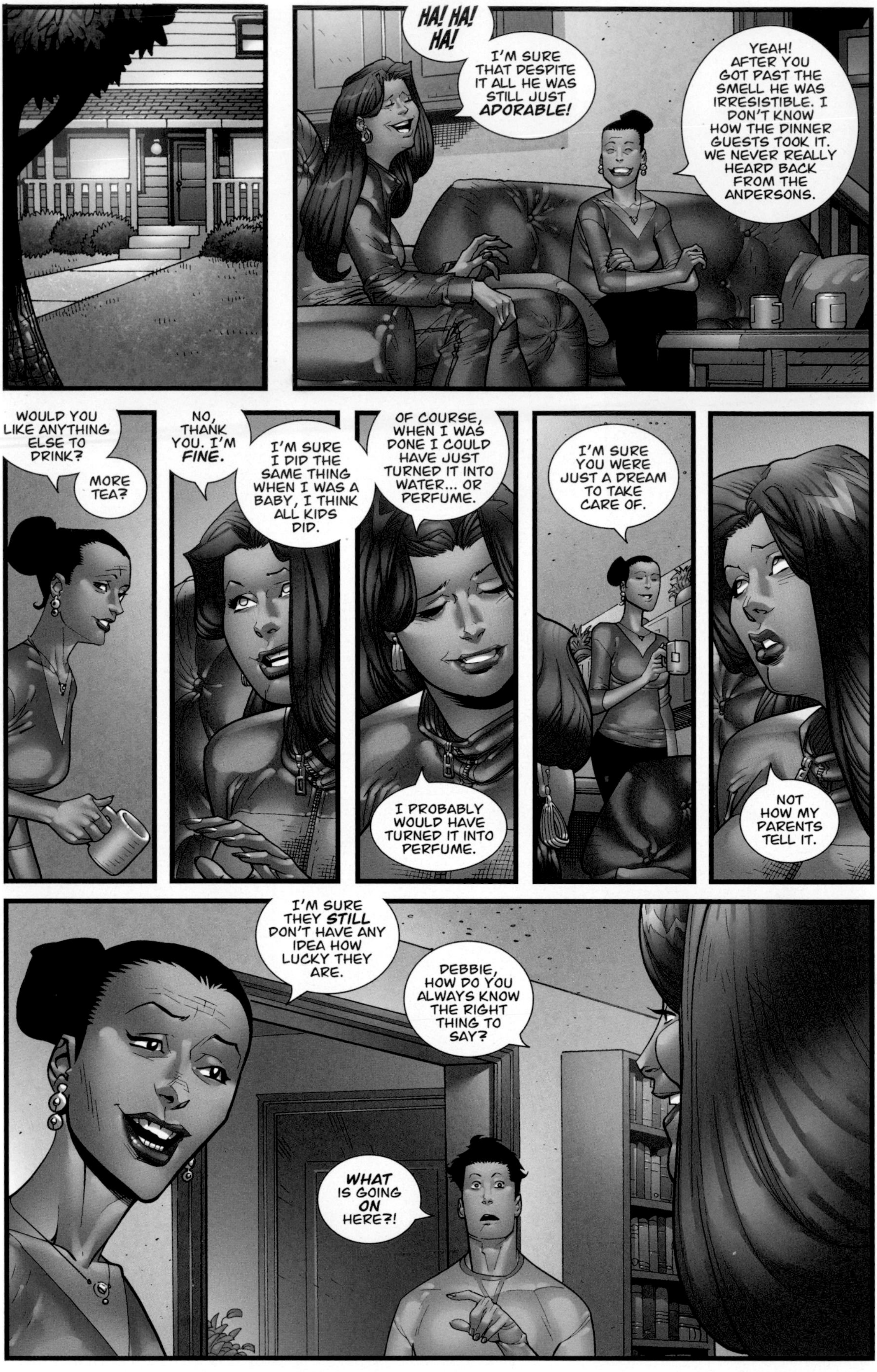
HA! HA! HA!
I'M SURE THAT DESPITE IT ALL HE WAS STILL JUST ADORABLE!
YEAH! AFTER YOU GOT PAST THE SMELL HE WAS IRRESISTIBLE. I DON'T KNOW HOW THE DINNER GUESTS TOOK IT. WE NEVER REALLY HEARD BACK FROM THE ANDERSONS.
WOULD YOU LIKE ANYTHING ELSE TO DRINK?
MORE TEA?
NO, THANK YOU. I'M FINE.
I'M SURE I DID THE SAME THING WHEN I WAS A BABY, I THINK ALL KIDS DID.
OF COURSE, WHEN I WAS DONE I COULD HAVE JUST TURNED IT INTO WATER... OR PERFUME.
I PROBABLY WOULD HAVE TURNED IT INTO PERFUME.
I'M SURE YOU WERE JUST A DREAM TO TAKE CARE OF.
NOT HOW MY PARENTS TELL IT.
I'M SURE THEY STILL DON'T HAVE ANY IDEA HOW LUCKY THEY ARE.
DEBBIE, HOW DO YOU ALWAYS KNOW THE RIGHT THING TO SAY?
WHAT IS GOING ON HERE?!

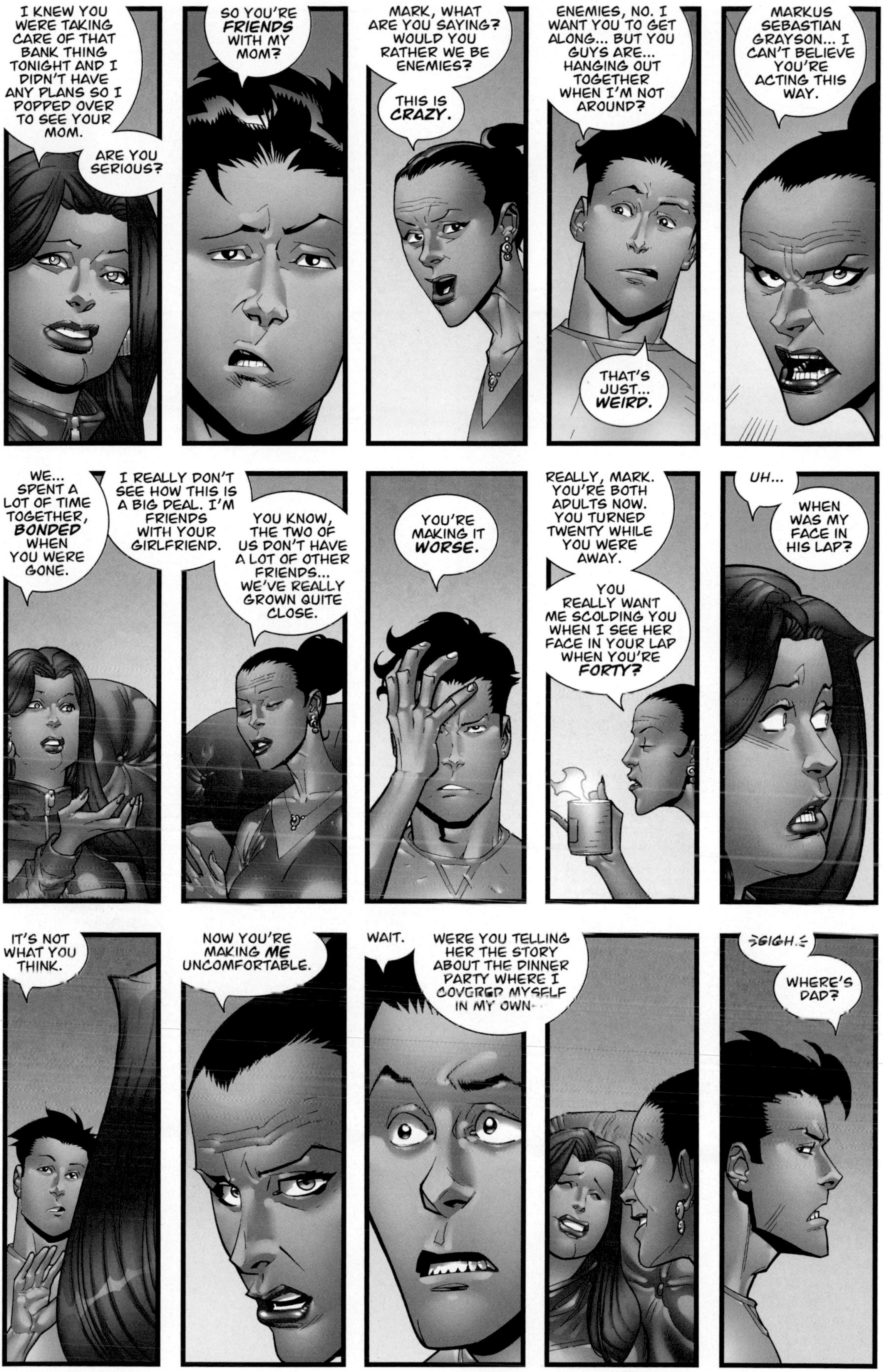

I KNEW YOU WERE TAKING CARE OF THAT BANK THING TONIGHT AND I DIDN'T HAVE ANY PLANS SO I POPPED OVER TO SEE YOUR MOM.
ARE YOU SERIOUS?
SO YOU'RE FRIENDS WITH MY MOM?
MARK, WHAT ARE YOU SAYING? WOULD YOU RATHER WE BE ENEMIES?
THIS IS CRAZY.
ENEMIES, NO. I WANT YOU TO GET ALONG... BUT YOU GUYS ARE... HANGING OUT TOGETHER WHEN I'M NOT AROUND?
THAT'S JUST... WEIRD.
MARKUS SEBASTIAN GRAYSON... I CAN'T BELIEVE YOU'RE ACTING THIS WAY.
WE... SPENT A LOT OF TIME TOGETHER, BONDED WHEN YOU WERE GONE.
I REALLY DON'T SEE HOW THIS IS A BIG DEAL. I'M FRIENDS WITH YOUR GIRLFRIEND.
YOU KNOW, THE TWO OF US DON'T HAVE A LOT OF OTHER FRIENDS... WE'VE REALLY GROWN QUITE CLOSE.
YOU'RE MAKING IT WORSE.
REALLY, MARK. YOU'RE BOTH ADULTS NOW. YOU TURNED TWENTY WHILE YOU WERE AWAY.
YOU REALLY WANT ME SCOLDING YOU WHEN I SEE HER FACE IN YOUR LAP WHEN YOU'RE FORTY?
UH...
WHEN WAS MY FACE IN HIS LAP?
IT'S NOT WHAT YOU THINK.
NOW YOU'RE MAKING ME UNCOMFORTABLE.
WAIT.
WERE YOU TELLING HER THE STORY ABOUT THE DINNER PARTY WHERE I COVERED MYSELF IN MY OWN--
SIGH.
WHERE'S DAD?

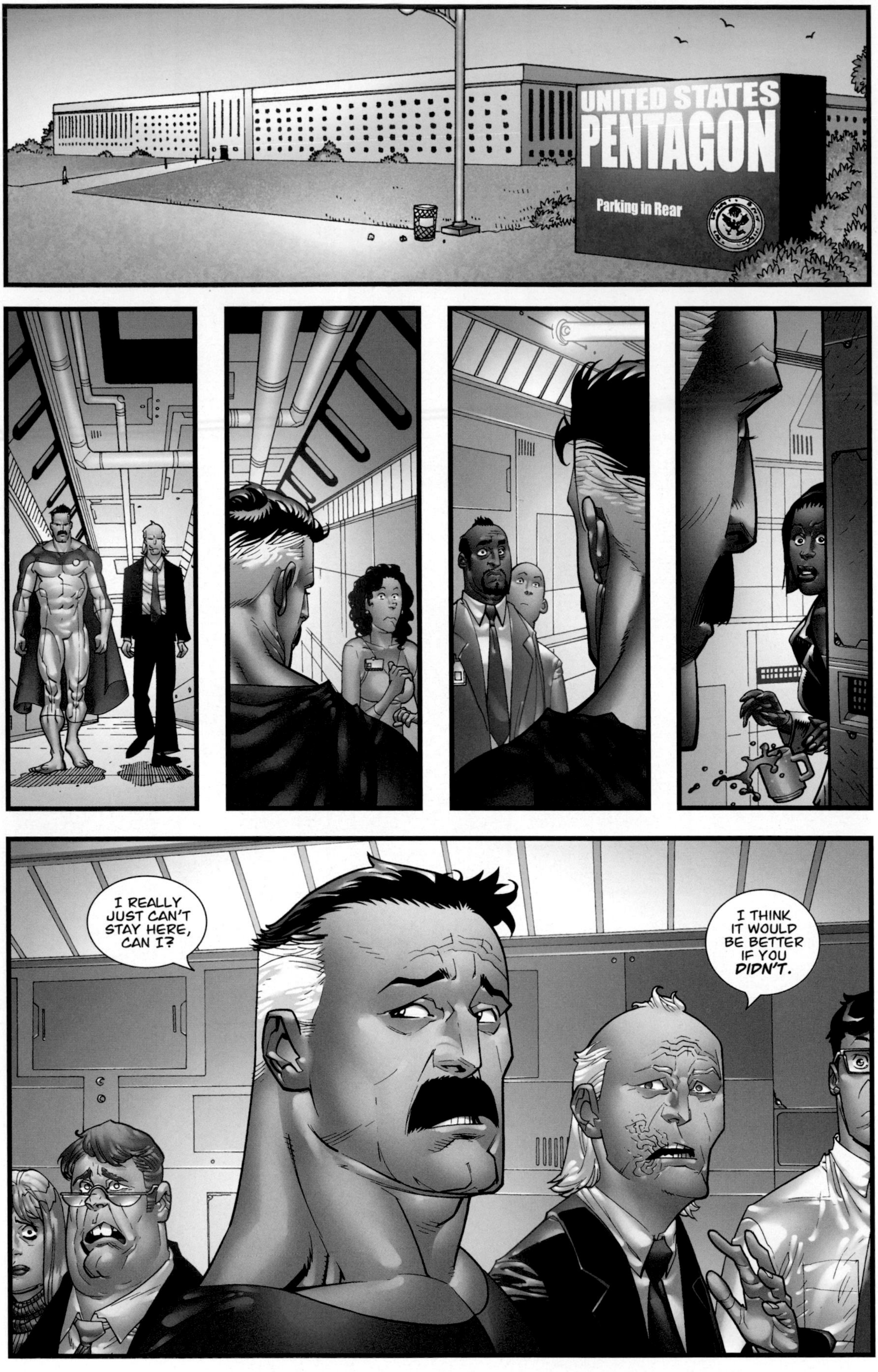
UNITED STATES PENTAGON
Parking in Rear
I REALLY JUST CAN'T STAY HERE, CAN I?
I THINK IT WOULD BE BETTER IF YOU DIDN'T.

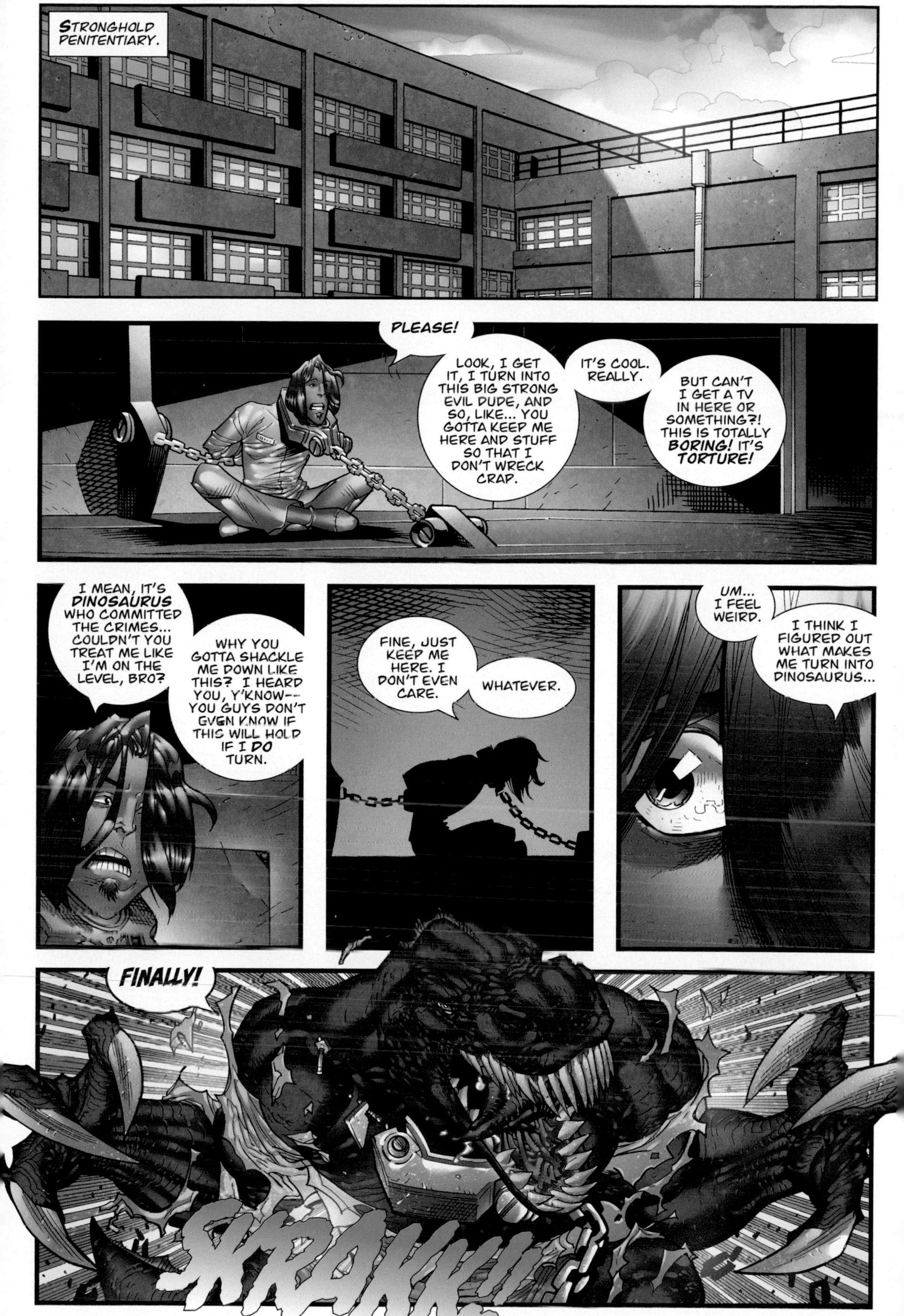
STRONGHOLD PENITENTIARY.
PLEASE!
LOOK, I GET IT, I TURN INTO THIS BIG STRONG EVIL DUDE, AND SO, LIKE... YOU GOTTA KEEP ME HERE AND STUFF SO THAT I DON'T WRECK CRAP.
IT'S COOL. REALLY.
BUT CAN'T I GET A TV IN HERE OR SOMETHING?! THIS IS TOTALLY BORING! IT'S TORTURE!
I MEAN, IT'S DINOSAURUS WHO COMMITTED THE CRIMES... COULDN'T YOU TREAT ME LIKE I'M ON THE LEVEL, BRO?
WHY YOU GOTTA SHACKLE ME DOWN LIKE THIS? I HEARD YOU, Y'KNOW-- YOU GUYS DON'T EVEN KNOW IF THIS WILL HOLD IF I DO TURN.
FINE, JUST KEEP ME HERE. I DON'T EVEN CARE.
WHATEVER.
UM... I FEEL WEIRD.
I THINK I FIGURED OUT WHAT MAKES ME TURN INTO DINOSAURUS...
FINALLY!
SKRAKK!!

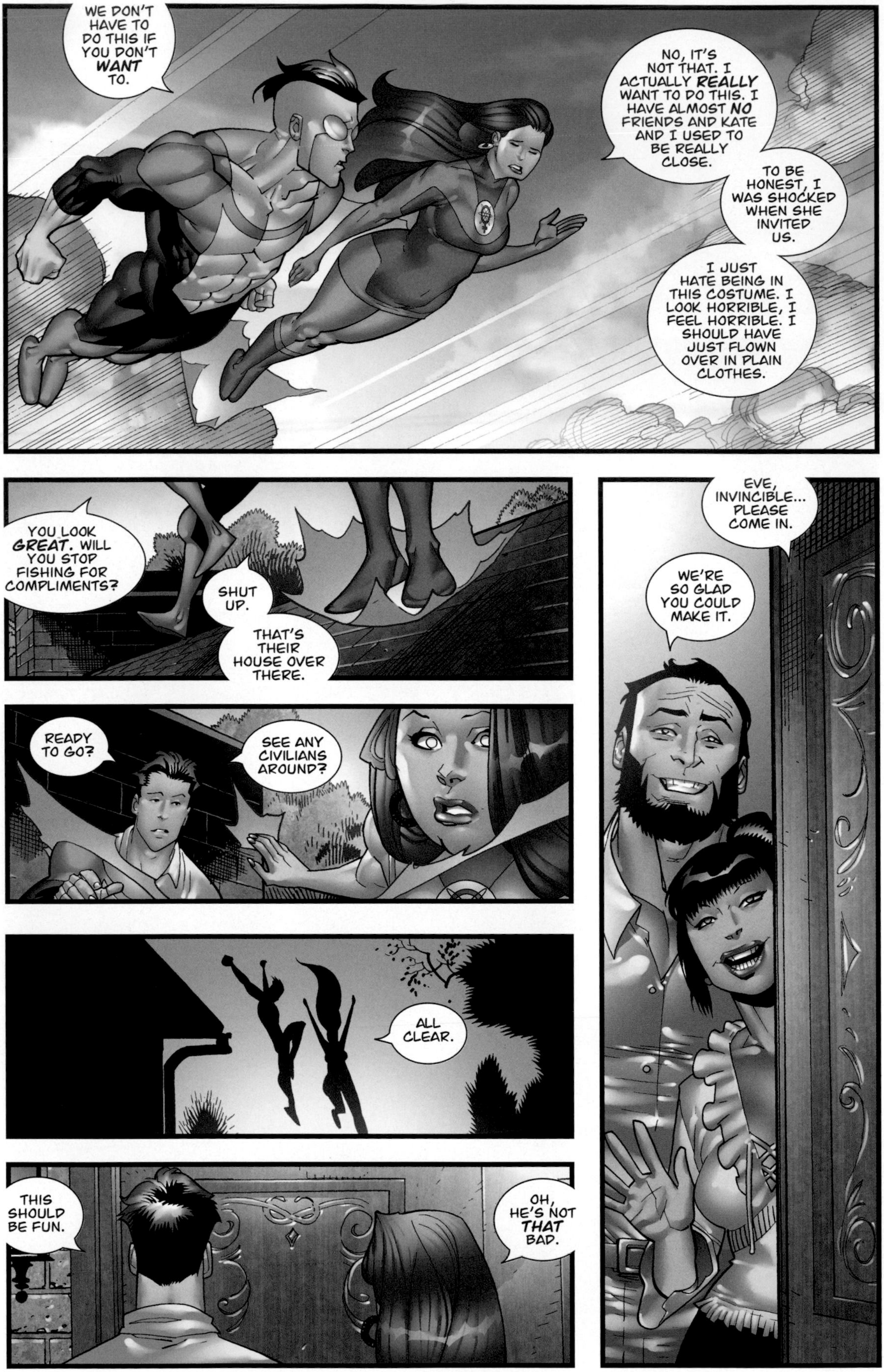
WE DON'T HAVE TO DO THIS IF YOU DON'T **WANT** TO.
NO, IT'S NOT THAT. I ACTUALLY **REALLY** WANT TO DO THIS. I HAVE ALMOST **NO** FRIENDS AND KATE AND I USED TO BE REALLY CLOSE.
TO BE HONEST, I WAS SHOCKED WHEN SHE INVITED US.
I JUST HATE BEING IN THIS COSTUME. I LOOK HORRIBLE, I FEEL HORRIBLE. I SHOULD HAVE JUST FLOWN OVER IN PLAIN CLOTHES.
YOU LOOK **GREAT.** WILL YOU STOP FISHING FOR COMPLIMENTS?
SHUT UP.
THAT'S THEIR HOUSE OVER THERE.
READY TO GO?
SEE ANY CIVILIANS AROUND?
ALL CLEAR.
THIS SHOULD BE FUN.
OH, HE'S NOT **THAT** BAD.
EVE, INVINCIBLE... PLEASE COME IN.
WE'RE SO GLAD YOU COULD MAKE IT.

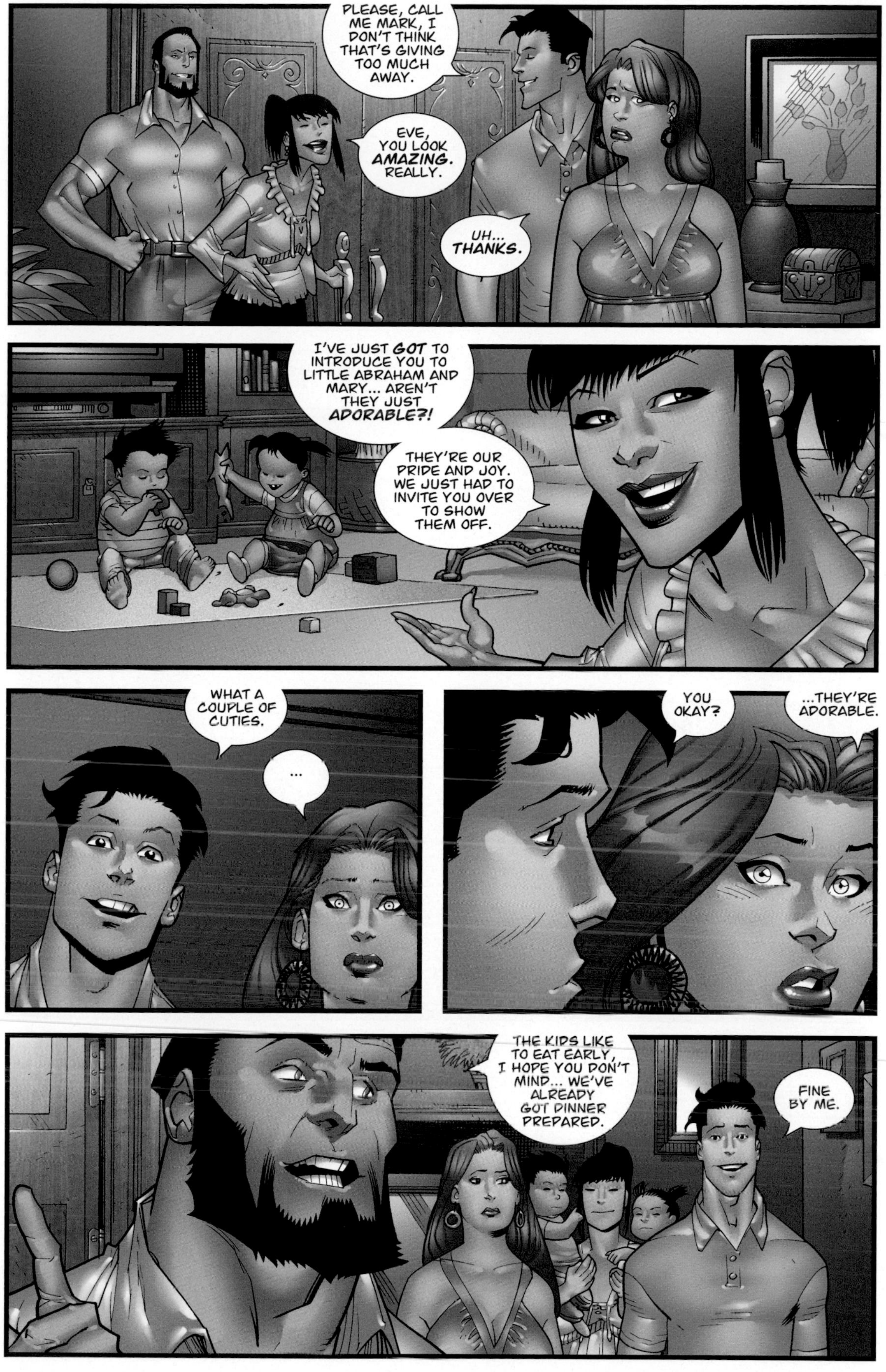
PLEASE, CALL ME MARK, I DON'T THINK THAT'S GIVING TOO MUCH AWAY.
EVE, YOU LOOK **AMAZING**. REALLY.
UH... **THANKS.**
I'VE JUST **GOT** TO INTRODUCE YOU TO LITTLE ABRAHAM AND MARY... AREN'T THEY JUST **ADORABLE?!**
THEY'RE OUR PRIDE AND JOY. WE JUST HAD TO INVITE YOU OVER TO SHOW THEM OFF.
WHAT A COUPLE OF CUTIES.
...
YOU OKAY?
...THEY'RE ADORABLE.
THE KIDS LIKE TO EAT EARLY, I HOPE YOU DON'T MIND... WE'VE ALREADY GOT DINNER PREPARED.
FINE BY ME.

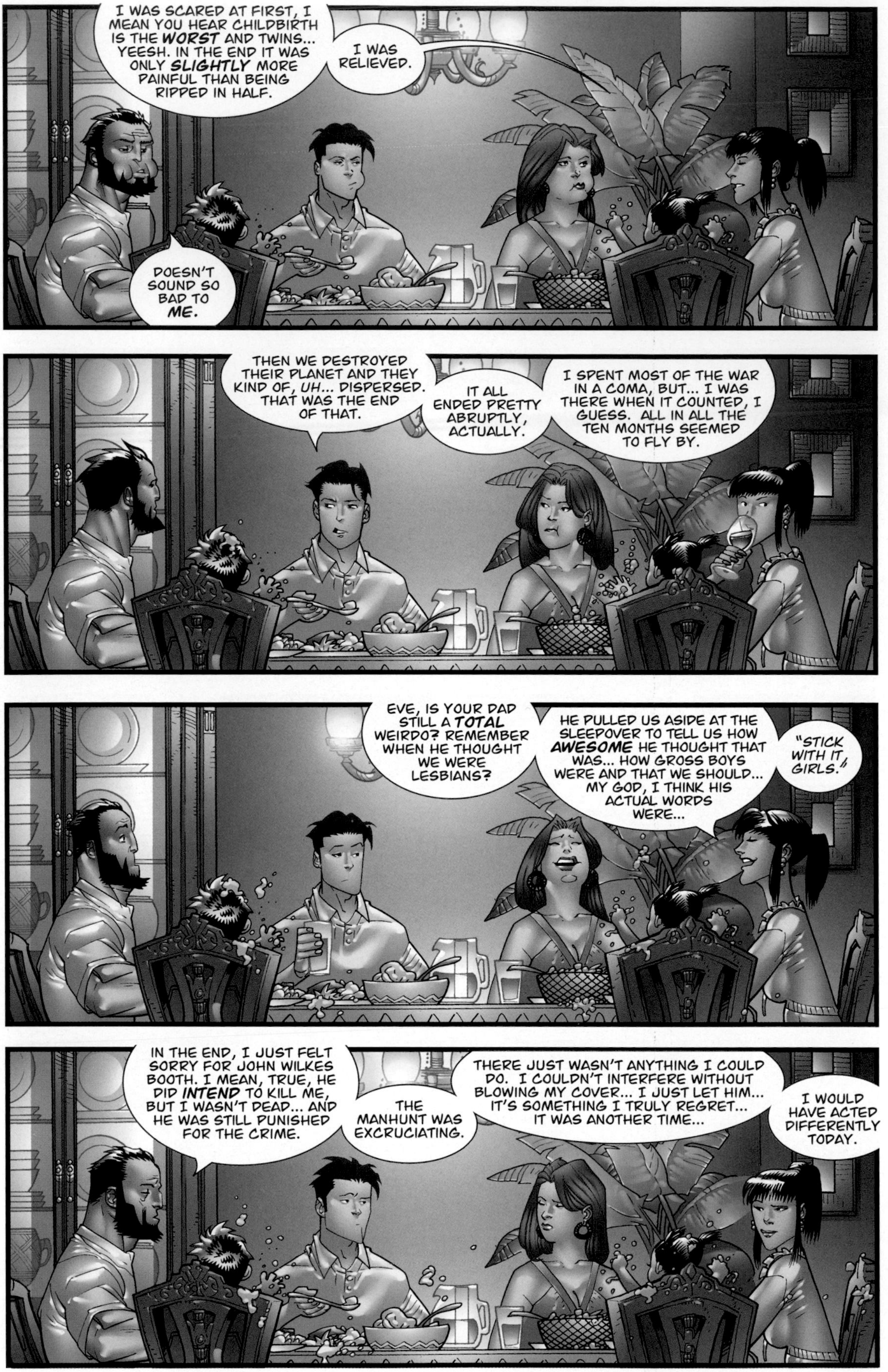
I WAS SCARED AT FIRST, I MEAN YOU HEAR CHILDBIRTH IS THE WORST AND TWINS... YEESH. IN THE END IT WAS ONLY SLIGHTLY MORE PAINFUL THAN BEING RIPPED IN HALF.
I WAS RELIEVED.
DOESN'T SOUND SO BAD TO ME.
THEN WE DESTROYED THEIR PLANET AND THEY KIND OF, UH... DISPERSED. THAT WAS THE END OF THAT.
IT ALL ENDED PRETTY ABRUPTLY, ACTUALLY.
I SPENT MOST OF THE WAR IN A COMA, BUT... I WAS THERE WHEN IT COUNTED, I GUESS. ALL IN ALL THE TEN MONTHS SEEMED TO FLY BY.
EVE, IS YOUR DAD STILL A TOTAL WEIRDO? REMEMBER WHEN HE THOUGHT WE WERE LESBIANS?
HE PULLED US ASIDE AT THE SLEEPOVER TO TELL US HOW AWESOME HE THOUGHT THAT WAS... HOW GROSS BOYS WERE AND THAT WE SHOULD... MY GOD, I THINK HIS ACTUAL WORDS WERE...
"STICK WITH IT, GIRLS."
IN THE END, I JUST FELT SORRY FOR JOHN WILKES BOOTH. I MEAN, TRUE, HE DID INTEND TO KILL ME, BUT I WASN'T DEAD... AND HE WAS STILL PUNISHED FOR THE CRIME.
THE MANHUNT WAS EXCRUCIATING.
THERE JUST WASN'T ANYTHING I COULD DO. I COULDN'T INTERFERE WITHOUT BLOWING MY COVER... I JUST LET HIM... IT'S SOMETHING I TRULY REGRET... IT WAS ANOTHER TIME...
I WOULD HAVE ACTED DIFFERENTLY TODAY.

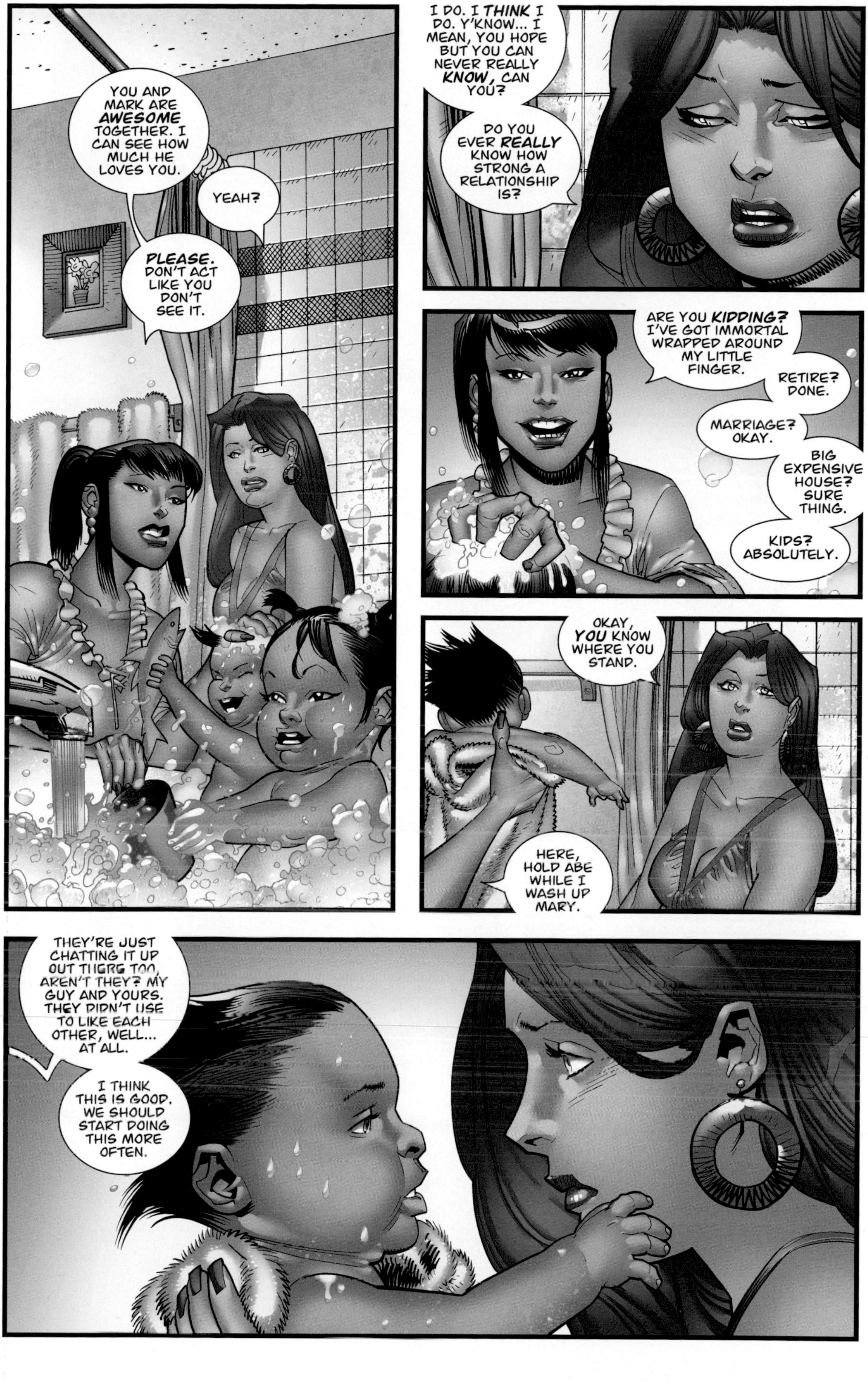

YOU AND MARK ARE **AWESOME** TOGETHER. I CAN SEE HOW MUCH HE LOVES YOU.
YEAH?
PLEASE. DON'T ACT LIKE YOU DON'T SEE IT.
I DO. I **THINK** I DO. Y'KNOW... I MEAN, YOU HOPE BUT YOU CAN NEVER REALLY **KNOW,** CAN YOU?
DO YOU EVER **REALLY** KNOW HOW STRONG A RELATIONSHIP IS?
ARE YOU **KIDDING?** I'VE GOT IMMORTAL WRAPPED AROUND MY LITTLE FINGER.
RETIRE? DONE.
MARRIAGE? OKAY.
BIG EXPENSIVE HOUSE? SURE THING.
KIDS? ABSOLUTELY.
OKAY, **YOU** KNOW WHERE YOU STAND.
HERE, HOLD ABE WHILE I WASH UP MARY.
THEY'RE JUST CHATTING IT UP OUT THERE TOO, AREN'T THEY? MY GUY AND YOURS. THEY DIDN'T USE TO LIKE EACH OTHER, WELL... AT ALL.
I THINK THIS IS GOOD. WE SHOULD START DOING THIS MORE OFTEN.

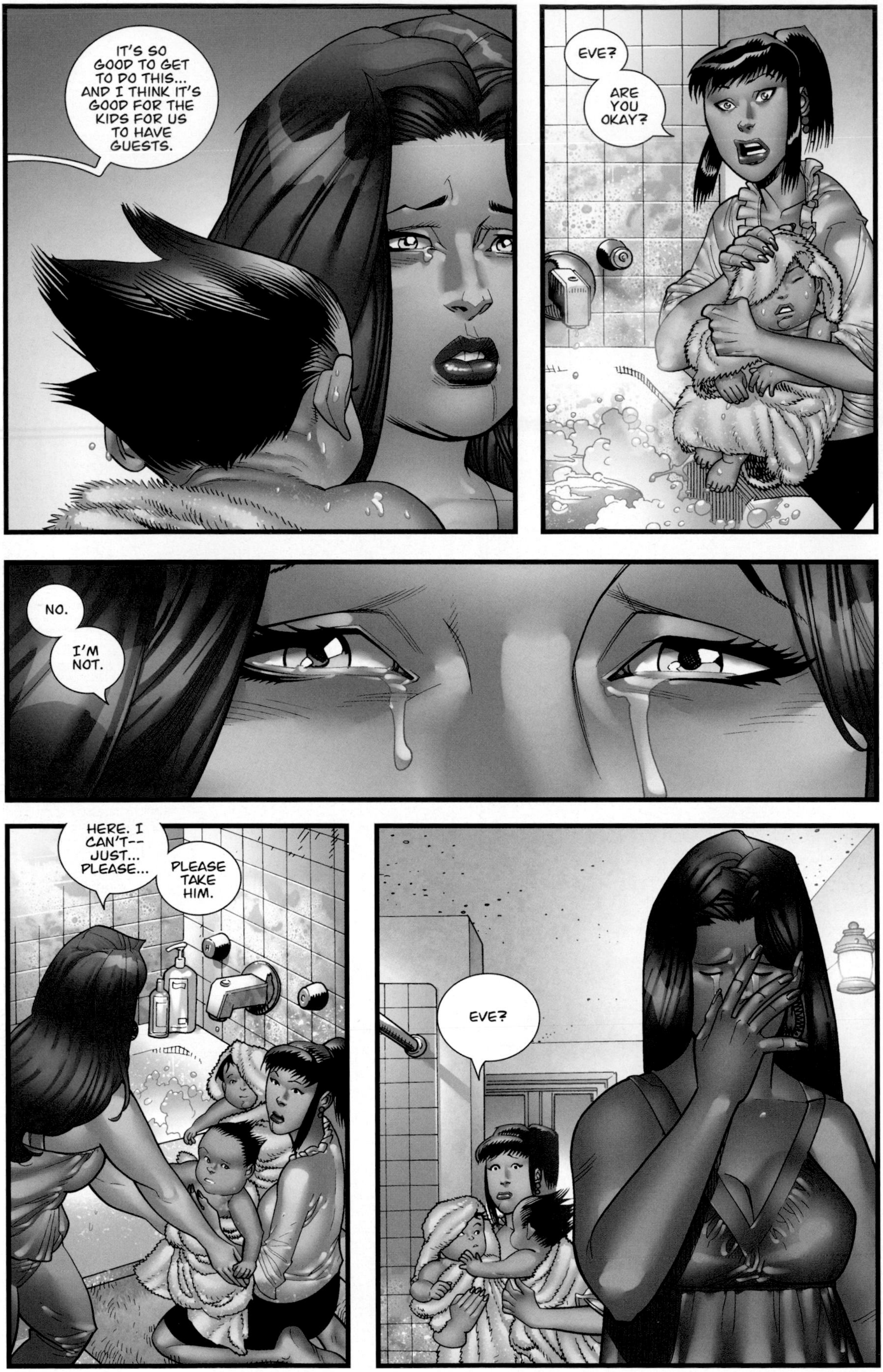
IT'S SO GOOD TO GET TO DO THIS... AND I THINK IT'S GOOD FOR THE KIDS FOR US TO HAVE GUESTS.
EVE?
ARE YOU OKAY?
NO.
I'M NOT.
HERE. I CAN'T-- JUST... PLEASE...
PLEASE TAKE HIM.
EVE?

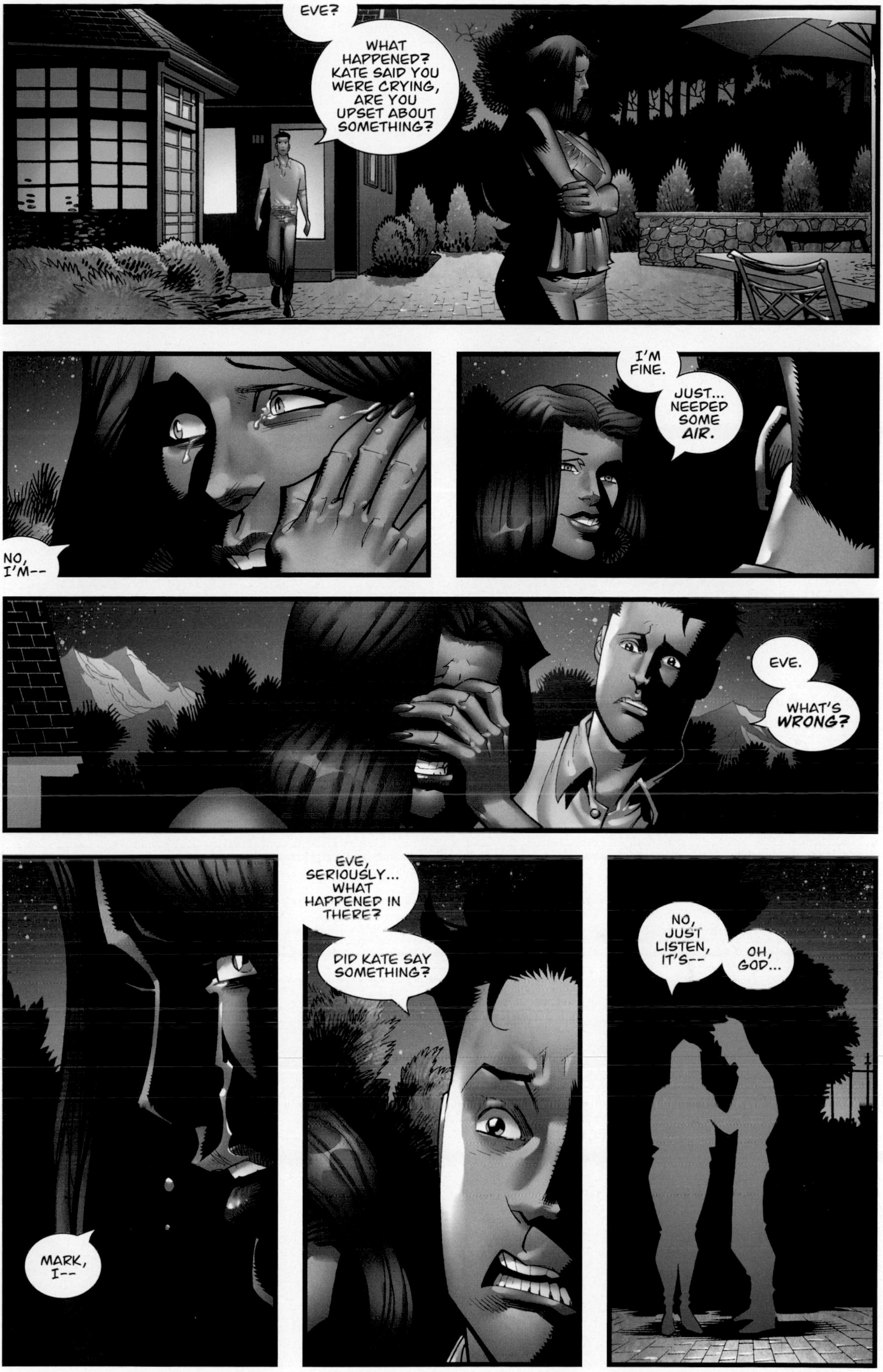
EVE?
WHAT HAPPENED? KATE SAID YOU WERE CRYING, ARE YOU UPSET ABOUT SOMETHING?
NO, I'M--
I'M FINE.
JUST... NEEDED SOME AIR.
EVE.
WHAT'S WRONG?
MARK, I--
EVE, SERIOUSLY... WHAT HAPPENED IN THERE?
DID KATE SAY SOMETHING?
NO, JUST LISTEN, IT'S--
OH, GOD...

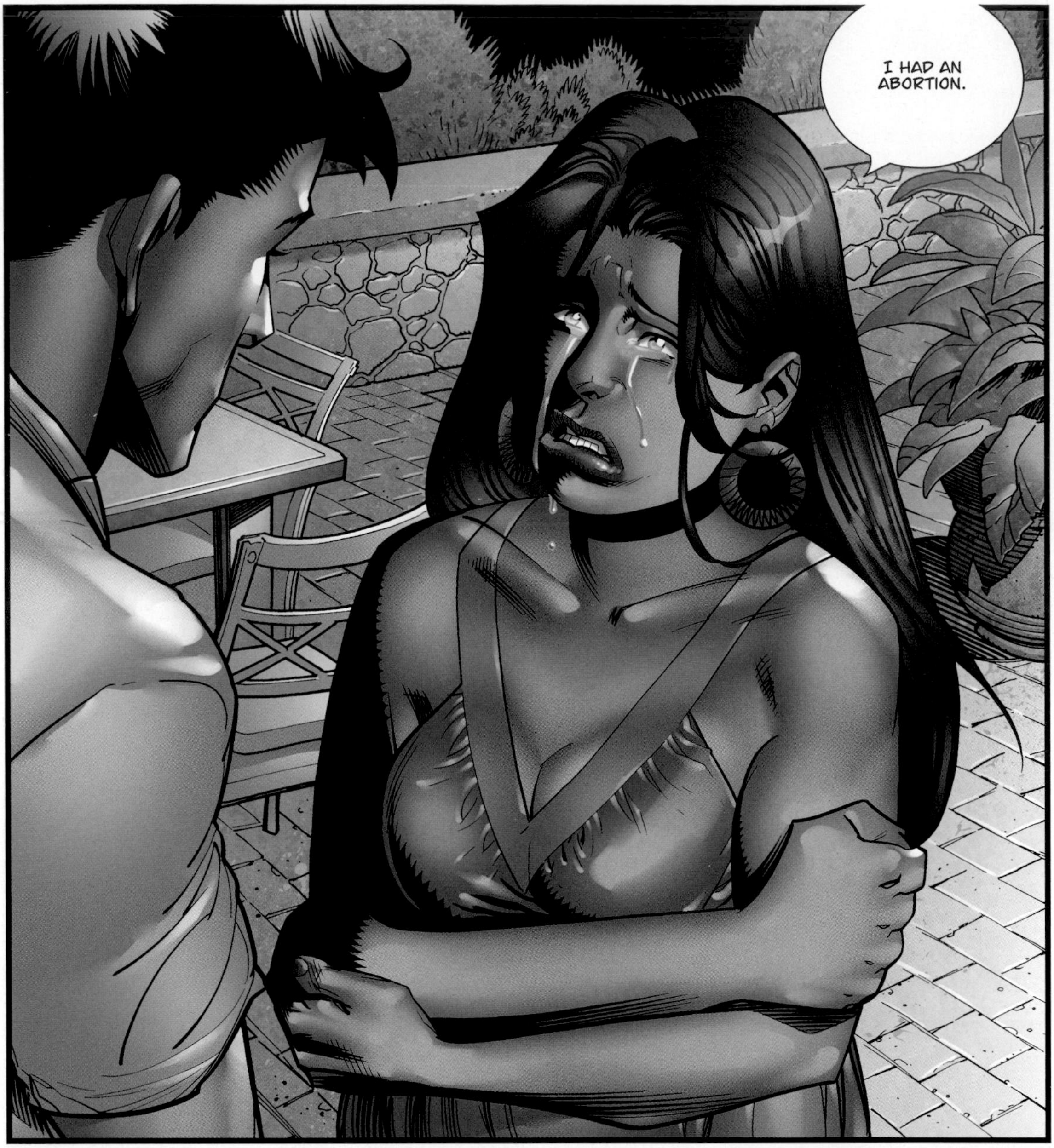
I HAD AN ABORTION.

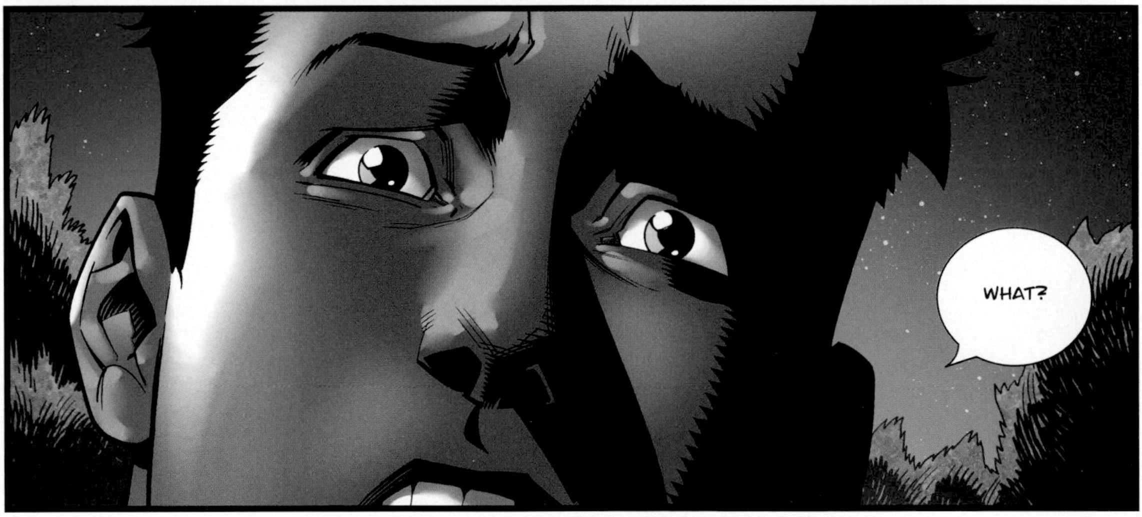
WHAT?

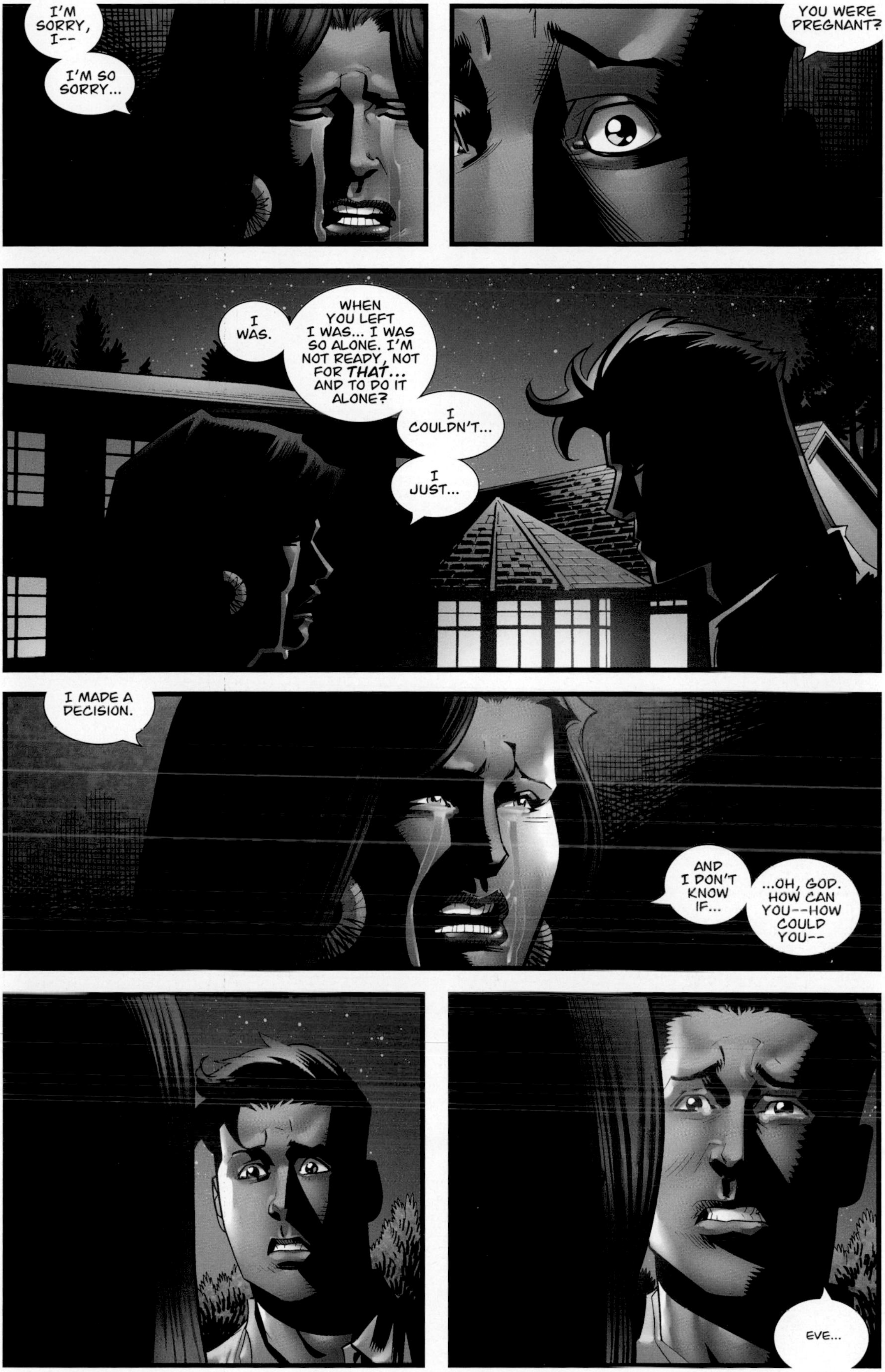
I'M SORRY, I--
I'M SO SORRY...
YOU WERE PREGNANT?
I WAS.
WHEN YOU LEFT I WAS... I WAS SO ALONE. I'M NOT READY, NOT FOR *THAT*... AND TO DO IT ALONE?
I COULDN'T...
I JUST...
I MADE A DECISION.
AND I DON'T KNOW IF...
...OH, GOD. HOW CAN YOU--HOW COULD YOU--
EVE...

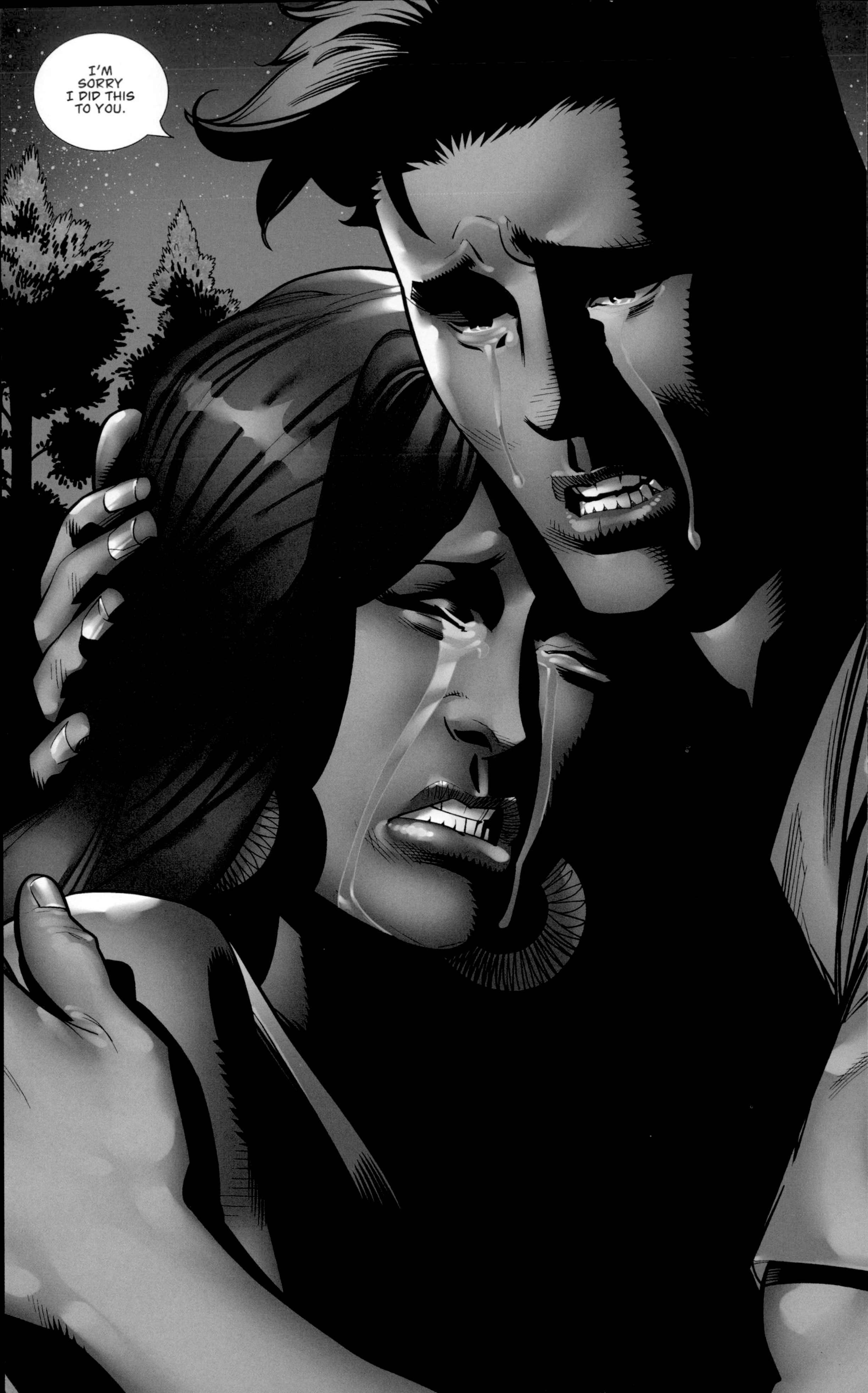
I'M SORRY I DID THIS TO YOU.

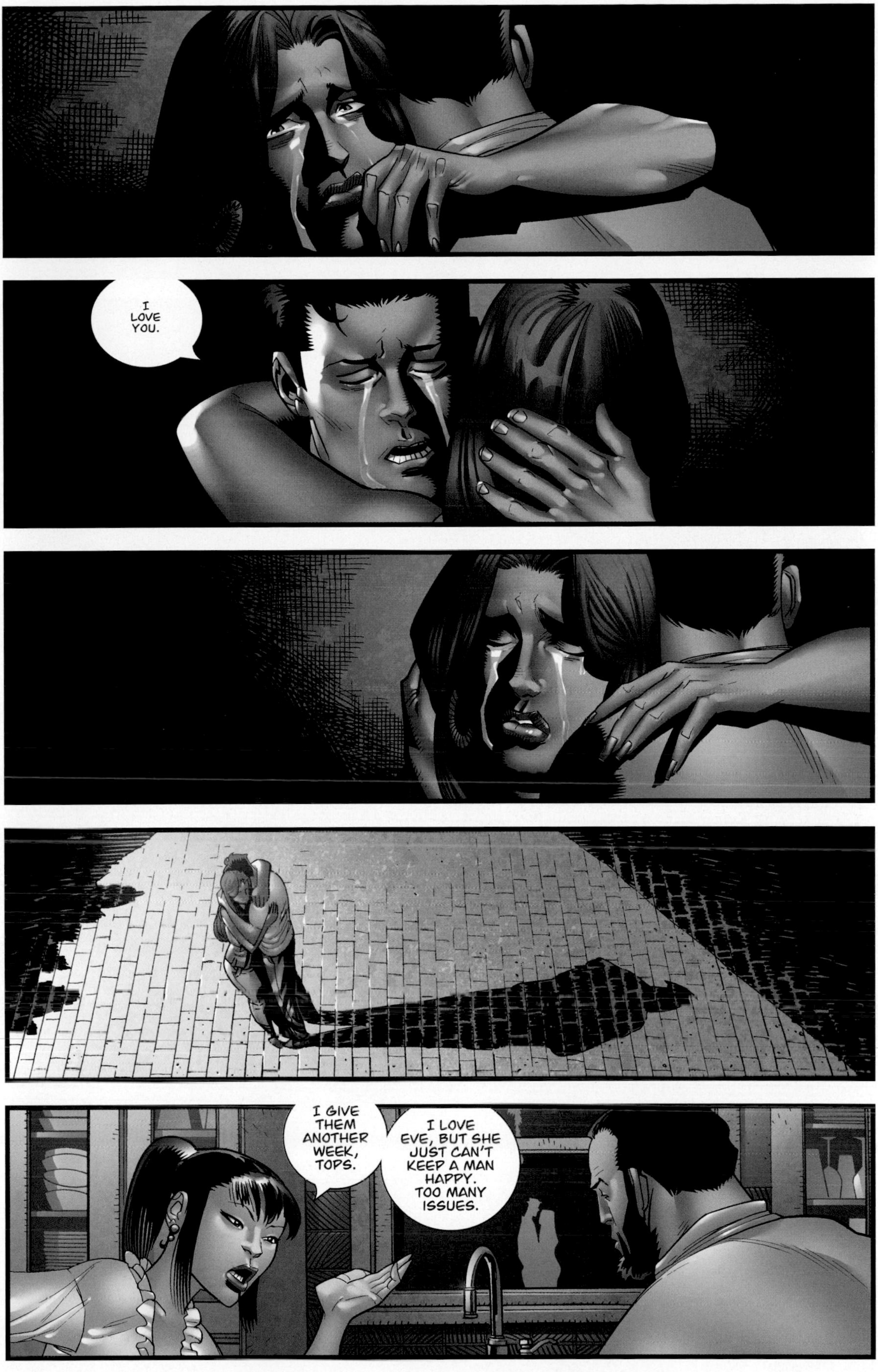
I LOVE YOU.
I GIVE THEM ANOTHER WEEK, TOPS.
I LOVE EVE, BUT SHE JUST CAN'T KEEP A MAN HAPPY. TOO MANY ISSUES.

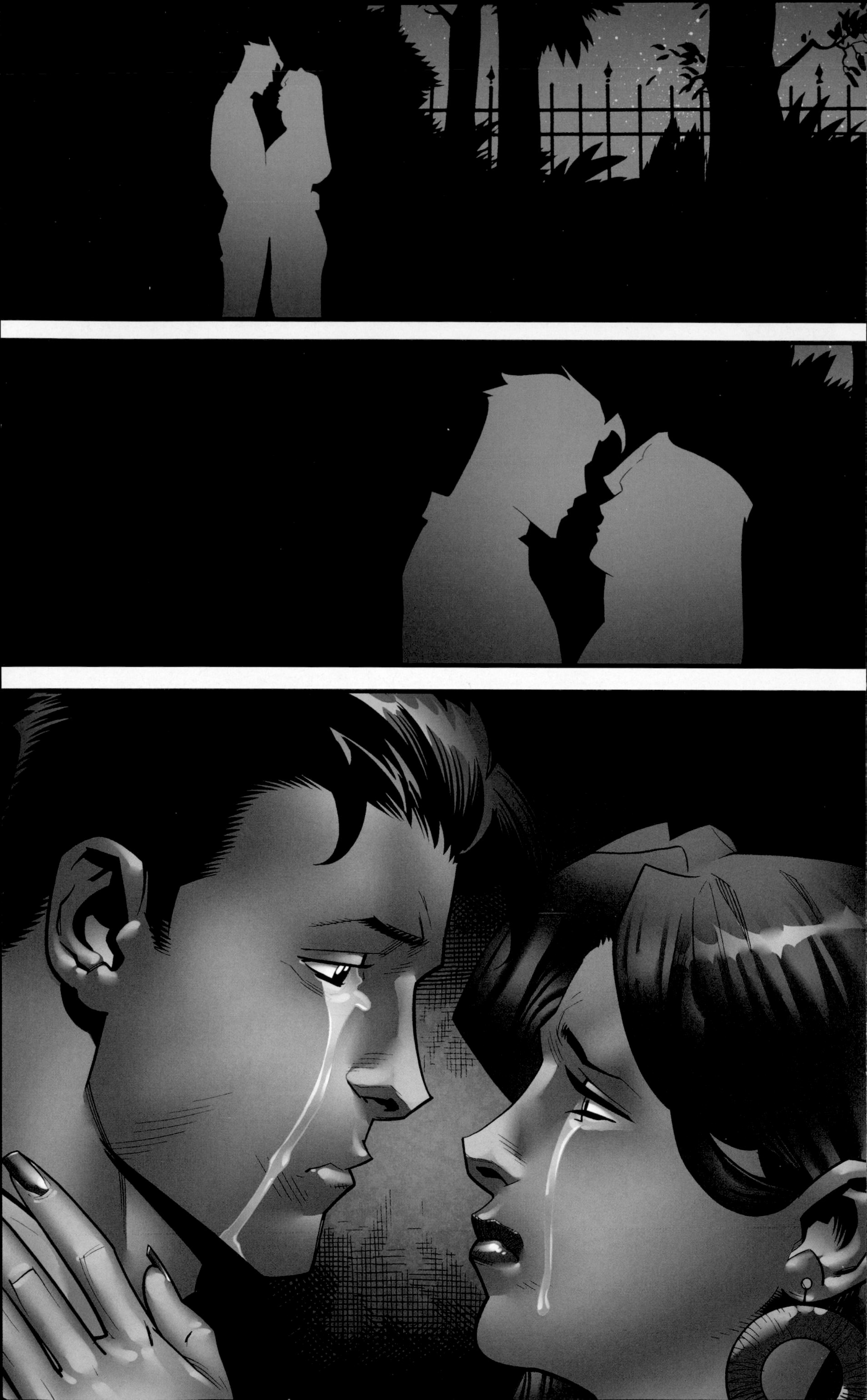

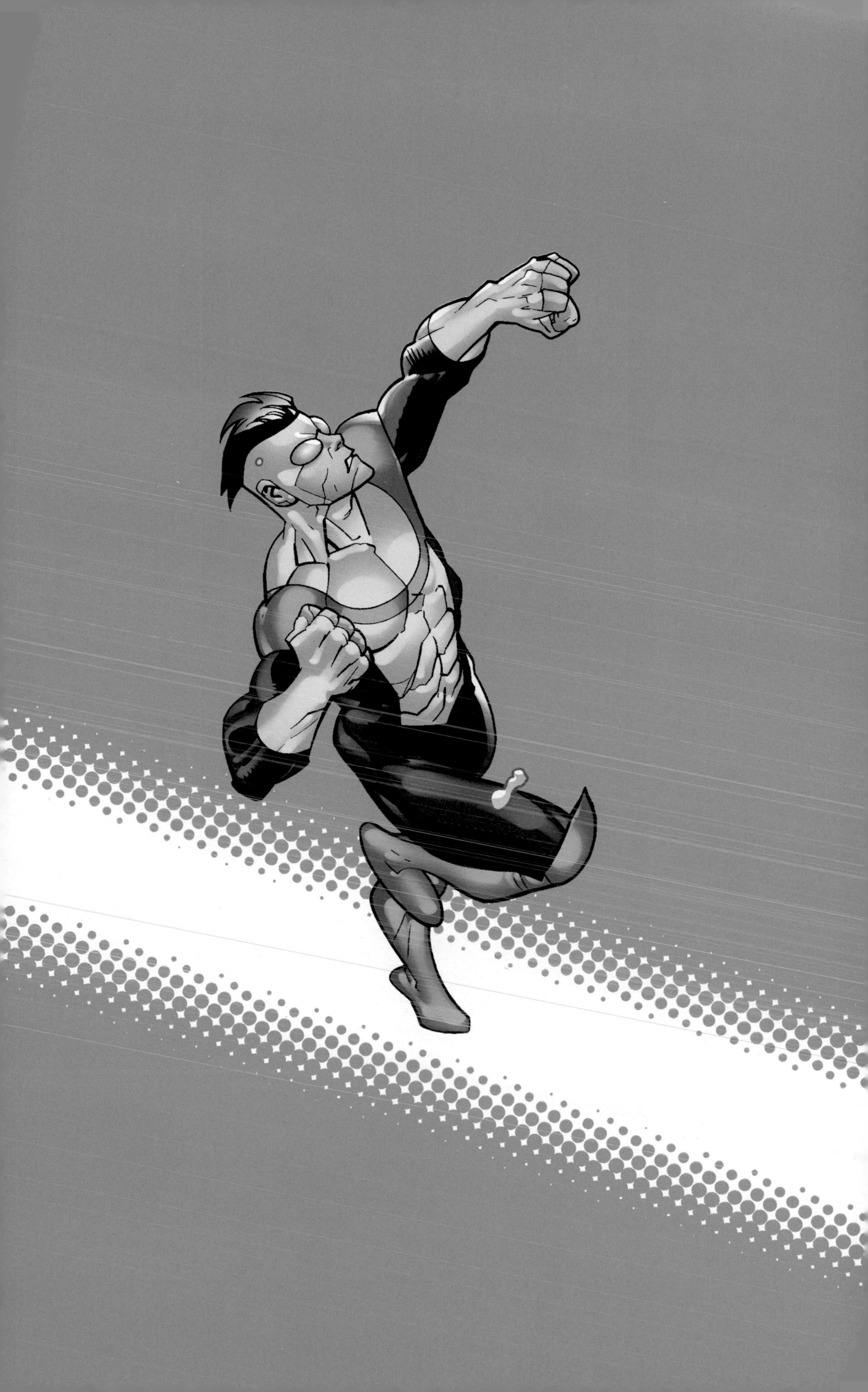

CHAPTER TWO

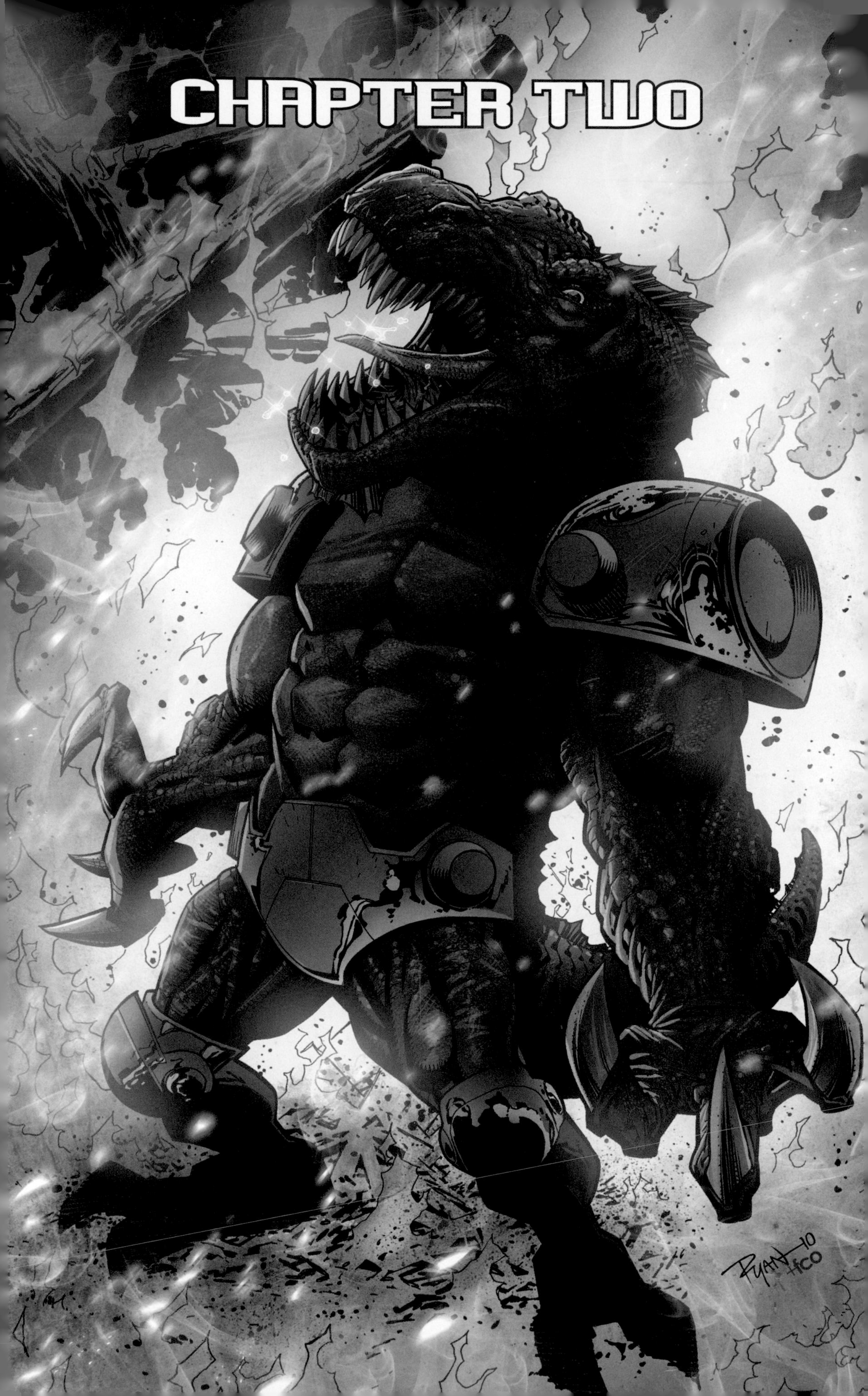

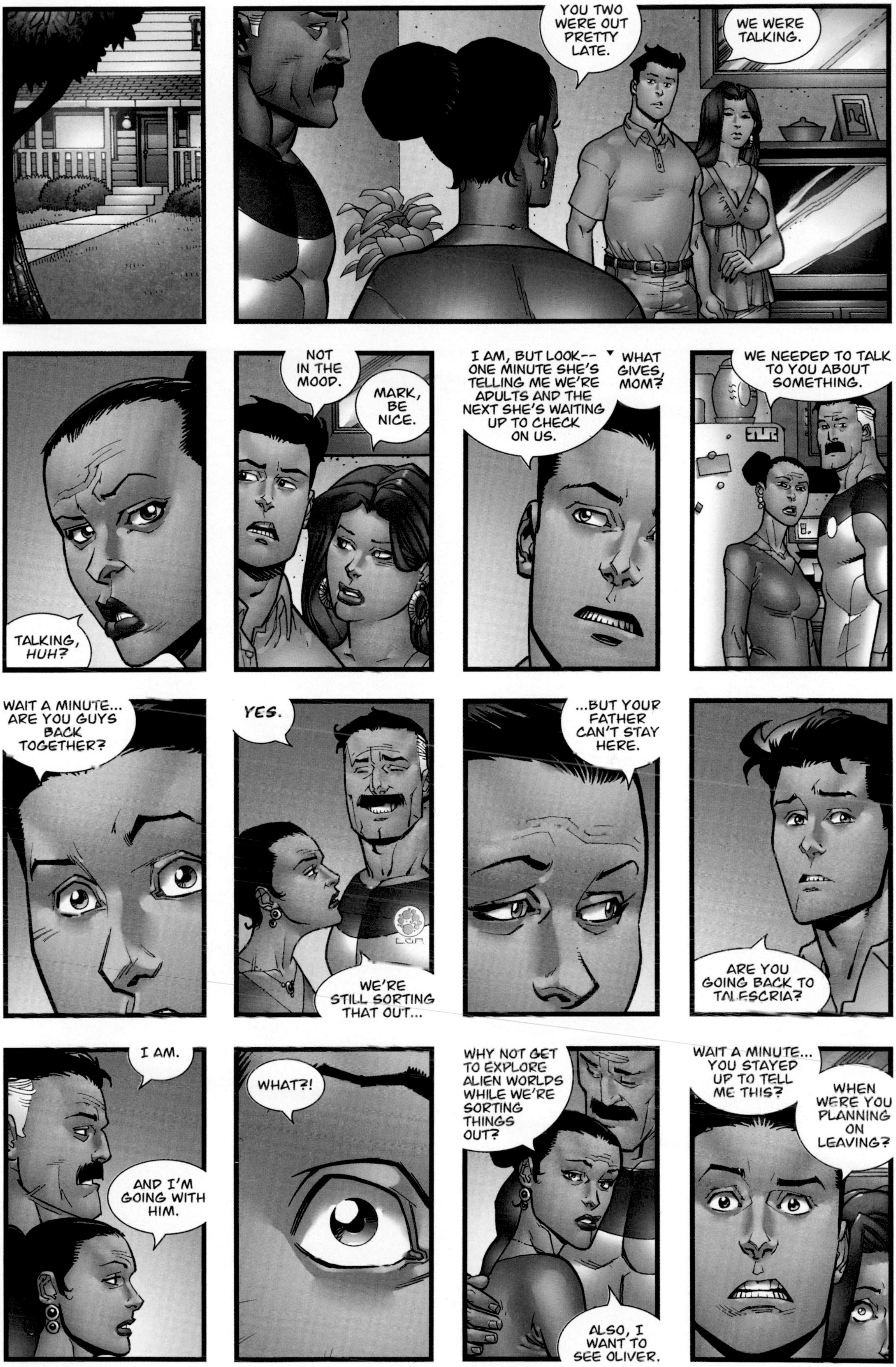
YOU TWO WERE OUT PRETTY LATE.
WE WERE TALKING.
TALKING, HUH?
NOT IN THE MOOD.
MARK, BE NICE.
I AM, BUT LOOK-- ONE MINUTE SHE'S TELLING ME WE'RE ADULTS AND THE NEXT SHE'S WAITING UP TO CHECK ON US.
WHAT GIVES, MOM?
WE NEEDED TO TALK TO YOU ABOUT SOMETHING.
WAIT A MINUTE... ARE YOU GUYS BACK TOGETHER?
YES.
WE'RE STILL SORTING THAT OUT...
...BUT YOUR FATHER CAN'T STAY HERE.
ARE YOU GOING BACK TO TALESCRIA?
I AM.
AND I'M GOING WITH HIM.
WHAT?!
WHY NOT GET TO EXPLORE ALIEN WORLDS WHILE WE'RE SORTING THINGS OUT?
ALSO, I WANT TO SEE OLIVER.
WAIT A MINUTE... YOU STAYED UP TO TELL ME THIS?
WHEN WERE YOU PLANNING ON LEAVING?

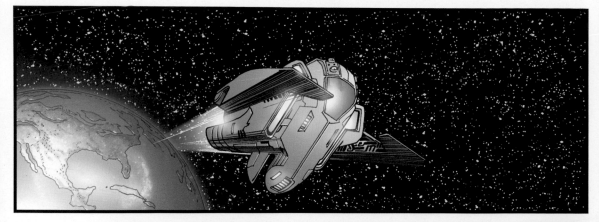

WELL... THIS HAS BEEN AN EVENTFUL FEW HOURS.

ARE YOU OKAY?

I'M FINE. I'M A LITTLE TOO OLD TO BE "MISSING MY MOMMY."

BUT YOU MISS HER ALREADY...

YEAH, OKAY... YOU GOT ME. BUT SHE'S ONLY GOING TO BE GONE SIX MONTHS, TOPS.

NICE OF HER TO LEAVE US THE HOUSE, THOUGH.

I'M *TOTALLY* MOVING IN, BY THE WAY. I'M SICK OF MY PARENTS' PLACE.

WE CAN MOVE INTO THE MASTER BEDROOM.

NO WAY.

MY PARENTS HAVE HAD SEX IN THERE.

FROM WHAT YOUR MOM TOLD ME, IF THAT'LL KEEP YOU OUT OF A ROOM WE SHOULD PROBABLY JUST STAY *OUTSIDE*.

WHAT *DON'T* YOU AND MY MOTHER TALK ABOUT?

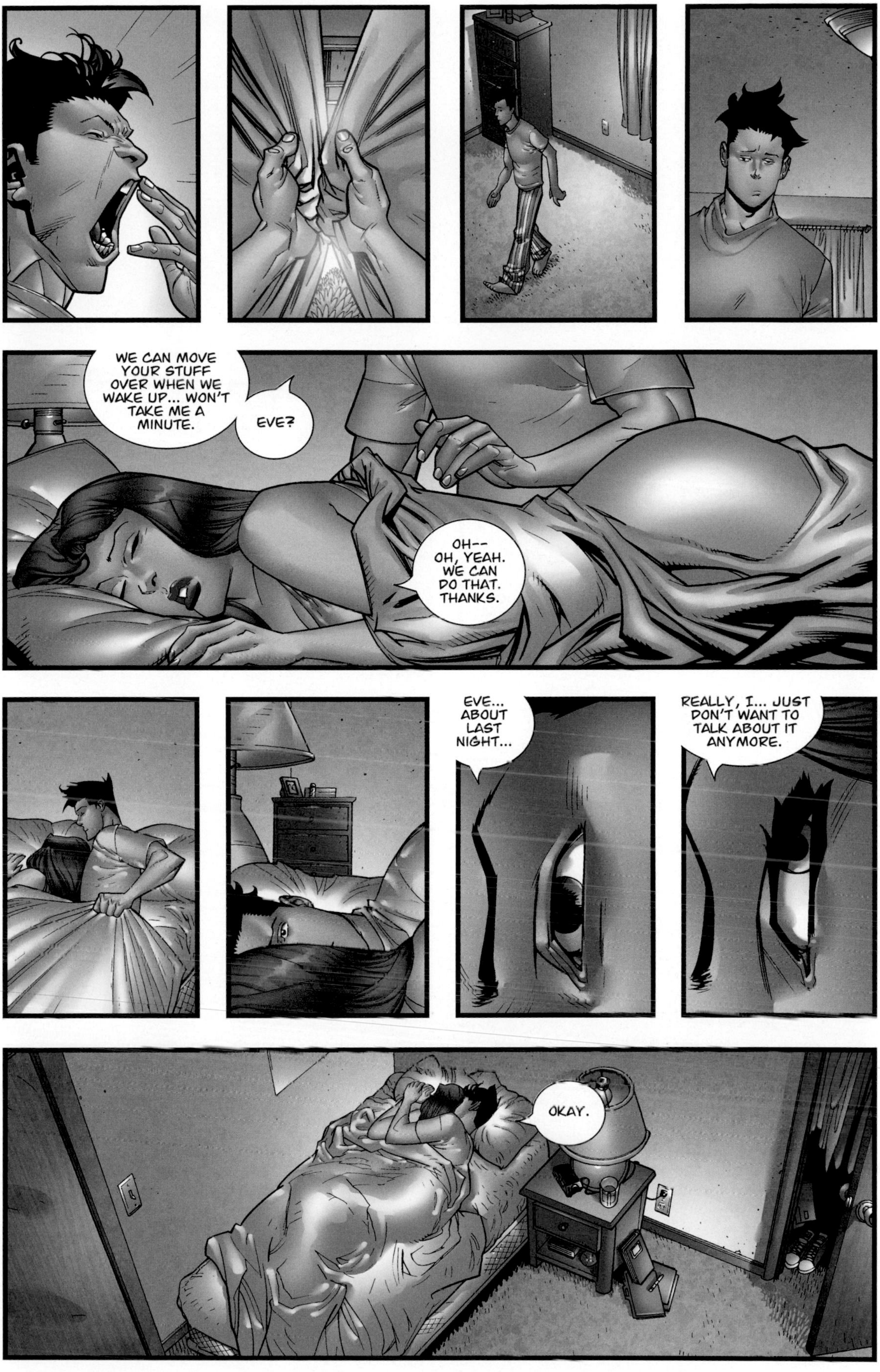

WE CAN MOVE YOUR STUFF OVER WHEN WE WAKE UP... WON'T TAKE ME A MINUTE.
EVE?
OH-- OH, YEAH. WE CAN DO THAT. THANKS.
EVE... ABOUT LAST NIGHT...
REALLY, I... JUST DON'T WANT TO TALK ABOUT IT ANYMORE.
OKAY.

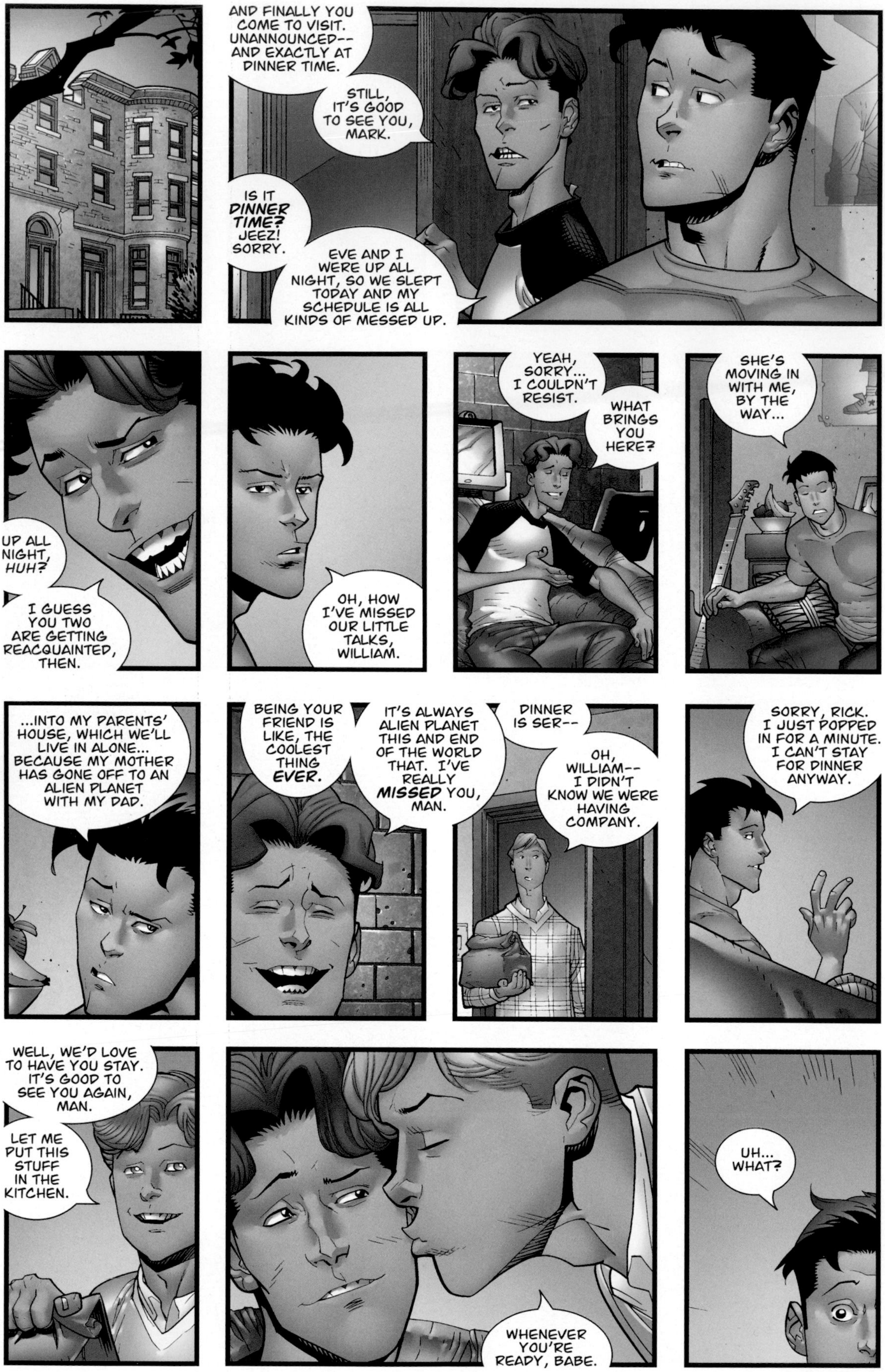

AND FINALLY YOU COME TO VISIT. UNANNOUNCED-- AND EXACTLY AT DINNER TIME.
STILL, IT'S GOOD TO SEE YOU, MARK.
IS IT DINNER TIME? JEEZ! SORRY.
EVE AND I WERE UP ALL NIGHT, SO WE SLEPT TODAY AND MY SCHEDULE IS ALL KINDS OF MESSED UP.
UP ALL NIGHT, HUH?
I GUESS YOU TWO ARE GETTING REACQUAINTED, THEN.
OH, HOW I'VE MISSED OUR LITTLE TALKS, WILLIAM.
YEAH, SORRY... I COULDN'T RESIST.
WHAT BRINGS YOU HERE?
SHE'S MOVING IN WITH ME, BY THE WAY...
...INTO MY PARENTS' HOUSE, WHICH WE'LL LIVE IN ALONE... BECAUSE MY MOTHER HAS GONE OFF TO AN ALIEN PLANET WITH MY DAD.
BEING YOUR FRIEND IS LIKE, THE COOLEST THING EVER.
IT'S ALWAYS ALIEN PLANET THIS AND END OF THE WORLD THAT. I'VE REALLY MISSED YOU, MAN.
DINNER IS SER--
OH, WILLIAM-- I DIDN'T KNOW WE WERE HAVING COMPANY.
SORRY, RICK. I JUST POPPED IN FOR A MINUTE. I CAN'T STAY FOR DINNER ANYWAY.
WELL, WE'D LOVE TO HAVE YOU STAY. IT'S GOOD TO SEE YOU AGAIN, MAN.
LET ME PUT THIS STUFF IN THE KITCHEN.
WHENEVER YOU'RE READY, BABE.
UH... WHAT?

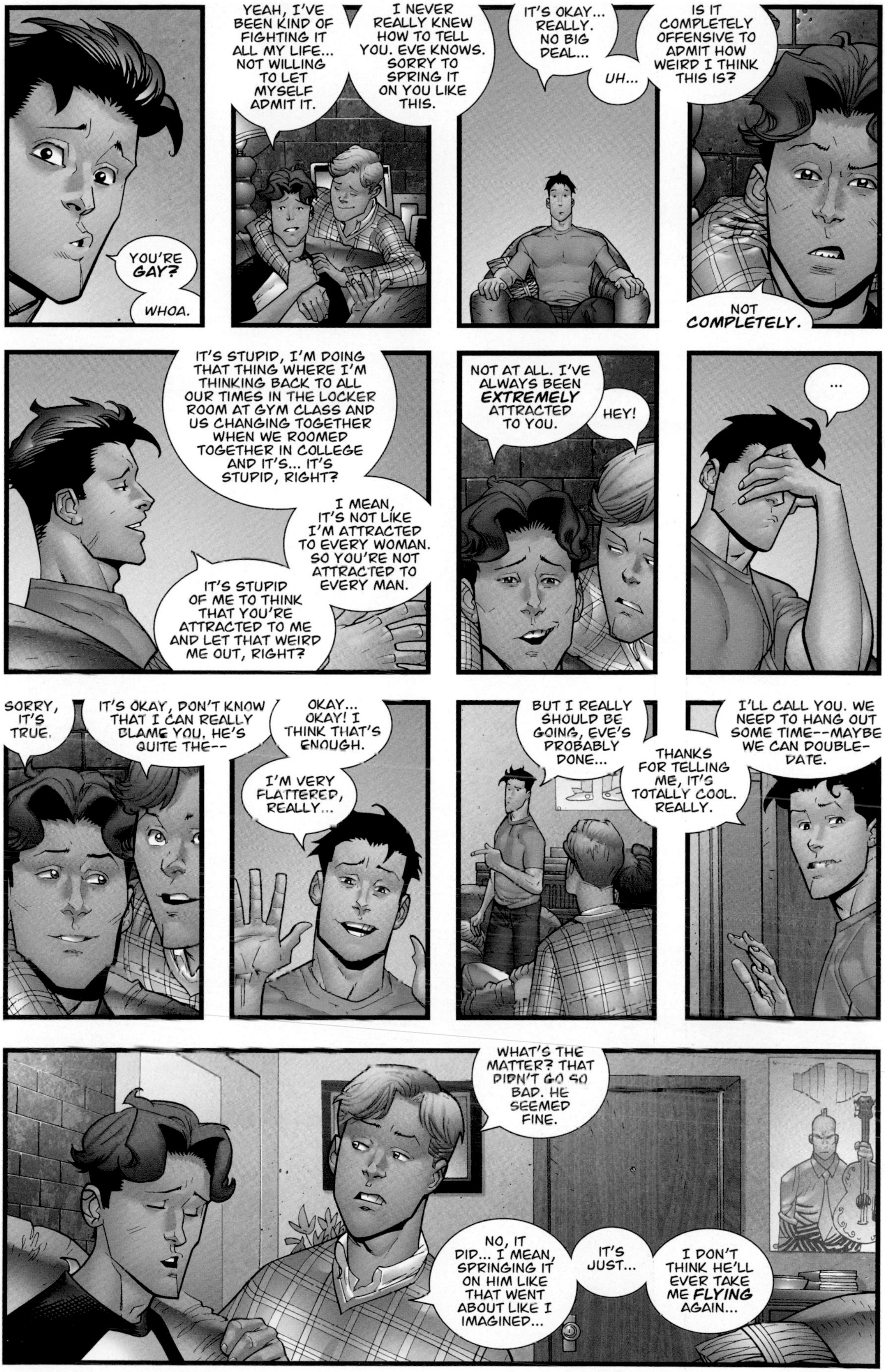
YOU'RE GAY?
WHOA.
YEAH, I'VE BEEN KIND OF FIGHTING IT ALL MY LIFE... NOT WILLING TO LET MYSELF ADMIT IT.
I NEVER REALLY KNEW HOW TO TELL YOU. EVE KNOWS. SORRY TO SPRING IT ON YOU LIKE THIS.
IT'S OKAY... REALLY. NO BIG DEAL...
UH...
IS IT COMPLETELY OFFENSIVE TO ADMIT HOW WEIRD I THINK THIS IS?
NOT COMPLETELY.
IT'S STUPID, I'M DOING THAT THING WHERE I'M THINKING BACK TO ALL OUR TIMES IN THE LOCKER ROOM AT GYM CLASS AND US CHANGING TOGETHER WHEN WE ROOMED TOGETHER IN COLLEGE AND IT'S... IT'S STUPID, RIGHT?
IT'S STUPID OF ME TO THINK THAT YOU'RE ATTRACTED TO ME AND LET THAT WEIRD ME OUT, RIGHT?
I MEAN, IT'S NOT LIKE I'M ATTRACTED TO EVERY WOMAN. SO YOU'RE NOT ATTRACTED TO EVERY MAN.
NOT AT ALL. I'VE ALWAYS BEEN EXTREMELY ATTRACTED TO YOU.
HEY!
...
SORRY, IT'S TRUE.
IT'S OKAY, DON'T KNOW THAT I CAN REALLY BLAME YOU. HE'S QUITE THE--
OKAY... OKAY! I THINK THAT'S ENOUGH.
I'M VERY FLATTERED, REALLY...
BUT I REALLY SHOULD BE GOING, EVE'S PROBABLY DONE...
THANKS FOR TELLING ME, IT'S TOTALLY COOL. REALLY.
I'LL CALL YOU. WE NEED TO HANG OUT SOME TIME--MAYBE WE CAN DOUBLE-DATE.
WHAT'S THE MATTER? THAT DIDN'T GO SO BAD. HE SEEMED FINE.
NO, IT DID... I MEAN, SPRINGING IT ON HIM LIKE THAT WENT ABOUT LIKE I IMAGINED...
IT'S JUST...
I DON'T THINK HE'LL EVER TAKE ME FLYING AGAIN...

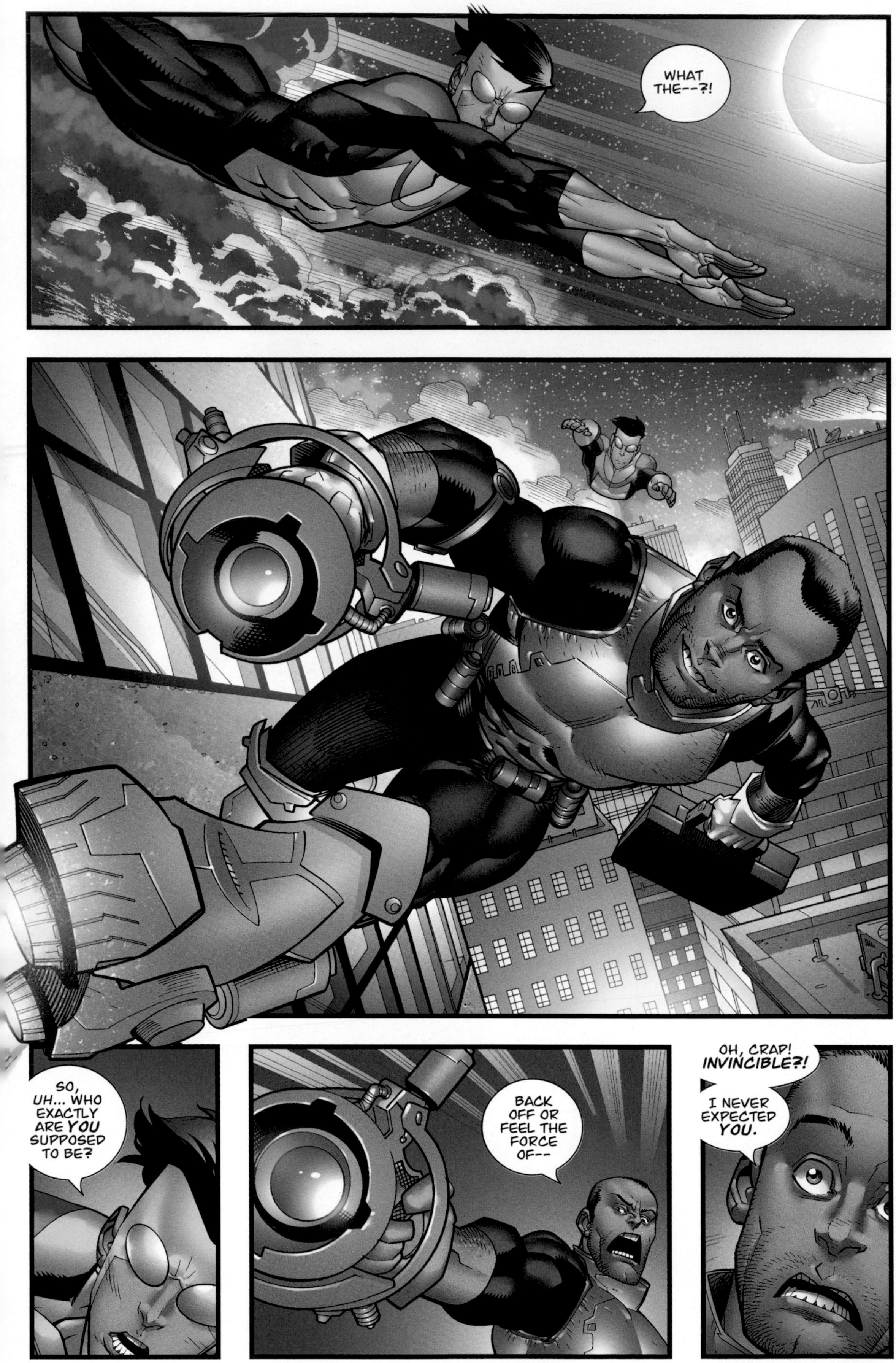
WHAT THE--?!
SO, UH... WHO EXACTLY ARE YOU SUPPOSED TO BE?
BACK OFF OR FEEL THE FORCE OF--
OH, CRAP! INVINCIBLE?!
I NEVER EXPECTED YOU.

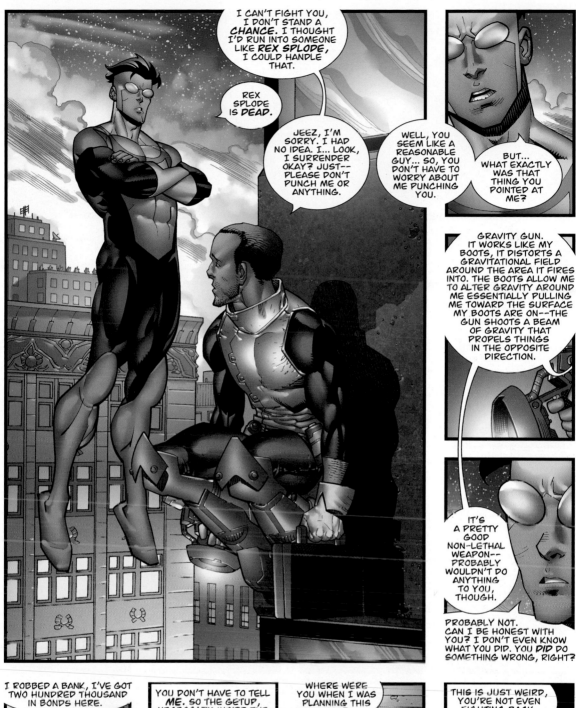

I CAN'T FIGHT YOU, I DON'T STAND A **CHANCE.** I THOUGHT I'D RUN INTO SOMEONE LIKE **REX SPLODE,** I COULD HANDLE THAT.

REX SPLODE IS **DEAD.**

JEEZ, I'M SORRY. I HAD NO IDEA. I... LOOK, I SURRENDER OKAY? JUST-- PLEASE DON'T PUNCH ME OR ANYTHING.

WELL, YOU SEEM LIKE A REASONABLE GUY... SO, YOU DON'T HAVE TO WORRY ABOUT ME PUNCHING YOU.

BUT... WHAT EXACTLY WAS THAT THING YOU POINTED AT ME?

GRAVITY GUN. IT WORKS LIKE MY BOOTS, IT DISTORTS A GRAVITATIONAL FIELD AROUND THE AREA IT FIRES INTO. THE BOOTS ALLOW ME TO ALTER GRAVITY AROUND ME ESSENTIALLY PULLING ME TOWARD THE SURFACE MY BOOTS ARE ON--THE GUN SHOOTS A BEAM OF GRAVITY THAT PROPELS THINGS IN THE OPPOSITE DIRECTION.

IT'S A PRETTY GOOD NON-LETHAL WEAPON-- PROBABLY WOULDN'T DO ANYTHING TO YOU, THOUGH.

PROBABLY NOT. CAN I BE HONEST WITH YOU? I DON'T EVEN KNOW WHAT YOU DID. YOU **DID** DO SOMETHING WRONG, RIGHT?

I ROBBED A BANK, I'VE GOT TWO HUNDRED THOUSAND IN BONDS HERE.

IT WAS A CINCH WITH THE BOOTS, NOBODY SAW ME, NO ONE LOOKS UP.

YOU DON'T HAVE TO TELL **ME.** SO THE GETUP, NECESSARY INSIDE THE BANK, SURE--BUT OUTSIDE?

I MEAN, IF YOU'D JUST BEEN WALKING DOWN THE STREET WITH A BRIEFCASE, I PROBABLY WOULDN'T HAVE EVEN **NOTICED** YOU.

JUST SAYING.

WHERE WERE YOU WHEN I WAS PLANNING THIS JOB?

THIS IS **SO** EMBARRASSING.

THIS IS JUST WEIRD, YOU'RE NOT EVEN FIGHTING BACK, YOU SEEM SO... REASONABLE.

WHY'D YOU DO IT? I'M CURIOUS.

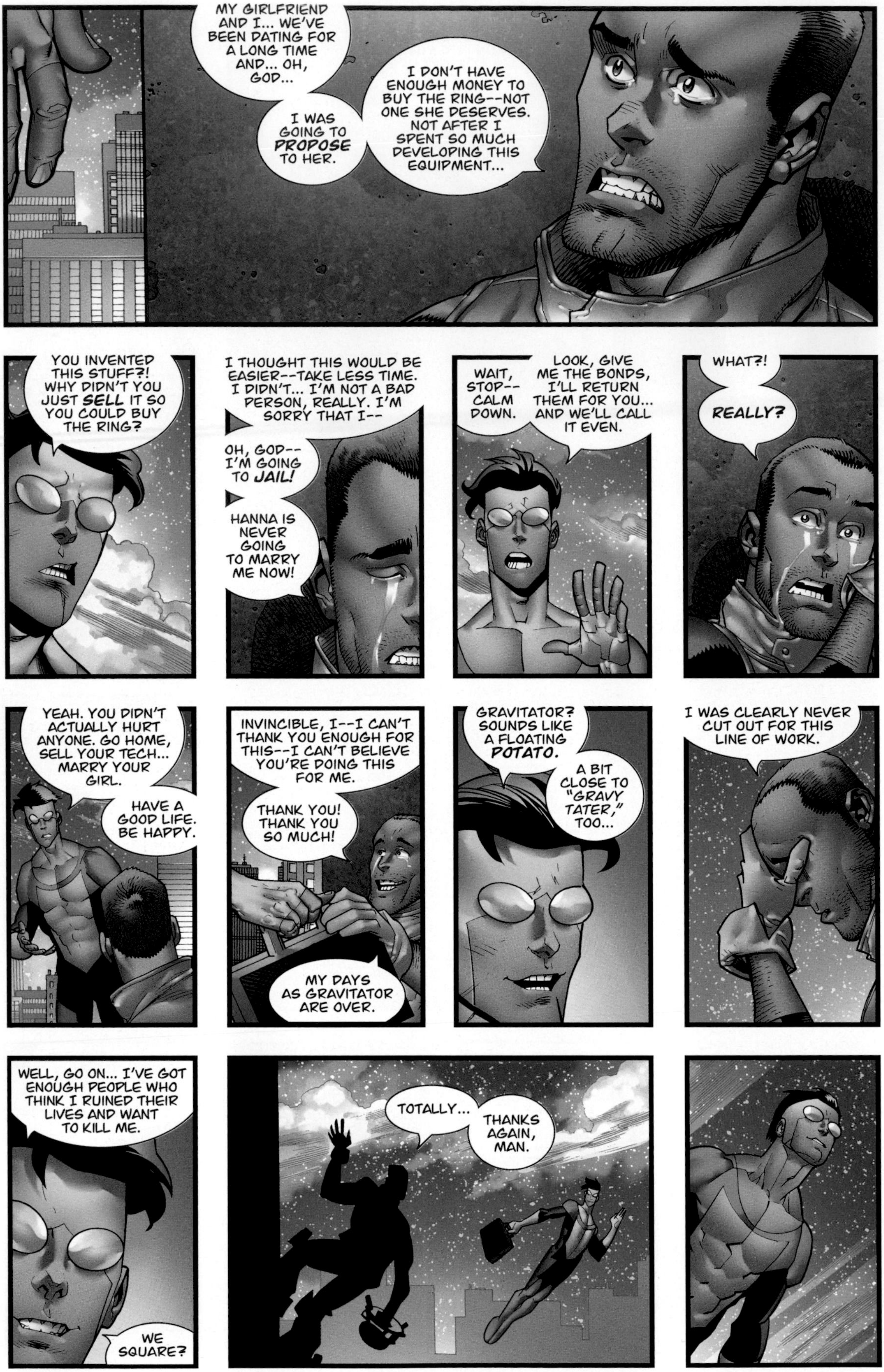
MY GIRLFRIEND AND I... WE'VE BEEN DATING FOR A LONG TIME AND... OH, GOD...
I WAS GOING TO PROPOSE TO HER.
I DON'T HAVE ENOUGH MONEY TO BUY THE RING--NOT ONE SHE DESERVES. NOT AFTER I SPENT SO MUCH DEVELOPING THIS EQUIPMENT...
YOU INVENTED THIS STUFF?! WHY DIDN'T YOU JUST SELL IT SO YOU COULD BUY THE RING?
I THOUGHT THIS WOULD BE EASIER--TAKE LESS TIME. I DIDN'T... I'M NOT A BAD PERSON, REALLY. I'M SORRY THAT I--
OH, GOD-- I'M GOING TO JAIL!
HANNA IS NEVER GOING TO MARRY ME NOW!
WAIT, STOP-- CALM DOWN.
LOOK, GIVE ME THE BONDS, I'LL RETURN THEM FOR YOU... AND WE'LL CALL IT EVEN.
WHAT?!
REALLY?
YEAH. YOU DIDN'T ACTUALLY HURT ANYONE. GO HOME, SELL YOUR TECH... MARRY YOUR GIRL.
HAVE A GOOD LIFE. BE HAPPY.
INVINCIBLE, I--I CAN'T THANK YOU ENOUGH FOR THIS--I CAN'T BELIEVE YOU'RE DOING THIS FOR ME.
THANK YOU! THANK YOU SO MUCH!
MY DAYS AS GRAVITATOR ARE OVER.
GRAVITATOR? SOUNDS LIKE A FLOATING POTATO.
A BIT CLOSE TO "GRAVY TATER," TOO...
I WAS CLEARLY NEVER CUT OUT FOR THIS LINE OF WORK.
WELL, GO ON... I'VE GOT ENOUGH PEOPLE WHO THINK I RUINED THEIR LIVES AND WANT TO KILL ME.
WE SQUARE?
TOTALLY...
THANKS AGAIN, MAN.

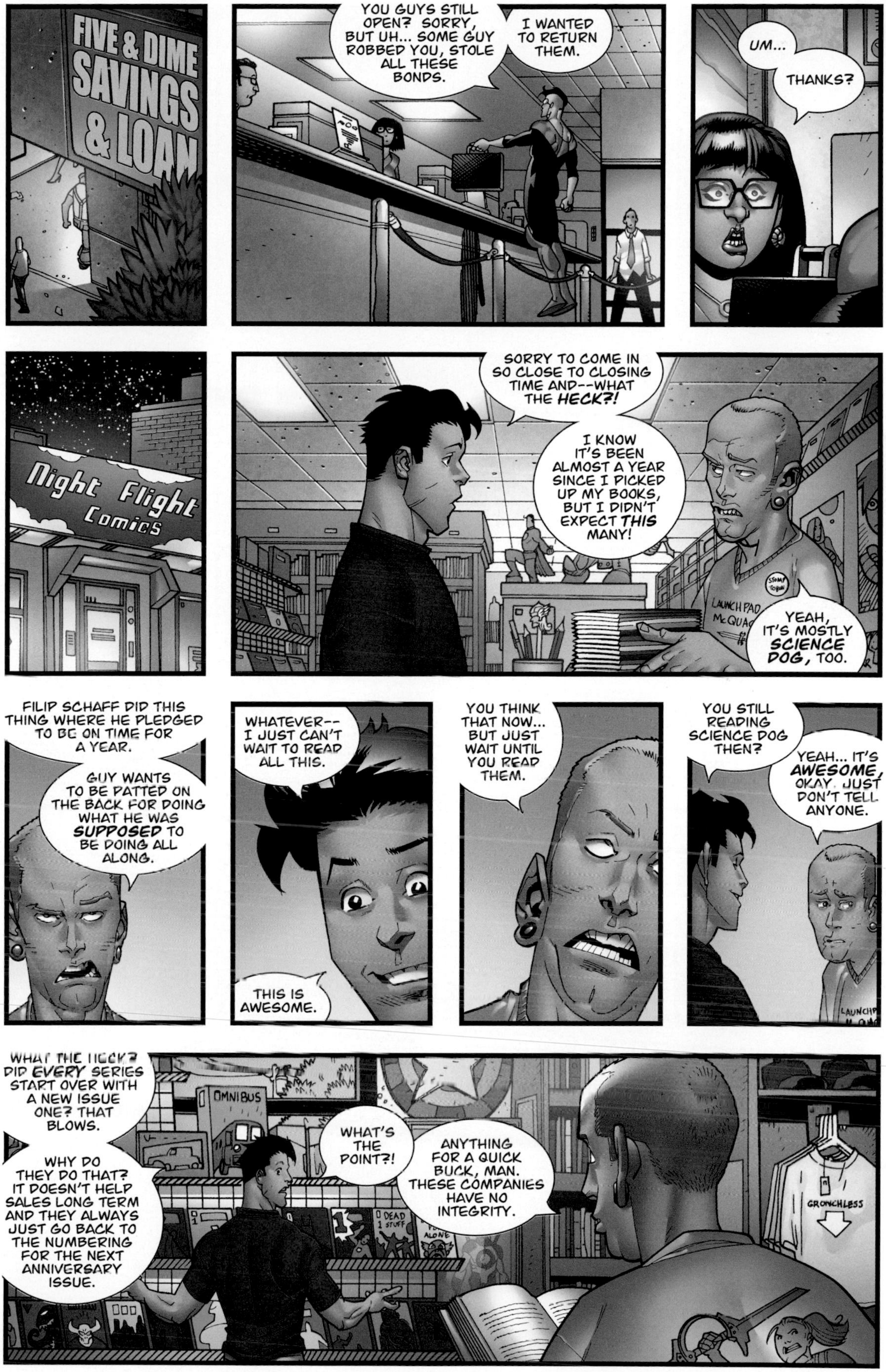
FIVE & DIME SAVINGS & LOAN
YOU GUYS STILL OPEN? SORRY, BUT UH... SOME GUY ROBBED YOU, STOLE ALL THESE BONDS.
I WANTED TO RETURN THEM.
UM...
THANKS?
Night Flight Comics
SORRY TO COME IN SO CLOSE TO CLOSING TIME AND--WHAT THE HECK?!
I KNOW IT'S BEEN ALMOST A YEAR SINCE I PICKED UP MY BOOKS, BUT I DIDN'T EXPECT THIS MANY!
YEAH, IT'S MOSTLY SCIENCE DOG, TOO.
FILIP SCHAFF DID THIS THING WHERE HE PLEDGED TO BE ON TIME FOR A YEAR.
GUY WANTS TO BE PATTED ON THE BACK FOR DOING WHAT HE WAS SUPPOSED TO BE DOING ALL ALONG.
WHATEVER-- I JUST CAN'T WAIT TO READ ALL THIS.
THIS IS AWESOME.
YOU THINK THAT NOW... BUT JUST WAIT UNTIL YOU READ THEM.
YOU STILL READING SCIENCE DOG THEN?
YEAH... IT'S AWESOME, OKAY. JUST DON'T TELL ANYONE.
WHAT THE HECK? DID EVERY SERIES START OVER WITH A NEW ISSUE ONE? THAT BLOWS.
WHY DO THEY DO THAT? IT DOESN'T HELP SALES LONG TERM AND THEY ALWAYS JUST GO BACK TO THE NUMBERING FOR THE NEXT ANNIVERSARY ISSUE.
WHAT'S THE POINT?!
ANYTHING FOR A QUICK BUCK, MAN. THESE COMPANIES HAVE NO INTEGRITY.
OMNIBUS
GRONCHLESS

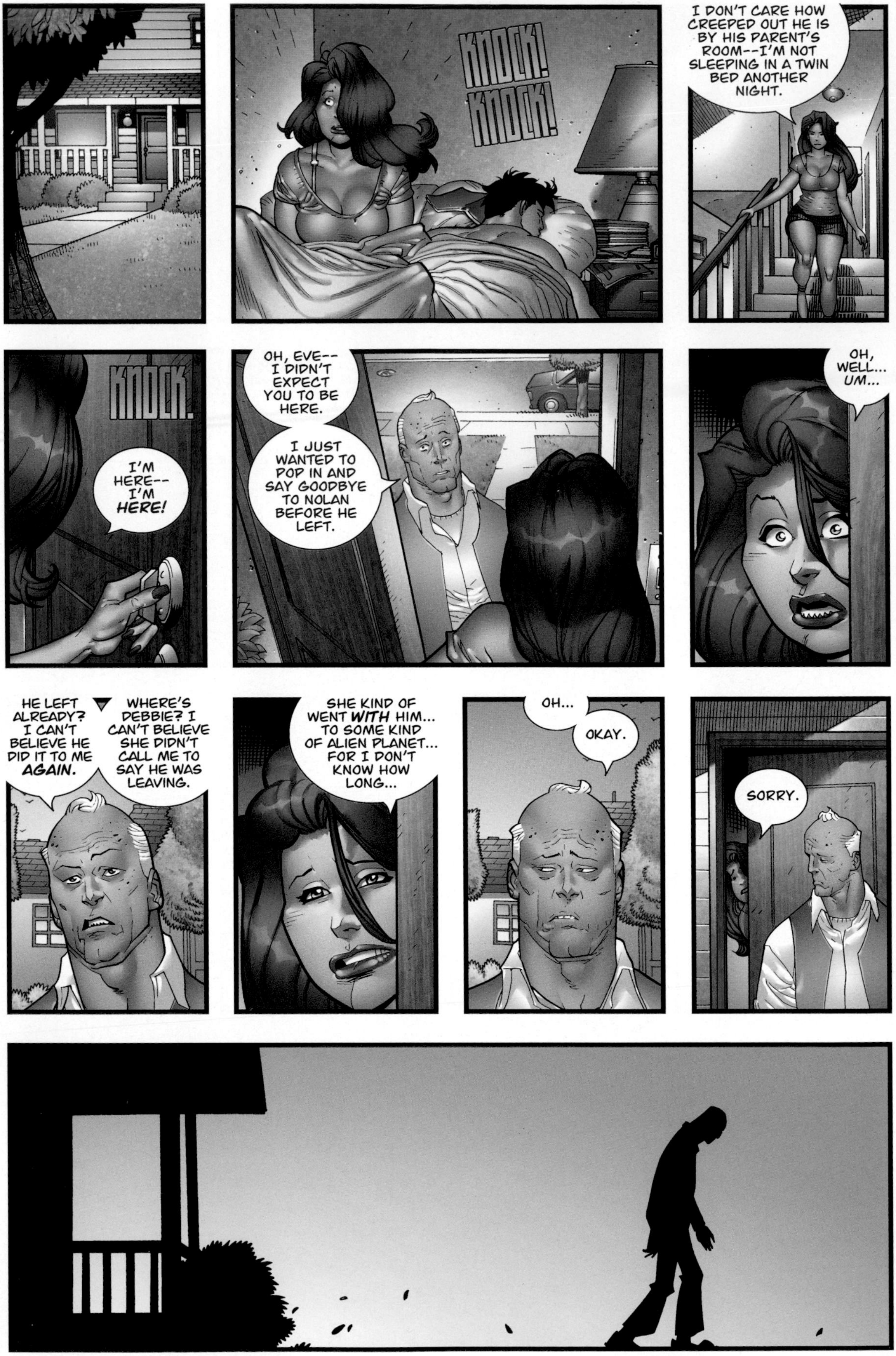
KNOCK! KNOCK!
I DON'T CARE HOW CREEPED OUT HE IS BY HIS PARENT'S ROOM--I'M NOT SLEEPING IN A TWIN BED ANOTHER NIGHT.
KNOCK.
I'M HERE-- I'M HERE!
OH, EVE-- I DIDN'T EXPECT YOU TO BE HERE.
I JUST WANTED TO POP IN AND SAY GOODBYE TO NOLAN BEFORE HE LEFT.
OH, WELL... UM...
HE LEFT ALREADY? I CAN'T BELIEVE HE DID IT TO ME AGAIN.
WHERE'S DEBBIE? I CAN'T BELIEVE SHE DIDN'T CALL ME TO SAY HE WAS LEAVING.
SHE KIND OF WENT WITH HIM... TO SOME KIND OF ALIEN PLANET... FOR I DON'T KNOW HOW LONG...
OH...
OKAY.
SORRY.

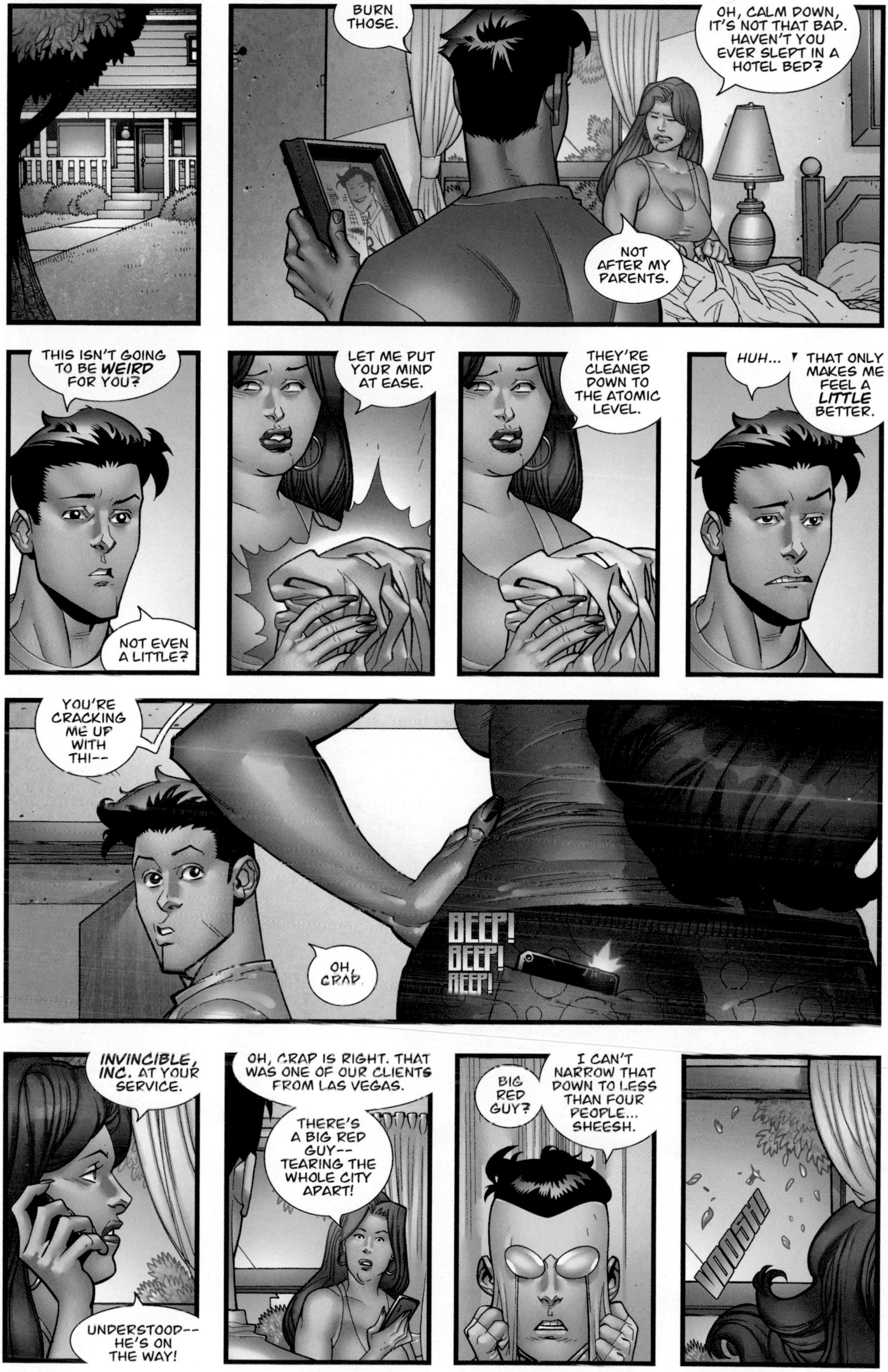
BURN THOSE.
OH, CALM DOWN, IT'S NOT THAT BAD. HAVEN'T YOU EVER SLEPT IN A HOTEL BED?
NOT AFTER MY PARENTS.
THIS ISN'T GOING TO BE WEIRD FOR YOU?
NOT EVEN A LITTLE?
LET ME PUT YOUR MIND AT EASE.
THEY'RE CLEANED DOWN TO THE ATOMIC LEVEL.
HUH...
THAT ONLY MAKES ME FEEL A LITTLE BETTER.
YOU'RE CRACKING ME UP WITH THI--
BEEP! BEEP! BEEP!
OH, CRAP.
INVINCIBLE, INC. AT YOUR SERVICE.
UNDERSTOOD-- HE'S ON THE WAY!
OH, CRAP IS RIGHT. THAT WAS ONE OF OUR CLIENTS FROM LAS VEGAS.
THERE'S A BIG RED GUY-- TEARING THE WHOLE CITY APART!
BIG RED GUY?
I CAN'T NARROW THAT DOWN TO LESS THAN FOUR PEOPLE... SHEESH.
VOOOSH!

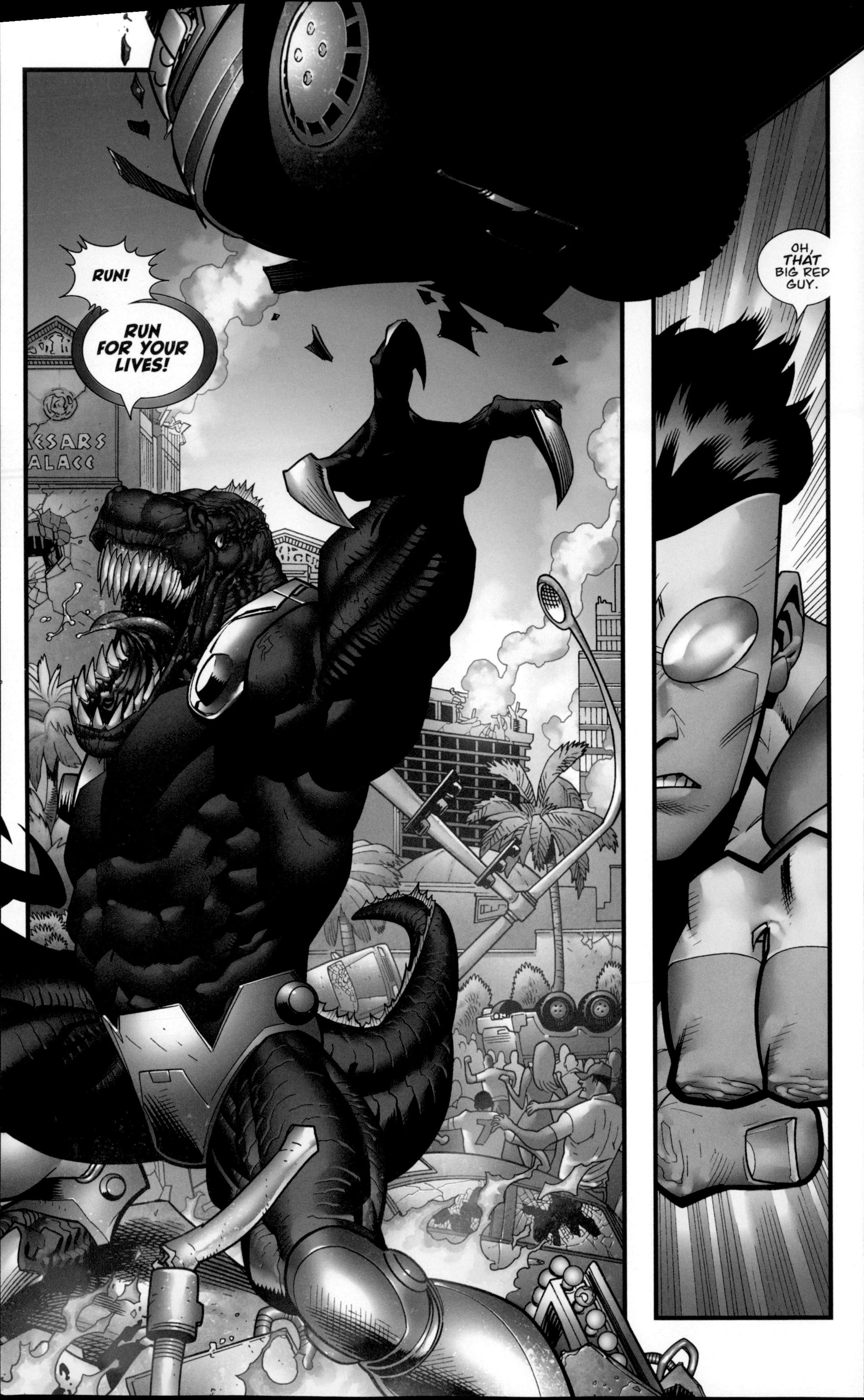
RUN!
RUN FOR YOUR LIVES!
OH, THAT BIG RED GUY.

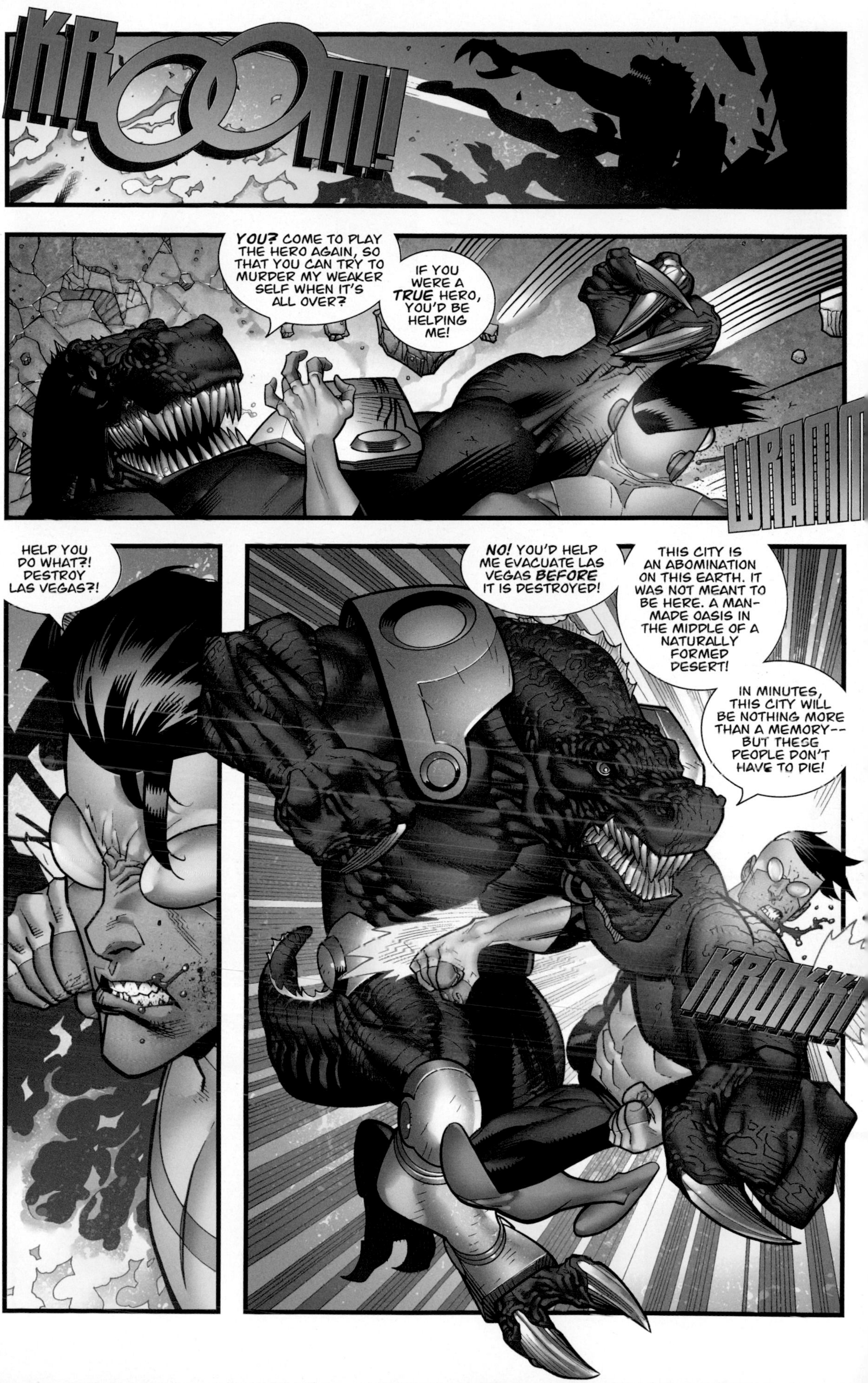
KROOM!
YOU? COME TO PLAY THE HERO AGAIN, SO THAT YOU CAN TRY TO MURDER MY WEAKER SELF WHEN IT'S ALL OVER?
IF YOU WERE A TRUE HERO, YOU'D BE HELPING ME!
WRAMM
HELP YOU DO WHAT?! DESTROY LAS VEGAS?!
NO! YOU'D HELP ME EVACUATE LAS VEGAS BEFORE IT IS DESTROYED!
THIS CITY IS AN ABOMINATION ON THIS EARTH. IT WAS NOT MEANT TO BE HERE. A MAN-MADE OASIS IN THE MIDDLE OF A NATURALLY FORMED DESERT!
IN MINUTES, THIS CITY WILL BE NOTHING MORE THAN A MEMORY-- BUT THESE PEOPLE DON'T HAVE TO DIE!
KRAKK!

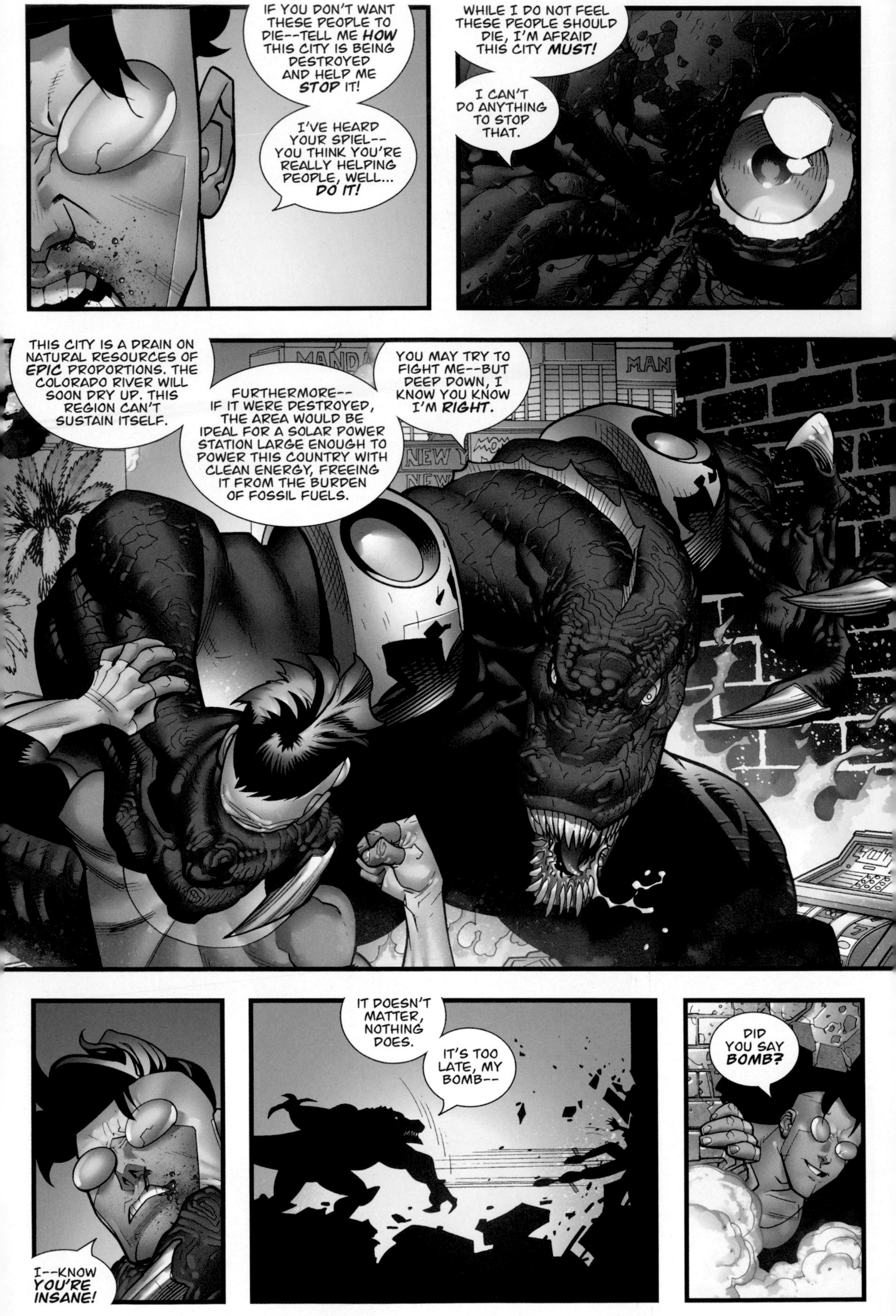
IF YOU DON'T WANT THESE PEOPLE TO DIE--TELL ME HOW THIS CITY IS BEING DESTROYED AND HELP ME STOP IT!
I'VE HEARD YOUR SPIEL--YOU THINK YOU'RE REALLY HELPING PEOPLE, WELL... DO IT!
WHILE I DO NOT FEEL THESE PEOPLE SHOULD DIE, I'M AFRAID THIS CITY MUST!
I CAN'T DO ANYTHING TO STOP THAT.
THIS CITY IS A DRAIN ON NATURAL RESOURCES OF EPIC PROPORTIONS. THE COLORADO RIVER WILL SOON DRY UP. THIS REGION CAN'T SUSTAIN ITSELF.
FURTHERMORE--IF IT WERE DESTROYED, THE AREA WOULD BE IDEAL FOR A SOLAR POWER STATION LARGE ENOUGH TO POWER THIS COUNTRY WITH CLEAN ENERGY, FREEING IT FROM THE BURDEN OF FOSSIL FUELS.
YOU MAY TRY TO FIGHT ME--BUT DEEP DOWN, I KNOW YOU KNOW I'M RIGHT.
I--KNOW YOU'RE INSANE!
IT DOESN'T MATTER, NOTHING DOES.
IT'S TOO LATE, MY BOMB--
DID YOU SAY BOMB?

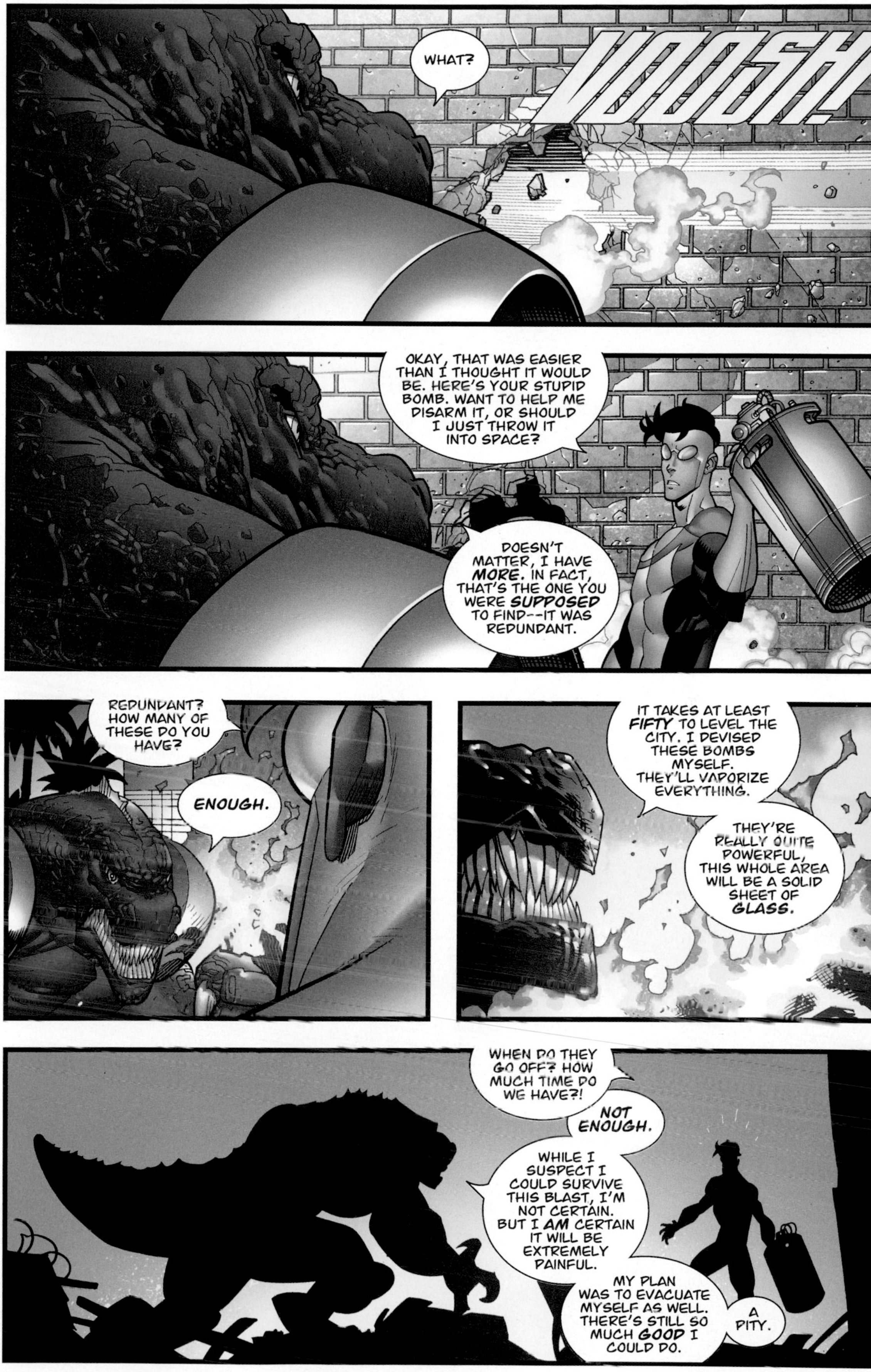

WHAT?
VOOSH!
OKAY, THAT WAS EASIER THAN I THOUGHT IT WOULD BE. HERE'S YOUR STUPID BOMB. WANT TO HELP ME DISARM IT, OR SHOULD I JUST THROW IT INTO SPACE?
DOESN'T MATTER, I HAVE MORE. IN FACT, THAT'S THE ONE YOU WERE SUPPOSED TO FIND--IT WAS REDUNDANT.
REDUNDANT? HOW MANY OF THESE DO YOU HAVE?
ENOUGH.
IT TAKES AT LEAST FIFTY TO LEVEL THE CITY. I DEVISED THESE BOMBS MYSELF. THEY'LL VAPORIZE EVERYTHING.
THEY'RE REALLY QUITE POWERFUL, THIS WHOLE AREA WILL BE A SOLID SHEET OF GLASS.
WHEN DO THEY GO OFF? HOW MUCH TIME DO WE HAVE?!
NOT ENOUGH.
WHILE I SUSPECT I COULD SURVIVE THIS BLAST, I'M NOT CERTAIN. BUT I AM CERTAIN IT WILL BE EXTREMELY PAINFUL.
MY PLAN WAS TO EVACUATE MYSELF AS WELL. THERE'S STILL SO MUCH GOOD I COULD DO.
A PITY.

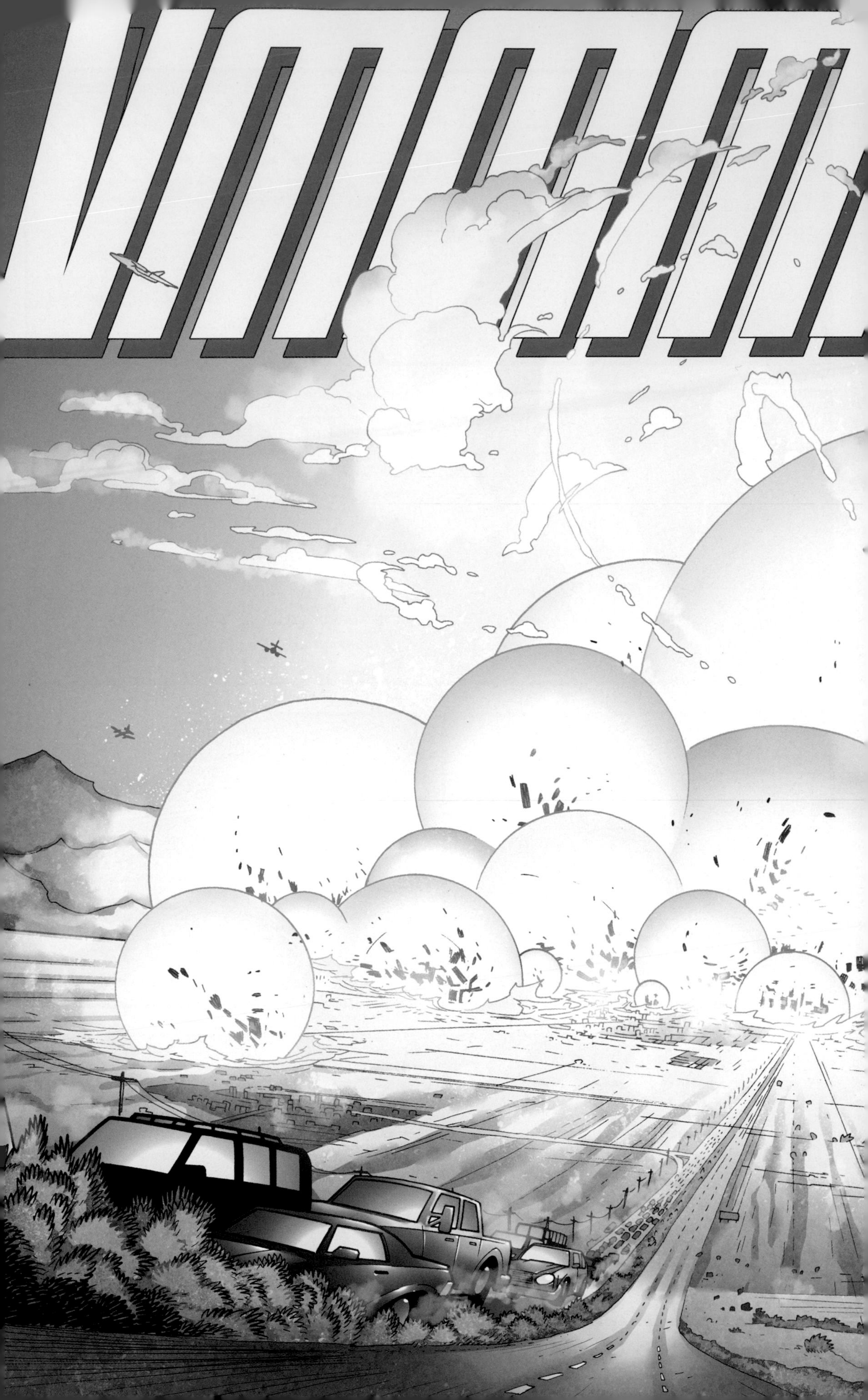

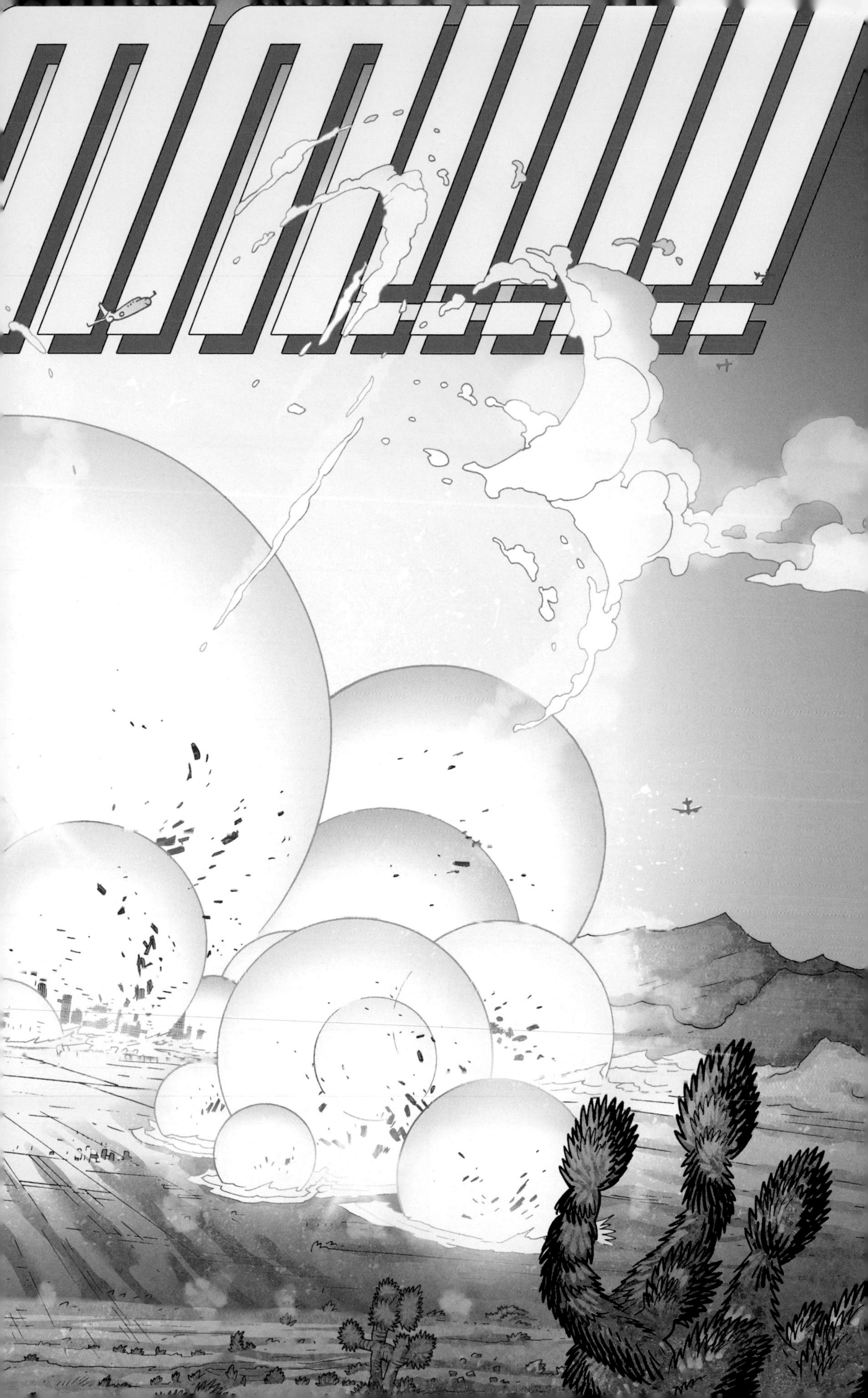

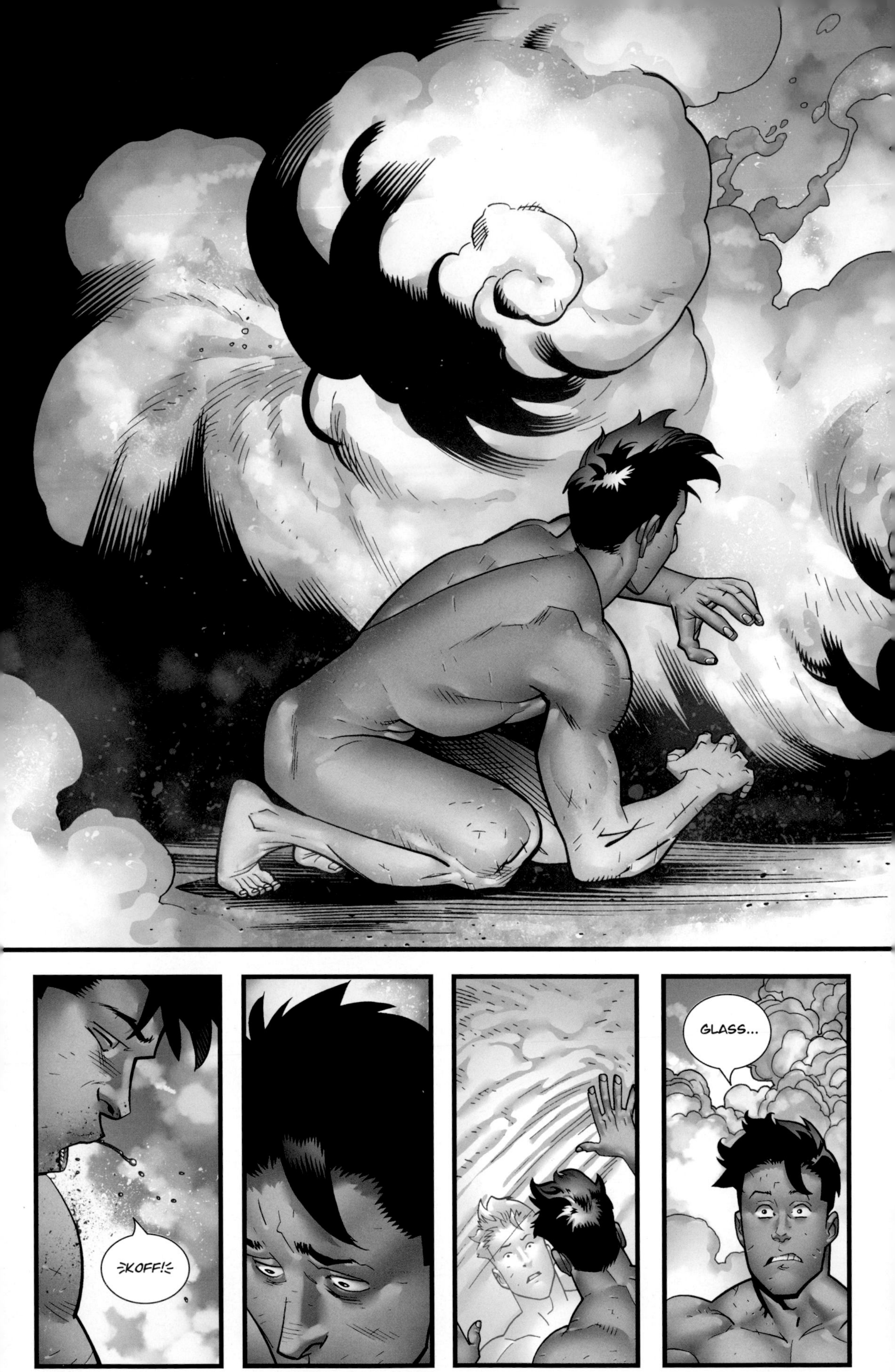
KOFF!
GLASS...

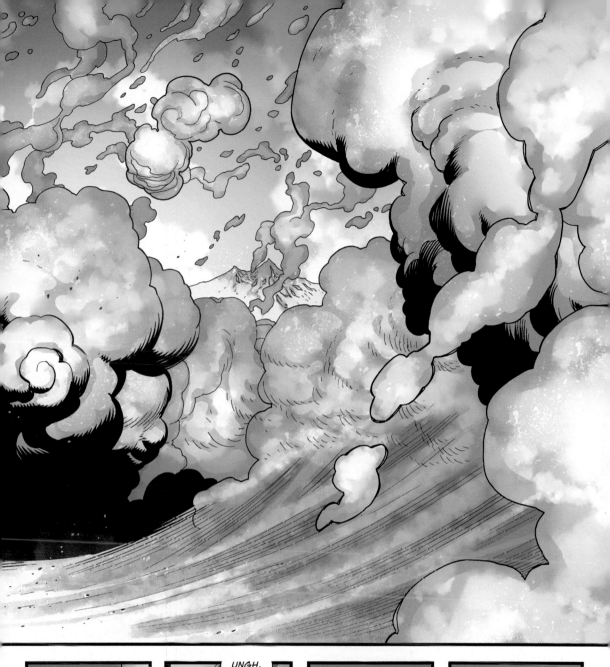

UNGH.

WHAT...?

MY GOD...

...IT'S ALL...

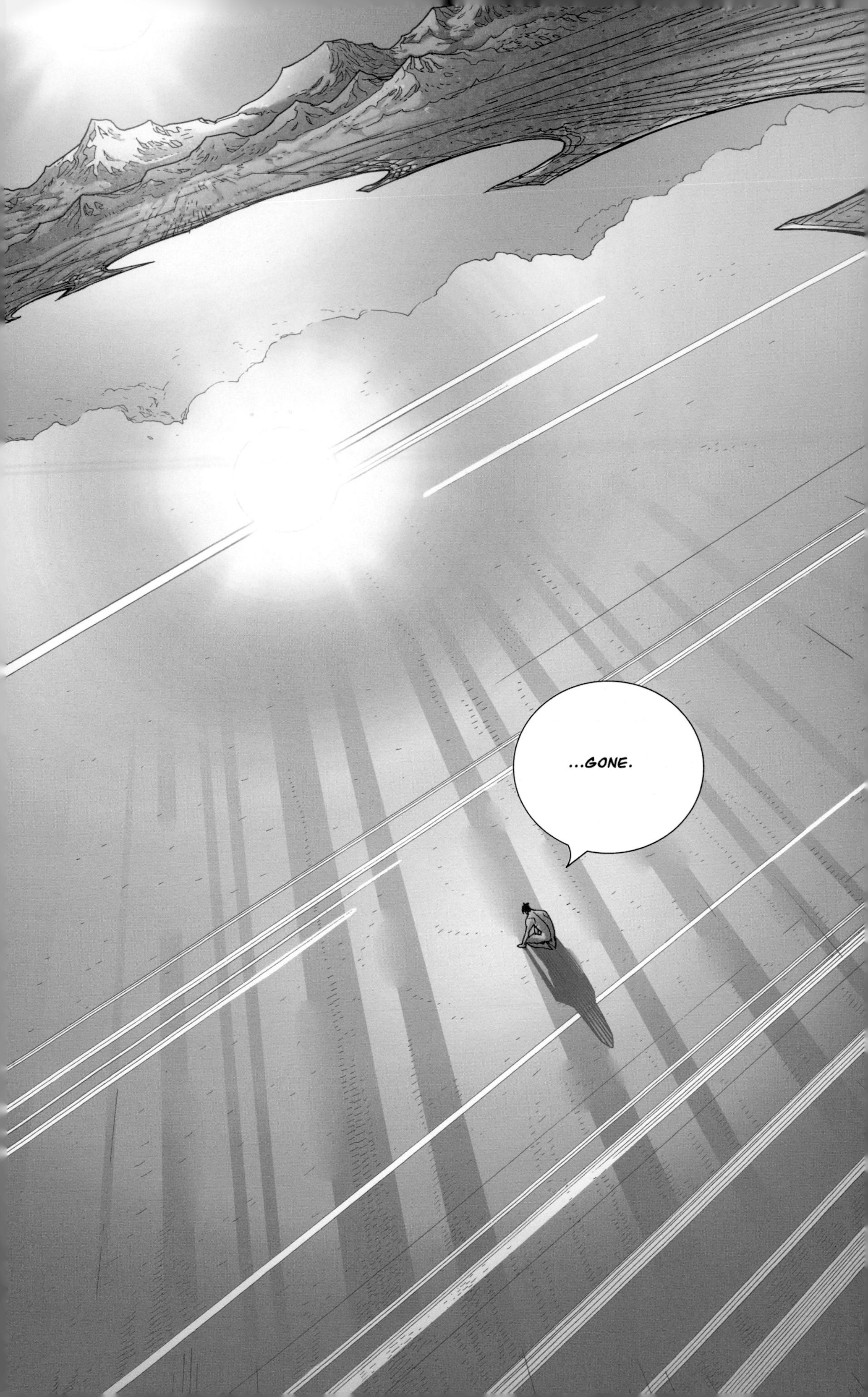
...GONE.

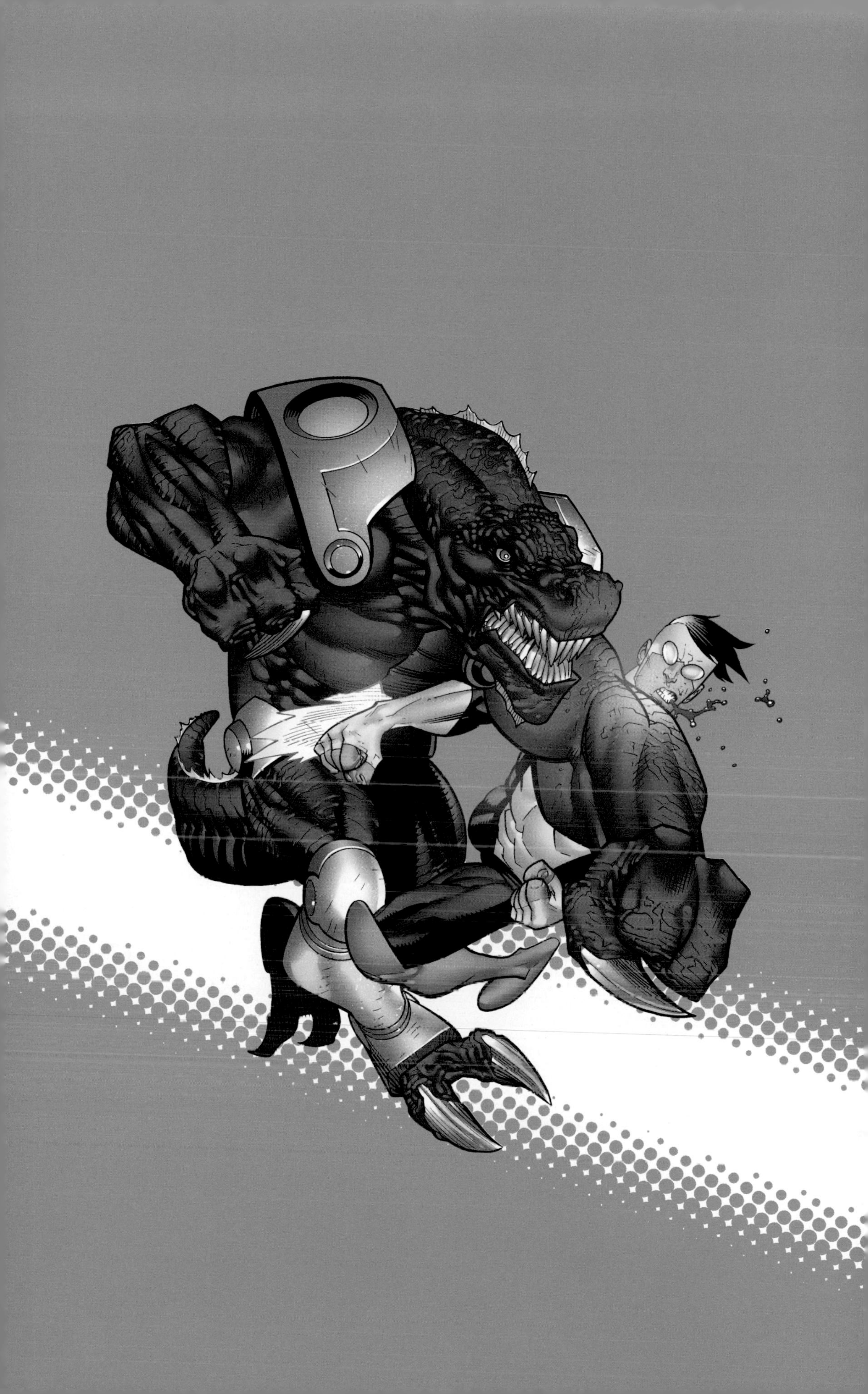

CHAPTER THREE

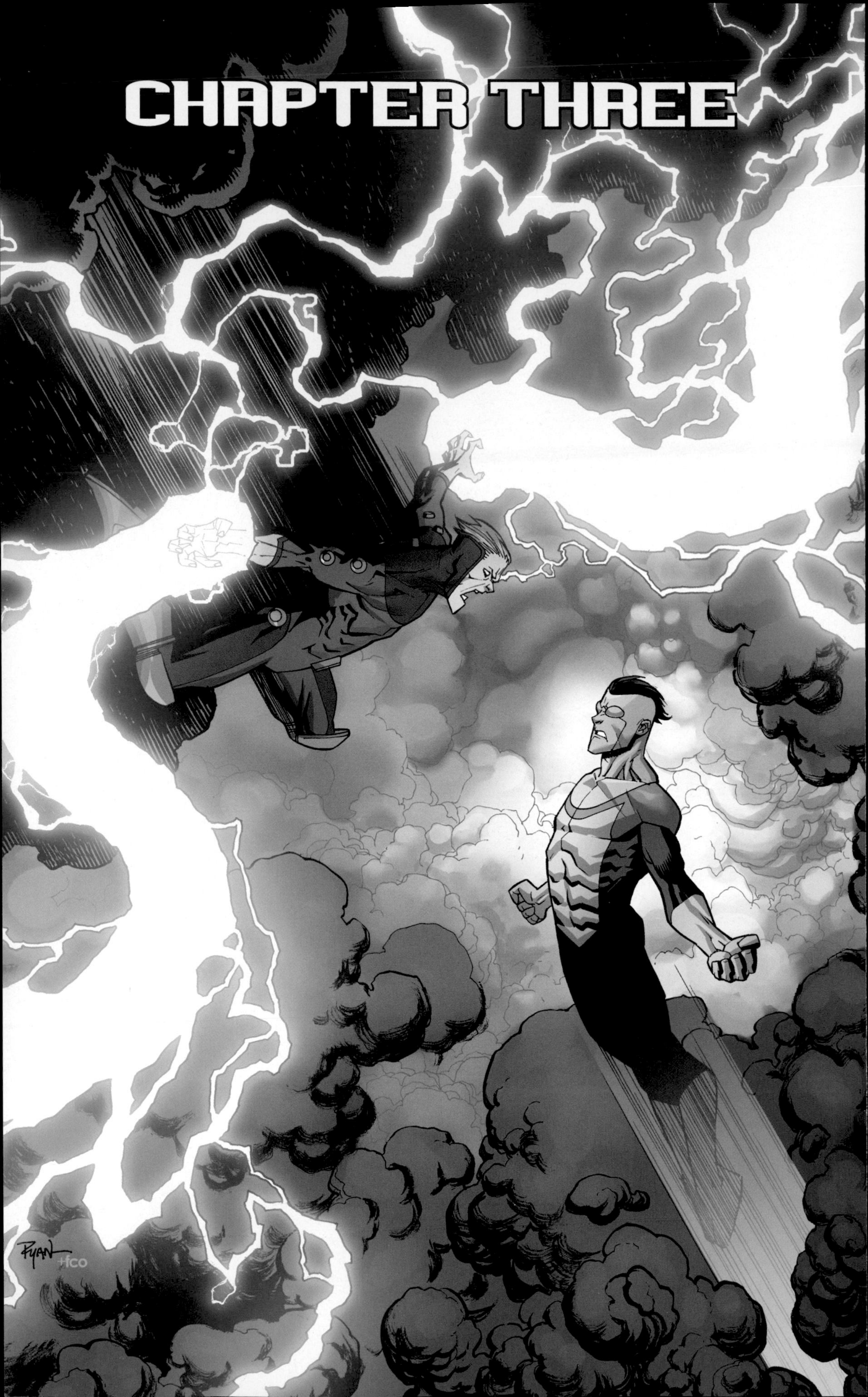

RYAN +fco

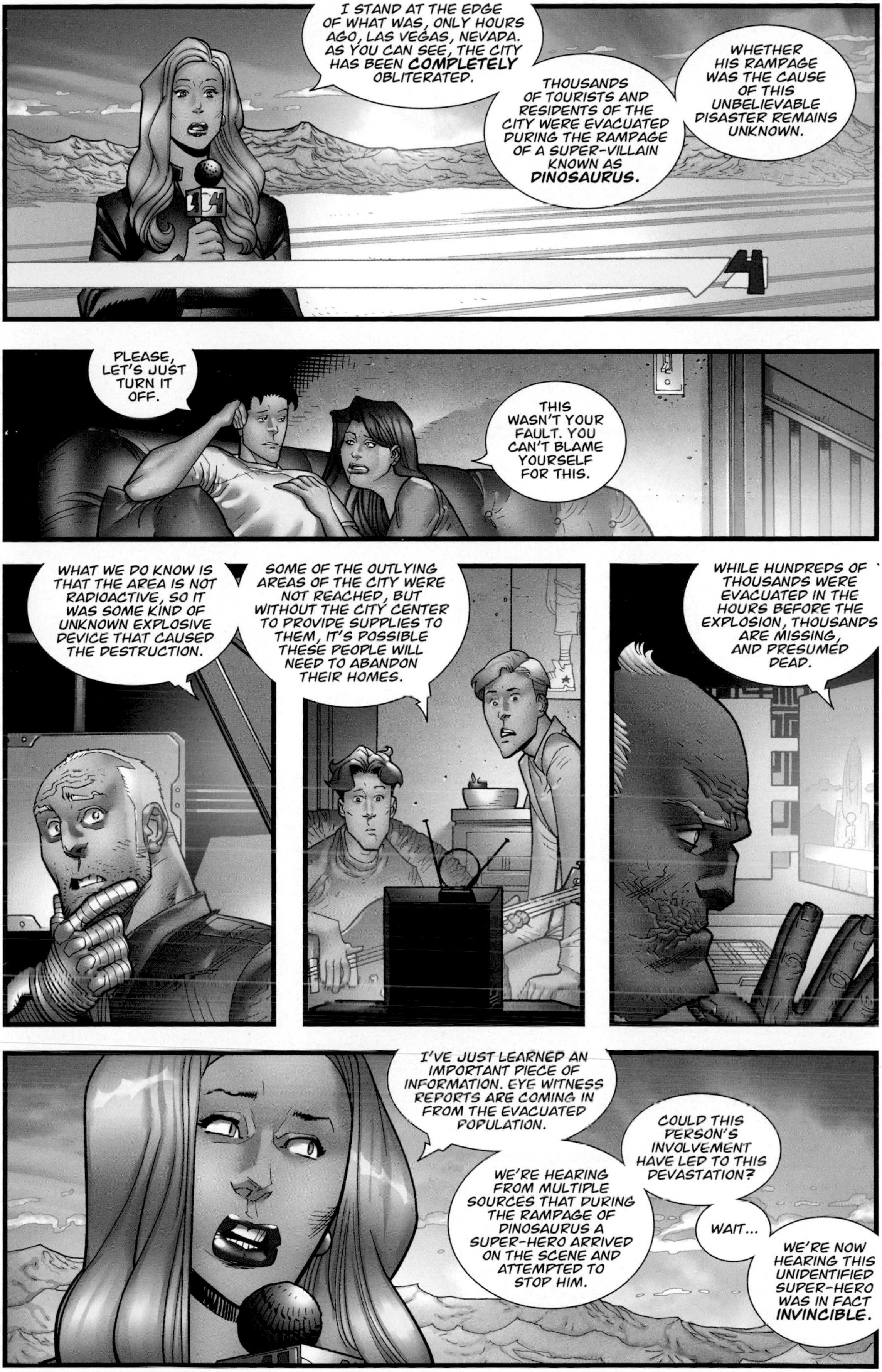
I STAND AT THE EDGE OF WHAT WAS, ONLY HOURS AGO, LAS VEGAS, NEVADA. AS YOU CAN SEE, THE CITY HAS BEEN COMPLETELY OBLITERATED.
THOUSANDS OF TOURISTS AND RESIDENTS OF THE CITY WERE EVACUATED DURING THE RAMPAGE OF A SUPER-VILLAIN KNOWN AS DINOSAURUS.
WHETHER HIS RAMPAGE WAS THE CAUSE OF THIS UNBELIEVABLE DISASTER REMAINS UNKNOWN.
PLEASE, LET'S JUST TURN IT OFF.
THIS WASN'T YOUR FAULT. YOU CAN'T BLAME YOURSELF FOR THIS.
WHAT WE DO KNOW IS THAT THE AREA IS NOT RADIOACTIVE, SO IT WAS SOME KIND OF UNKNOWN EXPLOSIVE DEVICE THAT CAUSED THE DESTRUCTION.
SOME OF THE OUTLYING AREAS OF THE CITY WERE NOT REACHED, BUT WITHOUT THE CITY CENTER TO PROVIDE SUPPLIES TO THEM, IT'S POSSIBLE THESE PEOPLE WILL NEED TO ABANDON THEIR HOMES.
WHILE HUNDREDS OF THOUSANDS WERE EVACUATED IN THE HOURS BEFORE THE EXPLOSION, THOUSANDS ARE MISSING, AND PRESUMED DEAD.
I'VE JUST LEARNED AN IMPORTANT PIECE OF INFORMATION. EYE WITNESS REPORTS ARE COMING IN FROM THE EVACUATED POPULATION.
WE'RE HEARING FROM MULTIPLE SOURCES THAT DURING THE RAMPAGE OF DINOSAURUS A SUPER-HERO ARRIVED ON THE SCENE AND ATTEMPTED TO STOP HIM.
COULD THIS PERSON'S INVOLVEMENT HAVE LED TO THIS DEVASTATION?
WAIT...
WE'RE NOW HEARING THIS UNIDENTIFIED SUPER-HERO WAS IN FACT INVINCIBLE.

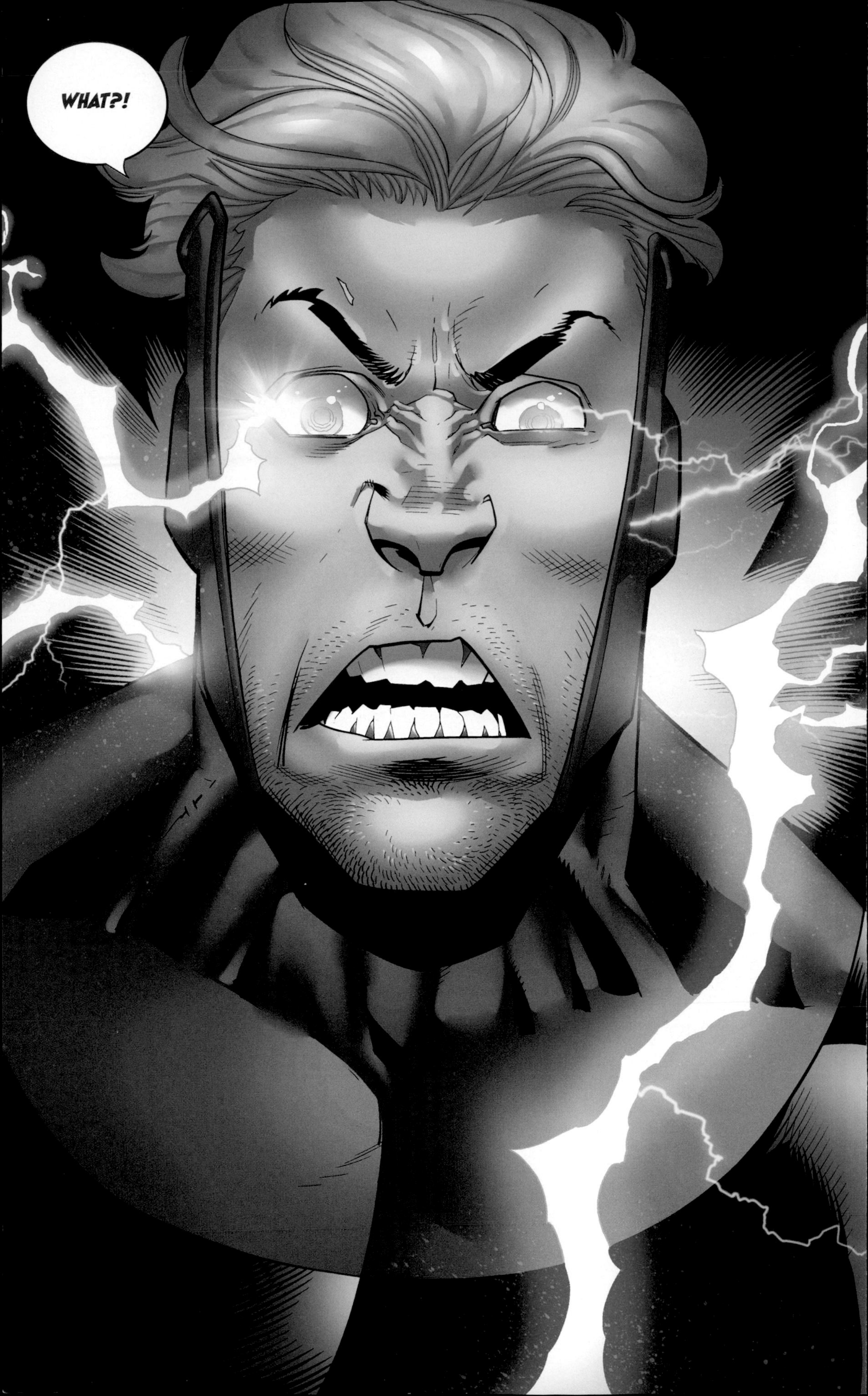
WHAT?!

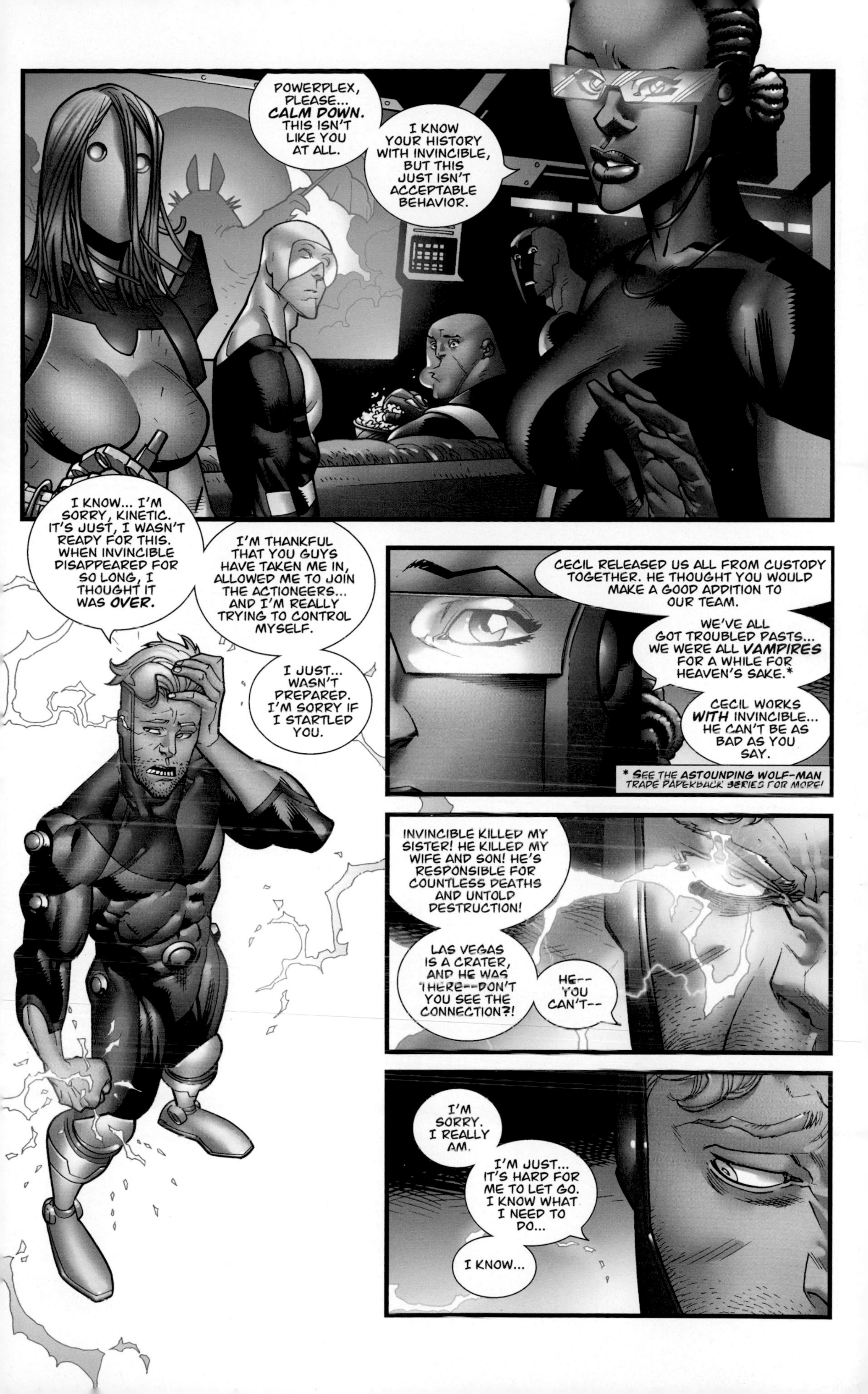
POWERPLEX, PLEASE... CALM DOWN. THIS ISN'T LIKE YOU AT ALL.
I KNOW YOUR HISTORY WITH INVINCIBLE, BUT THIS JUST ISN'T ACCEPTABLE BEHAVIOR.
I KNOW... I'M SORRY, KINETIC. IT'S JUST, I WASN'T READY FOR THIS. WHEN INVINCIBLE DISAPPEARED FOR SO LONG, I THOUGHT IT WAS OVER.
I'M THANKFUL THAT YOU GUYS HAVE TAKEN ME IN, ALLOWED ME TO JOIN THE ACTIONEERS... AND I'M REALLY TRYING TO CONTROL MYSELF.
I JUST... WASN'T PREPARED. I'M SORRY IF I STARTLED YOU.
CECIL RELEASED US ALL FROM CUSTODY TOGETHER. HE THOUGHT YOU WOULD MAKE A GOOD ADDITION TO OUR TEAM.
WE'VE ALL GOT TROUBLED PASTS... WE WERE ALL VAMPIRES FOR A WHILE FOR HEAVEN'S SAKE.*
CECIL WORKS WITH INVINCIBLE... HE CAN'T BE AS BAD AS YOU SAY.
* SEE THE ASTOUNDING WOLF-MAN TRADE PAPERBACK SERIES FOR MORE!
INVINCIBLE KILLED MY SISTER! HE KILLED MY WIFE AND SON! HE'S RESPONSIBLE FOR COUNTLESS DEATHS AND UNTOLD DESTRUCTION!
LAS VEGAS IS A CRATER, AND HE WAS THERE--DON'T YOU SEE THE CONNECTION?!
HE-- YOU CAN'T--
I'M SORRY. I REALLY AM.
I'M JUST... IT'S HARD FOR ME TO LET GO. I KNOW WHAT I NEED TO DO...
I KNOW...

UNITED STATES
PENTAGON

Parking in Rear

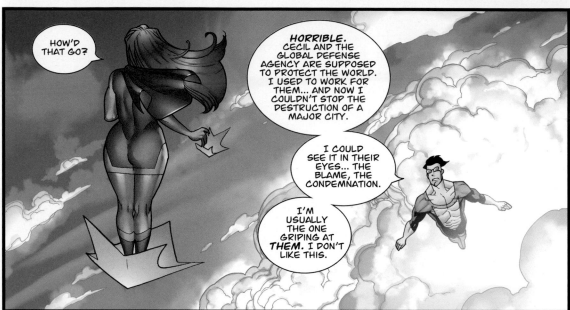

HOW'D THAT GO?

HORRIBLE. CECIL AND THE GLOBAL DEFENSE AGENCY ARE SUPPOSED TO PROTECT THE WORLD. I USED TO WORK FOR THEM... AND NOW I COULDN'T STOP THE DESTRUCTION OF A MAJOR CITY.

I COULD SEE IT IN THEIR EYES... THE BLAME, THE CONDEMNATION.

I'M USUALLY THE ONE GRIPING AT **THEM.** I DON'T LIKE THIS.

I'M SURE IT'S NOT THAT BAD. YOU'RE READING INTO THINGS.

STOP BEATING YOURSELF UP.

IT'S JUST GOT ME THINKING ABOUT EVERYTHING. WHAT WE'RE DOING... INVINCIBLE, INC... FIGHTING BAD GUYS...

TRYING TO HELP PEOPLE...

THERE HAS TO BE A BETTER WAY.

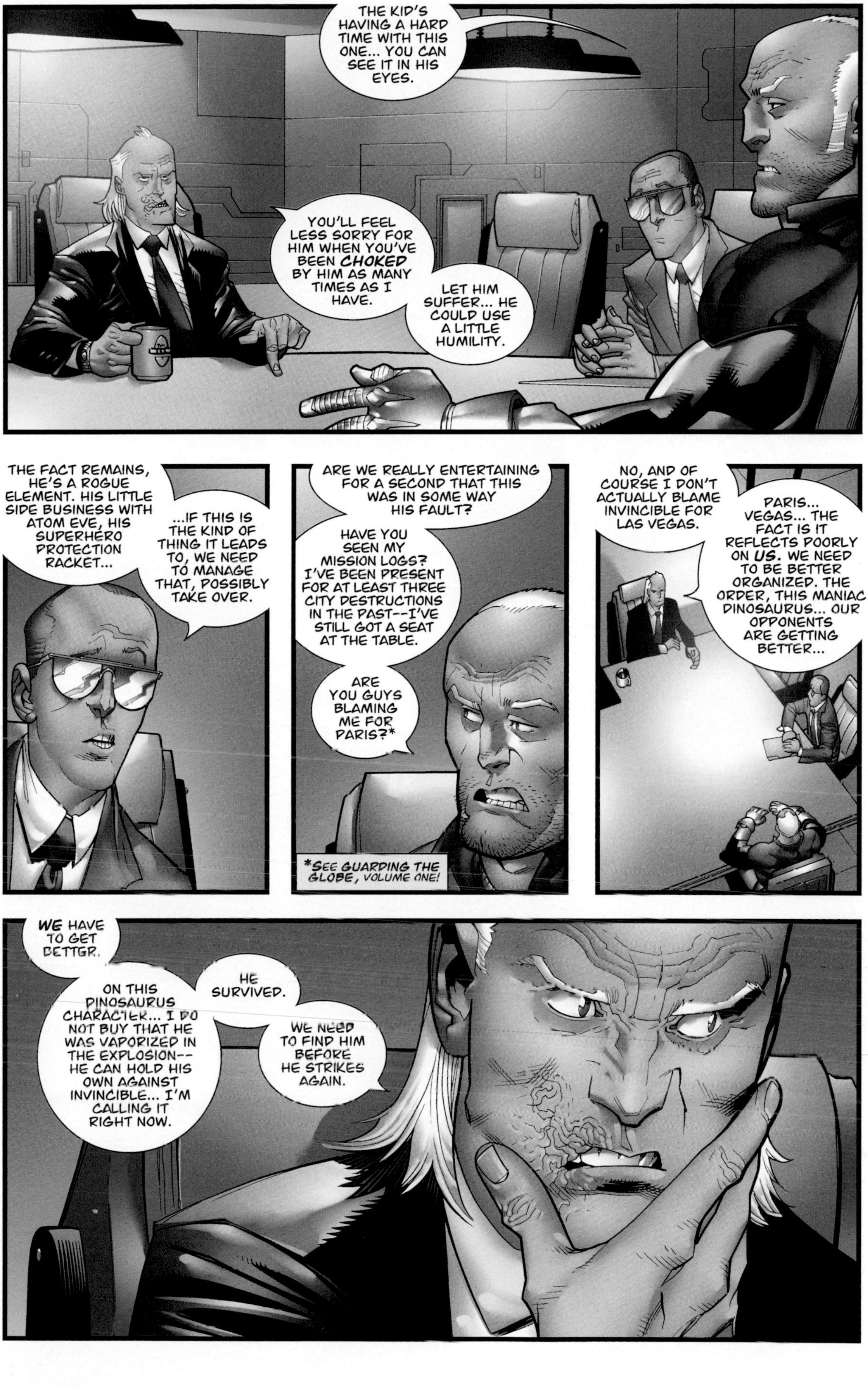

THE KID'S HAVING A HARD TIME WITH THIS ONE... YOU CAN SEE IT IN HIS EYES.
YOU'LL FEEL LESS SORRY FOR HIM WHEN YOU'VE BEEN CHOKED BY HIM AS MANY TIMES AS I HAVE.
LET HIM SUFFER... HE COULD USE A LITTLE HUMILITY.
THE FACT REMAINS, HE'S A ROGUE ELEMENT. HIS LITTLE SIDE BUSINESS WITH ATOM EVE, HIS SUPERHERO PROTECTION RACKET...
...IF THIS IS THE KIND OF THING IT LEADS TO, WE NEED TO MANAGE THAT, POSSIBLY TAKE OVER.
ARE WE REALLY ENTERTAINING FOR A SECOND THAT THIS WAS IN SOME WAY HIS FAULT?
HAVE YOU SEEN MY MISSION LOGS? I'VE BEEN PRESENT FOR AT LEAST THREE CITY DESTRUCTIONS IN THE PAST--I'VE STILL GOT A SEAT AT THE TABLE.
ARE YOU GUYS BLAMING ME FOR PARIS?*
*SEE GUARDING THE GLOBE, VOLUME ONE!
NO, AND OF COURSE I DON'T ACTUALLY BLAME INVINCIBLE FOR LAS VEGAS.
PARIS... VEGAS... THE FACT IS IT REFLECTS POORLY ON US. WE NEED TO BE BETTER ORGANIZED. THE ORDER, THIS MANIAC DINOSAURUS... OUR OPPONENTS ARE GETTING BETTER...
WE HAVE TO GET BETTER.
ON THIS DINOSAURUS CHARACTER... I DO NOT BUY THAT HE WAS VAPORIZED IN THE EXPLOSION--HE CAN HOLD HIS OWN AGAINST INVINCIBLE... I'M CALLING IT RIGHT NOW.
HE SURVIVED.
WE NEED TO FIND HIM BEFORE HE STRIKES AGAIN.

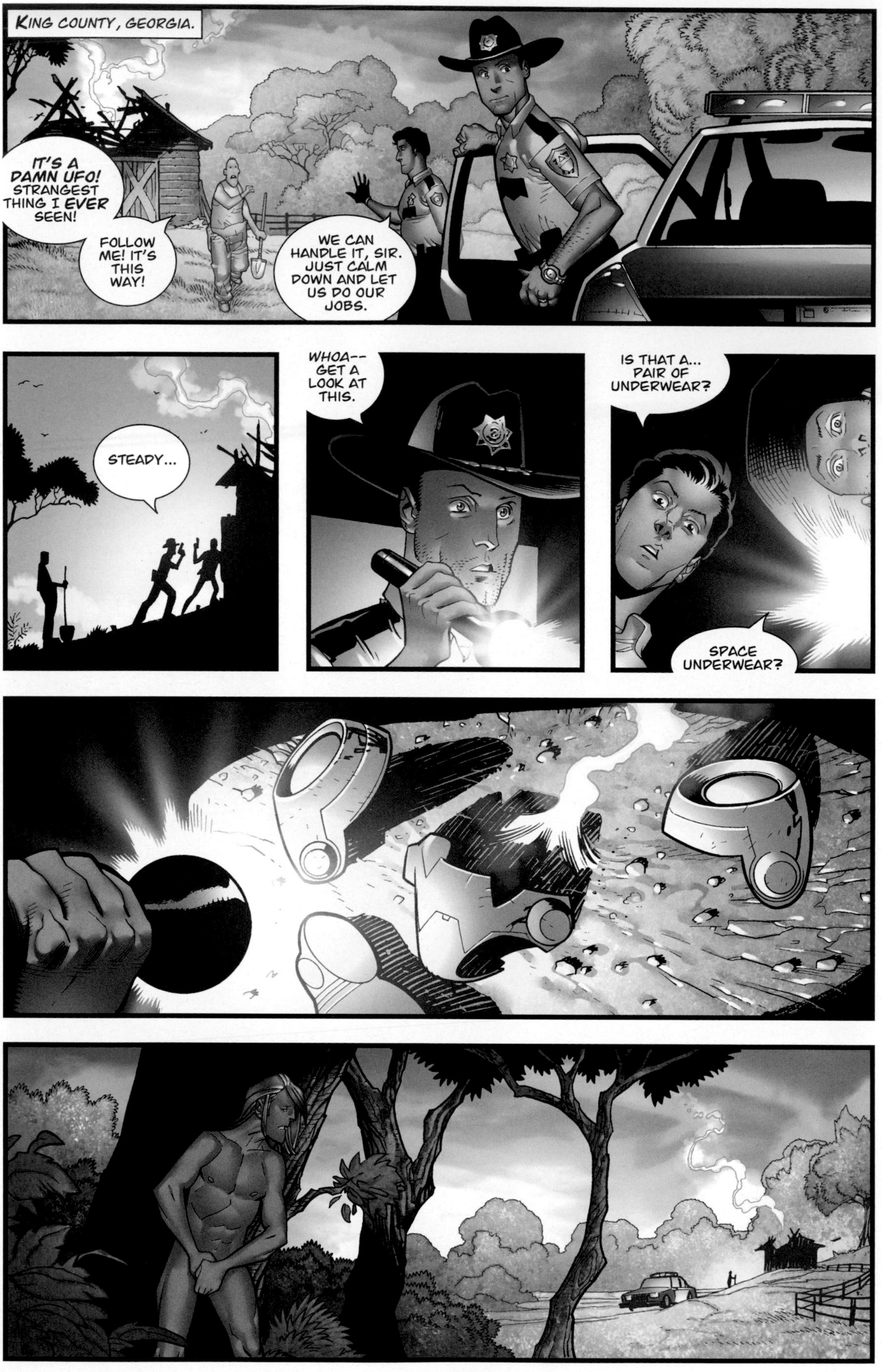
King county, Georgia.
It's a damn UFO! Strangest thing I ever seen!
Follow me! It's this way!
We can handle it, sir. Just calm down and let us do our jobs.
Steady...
Whoa-- get a look at this.
Is that a... pair of underwear?
Space underwear?

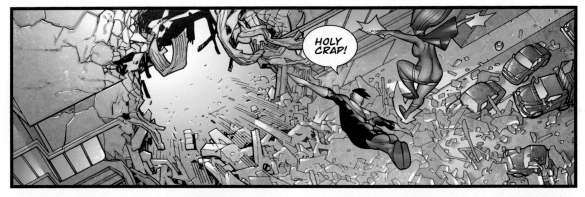

HOLY CRAP!

ARE YOU OKAY, MA'AM?

HIS GUN-- AND THE BUILDING... I'LL BE OKAY. IT HAPPENED SO FAST--AND...

WHO IS--

INVINCIBLE...

OH-- WHAT THE HECK?!

TREMBLE BEFORE THE AWESOME MIGHT OF GRAVITATOR!

AND FILL THOSE BAGS, JERKS! TREMBLE AND THEN FILL-- IN THAT ORDER!

HOP TO IT!

WHAT? WHERE DID HE GET--?

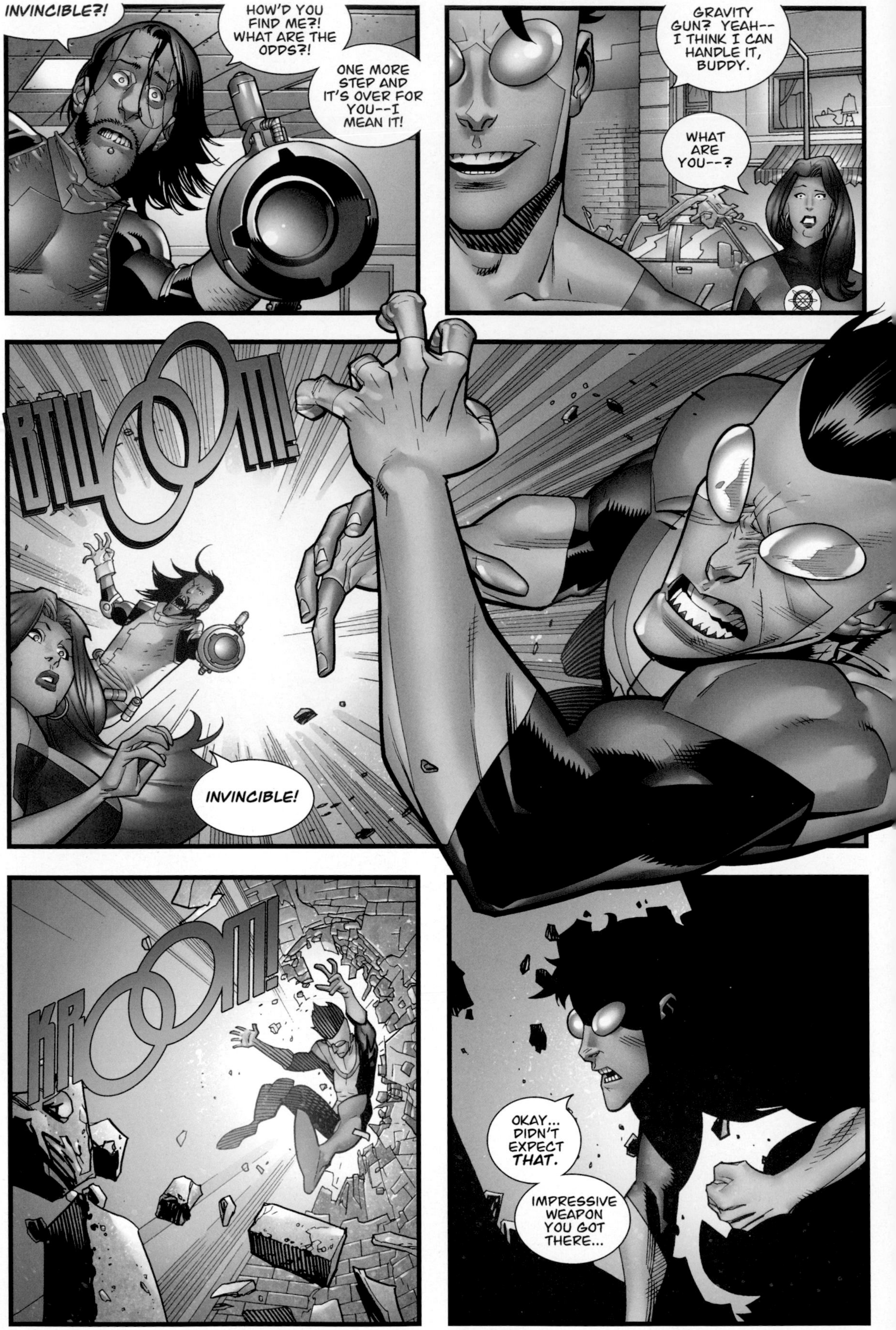
INVINCIBLE?!
HOW'D YOU FIND ME?! WHAT ARE THE ODDS?!
ONE MORE STEP AND IT'S OVER FOR YOU--I MEAN IT!
GRAVITY GUN? YEAH-- I THINK I CAN HANDLE IT, BUDDY.
WHAT ARE YOU--?
BTWOOM!!
INVINCIBLE!
KROOM!
OKAY... DIDN'T EXPECT THAT.
IMPRESSIVE WEAPON YOU GOT THERE...

...BUT I KNOW *YOU* DIDN'T INVENT IT!

I GOT HIM--THIS GUY'S NO EXPERT!

HEY-- HEY!

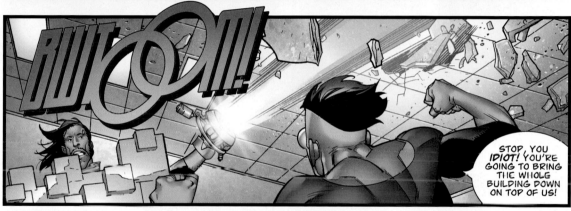

STOP, YOU *IDIOT!* YOU'RE GOING TO BRING THE WHOLE BUILDING DOWN ON TOP OF US!

KROOM!

TELL ME WHERE YOU GOT THIS TECH!

I HAVE IT, NOW.

I *MADE* ALL THIS STUFF-- I'M AN *INVENTOR!*

YOU *BOUGHT* IT ALL, AND YOU'RE GOING TO TELL ME EVERYTHING YOU KNOW ABOUT THE GUY WHO SOLD IT TO YOU...

...OR I STOP HOLDING BACK.

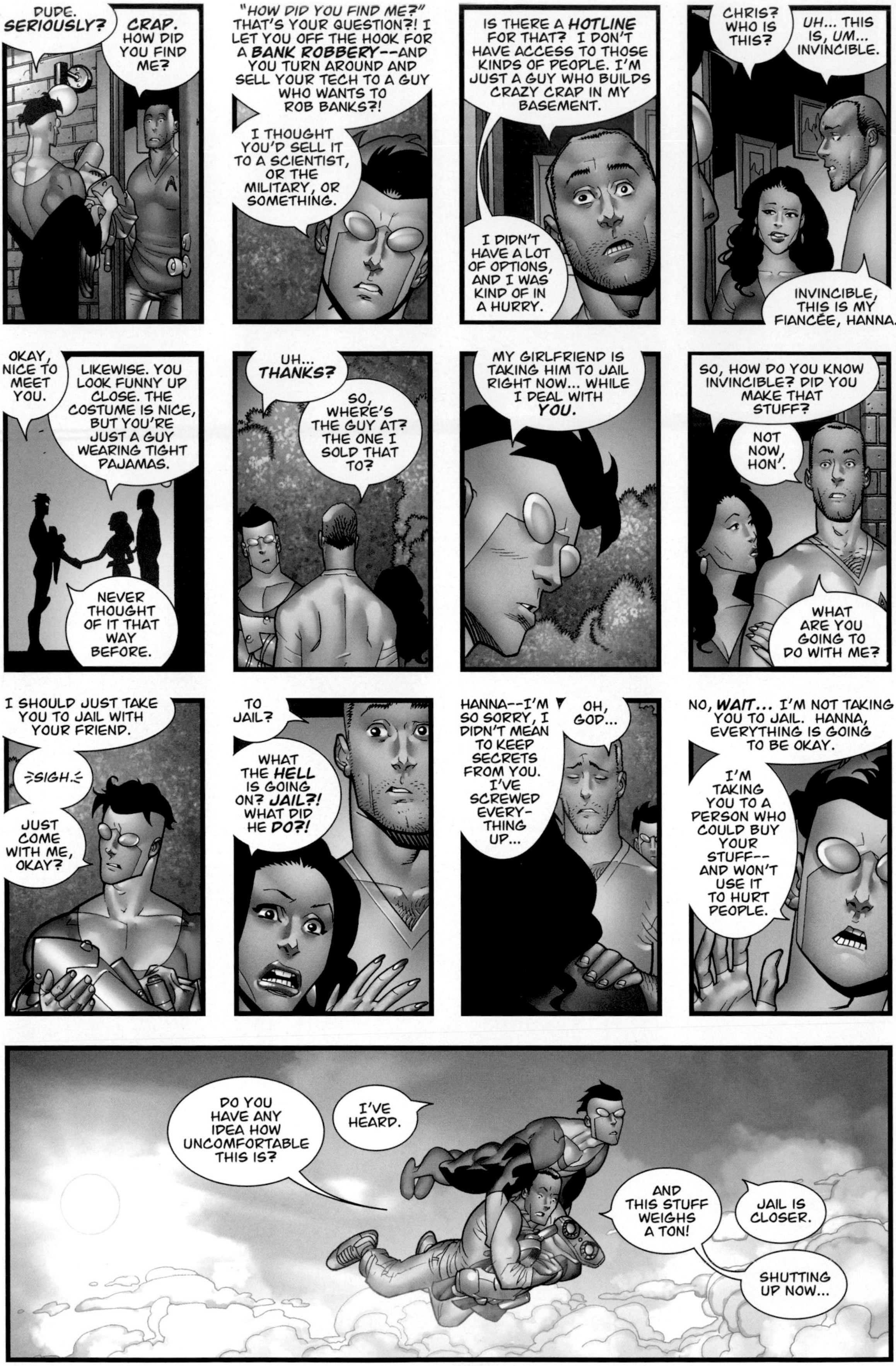
DUDE. SERIOUSLY?
CRAP. HOW DID YOU FIND ME?
"HOW DID YOU FIND ME?" THAT'S YOUR QUESTION?! I LET YOU OFF THE HOOK FOR A BANK ROBBERY--AND YOU TURN AROUND AND SELL YOUR TECH TO A GUY WHO WANTS TO ROB BANKS?!
I THOUGHT YOU'D SELL IT TO A SCIENTIST, OR THE MILITARY, OR SOMETHING.
IS THERE A HOTLINE FOR THAT? I DON'T HAVE ACCESS TO THOSE KINDS OF PEOPLE. I'M JUST A GUY WHO BUILDS CRAZY CRAP IN MY BASEMENT.
I DIDN'T HAVE A LOT OF OPTIONS, AND I WAS KIND OF IN A HURRY.
CHRIS? WHO IS THIS?
UH... THIS IS, UM... INVINCIBLE.
INVINCIBLE, THIS IS MY FIANCÉE, HANNA.
OKAY, NICE TO MEET YOU.
LIKEWISE. YOU LOOK FUNNY UP CLOSE. THE COSTUME IS NICE, BUT YOU'RE JUST A GUY WEARING TIGHT PAJAMAS.
NEVER THOUGHT OF IT THAT WAY BEFORE.
UH... THANKS?
SO, WHERE'S THE GUY AT? THE ONE I SOLD THAT TO?
MY GIRLFRIEND IS TAKING HIM TO JAIL RIGHT NOW... WHILE I DEAL WITH YOU.
SO, HOW DO YOU KNOW INVINCIBLE? DID YOU MAKE THAT STUFF?
NOT NOW, HON'.
WHAT ARE YOU GOING TO DO WITH ME?
I SHOULD JUST TAKE YOU TO JAIL WITH YOUR FRIEND.
SIGH.
JUST COME WITH ME, OKAY?
TO JAIL?
WHAT THE HELL IS GOING ON? JAIL?! WHAT DID HE DO?!
HANNA--I'M SO SORRY, I DIDN'T MEAN TO KEEP SECRETS FROM YOU. I'VE SCREWED EVERY-THING UP...
OH, GOD...
NO, WAIT... I'M NOT TAKING YOU TO JAIL. HANNA, EVERYTHING IS GOING TO BE OKAY.
I'M TAKING YOU TO A PERSON WHO COULD BUY YOUR STUFF--AND WON'T USE IT TO HURT PEOPLE.
DO YOU HAVE ANY IDEA HOW UNCOMFORTABLE THIS IS?
I'VE HEARD.
AND THIS STUFF WEIGHS A TON!
JAIL IS CLOSER.
SHUTTING UP NOW...

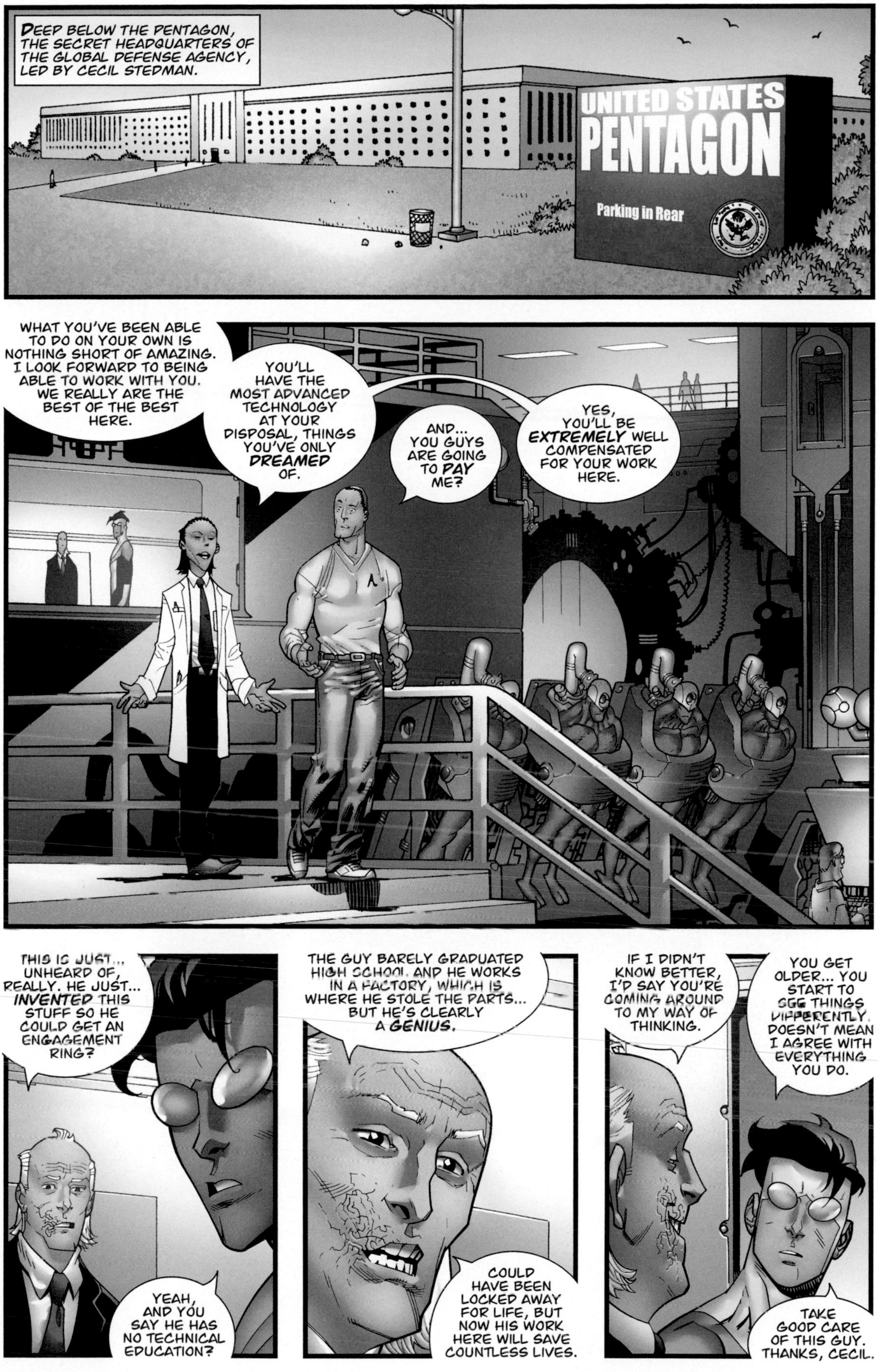
DEEP BELOW THE PENTAGON, THE SECRET HEADQUARTERS OF THE GLOBAL DEFENSE AGENCY, LED BY CECIL STEDMAN.
UNITED STATES PENTAGON
Parking in Rear
WHAT YOU'VE BEEN ABLE TO DO ON YOUR OWN IS NOTHING SHORT OF AMAZING. I LOOK FORWARD TO BEING ABLE TO WORK WITH YOU. WE REALLY ARE THE BEST OF THE BEST HERE.
YOU'LL HAVE THE MOST ADVANCED TECHNOLOGY AT YOUR DISPOSAL, THINGS YOU'VE ONLY DREAMED OF.
AND... YOU GUYS ARE GOING TO PAY ME?
YES, YOU'LL BE EXTREMELY WELL COMPENSATED FOR YOUR WORK HERE.
THIS IS JUST... UNHEARD OF, REALLY. HE JUST... INVENTED THIS STUFF SO HE COULD GET AN ENGAGEMENT RING?
YEAH, AND YOU SAY HE HAS NO TECHNICAL EDUCATION?
THE GUY BARELY GRADUATED HIGH SCHOOL AND HE WORKS IN A FACTORY, WHICH IS WHERE HE STOLE THE PARTS... BUT HE'S CLEARLY A GENIUS.
COULD HAVE BEEN LOCKED AWAY FOR LIFE, BUT NOW HIS WORK HERE WILL SAVE COUNTLESS LIVES.
IF I DIDN'T KNOW BETTER, I'D SAY YOU'RE COMING AROUND TO MY WAY OF THINKING.
YOU GET OLDER... YOU START TO SEE THINGS DIFFERENTLY. DOESN'T MEAN I AGREE WITH EVERYTHING YOU DO.
TAKE GOOD CARE OF THIS GUY. THANKS, CECIL.

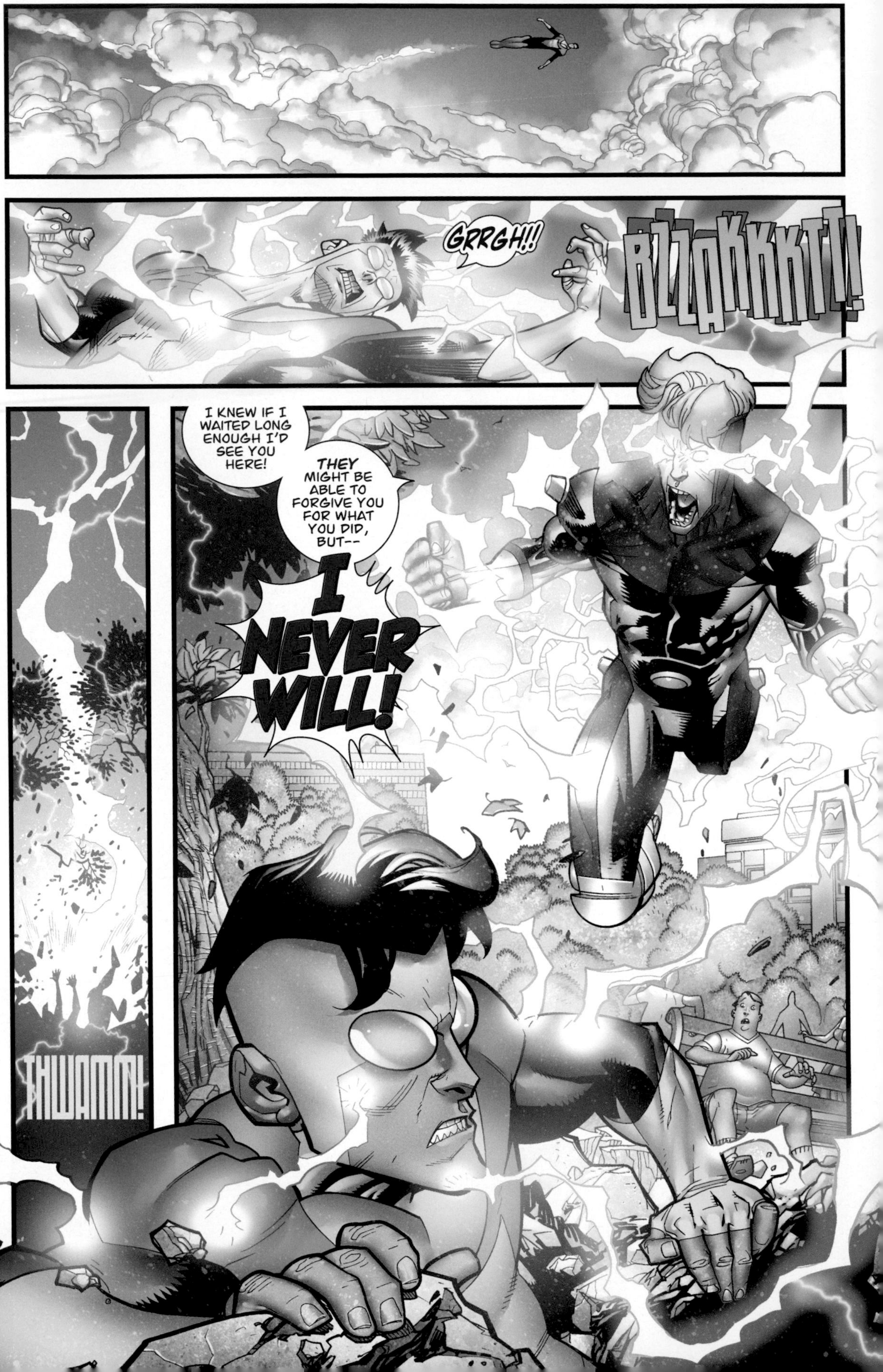
GRRGH!!
BZZAKKKKTT!!
I KNEW IF I WAITED LONG ENOUGH I'D SEE YOU HERE!
THEY MIGHT BE ABLE TO FORGIVE YOU FOR WHAT YOU DID, BUT--
I NEVER WILL!
THWAMM!

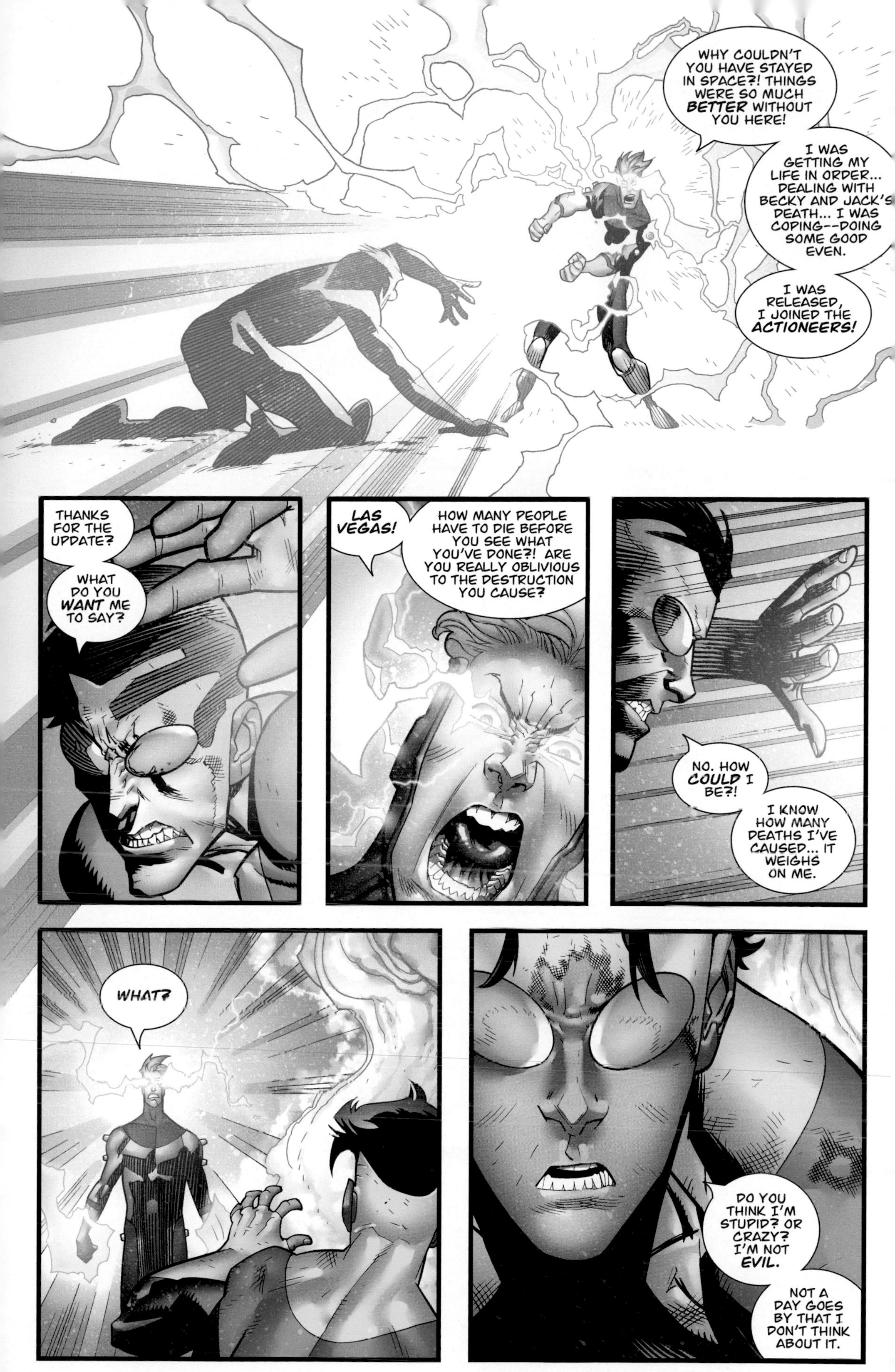
WHY COULDN'T YOU HAVE STAYED IN SPACE?! THINGS WERE SO MUCH BETTER WITHOUT YOU HERE!
I WAS GETTING MY LIFE IN ORDER... DEALING WITH BECKY AND JACK'S DEATH... I WAS COPING--DOING SOME GOOD EVEN.
I WAS RELEASED, I JOINED THE ACTIONEERS!
THANKS FOR THE UPDATE?
WHAT DO YOU WANT ME TO SAY?
LAS VEGAS!
HOW MANY PEOPLE HAVE TO DIE BEFORE YOU SEE WHAT YOU'VE DONE?! ARE YOU REALLY OBLIVIOUS TO THE DESTRUCTION YOU CAUSE?
NO. HOW COULD I BE?!
I KNOW HOW MANY DEATHS I'VE CAUSED... IT WEIGHS ON ME.
WHAT?
DO YOU THINK I'M STUPID? OR CRAZY? I'M NOT EVIL.
NOT A DAY GOES BY THAT I DON'T THINK ABOUT IT.

HERE'S WHAT YOU'RE IGNORING, THOUGH... THE WORLD IS A **HORRIBLE** PLACE.

EVERY TIME I WAS INVOLVED IN A FIGHT THAT LED TO DEATHS, BE IT ONE OR ONE-THOUSAND, IF I'D DONE NOTHING, IT WOULD HAVE BEEN **WORSE.**

YOUR SISTER DIED WHEN I FOUGHT MY FATHER, THAT WAS UNFORTUNATE, BUT I WAS STOPPING HIM FROM TAKING OVER THE WHOLE PLANET. HUNDREDS DIED IN THAT FIGHT--COULD HAVE BEEN HUNDREDS OF THOUSANDS IF HE'D WON.

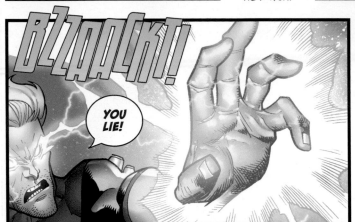

BZZAACKT!

YOU LIE!

ACK!

I'M NOT-- LYING--AND I'M--NOT GOING TO FIGHT YOU--I KNOW HOW YOU ABSORB ENERGY.

COUNTLESS DEATHS ARE THE RESULT OF YOUR BATTLES! I REFUSE TO BELIEVE THINGS WOULDN'T BE BETTER WITHOUT YOU!

YOU'RE RECKLESS, SLOPPY-- YOU MAKE SITUATIONS **WORSE!**

BZZKKT!

YOU'RE **WRONG**-- AND YOU'RE ALMOST OUT OF ENERGY, YOUR BLASTS ARE-- WEAKER.

I'VE SAVED THE **WORLD,** POWERPLEX!

THAT'S WHAT I WAS DOING IN SPACE-- THAT'S WHAT I **DO**--WHAT I WAS TRYING TO DO IN LAS VEGAS.

I DIDN'T PLANT THOSE BOMBS THERE, I DIDN'T TURN THEM ON--ALL I DID WAS FAIL TO STOP THEM.

I FAILED... BUT YOU CAN'T BLAME *ME* FOR THAT--JUST LIKE YOU CAN'T BLAME ME FOR WHAT HAPPENED TO YOUR FAMILY.

...

I DIDN'T BRING THEM TO THAT PLACE... I DIDN'T TIE THEM UP... I DIDN'T SHOOT ELECTRICAL CURRENT INTO THEIR BODIES.

I'M SORRY...

...BUT *YOU* DID THAT.

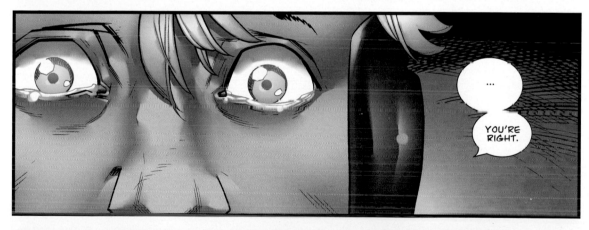

...

YOU'RE RIGHT.

OH, GOD... YOU'RE RIGHT.

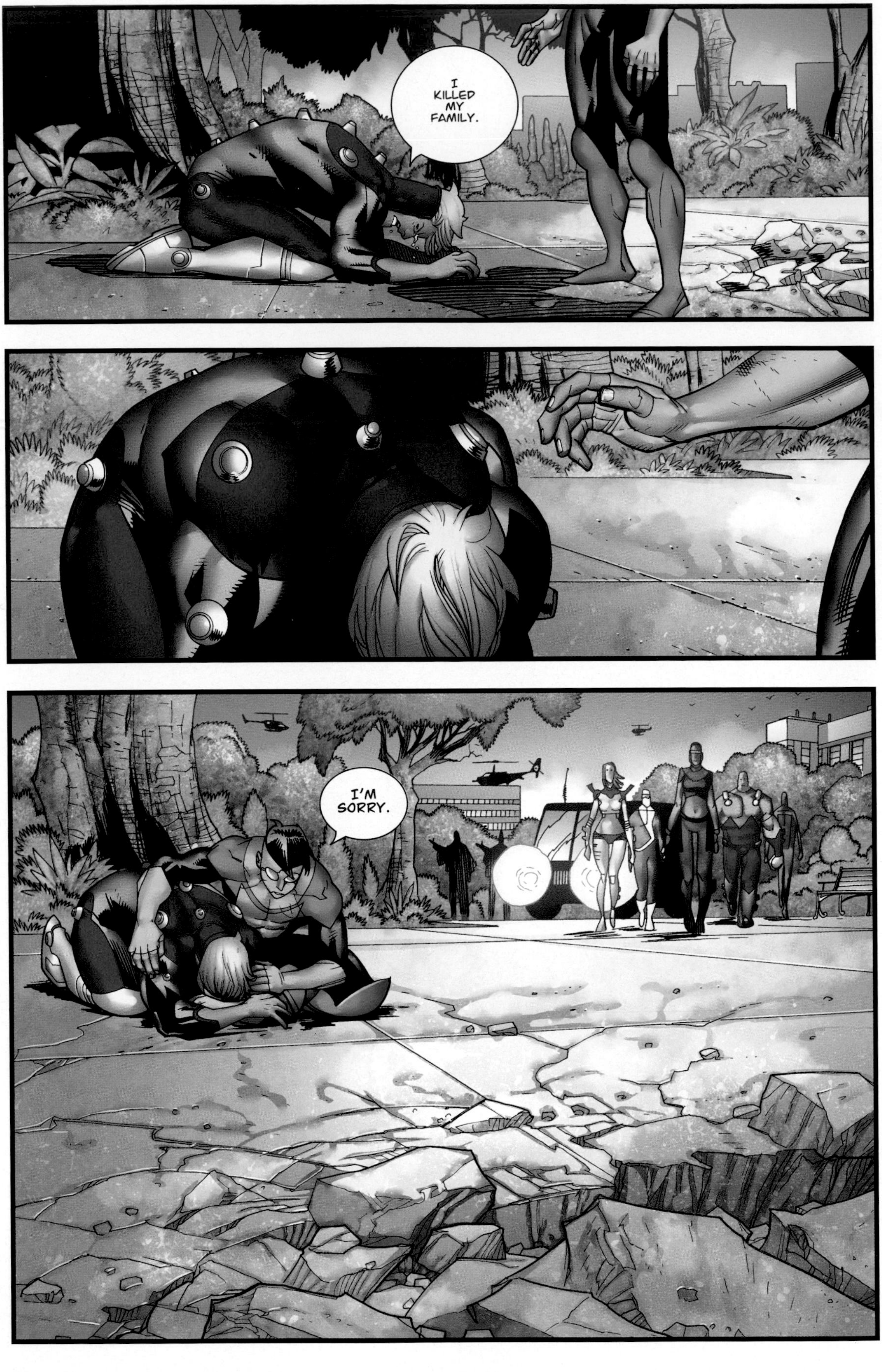
I KILLED MY FAMILY.
I'M SORRY.

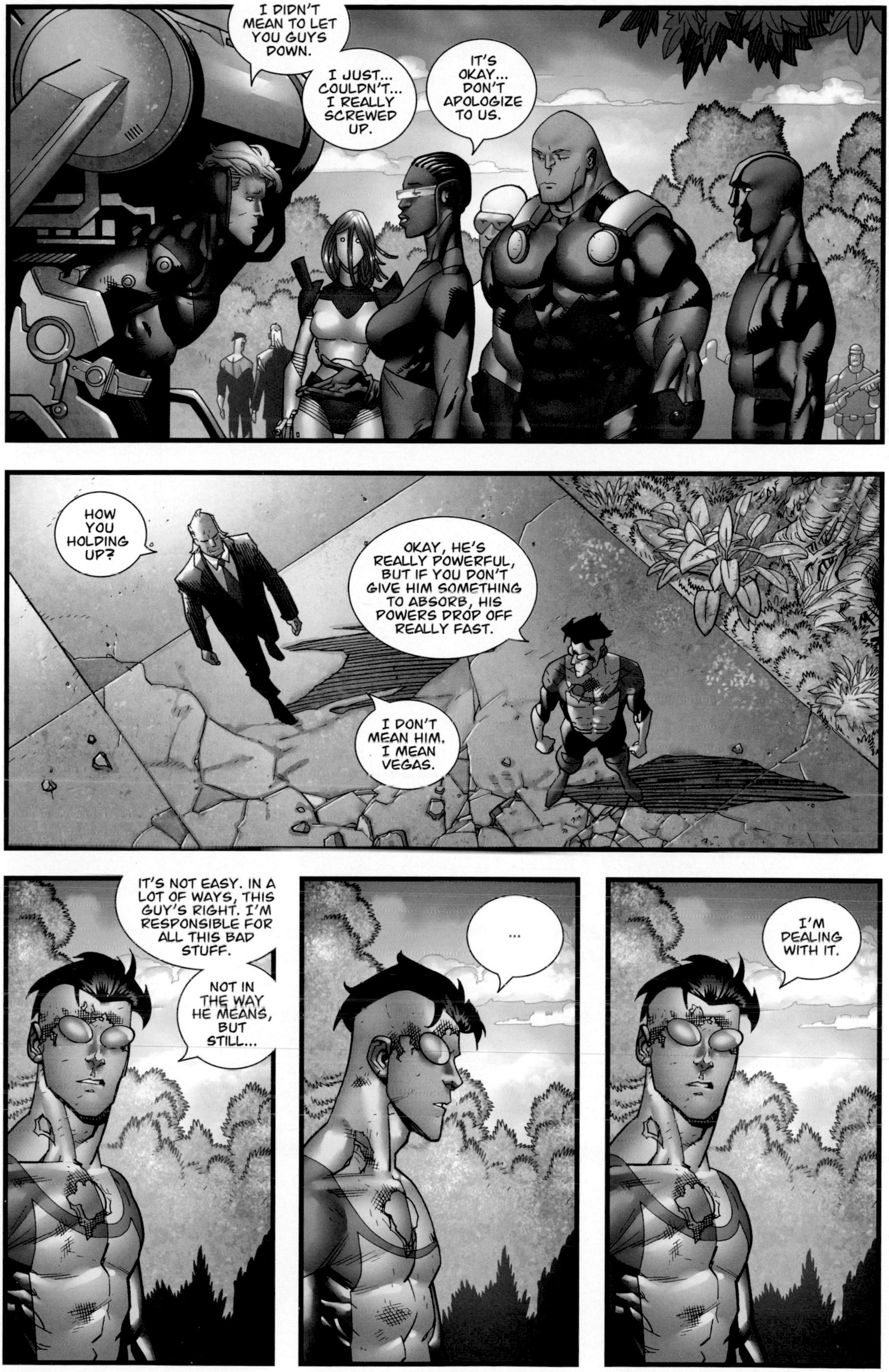
I DIDN'T MEAN TO LET YOU GUYS DOWN.
I JUST... COULDN'T... I REALLY SCREWED UP.
IT'S OKAY... DON'T APOLOGIZE TO US.
HOW YOU HOLDING UP?
OKAY, HE'S REALLY POWERFUL, BUT IF YOU DON'T GIVE HIM SOMETHING TO ABSORB, HIS POWERS DROP OFF REALLY FAST.
I DON'T MEAN HIM. I MEAN VEGAS.
IT'S NOT EASY. IN A LOT OF WAYS, THIS GUY'S RIGHT. I'M RESPONSIBLE FOR ALL THIS BAD STUFF.
NOT IN THE WAY HE MEANS, BUT STILL...
...
I'M DEALING WITH IT.

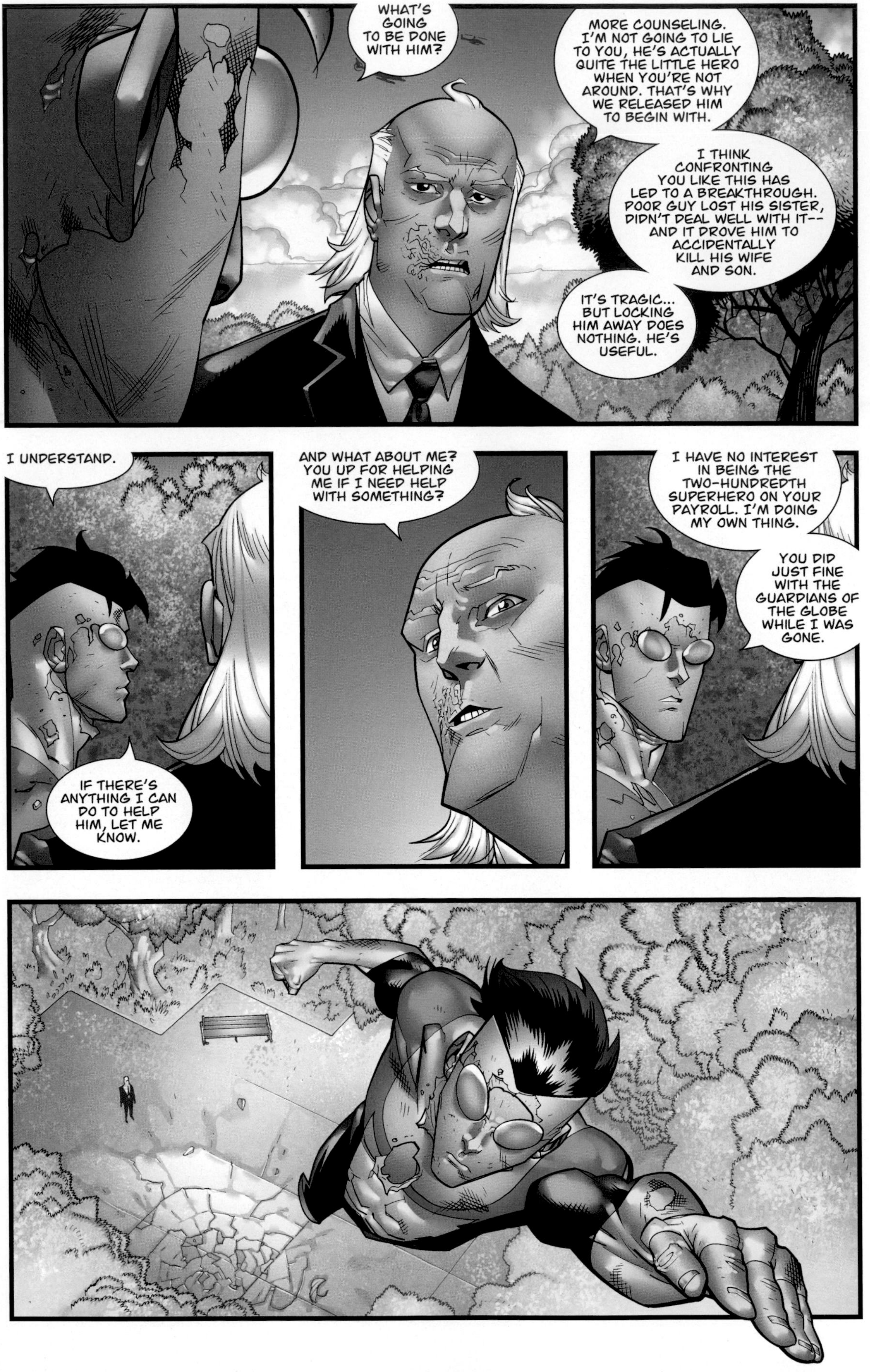
WHAT'S GOING TO BE DONE WITH HIM?
MORE COUNSELING. I'M NOT GOING TO LIE TO YOU, HE'S ACTUALLY QUITE THE LITTLE HERO WHEN YOU'RE NOT AROUND. THAT'S WHY WE RELEASED HIM TO BEGIN WITH.
I THINK CONFRONTING YOU LIKE THIS HAS LED TO A BREAKTHROUGH. POOR GUY LOST HIS SISTER, DIDN'T DEAL WELL WITH IT-- AND IT DROVE HIM TO ACCIDENTALLY KILL HIS WIFE AND SON.
IT'S TRAGIC... BUT LOCKING HIM AWAY DOES NOTHING. HE'S USEFUL.
I UNDERSTAND.
IF THERE'S ANYTHING I CAN DO TO HELP HIM, LET ME KNOW.
AND WHAT ABOUT ME? YOU UP FOR HELPING ME IF I NEED HELP WITH SOMETHING?
I HAVE NO INTEREST IN BEING THE TWO-HUNDREDTH SUPERHERO ON YOUR PAYROLL. I'M DOING MY OWN THING.
YOU DID JUST FINE WITH THE GUARDIANS OF THE GLOBE WHILE I WAS GONE.

DO I EVEN WANT TO KNOW WHAT KEPT YOU OUT?

ANOTHER VILLAIN, POWERPLEX-- IT'S TAKEN CARE OF.

NO LEVELED CITIES THIS TIME.

BAD JOKE.

YOU'RE NOT STILL BLAMING YOURSELF FOR THAT ARE YOU?

OF COURSE I AM, EVE... AND I SHOULD BE.

I DIDN'T JUST START DOING THIS BECAUSE OF MY DAD--OR BECAUSE I GOT POWERS. THIS WORLD SUCKS AND I WANT TO HELP PEOPLE.

ALL I WANT TO DO IS HELP PEOPLE.

WHEN I'M TEARING DOWN BUILDINGS, PUNCHING GIANT MONSTERS, BEATING THE SNOT OUT OF PEOPLE WHO ARE JUST CRAZY OR DISTURBED...

THAT'S NOT IT... THAT'S NOT WHAT I WANT TO DO.

MARK?

WHAT ARE YOU SAYING?

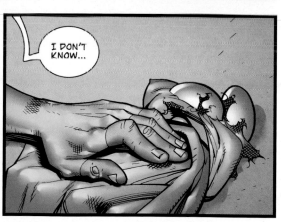

I DON'T KNOW...

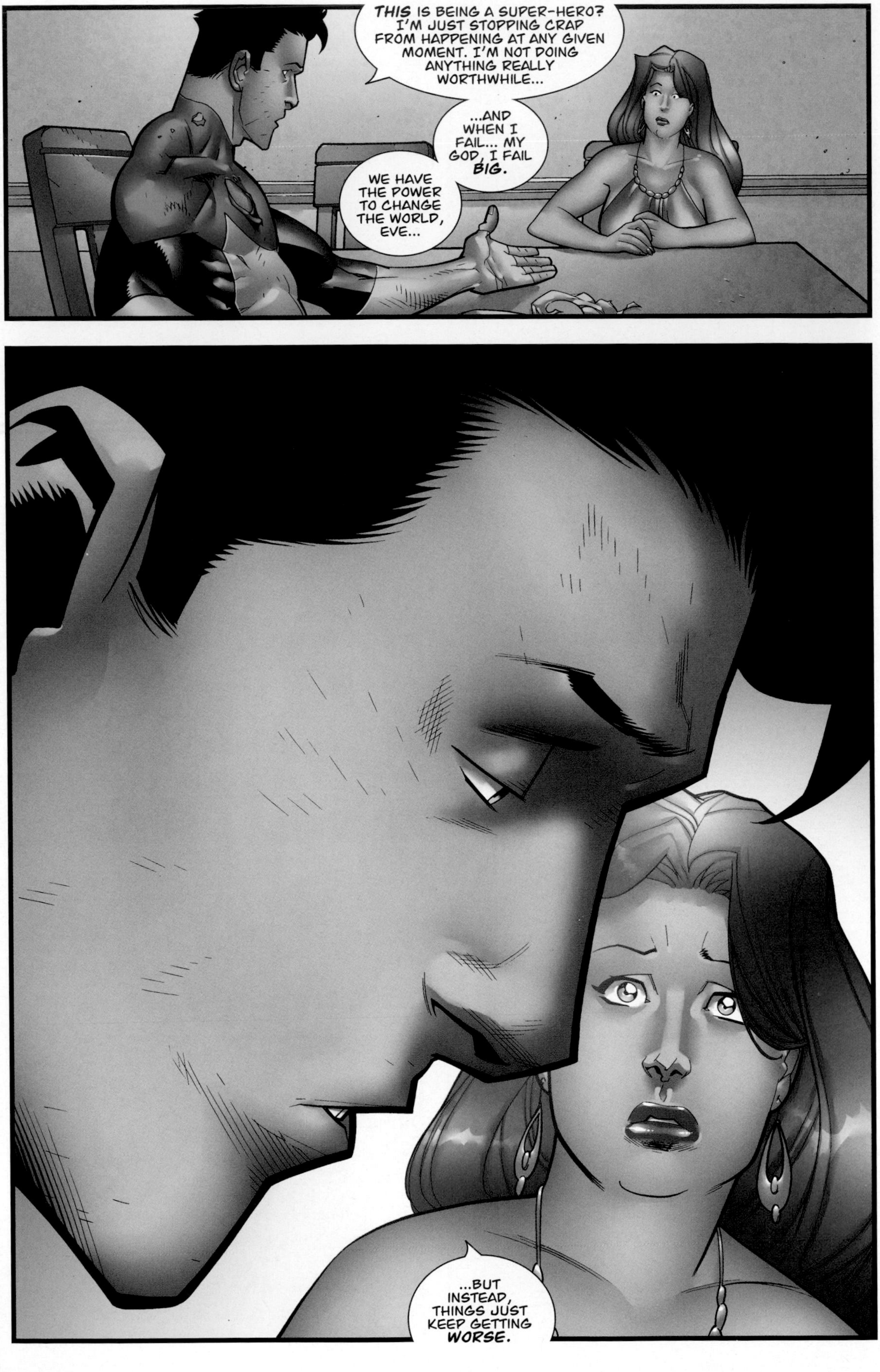
THIS IS BEING A SUPER-HERO? I'M JUST STOPPING CRAP FROM HAPPENING AT ANY GIVEN MOMENT. I'M NOT DOING ANYTHING REALLY WORTHWHILE...
...AND WHEN I FAIL... MY GOD, I FAIL BIG.
WE HAVE THE POWER TO CHANGE THE WORLD, EVE...
...BUT INSTEAD, THINGS JUST KEEP GETTING WORSE.

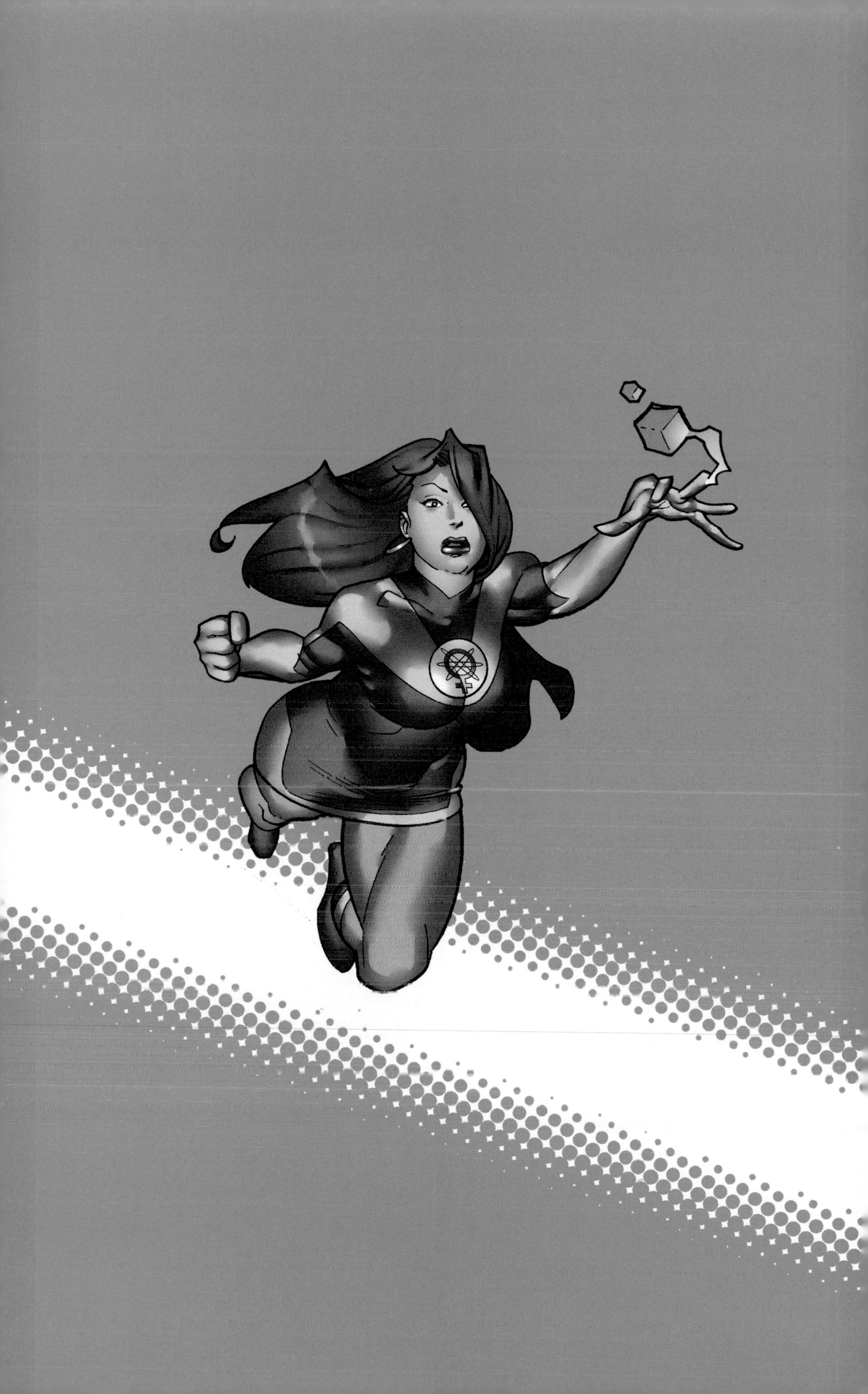

CHAPTER FOUR

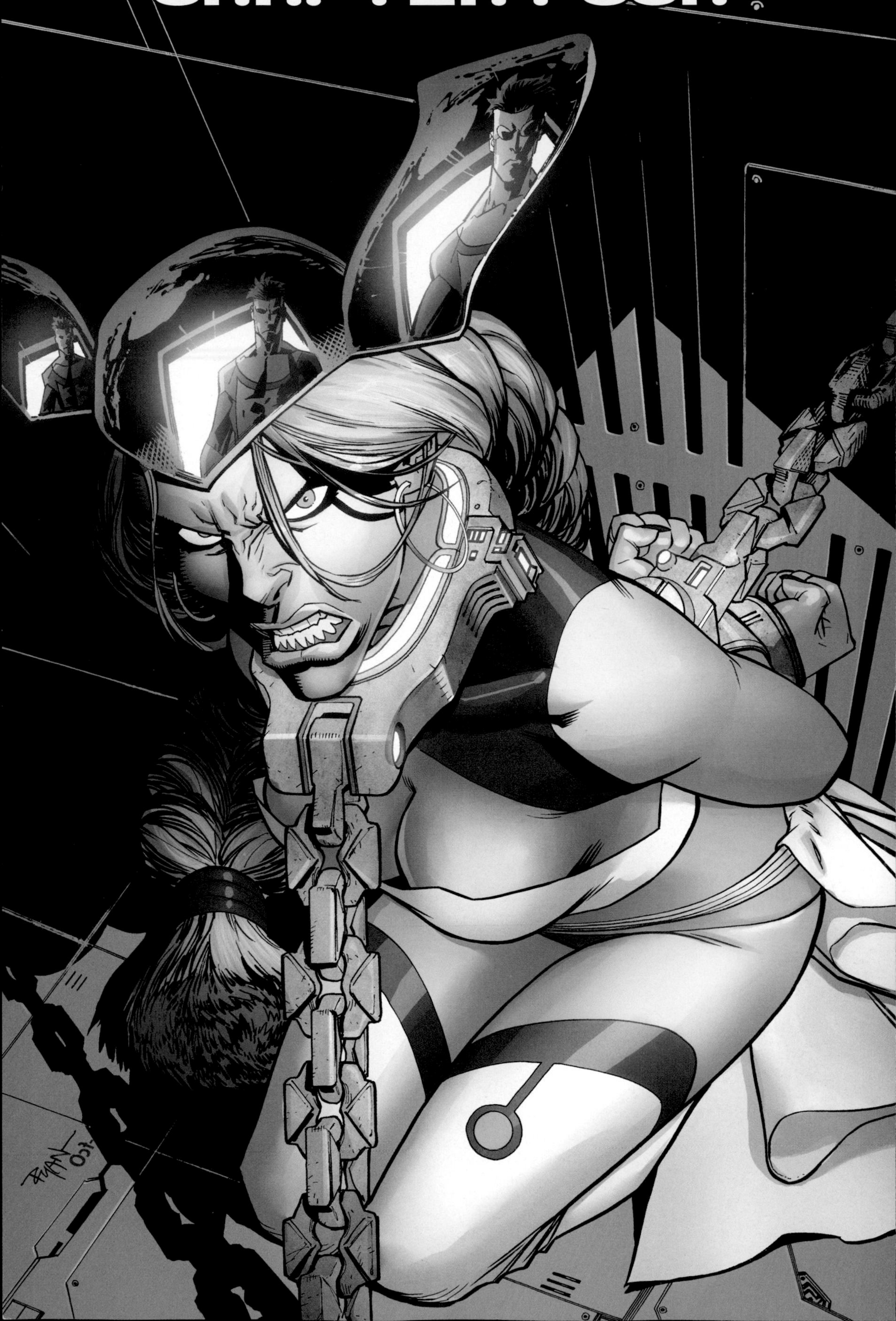

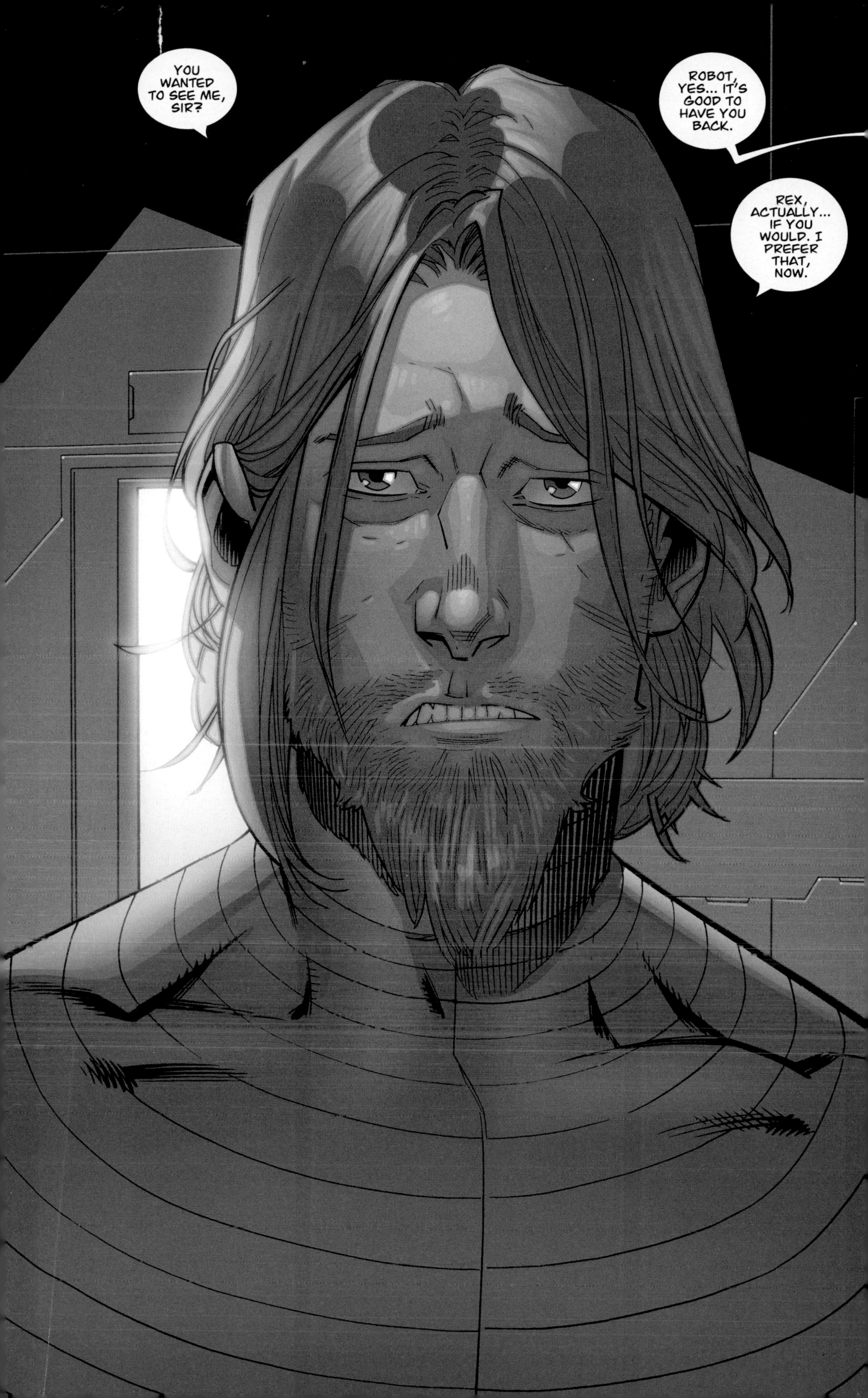
YOU WANTED TO SEE ME, SIR?
ROBOT, YES... IT'S GOOD TO HAVE YOU BACK.
REX, ACTUALLY... IF YOU WOULD. I PREFER THAT, NOW.

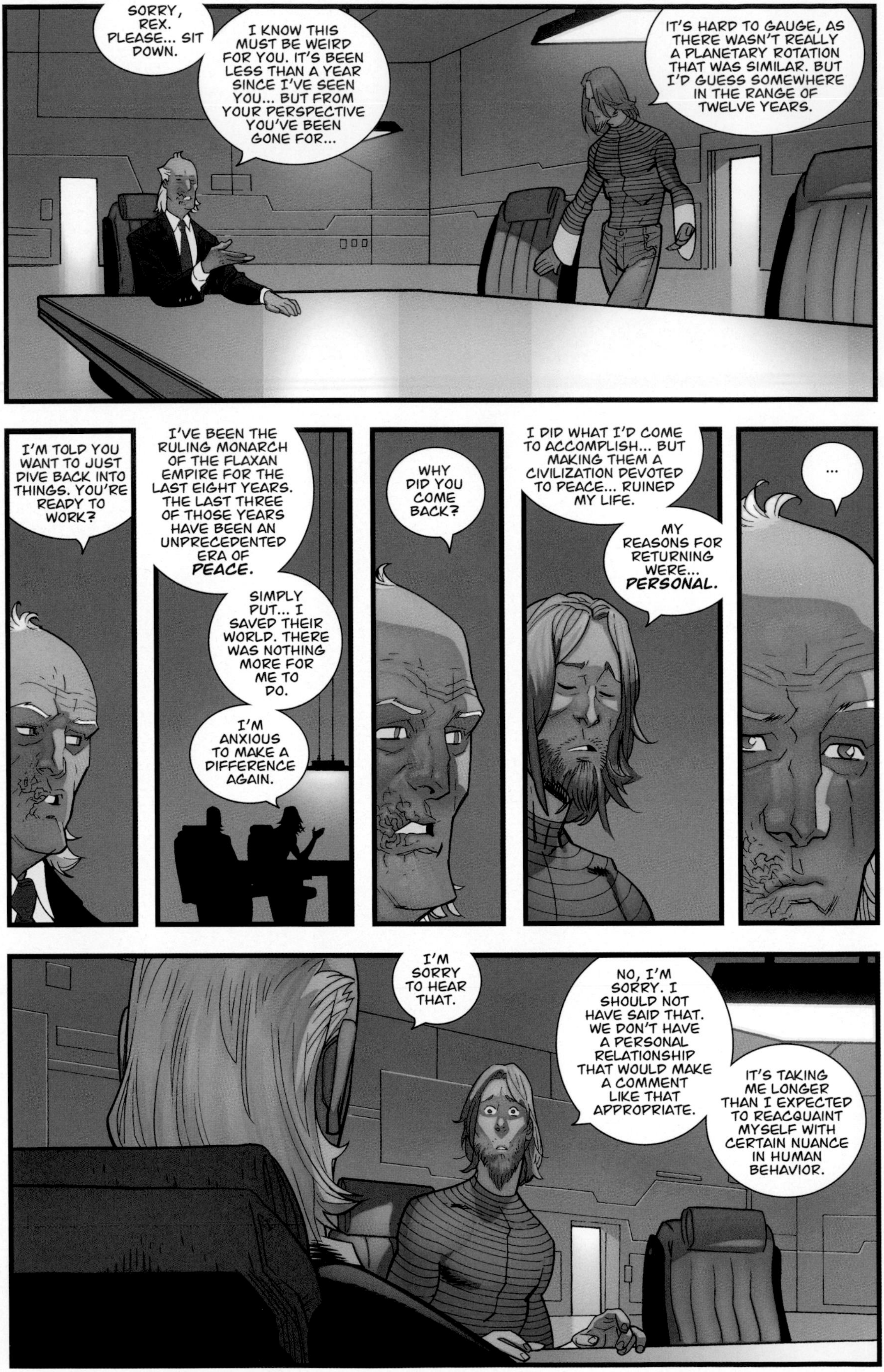
SORRY, REX. PLEASE... SIT DOWN.
I KNOW THIS MUST BE WEIRD FOR YOU. IT'S BEEN LESS THAN A YEAR SINCE I'VE SEEN YOU... BUT FROM YOUR PERSPECTIVE YOU'VE BEEN GONE FOR...
IT'S HARD TO GAUGE, AS THERE WASN'T REALLY A PLANETARY ROTATION THAT WAS SIMILAR. BUT I'D GUESS SOMEWHERE IN THE RANGE OF TWELVE YEARS.
I'M TOLD YOU WANT TO JUST DIVE BACK INTO THINGS. YOU'RE READY TO WORK?
I'VE BEEN THE RULING MONARCH OF THE FLAXAN EMPIRE FOR THE LAST EIGHT YEARS. THE LAST THREE OF THOSE YEARS HAVE BEEN AN UNPRECEDENTED ERA OF PEACE.
SIMPLY PUT... I SAVED THEIR WORLD. THERE WAS NOTHING MORE FOR ME TO DO.
I'M ANXIOUS TO MAKE A DIFFERENCE AGAIN.
WHY DID YOU COME BACK?
I DID WHAT I'D COME TO ACCOMPLISH... BUT MAKING THEM A CIVILIZATION DEVOTED TO PEACE... RUINED MY LIFE.
MY REASONS FOR RETURNING WERE... PERSONAL.
...
I'M SORRY TO HEAR THAT.
NO, I'M SORRY. I SHOULD NOT HAVE SAID THAT. WE DON'T HAVE A PERSONAL RELATIONSHIP THAT WOULD MAKE A COMMENT LIKE THAT APPROPRIATE.
IT'S TAKING ME LONGER THAN I EXPECTED TO REACQUAINT MYSELF WITH CERTAIN NUANCE IN HUMAN BEHAVIOR.

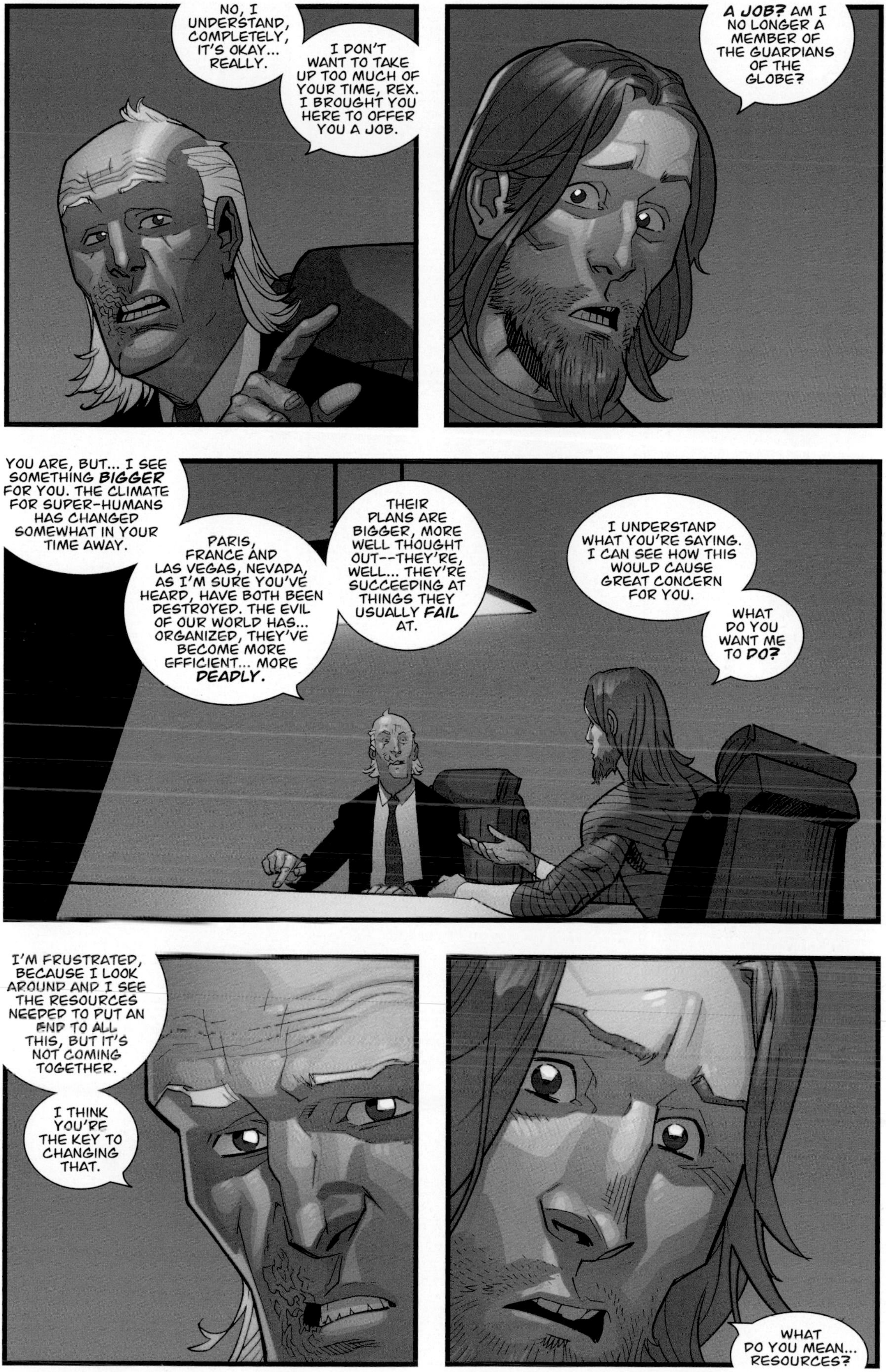
NO, I UNDERSTAND, COMPLETELY, IT'S OKAY... REALLY.
I DON'T WANT TO TAKE UP TOO MUCH OF YOUR TIME, REX. I BROUGHT YOU HERE TO OFFER YOU A JOB.
A JOB? AM I NO LONGER A MEMBER OF THE GUARDIANS OF THE GLOBE?
YOU ARE, BUT... I SEE SOMETHING BIGGER FOR YOU. THE CLIMATE FOR SUPER-HUMANS HAS CHANGED SOMEWHAT IN YOUR TIME AWAY.
PARIS, FRANCE AND LAS VEGAS, NEVADA, AS I'M SURE YOU'VE HEARD, HAVE BOTH BEEN DESTROYED. THE EVIL OF OUR WORLD HAS... ORGANIZED, THEY'VE BECOME MORE EFFICIENT... MORE DEADLY.
THEIR PLANS ARE BIGGER, MORE WELL THOUGHT OUT--THEY'RE, WELL... THEY'RE SUCCEEDING AT THINGS THEY USUALLY FAIL AT.
I UNDERSTAND WHAT YOU'RE SAYING. I CAN SEE HOW THIS WOULD CAUSE GREAT CONCERN FOR YOU.
WHAT DO YOU WANT ME TO DO?
I'M FRUSTRATED, BECAUSE I LOOK AROUND AND I SEE THE RESOURCES NEEDED TO PUT AN END TO ALL THIS, BUT IT'S NOT COMING TOGETHER.
I THINK YOU'RE THE KEY TO CHANGING THAT.
WHAT DO YOU MEAN... RESOURCES?

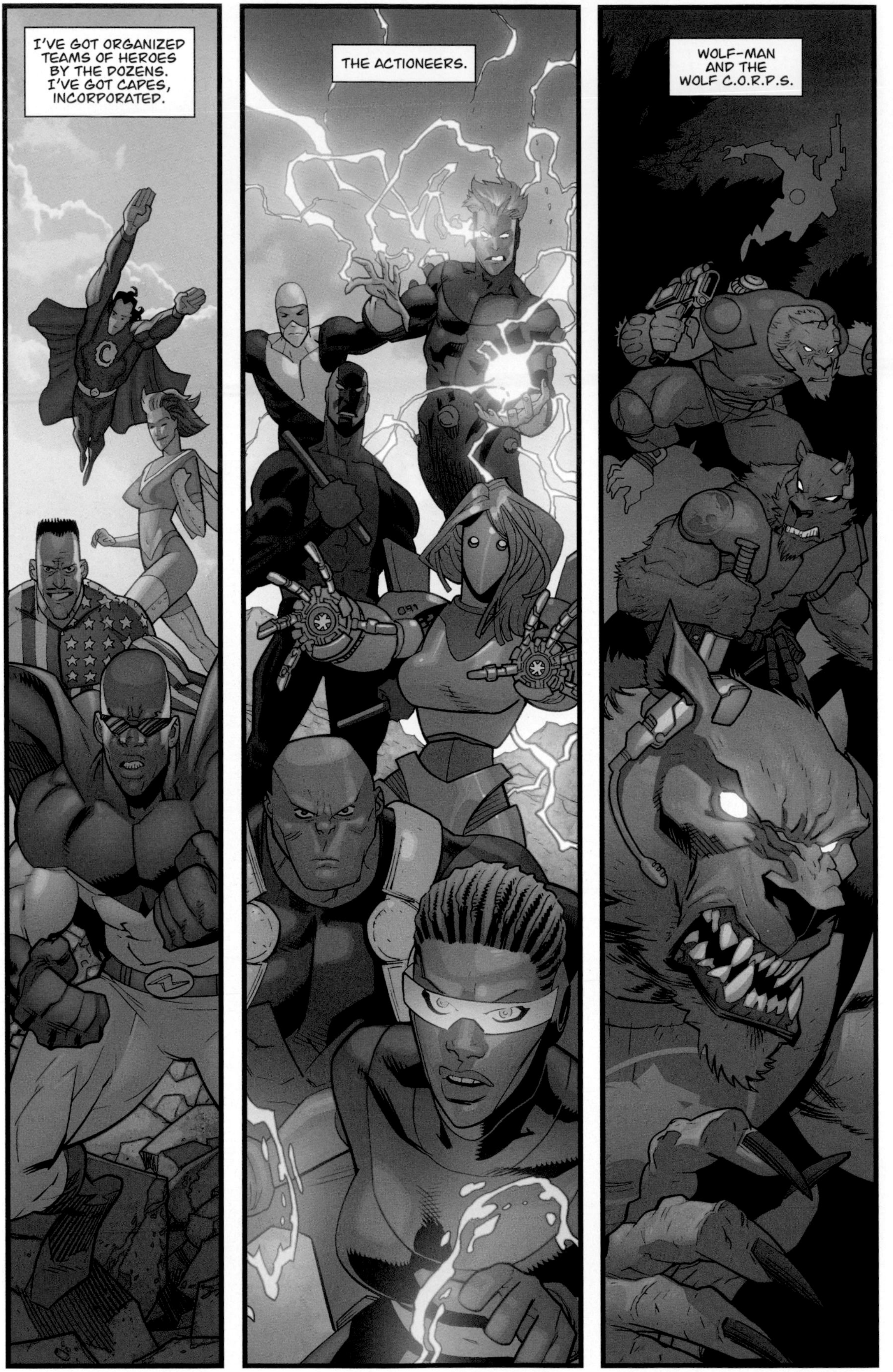

I'VE GOT ORGANIZED TEAMS OF HEROES BY THE DOZENS. I'VE GOT CAPES, INCORPORATED.
THE ACTIONEERS.
WOLF-MAN AND THE WOLF C.O.R.P.S.

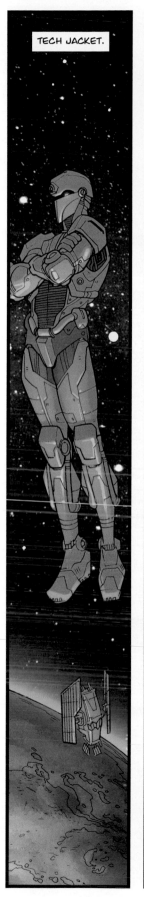

TECH JACKET.

THOUGH HE DOESN'T *DIRECTLY* ANSWER TO ME, THERE'S ALSO INVINCIBLE.

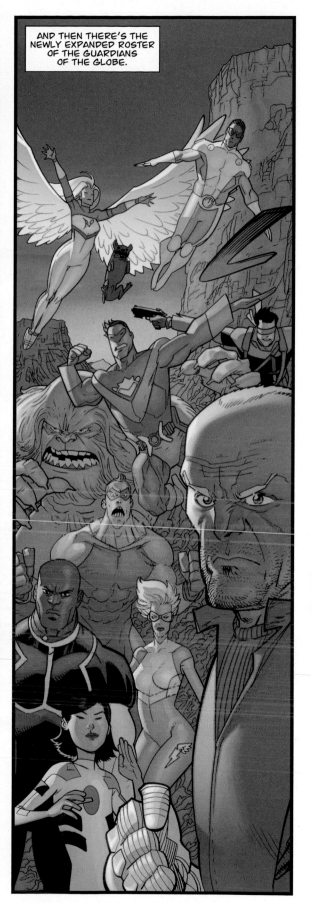

AND THEN THERE'S THE NEWLY EXPANDED ROSTER OF THE GUARDIANS OF THE GLOBE.

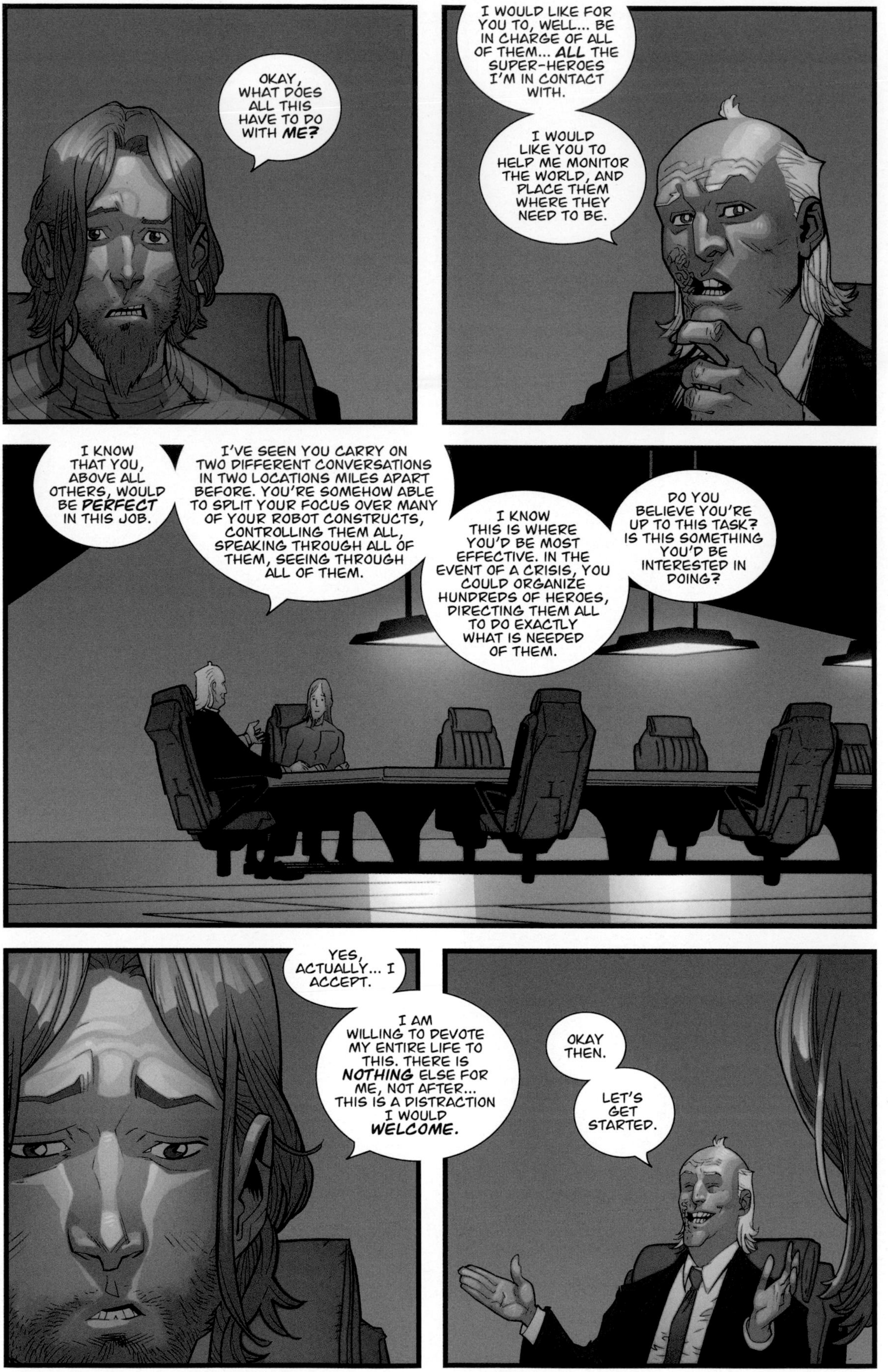
OKAY, WHAT DOES ALL THIS HAVE TO DO WITH ME?
I WOULD LIKE FOR YOU TO, WELL... BE IN CHARGE OF ALL OF THEM... ALL THE SUPER-HEROES I'M IN CONTACT WITH.
I WOULD LIKE YOU TO HELP ME MONITOR THE WORLD, AND PLACE THEM WHERE THEY NEED TO BE.
I KNOW THAT YOU, ABOVE ALL OTHERS, WOULD BE PERFECT IN THIS JOB.
I'VE SEEN YOU CARRY ON TWO DIFFERENT CONVERSATIONS IN TWO LOCATIONS MILES APART BEFORE. YOU'RE SOMEHOW ABLE TO SPLIT YOUR FOCUS OVER MANY OF YOUR ROBOT CONSTRUCTS, CONTROLLING THEM ALL, SPEAKING THROUGH ALL OF THEM, SEEING THROUGH ALL OF THEM.
I KNOW THIS IS WHERE YOU'D BE MOST EFFECTIVE. IN THE EVENT OF A CRISIS, YOU COULD ORGANIZE HUNDREDS OF HEROES, DIRECTING THEM ALL TO DO EXACTLY WHAT IS NEEDED OF THEM.
DO YOU BELIEVE YOU'RE UP TO THIS TASK? IS THIS SOMETHING YOU'D BE INTERESTED IN DOING?
YES, ACTUALLY... I ACCEPT.
I AM WILLING TO DEVOTE MY ENTIRE LIFE TO THIS. THERE IS NOTHING ELSE FOR ME, NOT AFTER... THIS IS A DISTRACTION I WOULD WELCOME.
OKAY THEN.
LET'S GET STARTED.

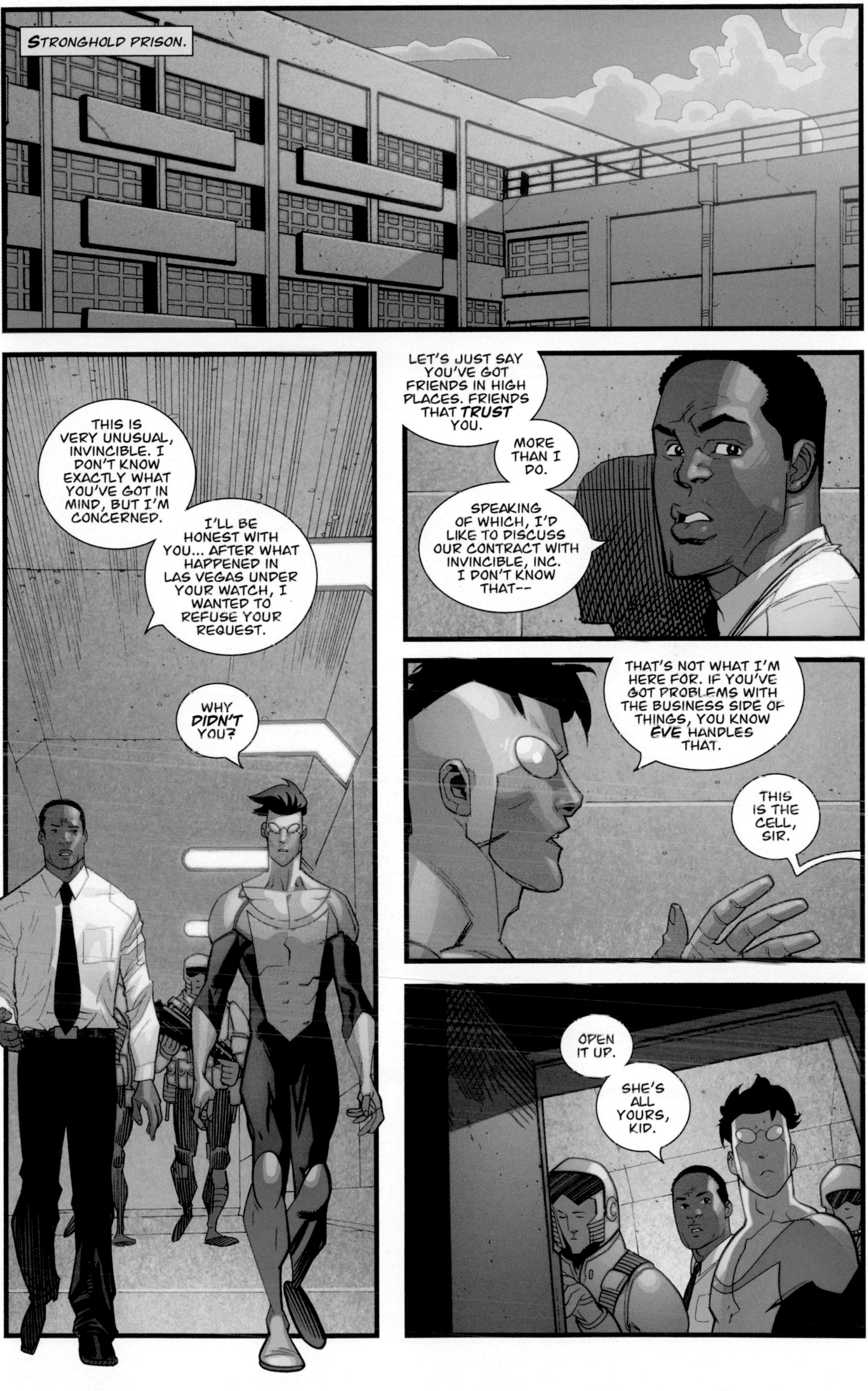
STRONGHOLD PRISON.
THIS IS VERY UNUSUAL, INVINCIBLE. I DON'T KNOW EXACTLY WHAT YOU'VE GOT IN MIND, BUT I'M CONCERNED.
I'LL BE HONEST WITH YOU... AFTER WHAT HAPPENED IN LAS VEGAS UNDER YOUR WATCH, I WANTED TO REFUSE YOUR REQUEST.
WHY DIDN'T YOU?
LET'S JUST SAY YOU'VE GOT FRIENDS IN HIGH PLACES. FRIENDS THAT TRUST YOU.
MORE THAN I DO.
SPEAKING OF WHICH, I'D LIKE TO DISCUSS OUR CONTRACT WITH INVINCIBLE, INC. I DON'T KNOW THAT--
THAT'S NOT WHAT I'M HERE FOR. IF YOU'VE GOT PROBLEMS WITH THE BUSINESS SIDE OF THINGS, YOU KNOW EVE HANDLES THAT.
THIS IS THE CELL, SIR.
OPEN IT UP.
SHE'S ALL YOURS, KID.

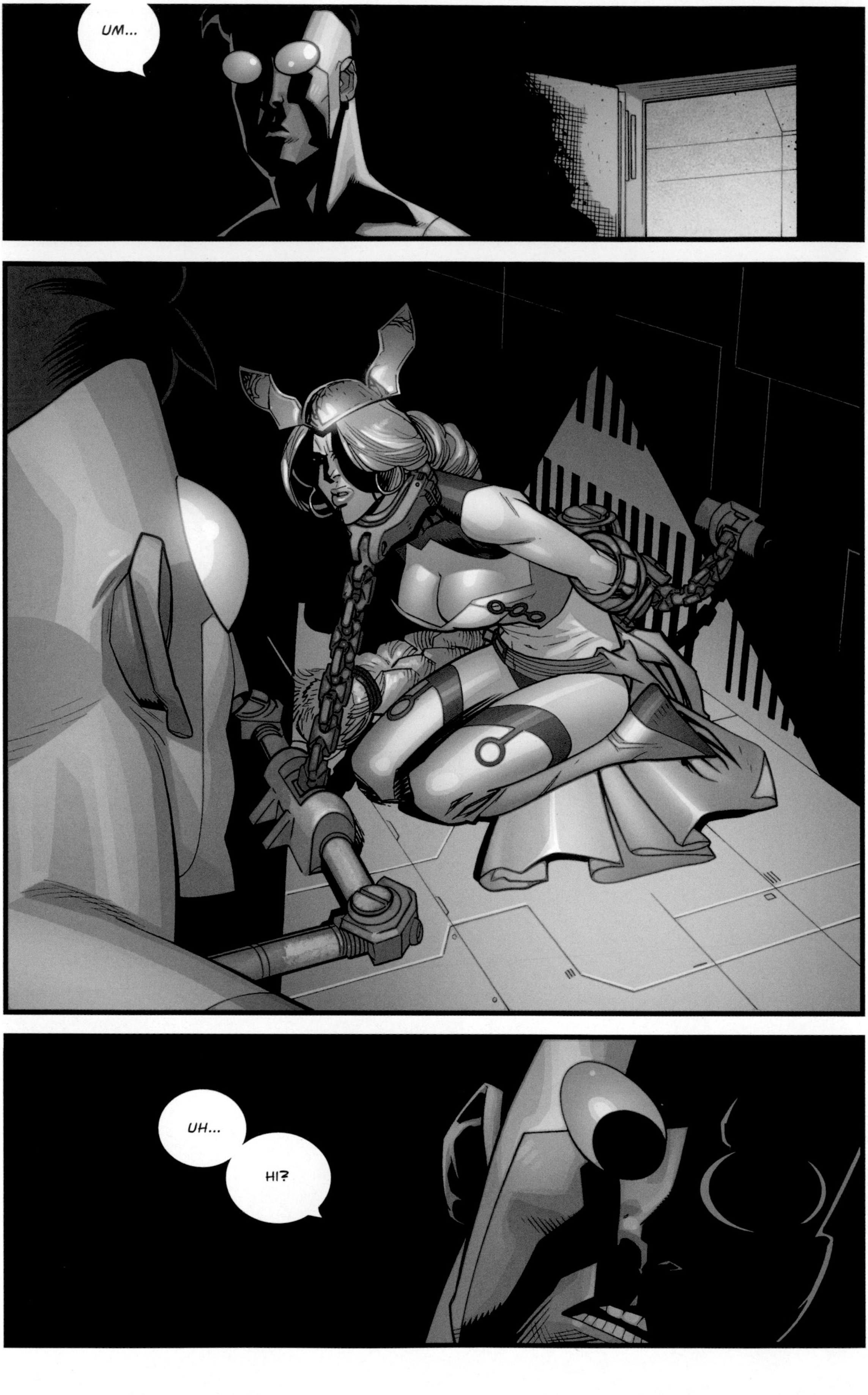
UM...
UH...
HI?

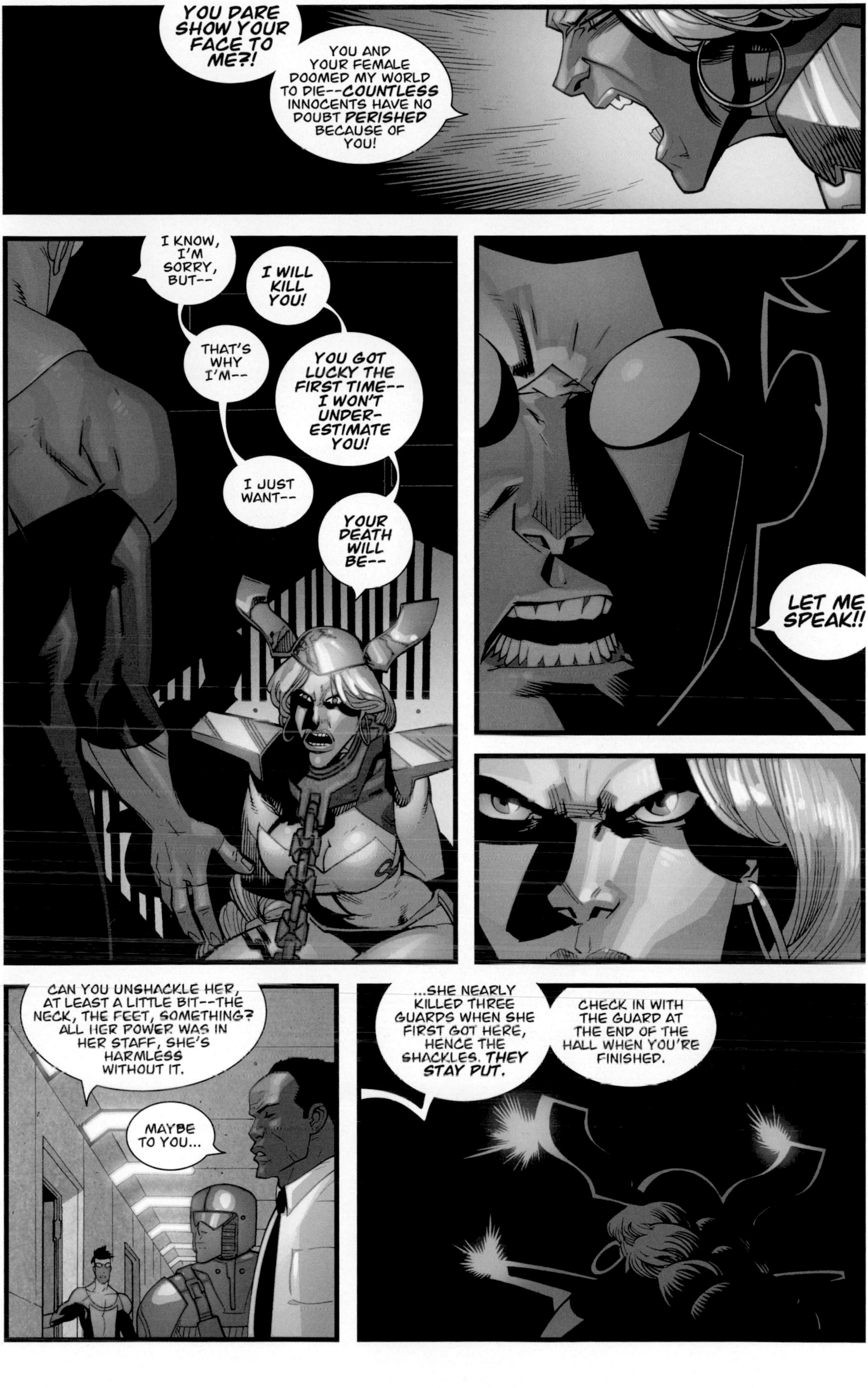
YOU DARE SHOW YOUR FACE TO ME?!
YOU AND YOUR FEMALE DOOMED MY WORLD TO DIE--COUNTLESS INNOCENTS HAVE NO DOUBT PERISHED BECAUSE OF YOU!
I KNOW, I'M SORRY, BUT--
I WILL KILL YOU!
THAT'S WHY I'M--
YOU GOT LUCKY THE FIRST TIME--I WON'T UNDER-ESTIMATE YOU!
I JUST WANT--
YOUR DEATH WILL BE--
LET ME SPEAK!!
CAN YOU UNSHACKLE HER, AT LEAST A LITTLE BIT--THE NECK, THE FEET, SOMETHING? ALL HER POWER WAS IN HER STAFF, SHE'S HARMLESS WITHOUT IT.
MAYBE TO YOU...
...SHE NEARLY KILLED THREE GUARDS WHEN SHE FIRST GOT HERE, HENCE THE SHACKLES. THEY STAY PUT.
CHECK IN WITH THE GUARD AT THE END OF THE HALL WHEN YOU'RE FINISHED.

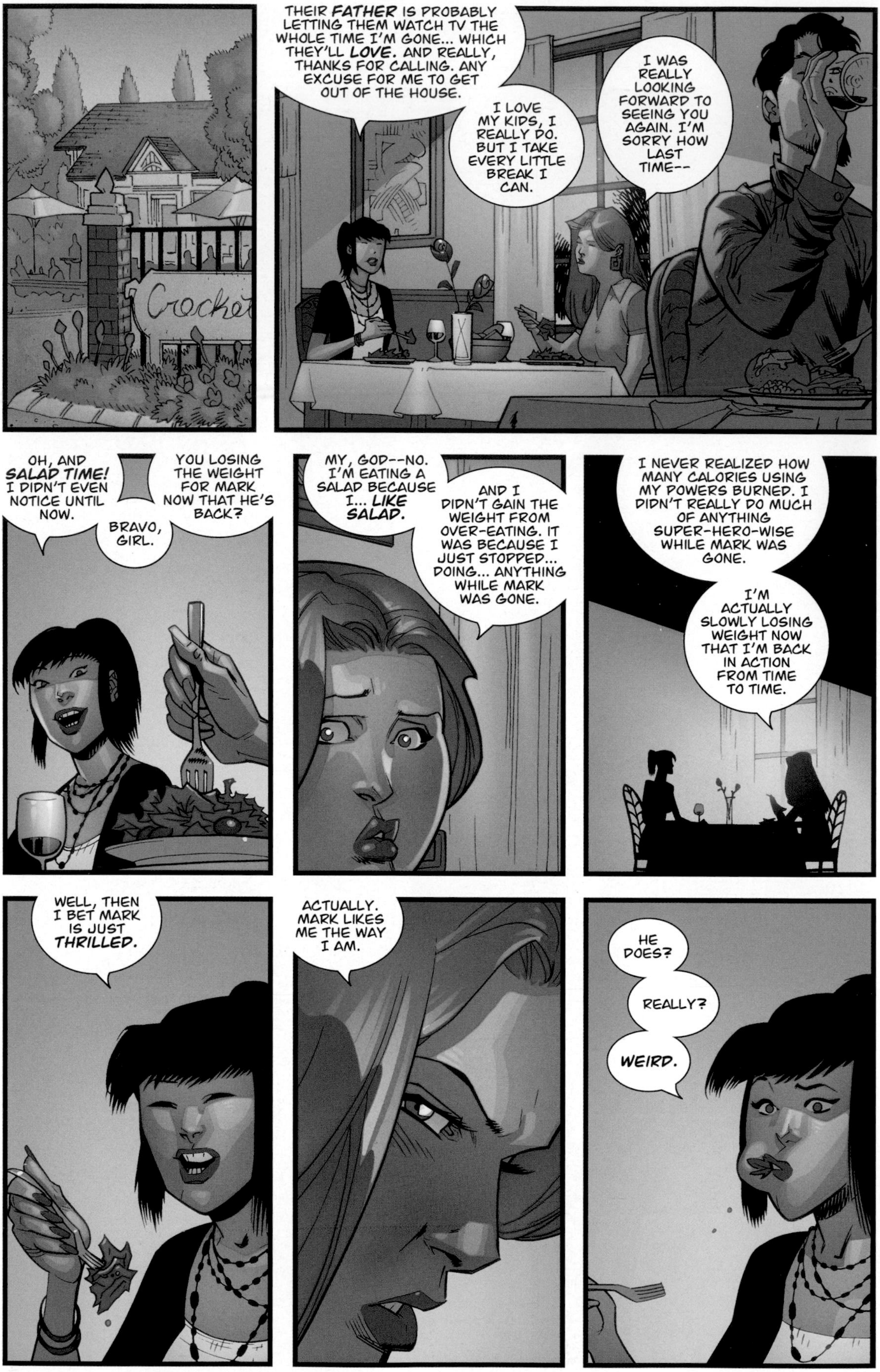
THEIR **FATHER** IS PROBABLY LETTING THEM WATCH TV THE WHOLE TIME I'M GONE... WHICH THEY'LL **LOVE.** AND REALLY, THANKS FOR CALLING. ANY EXCUSE FOR ME TO GET OUT OF THE HOUSE.
I LOVE MY KIDS, I REALLY DO. BUT I TAKE EVERY LITTLE BREAK I CAN.
I WAS REALLY LOOKING FORWARD TO SEEING YOU AGAIN. I'M SORRY HOW LAST TIME--
OH, AND **SALAD TIME!** I DIDN'T EVEN NOTICE UNTIL NOW.
BRAVO, GIRL.
YOU LOSING THE WEIGHT FOR MARK NOW THAT HE'S BACK?
MY, GOD--NO. I'M EATING A SALAD BECAUSE I... **LIKE SALAD.**
AND I DIDN'T GAIN THE WEIGHT FROM OVER-EATING. IT WAS BECAUSE I JUST STOPPED... DOING... ANYTHING WHILE MARK WAS GONE.
I NEVER REALIZED HOW MANY CALORIES USING MY POWERS BURNED. I DIDN'T REALLY DO MUCH OF ANYTHING SUPER-HERO-WISE WHILE MARK WAS GONE.
I'M ACTUALLY SLOWLY LOSING WEIGHT NOW THAT I'M BACK IN ACTION FROM TIME TO TIME.
WELL, THEN I BET MARK IS JUST **THRILLED.**
ACTUALLY. MARK LIKES ME THE WAY I AM.
HE DOES?
REALLY?
WEIRD.

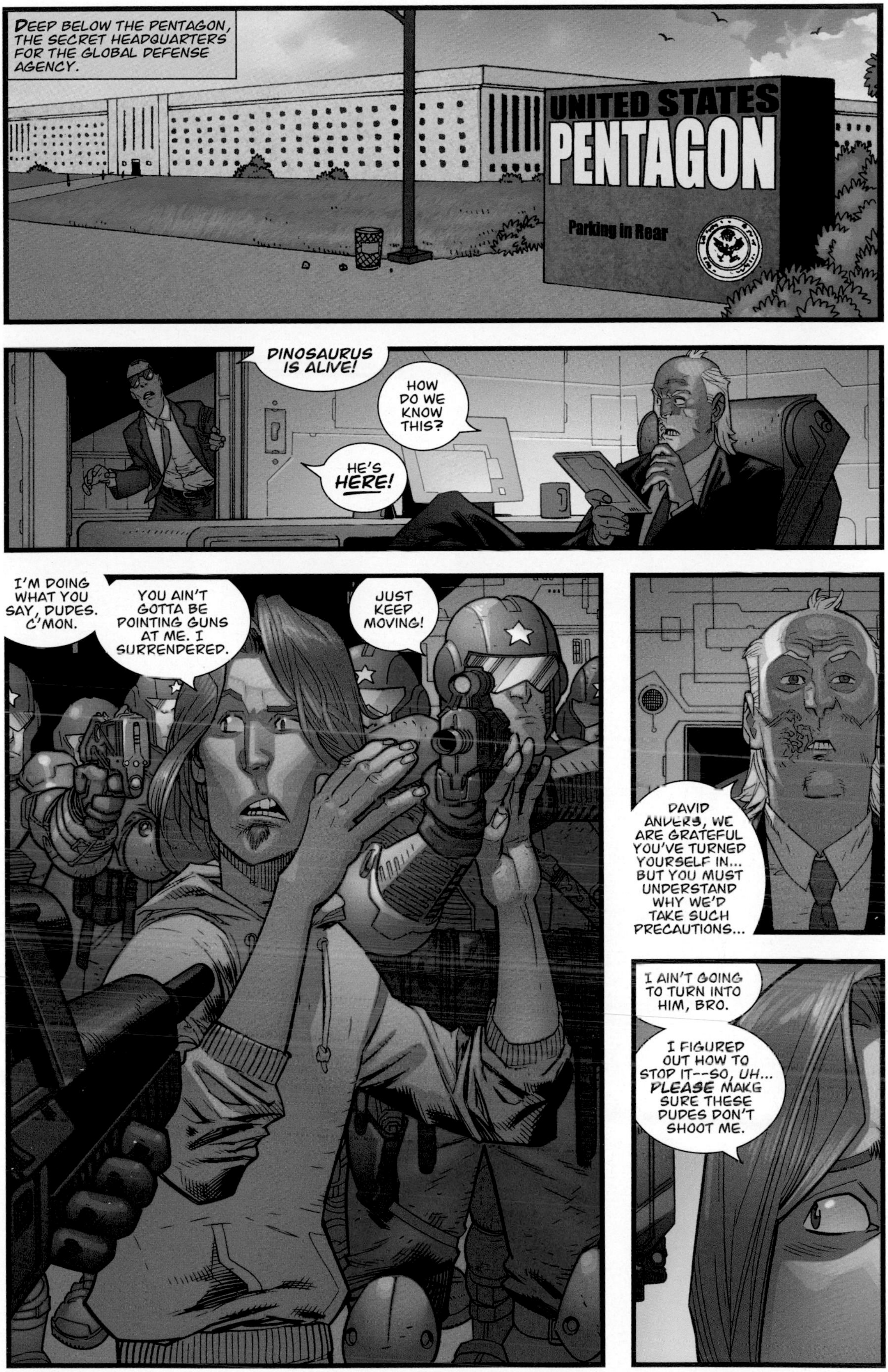
DEEP BELOW THE PENTAGON, THE SECRET HEADQUARTERS FOR THE GLOBAL DEFENSE AGENCY.
UNITED STATES
PENTAGON
Parking in Rear
DINOSAURUS IS ALIVE!
HOW DO WE KNOW THIS?
HE'S HERE!
I'M DOING WHAT YOU SAY, DUDES. C'MON.
YOU AIN'T GOTTA BE POINTING GUNS AT ME. I SURRENDERED.
JUST KEEP MOVING!
DAVID ANDERS, WE ARE GRATEFUL YOU'VE TURNED YOURSELF IN... BUT YOU MUST UNDERSTAND WHY WE'D TAKE SUCH PRECAUTIONS...
I AIN'T GOING TO TURN INTO HIM, BRO.
I FIGURED OUT HOW TO STOP IT--SO, UH... PLEASE MAKE SURE THESE DUDES DON'T SHOOT ME.

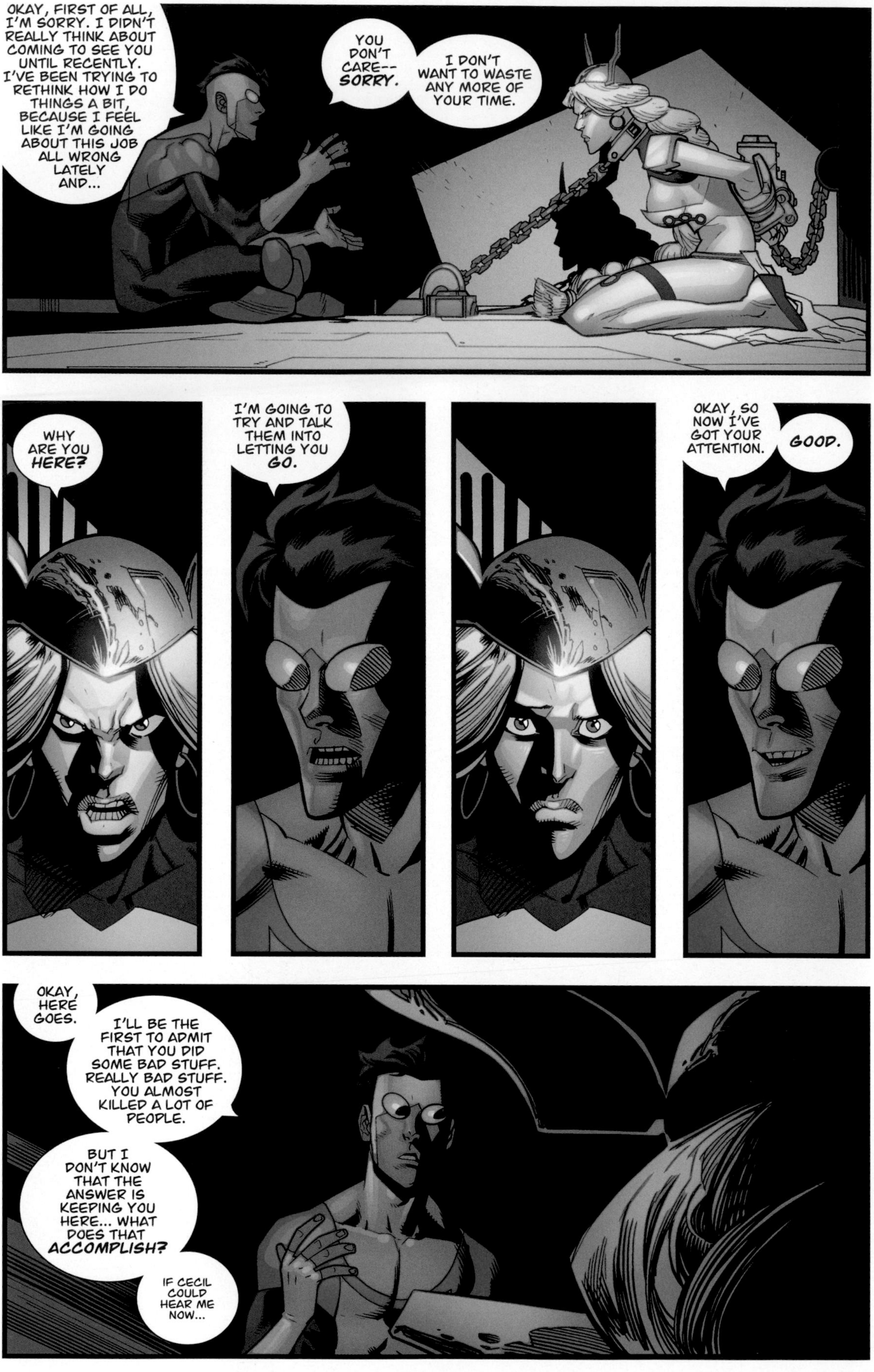
OKAY, FIRST OF ALL, I'M SORRY. I DIDN'T REALLY THINK ABOUT COMING TO SEE YOU UNTIL RECENTLY. I'VE BEEN TRYING TO RETHINK HOW I DO THINGS A BIT, BECAUSE I FEEL LIKE I'M GOING ABOUT THIS JOB ALL WRONG LATELY AND...
YOU DON'T CARE-- SORRY.
I DON'T WANT TO WASTE ANY MORE OF YOUR TIME.
WHY ARE YOU HERE?
I'M GOING TO TRY AND TALK THEM INTO LETTING YOU GO.
OKAY, SO NOW I'VE GOT YOUR ATTENTION.
GOOD.
OKAY, HERE GOES.
I'LL BE THE FIRST TO ADMIT THAT YOU DID SOME BAD STUFF. REALLY BAD STUFF. YOU ALMOST KILLED A LOT OF PEOPLE.
BUT I DON'T KNOW THAT THE ANSWER IS KEEPING YOU HERE... WHAT DOES THAT ACCOMPLISH?
IF CECIL COULD HEAR ME NOW...

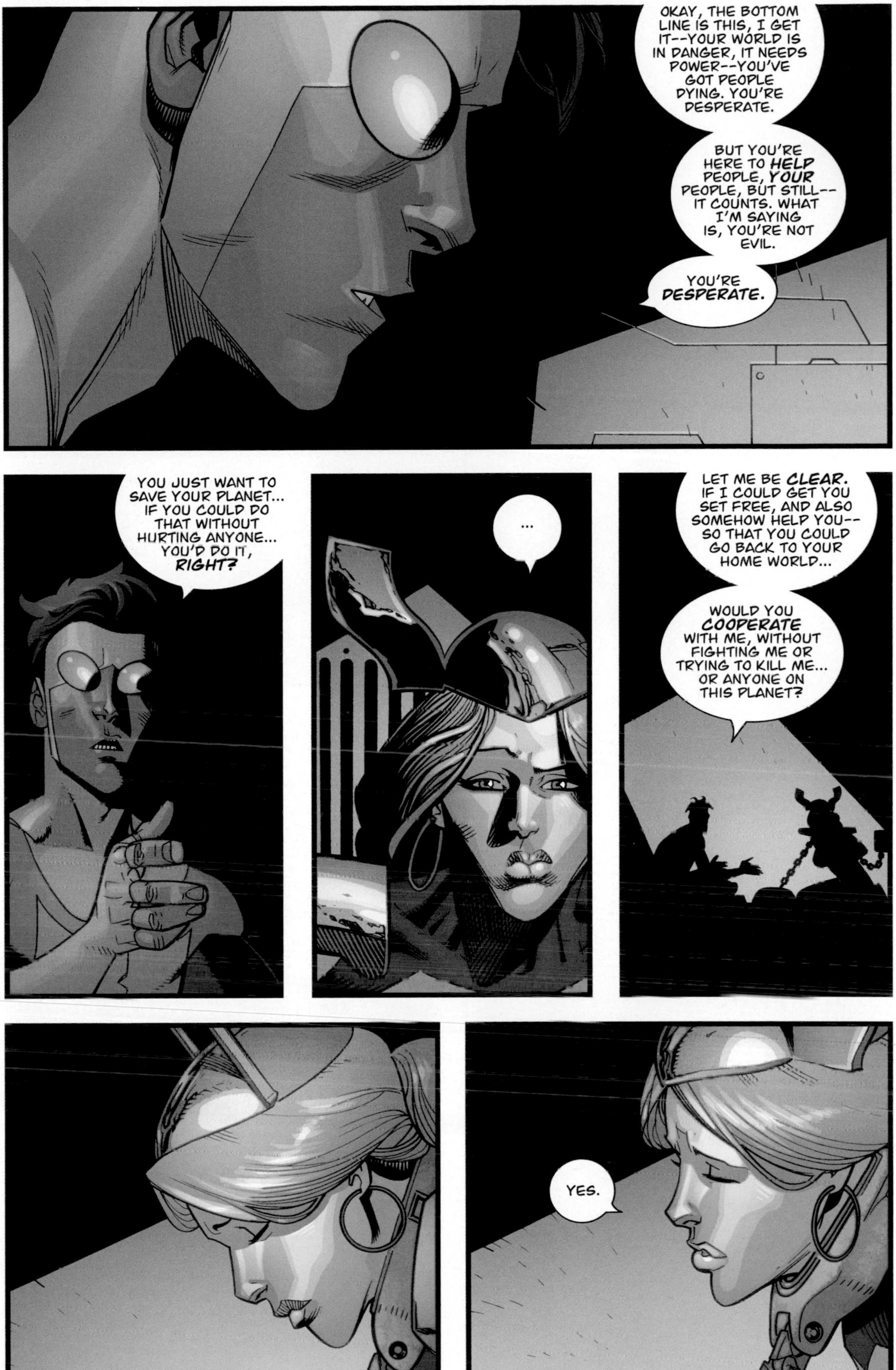
OKAY, THE BOTTOM LINE IS THIS, I GET IT--YOUR WORLD IS IN DANGER, IT NEEDS POWER--YOU'VE GOT PEOPLE DYING. YOU'RE DESPERATE.
BUT YOU'RE HERE TO HELP PEOPLE, YOUR PEOPLE, BUT STILL-- IT COUNTS. WHAT I'M SAYING IS, YOU'RE NOT EVIL.
YOU'RE DESPERATE.
YOU JUST WANT TO SAVE YOUR PLANET... IF YOU COULD DO THAT WITHOUT HURTING ANYONE... YOU'D DO IT, RIGHT?
...
LET ME BE CLEAR. IF I COULD GET YOU SET FREE, AND ALSO SOMEHOW HELP YOU-- SO THAT YOU COULD GO BACK TO YOUR HOME WORLD...
WOULD YOU COOPERATE WITH ME, WITHOUT FIGHTING ME OR TRYING TO KILL ME... OR ANYONE ON THIS PLANET?
YES.

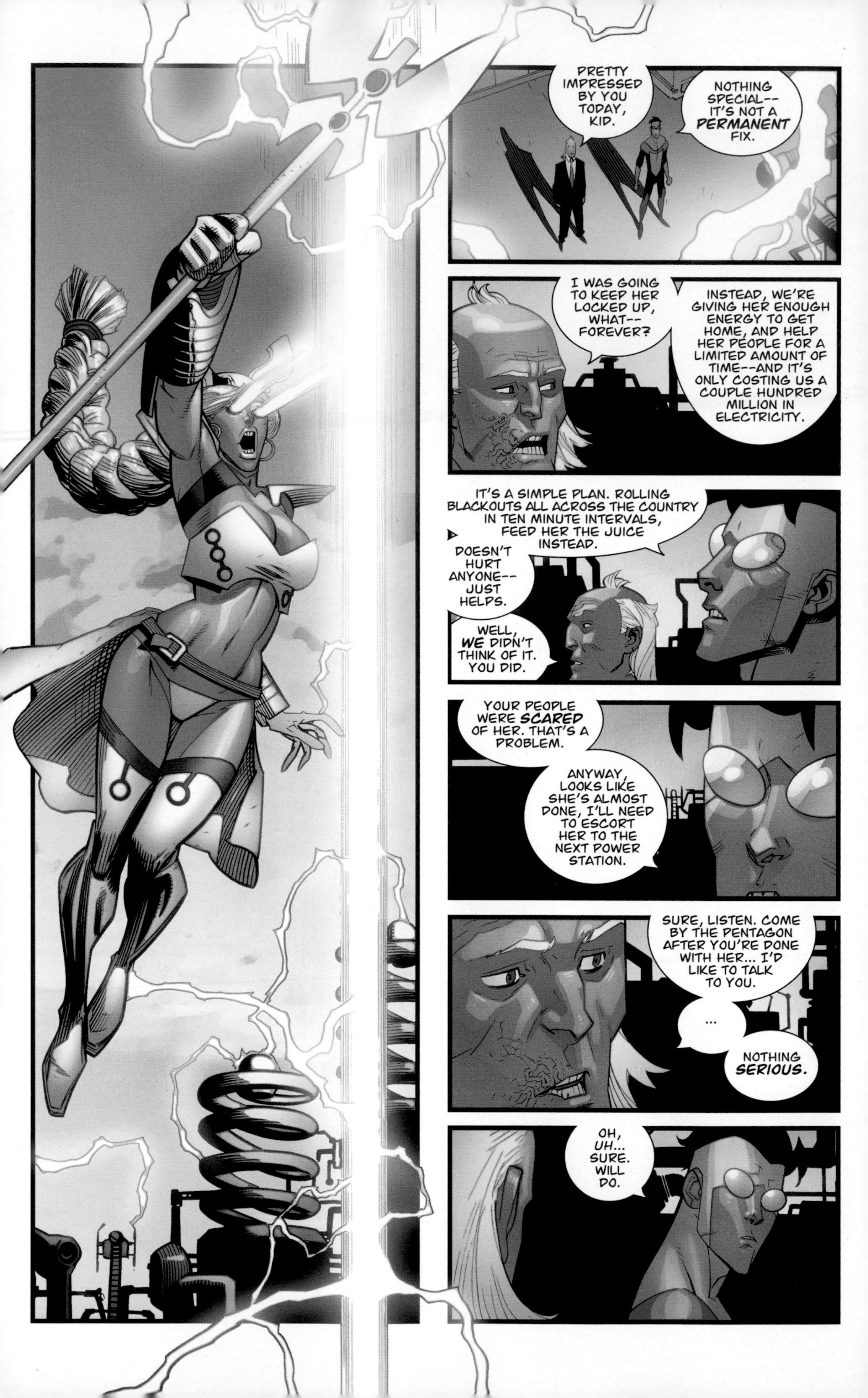
PRETTY IMPRESSED BY YOU TODAY, KID.
NOTHING SPECIAL-- IT'S NOT A PERMANENT FIX.
I WAS GOING TO KEEP HER LOCKED UP, WHAT-- FOREVER?
INSTEAD, WE'RE GIVING HER ENOUGH ENERGY TO GET HOME, AND HELP HER PEOPLE FOR A LIMITED AMOUNT OF TIME--AND IT'S ONLY COSTING US A COUPLE HUNDRED MILLION IN ELECTRICITY.
IT'S A SIMPLE PLAN. ROLLING BLACKOUTS ALL ACROSS THE COUNTRY IN TEN MINUTE INTERVALS, FEED HER THE JUICE INSTEAD.
DOESN'T HURT ANYONE-- JUST HELPS.
WELL, WE DIDN'T THINK OF IT. YOU DID.
YOUR PEOPLE WERE SCARED OF HER. THAT'S A PROBLEM.
ANYWAY, LOOKS LIKE SHE'S ALMOST DONE, I'LL NEED TO ESCORT HER TO THE NEXT POWER STATION.
SURE, LISTEN. COME BY THE PENTAGON AFTER YOU'RE DONE WITH HER... I'D LIKE TO TALK TO YOU.
...
NOTHING SERIOUS.
OH, UH... SURE. WILL DO.

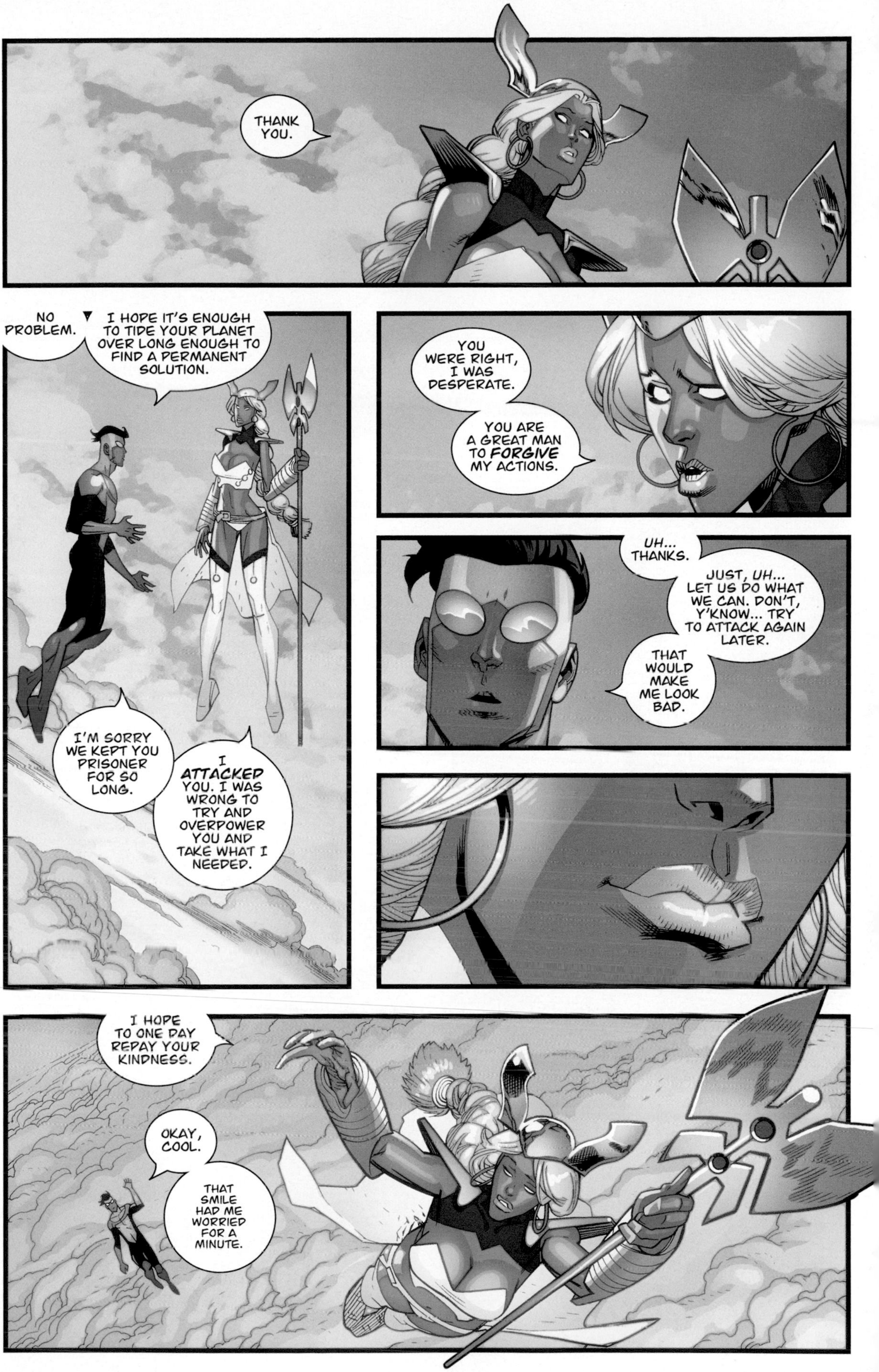

THANK YOU.
NO PROBLEM.
I HOPE IT'S ENOUGH TO TIDE YOUR PLANET OVER LONG ENOUGH TO FIND A PERMANENT SOLUTION.
I'M SORRY WE KEPT YOU PRISONER FOR SO LONG.
I ATTACKED YOU. I WAS WRONG TO TRY AND OVERPOWER YOU AND TAKE WHAT I NEEDED.
YOU WERE RIGHT, I WAS DESPERATE.
YOU ARE A GREAT MAN TO FORGIVE MY ACTIONS.
UH... THANKS.
JUST, UH... LET US DO WHAT WE CAN. DON'T, Y'KNOW... TRY TO ATTACK AGAIN LATER.
THAT WOULD MAKE ME LOOK BAD.
I HOPE TO ONE DAY REPAY YOUR KINDNESS.
OKAY, COOL.
THAT SMILE HAD ME WORRIED FOR A MINUTE.

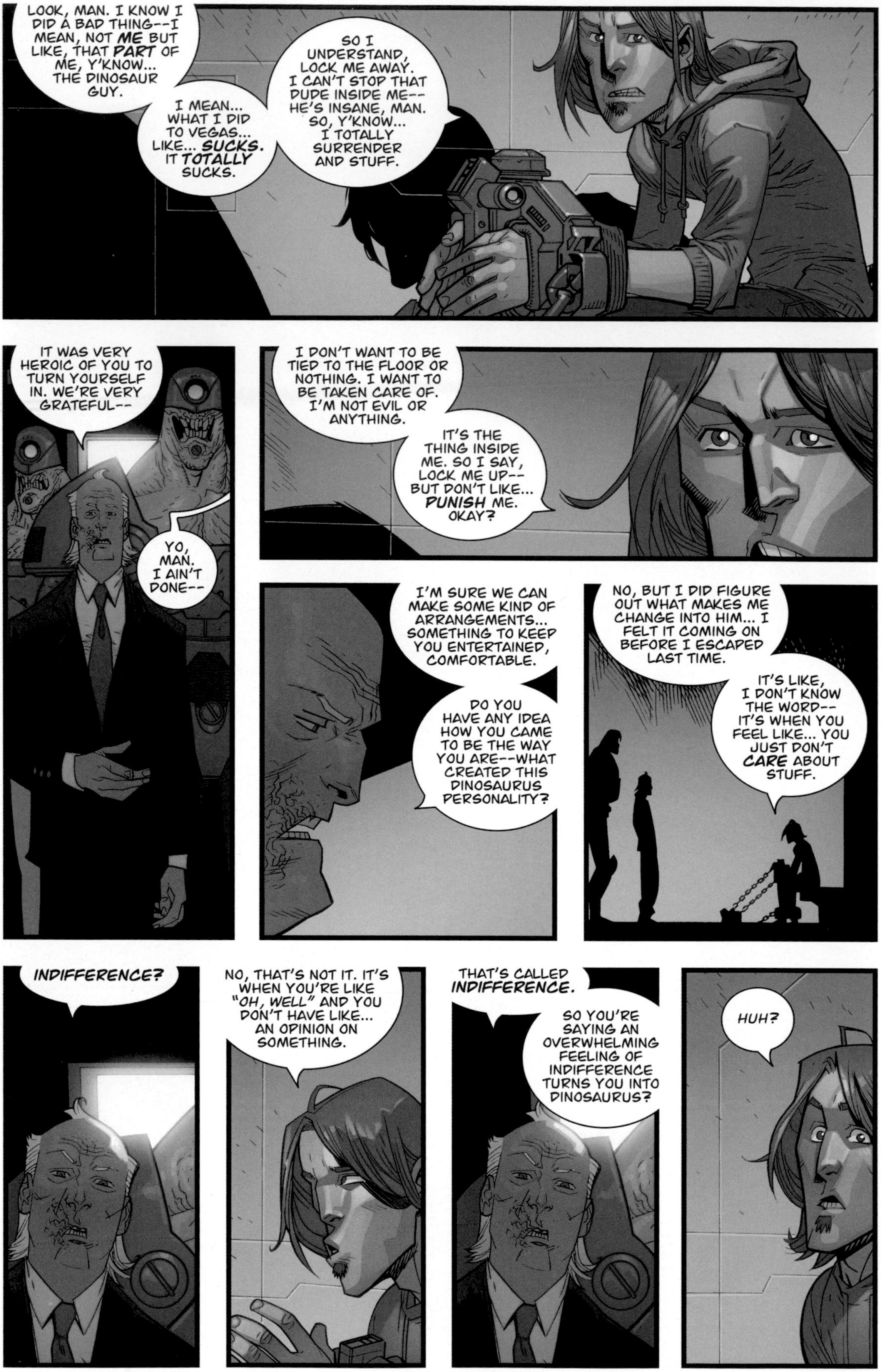
LOOK, MAN. I KNOW I DID A BAD THING--I MEAN, NOT ME BUT LIKE, THAT PART OF ME, Y'KNOW... THE DINOSAUR GUY.
I MEAN... WHAT I DID TO VEGAS... LIKE... SUCKS. IT TOTALLY SUCKS.
SO I UNDERSTAND, LOCK ME AWAY. I CAN'T STOP THAT DUDE INSIDE ME--HE'S INSANE, MAN. SO, Y'KNOW... I TOTALLY SURRENDER AND STUFF.
IT WAS VERY HEROIC OF YOU TO TURN YOURSELF IN. WE'RE VERY GRATEFUL--
YO, MAN. I AIN'T DONE--
I DON'T WANT TO BE TIED TO THE FLOOR OR NOTHING. I WANT TO BE TAKEN CARE OF. I'M NOT EVIL OR ANYTHING.
IT'S THE THING INSIDE ME. SO I SAY, LOCK ME UP--BUT DON'T LIKE... PUNISH ME. OKAY?
I'M SURE WE CAN MAKE SOME KIND OF ARRANGEMENTS... SOMETHING TO KEEP YOU ENTERTAINED, COMFORTABLE.
DO YOU HAVE ANY IDEA HOW YOU CAME TO BE THE WAY YOU ARE--WHAT CREATED THIS DINOSAURUS PERSONALITY?
NO, BUT I DID FIGURE OUT WHAT MAKES ME CHANGE INTO HIM... I FELT IT COMING ON BEFORE I ESCAPED LAST TIME.
IT'S LIKE, I DON'T KNOW THE WORD--IT'S WHEN YOU FEEL LIKE... YOU JUST DON'T CARE ABOUT STUFF.
INDIFFERENCE?
NO, THAT'S NOT IT. IT'S WHEN YOU'RE LIKE "OH, WELL" AND YOU DON'T HAVE LIKE... AN OPINION ON SOMETHING.
THAT'S CALLED INDIFFERENCE.
SO YOU'RE SAYING AN OVERWHELMING FEELING OF INDIFFERENCE TURNS YOU INTO DINOSAURUS?
HUH?

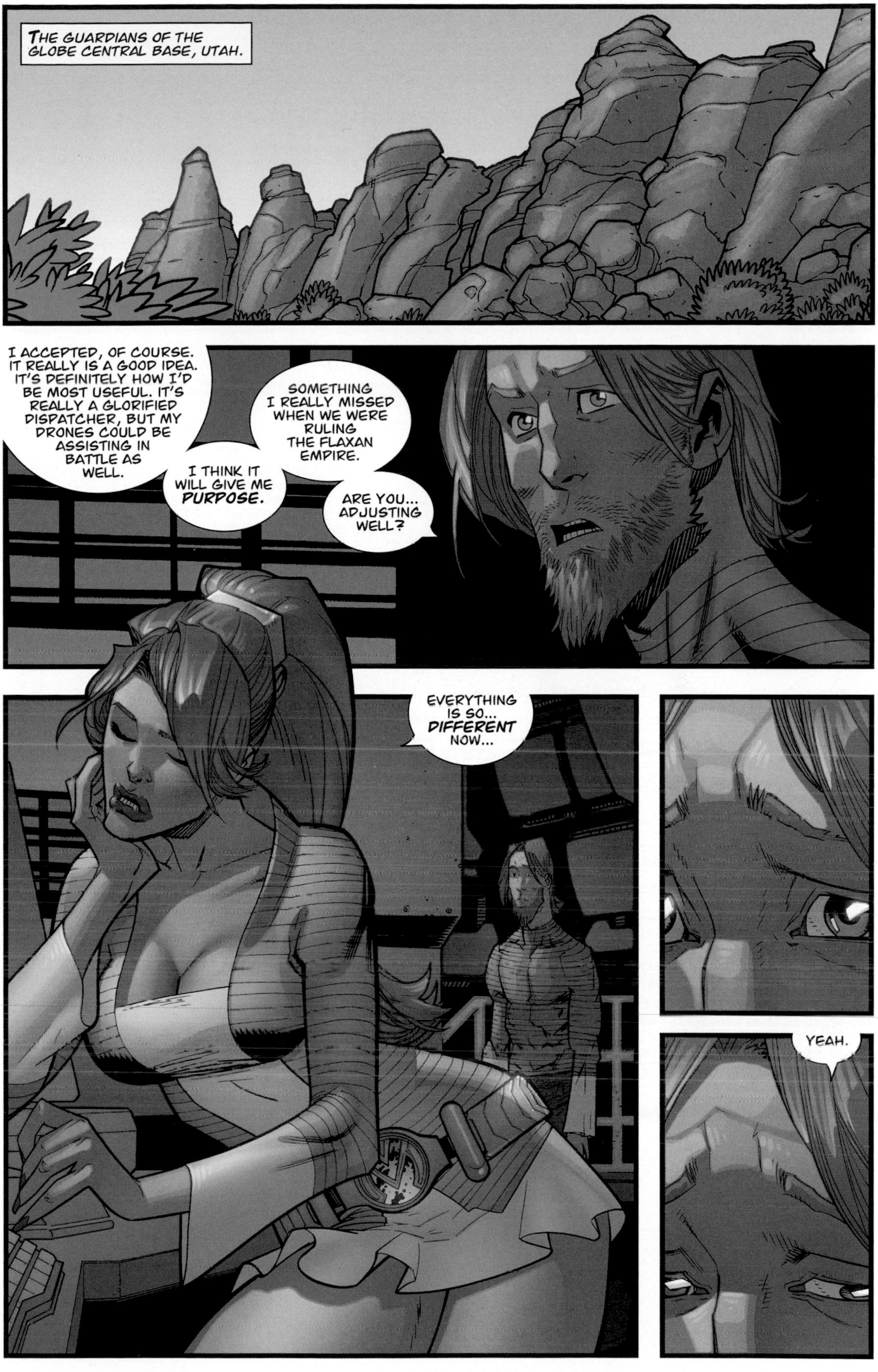

THE GUARDIANS OF THE GLOBE CENTRAL BASE, UTAH.
I ACCEPTED, OF COURSE. IT REALLY IS A GOOD IDEA. IT'S DEFINITELY HOW I'D BE MOST USEFUL. IT'S REALLY A GLORIFIED DISPATCHER, BUT MY DRONES COULD BE ASSISTING IN BATTLE AS WELL.
I THINK IT WILL GIVE ME PURPOSE.
SOMETHING I REALLY MISSED WHEN WE WERE RULING THE FLAXAN EMPIRE.
ARE YOU... ADJUSTING WELL?
EVERYTHING IS SO... DIFFERENT NOW...
YEAH.

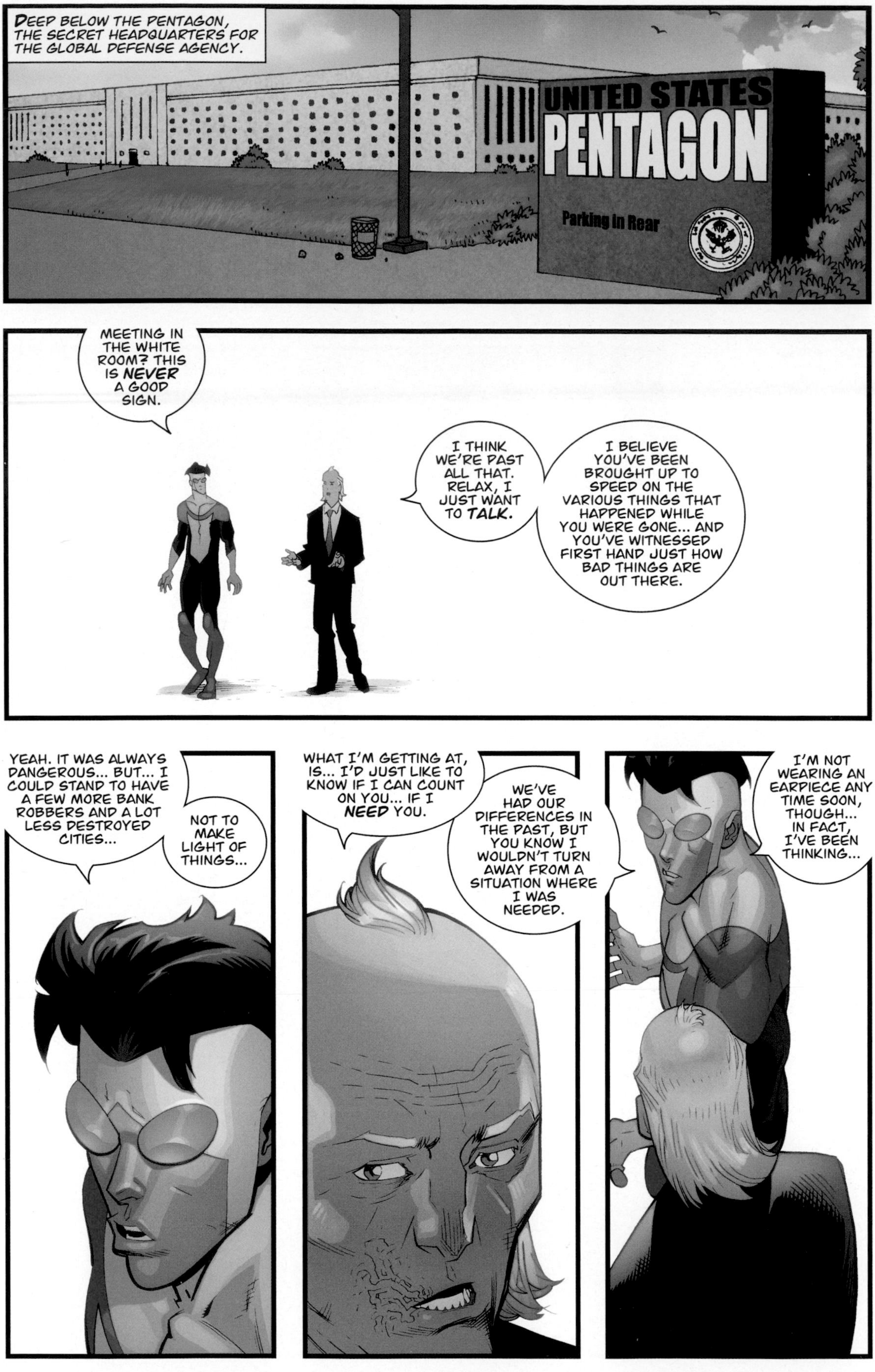
DEEP BELOW THE PENTAGON, THE SECRET HEADQUARTERS FOR THE GLOBAL DEFENSE AGENCY.
UNITED STATES PENTAGON
Parking in Rear
MEETING IN THE WHITE ROOM? THIS IS NEVER A GOOD SIGN.
I THINK WE'RE PAST ALL THAT. RELAX, I JUST WANT TO TALK.
I BELIEVE YOU'VE BEEN BROUGHT UP TO SPEED ON THE VARIOUS THINGS THAT HAPPENED WHILE YOU WERE GONE... AND YOU'VE WITNESSED FIRST HAND JUST HOW BAD THINGS ARE OUT THERE.
YEAH. IT WAS ALWAYS DANGEROUS... BUT... I COULD STAND TO HAVE A FEW MORE BANK ROBBERS AND A LOT LESS DESTROYED CITIES...
NOT TO MAKE LIGHT OF THINGS...
WHAT I'M GETTING AT, IS... I'D JUST LIKE TO KNOW IF I CAN COUNT ON YOU... IF I NEED YOU.
WE'VE HAD OUR DIFFERENCES IN THE PAST, BUT YOU KNOW I WOULDN'T TURN AWAY FROM A SITUATION WHERE I WAS NEEDED.
I'M NOT WEARING AN EARPIECE ANY TIME SOON, THOUGH... IN FACT, I'VE BEEN THINKING...

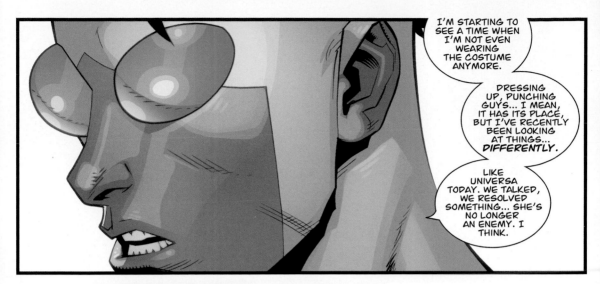

I'M STARTING TO SEE A TIME WHEN I'M NOT EVEN WEARING THE COSTUME ANYMORE.

DRESSING UP, PUNCHING GUYS... I MEAN, IT HAS ITS PLACE, BUT I'VE RECENTLY BEEN LOOKING AT THINGS... *DIFFERENTLY.*

LIKE *UNIVERSA* TODAY. WE TALKED, WE RESOLVED SOMETHING... SHE'S NO LONGER AN ENEMY. I THINK.

THAT SEEMS SO MUCH *SMARTER* THAN... FIGHTING.

MAYBE IF I'D TRIED A DIFFERENT APPROACH WITH DINOSAURUS...

THAT THING IS A *MANIAC.* NOTHING WOULD GET THROUGH TO HIM.

HOW CAN YOU BE SO CERTAIN? EVERYONE *WANTS* SOMETHING... AND THESE GUYS ARE JUST TRYING TO GET IT.

I DON'T AGREE WITH HIS METHODS, BUT FROM WHAT HE SAYS, DINOSAURUS THINKS HE'S ACTUALLY *HELPING* HUMANITY.

I THINK THERE MIGHT BE SOMETHING TO THAT...

THAT'S AN ARGUMENT FOR ANOTHER TIME, THEN.

SO, TO WRAP UP... I CAN COUNT ON YOU IF I NEED YOU?

OF COURSE... YES.

GOOD. NOW THAT WE'RE ON SPEAKING TERMS AGAIN, I FIGURE IT'S BEST TO JUST *TELL* YOU THINGS UP FRONT THAT I FEEL MIGHT UPSET YOU.

DON'T BE ALARMED, BUT...

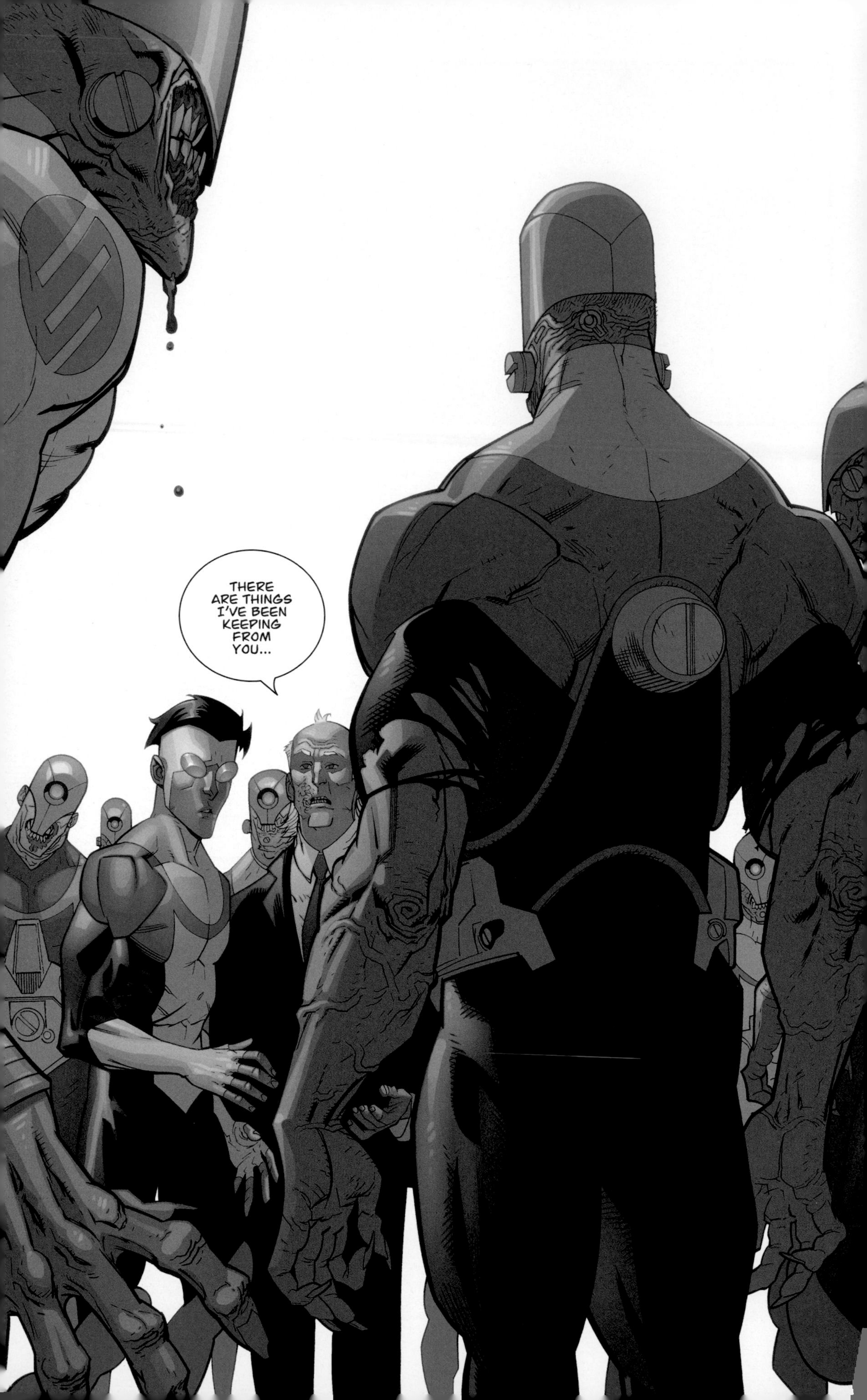
THERE ARE THINGS I'VE BEEN KEEPING FROM YOU...

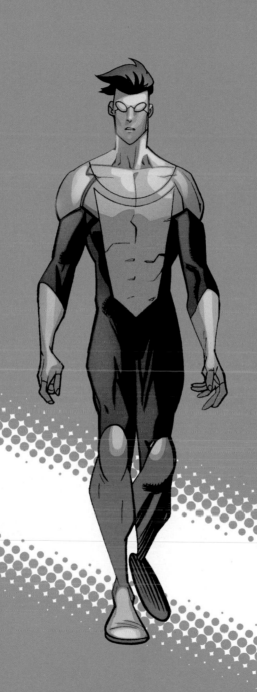

CHAPTER FIVE

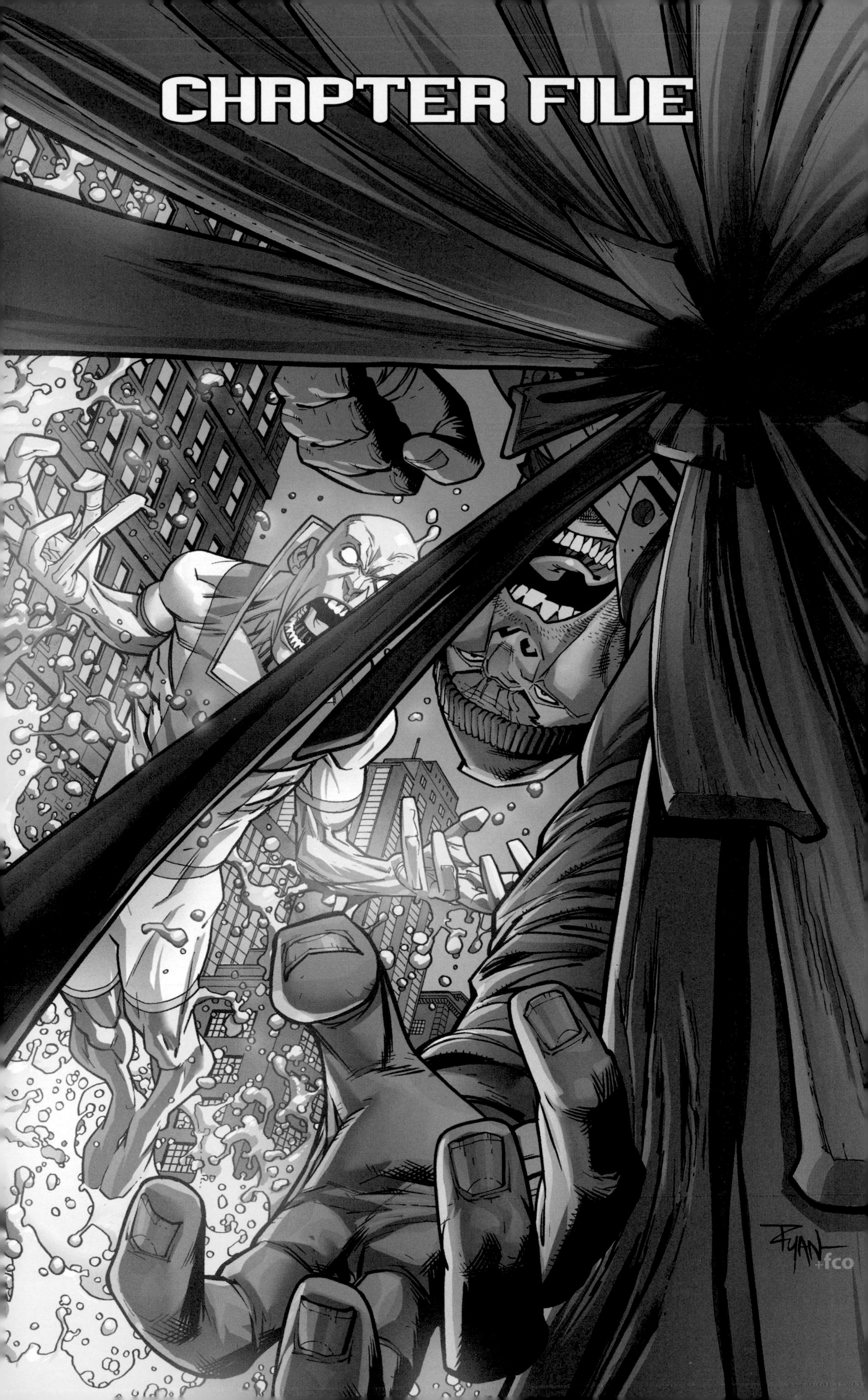
RYAN
+fco

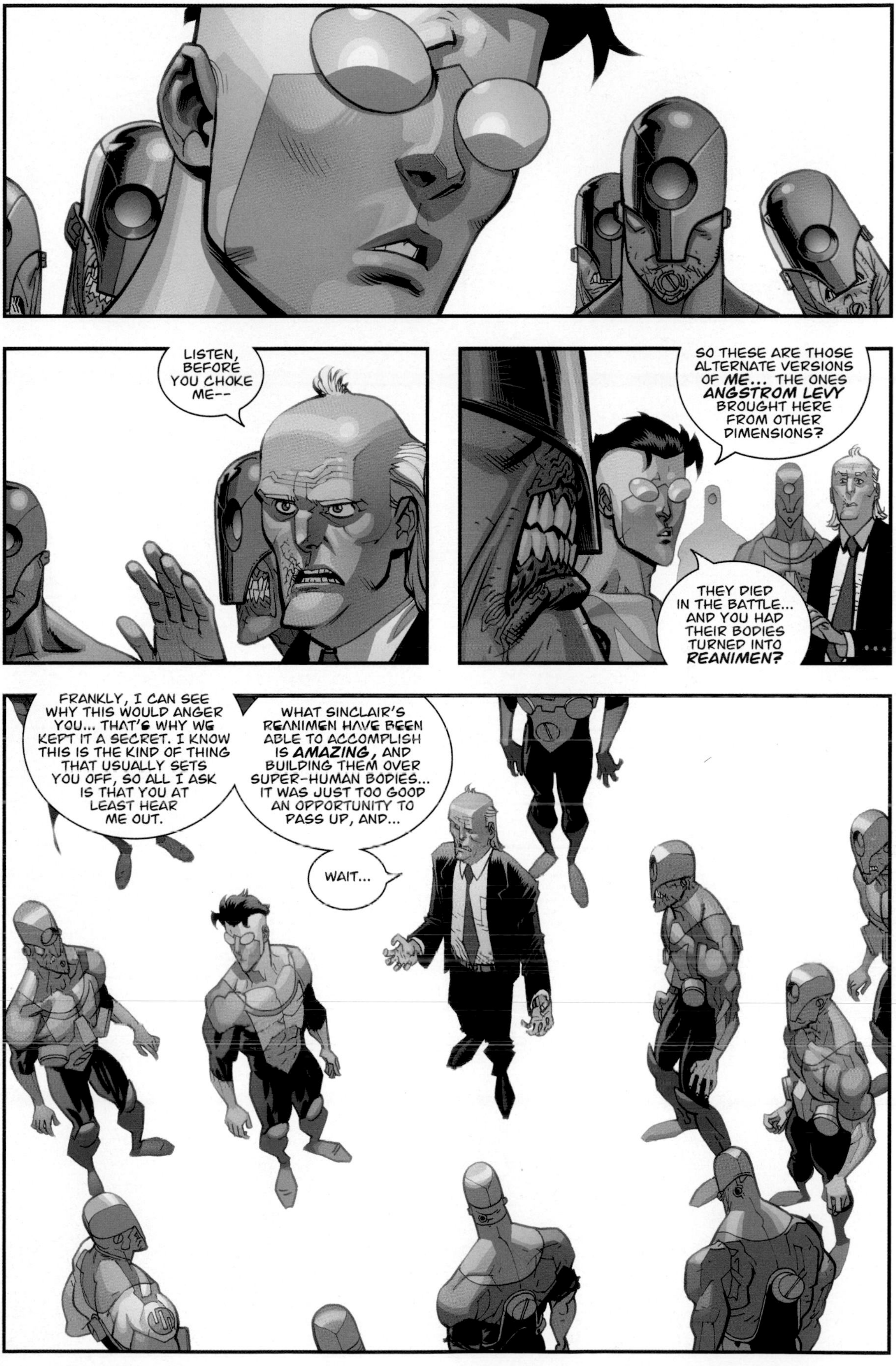
LISTEN, BEFORE YOU CHOKE ME--
SO THESE ARE THOSE ALTERNATE VERSIONS OF ME... THE ONES ANGSTROM LEVY BROUGHT HERE FROM OTHER DIMENSIONS?
THEY DIED IN THE BATTLE... AND YOU HAD THEIR BODIES TURNED INTO REANIMEN?
FRANKLY, I CAN SEE WHY THIS WOULD ANGER YOU... THAT'S WHY WE KEPT IT A SECRET. I KNOW THIS IS THE KIND OF THING THAT USUALLY SETS YOU OFF, SO ALL I ASK IS THAT YOU AT LEAST HEAR ME OUT.
WHAT SINCLAIR'S REANIMEN HAVE BEEN ABLE TO ACCOMPLISH IS AMAZING, AND BUILDING THEM OVER SUPER-HUMAN BODIES... IT WAS JUST TOO GOOD AN OPPORTUNITY TO PASS UP, AND...
WAIT...

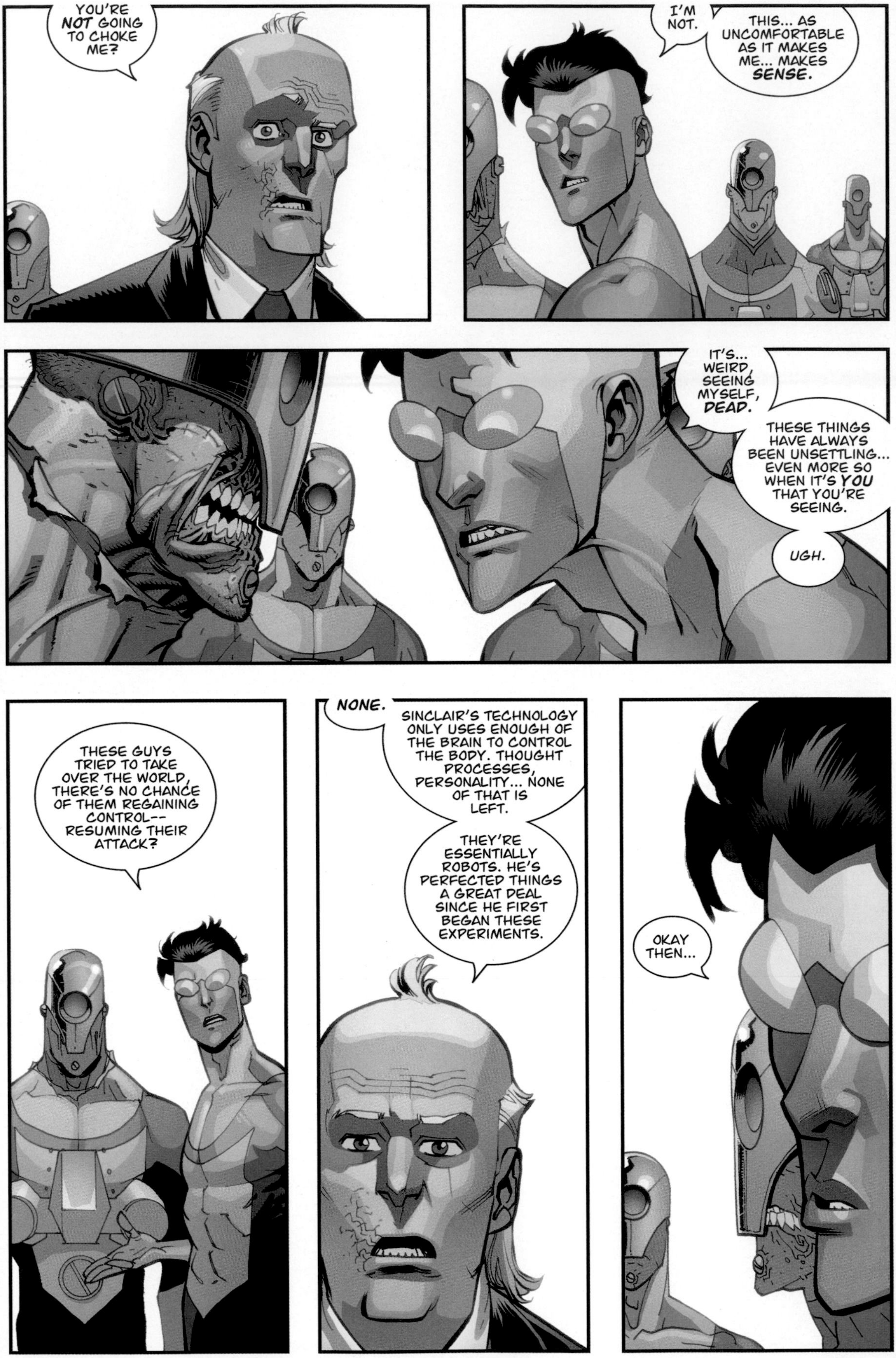
YOU'RE NOT GOING TO CHOKE ME?
I'M NOT.
THIS... AS UNCOMFORTABLE AS IT MAKES ME... MAKES SENSE.
IT'S... WEIRD, SEEING MYSELF, DEAD.
THESE THINGS HAVE ALWAYS BEEN UNSETTLING... EVEN MORE SO WHEN IT'S YOU THAT YOU'RE SEEING.
UGH.
THESE GUYS TRIED TO TAKE OVER THE WORLD, THERE'S NO CHANCE OF THEM REGAINING CONTROL-- RESUMING THEIR ATTACK?
NONE.
SINCLAIR'S TECHNOLOGY ONLY USES ENOUGH OF THE BRAIN TO CONTROL THE BODY. THOUGHT PROCESSES, PERSONALITY... NONE OF THAT IS LEFT.
THEY'RE ESSENTIALLY ROBOTS. HE'S PERFECTED THINGS A GREAT DEAL SINCE HE FIRST BEGAN THESE EXPERIMENTS.
OKAY THEN...

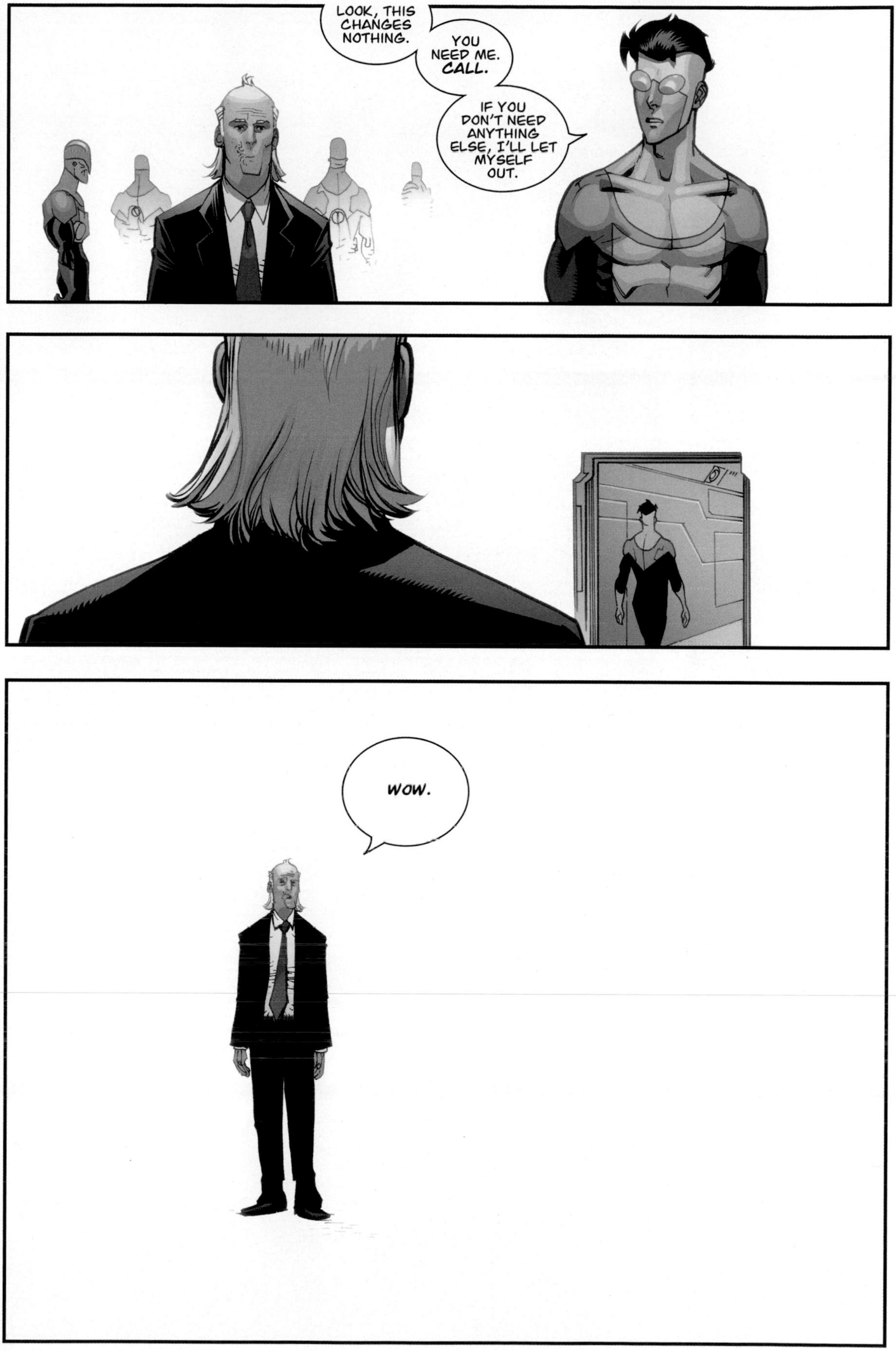
LOOK, THIS CHANGES NOTHING.
YOU NEED ME. CALL.
IF YOU DON'T NEED ANYTHING ELSE, I'LL LET MYSELF OUT.
WOW.

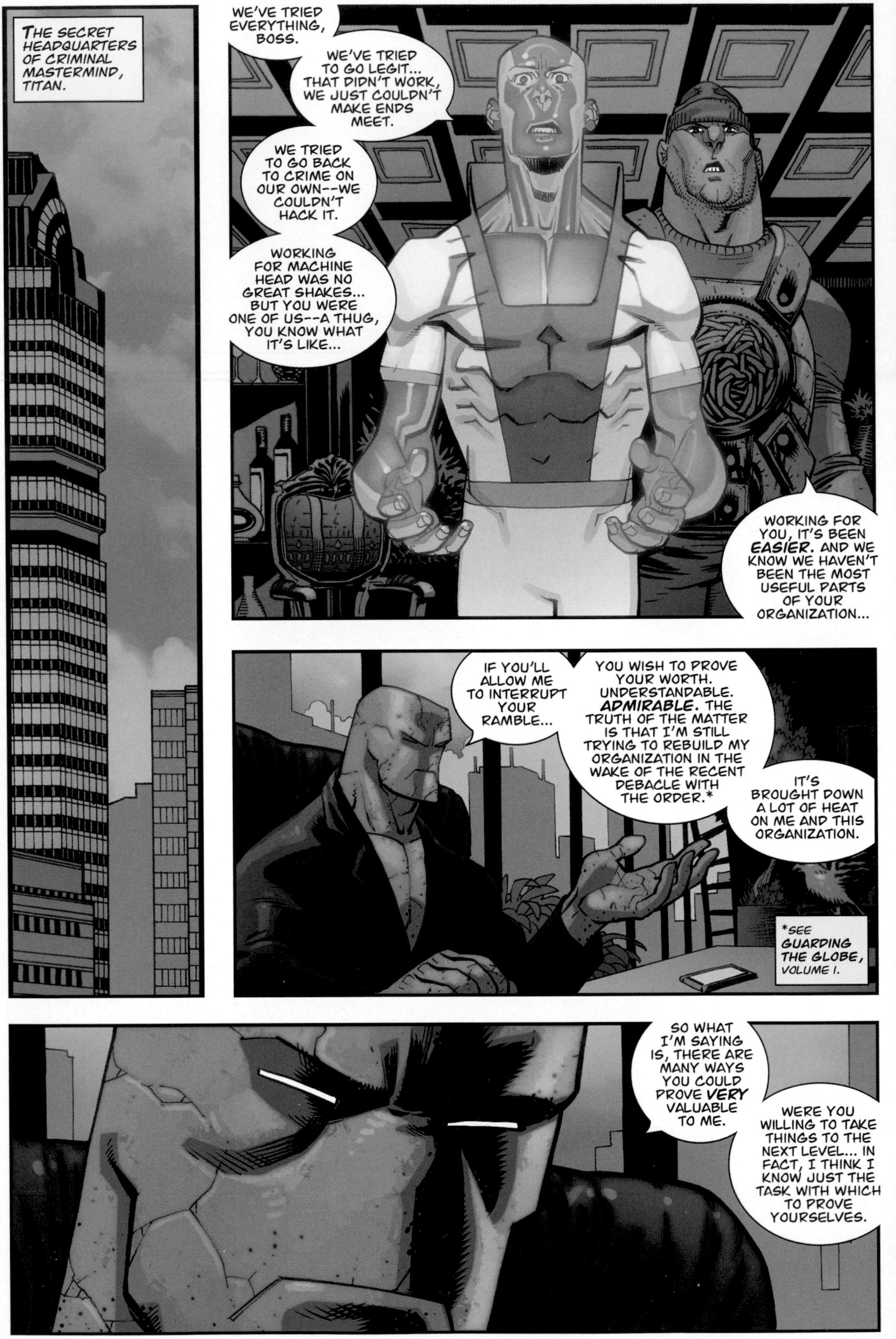
THE SECRET HEADQUARTERS OF CRIMINAL MASTERMIND, TITAN.
WE'VE TRIED EVERYTHING, BOSS.
WE'VE TRIED TO GO LEGIT... THAT DIDN'T WORK, WE JUST COULDN'T MAKE ENDS MEET.
WE TRIED TO GO BACK TO CRIME ON OUR OWN--WE COULDN'T HACK IT.
WORKING FOR MACHINE HEAD WAS NO GREAT SHAKES... BUT YOU WERE ONE OF US--A THUG, YOU KNOW WHAT IT'S LIKE...
WORKING FOR YOU, IT'S BEEN EASIER. AND WE KNOW WE HAVEN'T BEEN THE MOST USEFUL PARTS OF YOUR ORGANIZATION...
IF YOU'LL ALLOW ME TO INTERRUPT YOUR RAMBLE...
YOU WISH TO PROVE YOUR WORTH. UNDERSTANDABLE. ADMIRABLE. THE TRUTH OF THE MATTER IS THAT I'M STILL TRYING TO REBUILD MY ORGANIZATION IN THE WAKE OF THE RECENT DEBACLE WITH THE ORDER.*
IT'S BROUGHT DOWN A LOT OF HEAT ON ME AND THIS ORGANIZATION.
*SEE GUARDING THE GLOBE, VOLUME I.
SO WHAT I'M SAYING IS, THERE ARE MANY WAYS YOU COULD PROVE VERY VALUABLE TO ME.
WERE YOU WILLING TO TAKE THINGS TO THE NEXT LEVEL... IN FACT, I THINK I KNOW JUST THE TASK WITH WHICH TO PROVE YOURSELVES.

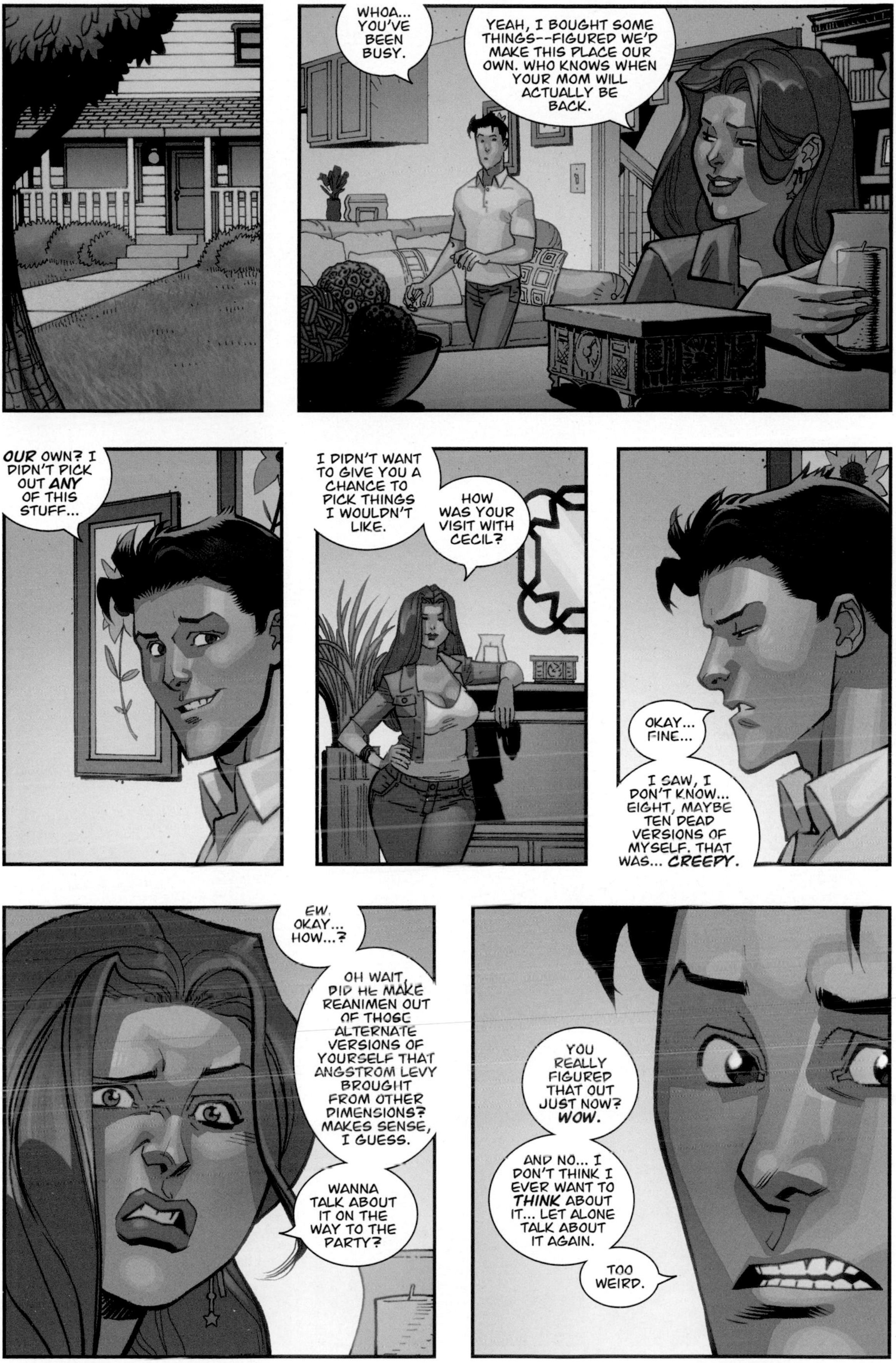
WHOA... YOU'VE BEEN BUSY.
YEAH, I BOUGHT SOME THINGS--FIGURED WE'D MAKE THIS PLACE OUR OWN. WHO KNOWS WHEN YOUR MOM WILL ACTUALLY BE BACK.
OUR OWN? I DIDN'T PICK OUT ANY OF THIS STUFF...
I DIDN'T WANT TO GIVE YOU A CHANCE TO PICK THINGS I WOULDN'T LIKE.
HOW WAS YOUR VISIT WITH CECIL?
OKAY... FINE...
I SAW, I DON'T KNOW... EIGHT, MAYBE TEN DEAD VERSIONS OF MYSELF. THAT WAS... CREEPY.
EW. OKAY... HOW...?
OH WAIT, DID HE MAKE REANIMEN OUT OF THOSE ALTERNATE VERSIONS OF YOURSELF THAT ANGSTROM LEVY BROUGHT FROM OTHER DIMENSIONS? MAKES SENSE, I GUESS.
WANNA TALK ABOUT IT ON THE WAY TO THE PARTY?
YOU REALLY FIGURED THAT OUT JUST NOW? WOW.
AND NO... I DON'T THINK I EVER WANT TO THINK ABOUT IT... LET ALONE TALK ABOUT IT AGAIN.
TOO WEIRD.

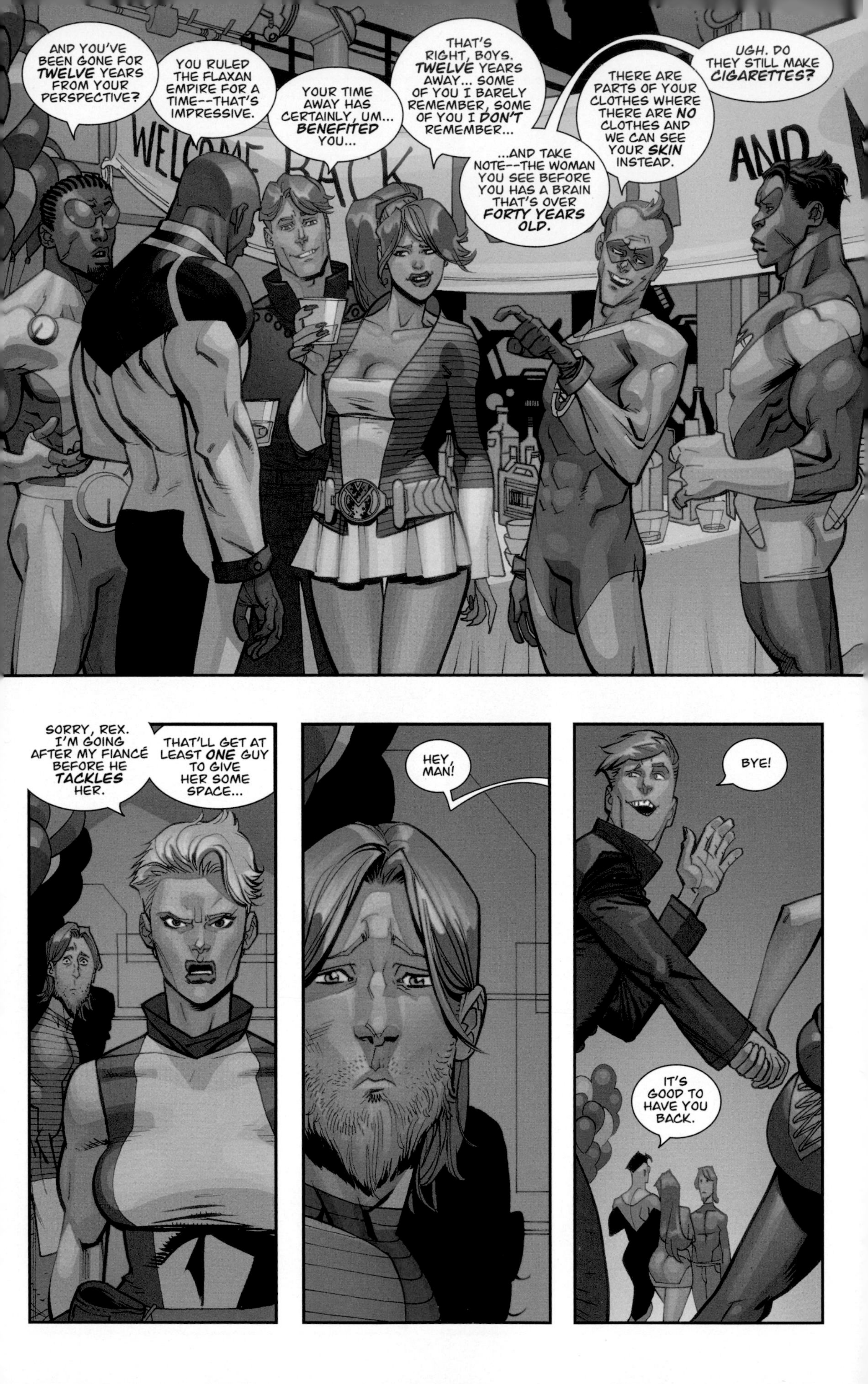
AND YOU'VE BEEN GONE FOR TWELVE YEARS FROM YOUR PERSPECTIVE?
YOU RULED THE FLAXAN EMPIRE FOR A TIME--THAT'S IMPRESSIVE.
YOUR TIME AWAY HAS CERTAINLY, UM... BENEFITED YOU...
THAT'S RIGHT, BOYS. TWELVE YEARS AWAY... SOME OF YOU I BARELY REMEMBER, SOME OF YOU I DON'T REMEMBER...
...AND TAKE NOTE--THE WOMAN YOU SEE BEFORE YOU HAS A BRAIN THAT'S OVER FORTY YEARS OLD.
THERE ARE PARTS OF YOUR CLOTHES WHERE THERE ARE NO CLOTHES AND WE CAN SEE YOUR SKIN INSTEAD.
UGH. DO THEY STILL MAKE CIGARETTES?
WELCOME BACK
AND
SORRY, REX. I'M GOING AFTER MY FIANCÉ BEFORE HE TACKLES HER.
THAT'LL GET AT LEAST ONE GUY TO GIVE HER SOME SPACE...
HEY, MAN!
BYE!
IT'S GOOD TO HAVE YOU BACK.

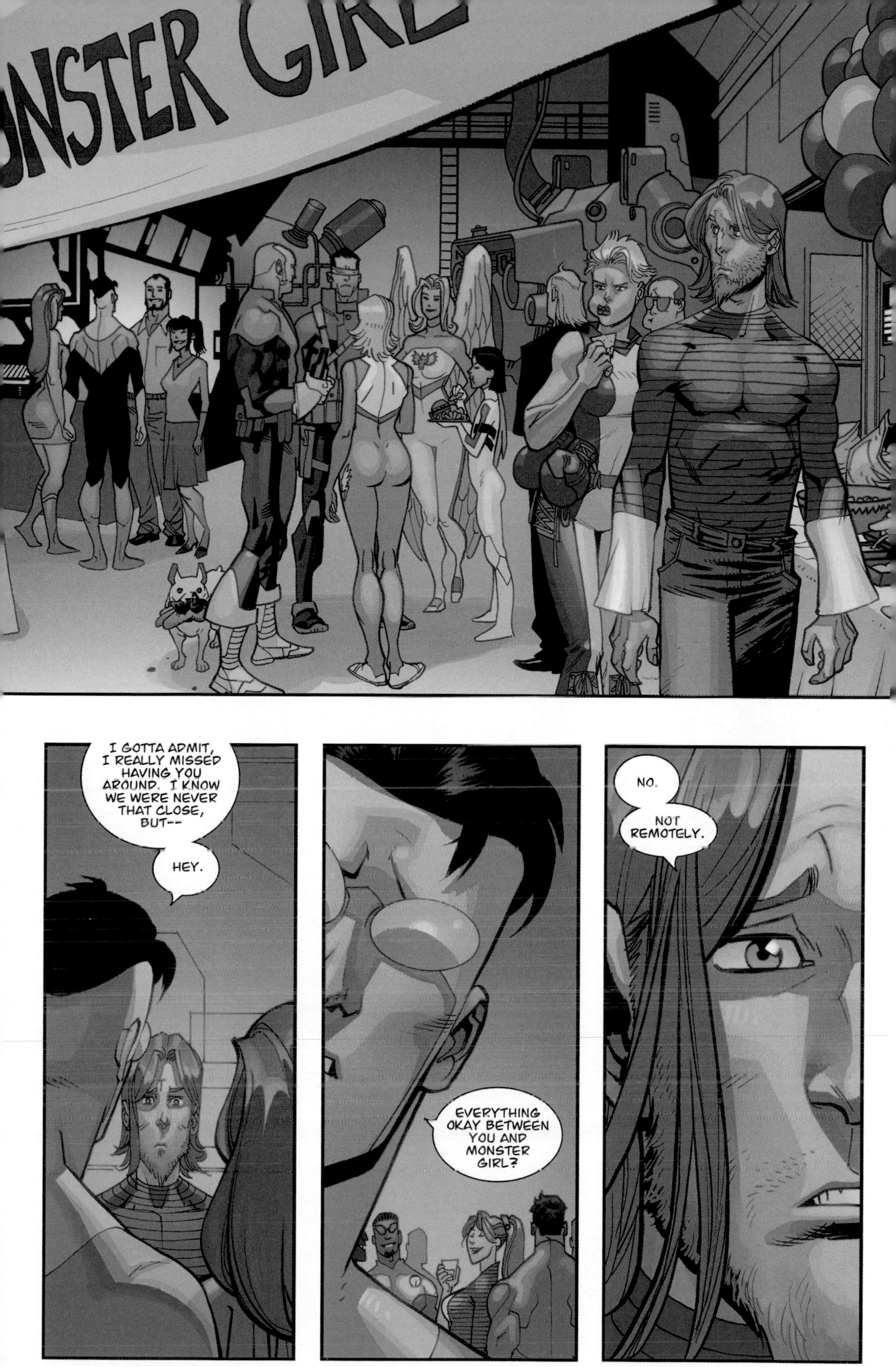

MONSTER GIRL
I GOTTA ADMIT, I REALLY MISSED HAVING YOU AROUND. I KNOW WE WERE NEVER THAT CLOSE, BUT--
HEY.
EVERYTHING OKAY BETWEEN YOU AND MONSTER GIRL?
NO.
NOT REMOTELY.

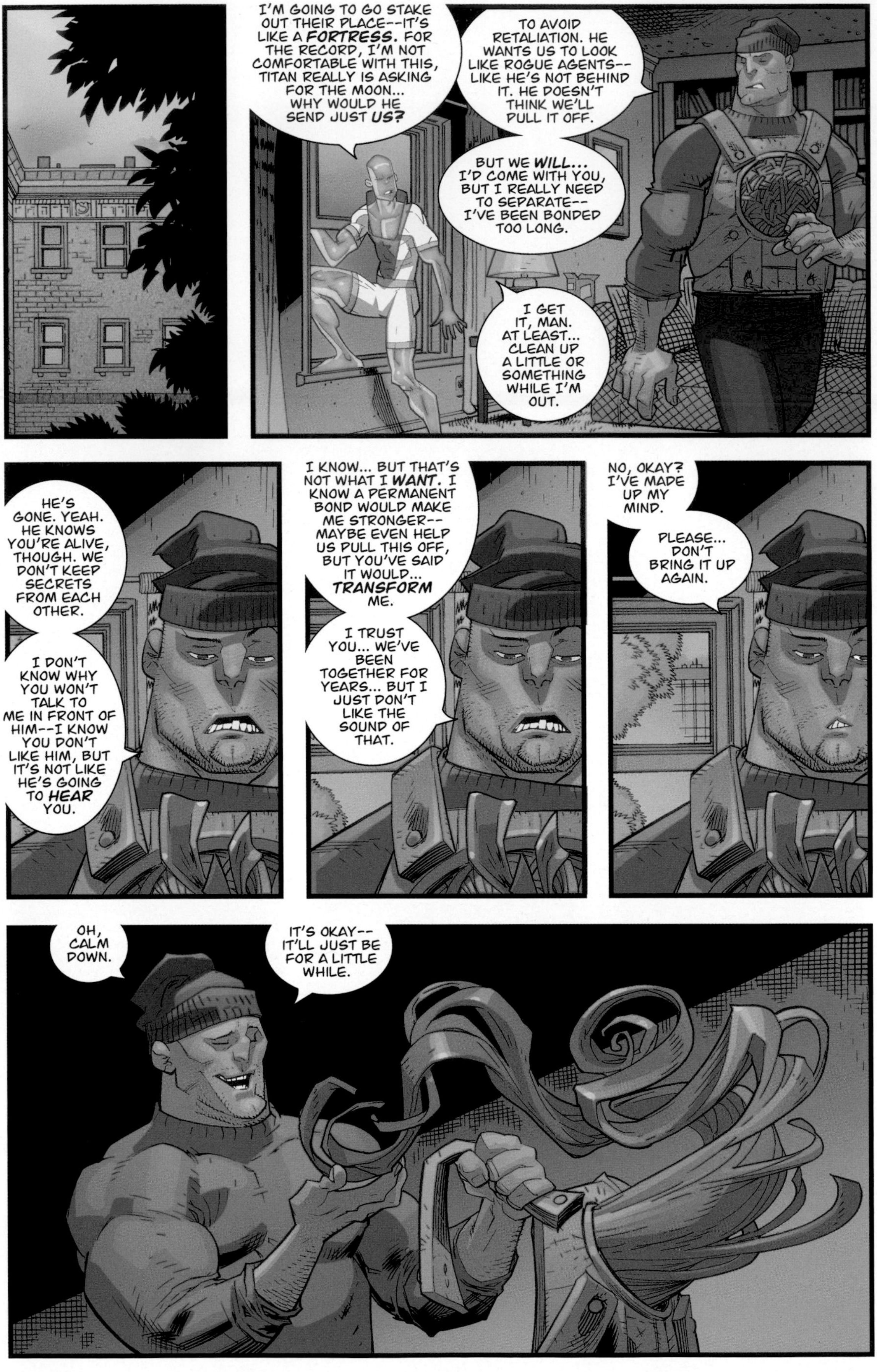
I'M GOING TO GO STAKE OUT THEIR PLACE--IT'S LIKE A FORTRESS. FOR THE RECORD, I'M NOT COMFORTABLE WITH THIS, TITAN REALLY IS ASKING FOR THE MOON... WHY WOULD HE SEND JUST US?
TO AVOID RETALIATION. HE WANTS US TO LOOK LIKE ROGUE AGENTS--LIKE HE'S NOT BEHIND IT. HE DOESN'T THINK WE'LL PULL IT OFF.
BUT WE WILL... I'D COME WITH YOU, BUT I REALLY NEED TO SEPARATE--I'VE BEEN BONDED TOO LONG.
I GET IT, MAN. AT LEAST... CLEAN UP A LITTLE OR SOMETHING WHILE I'M OUT.
HE'S GONE. YEAH. HE KNOWS YOU'RE ALIVE, THOUGH. WE DON'T KEEP SECRETS FROM EACH OTHER.
I DON'T KNOW WHY YOU WON'T TALK TO ME IN FRONT OF HIM--I KNOW YOU DON'T LIKE HIM, BUT IT'S NOT LIKE HE'S GOING TO HEAR YOU.
I KNOW... BUT THAT'S NOT WHAT I WANT. I KNOW A PERMANENT BOND WOULD MAKE ME STRONGER--MAYBE EVEN HELP US PULL THIS OFF, BUT YOU'VE SAID IT WOULD... TRANSFORM ME.
I TRUST YOU... WE'VE BEEN TOGETHER FOR YEARS... BUT I JUST DON'T LIKE THE SOUND OF THAT.
NO, OKAY? I'VE MADE UP MY MIND.
PLEASE... DON'T BRING IT UP AGAIN.
OH, CALM DOWN.
IT'S OKAY--IT'LL JUST BE FOR A LITTLE WHILE.

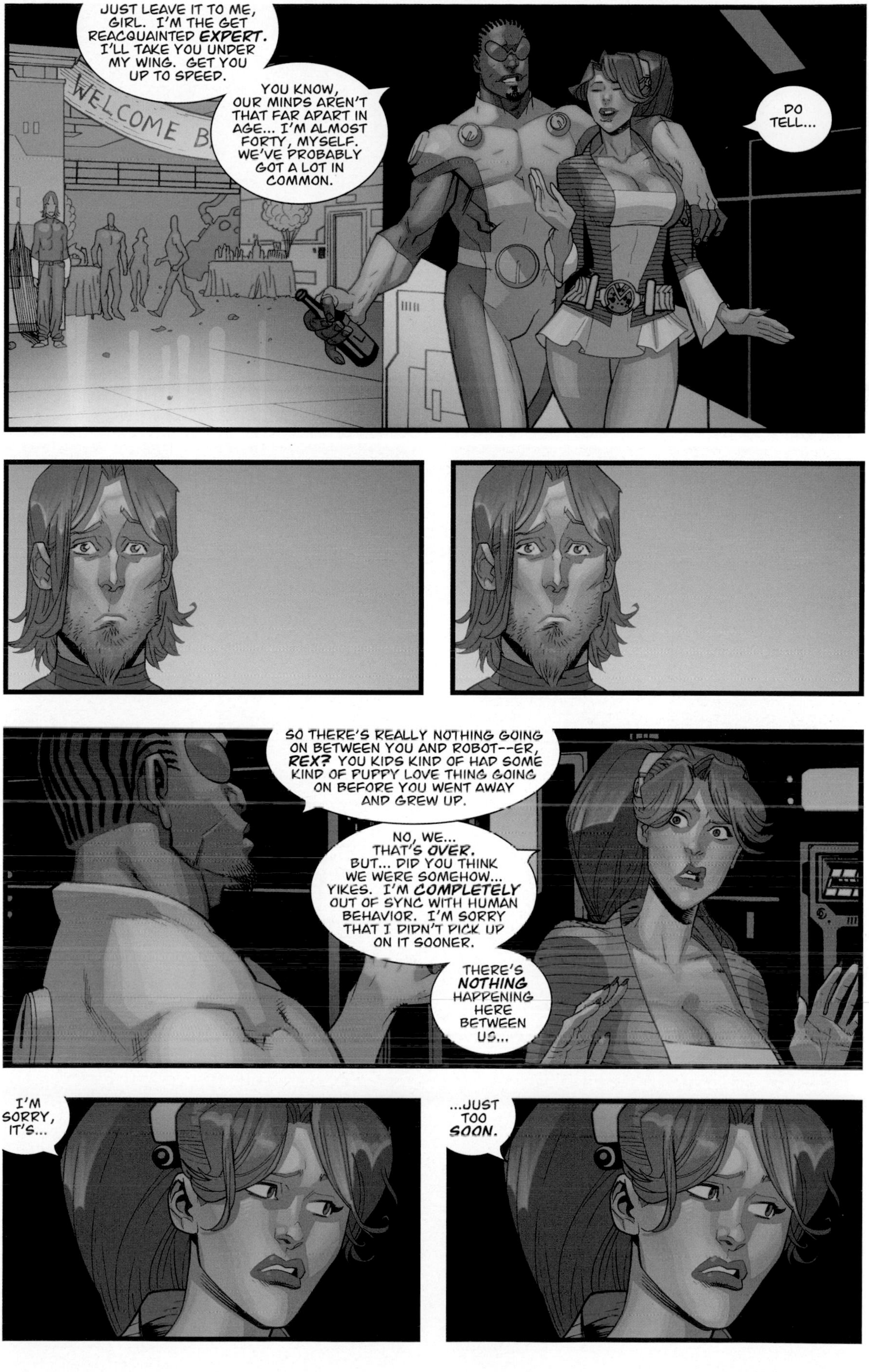
JUST LEAVE IT TO ME, GIRL. I'M THE GET REACQUAINTED EXPERT. I'LL TAKE YOU UNDER MY WING. GET YOU UP TO SPEED.
YOU KNOW, OUR MINDS AREN'T THAT FAR APART IN AGE... I'M ALMOST FORTY, MYSELF. WE'VE PROBABLY GOT A LOT IN COMMON.
DO TELL...
SO THERE'S REALLY NOTHING GOING ON BETWEEN YOU AND ROBOT--ER, REX? YOU KIDS KIND OF HAD SOME KIND OF PUPPY LOVE THING GOING ON BEFORE YOU WENT AWAY AND GREW UP.
NO, WE... THAT'S OVER. BUT... DID YOU THINK WE WERE SOMEHOW... YIKES. I'M COMPLETELY OUT OF SYNC WITH HUMAN BEHAVIOR. I'M SORRY THAT I DIDN'T PICK UP ON IT SOONER.
THERE'S NOTHING HAPPENING HERE BETWEEN US...
I'M SORRY, IT'S...
...JUST TOO SOON.

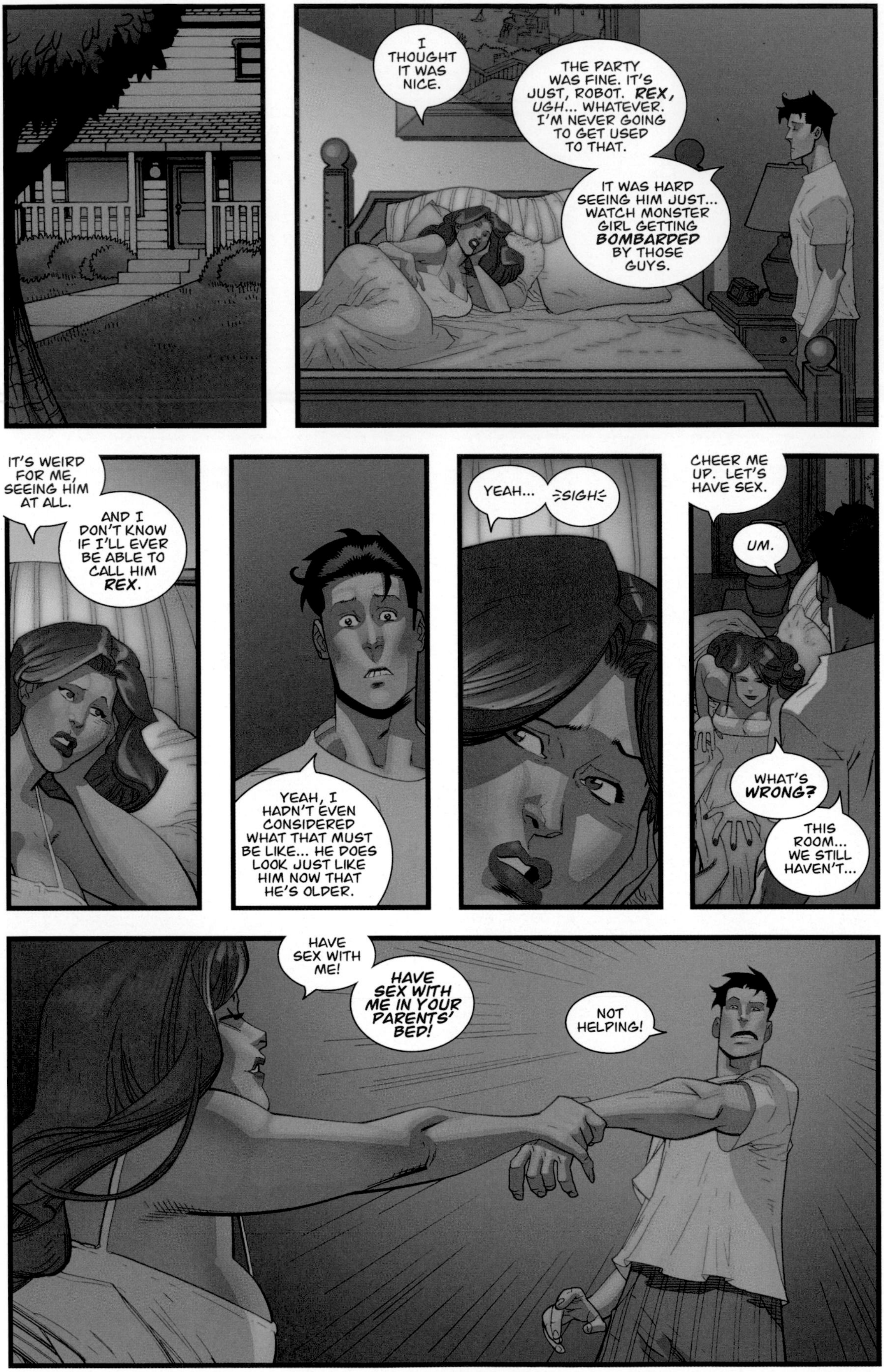
I THOUGHT IT WAS NICE.
THE PARTY WAS FINE. IT'S JUST, ROBOT. REX, UGH... WHATEVER. I'M NEVER GOING TO GET USED TO THAT.
IT WAS HARD SEEING HIM JUST... WATCH MONSTER GIRL GETTING BOMBARDED BY THOSE GUYS.
IT'S WEIRD FOR ME, SEEING HIM AT ALL.
AND I DON'T KNOW IF I'LL EVER BE ABLE TO CALL HIM REX.
YEAH, I HADN'T EVEN CONSIDERED WHAT THAT MUST BE LIKE... HE DOES LOOK JUST LIKE HIM NOW THAT HE'S OLDER.
YEAH...
SIGH
CHEER ME UP. LET'S HAVE SEX.
UM.
WHAT'S WRONG?
THIS ROOM... WE STILL HAVEN'T...
HAVE SEX WITH ME!
HAVE SEX WITH ME IN YOUR PARENTS' BED!
NOT HELPING!

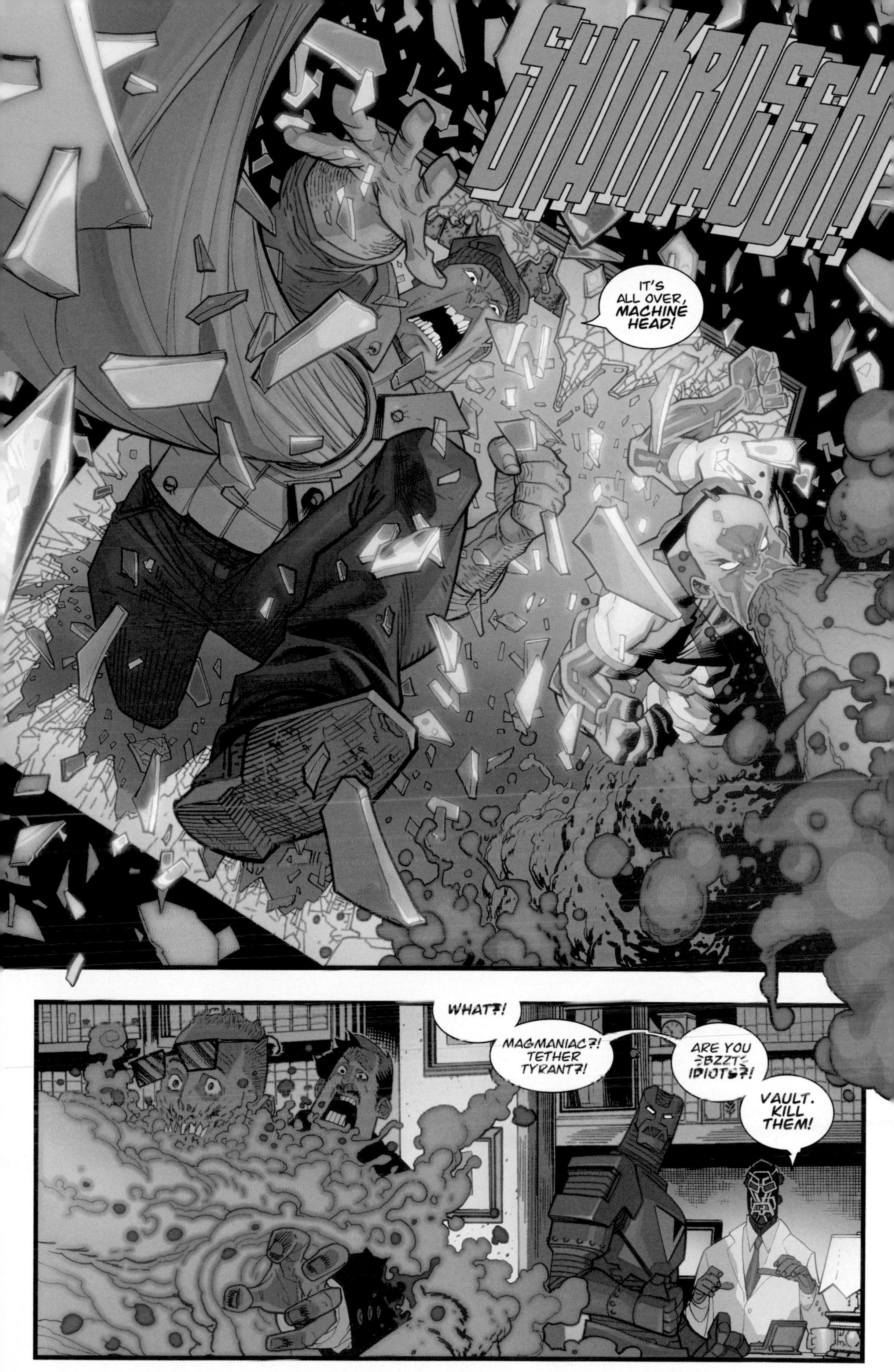
SHUNKROSCH
IT'S ALL OVER, MACHINE HEAD!
WHAT?!
MAGMANIAC?! TETHER TYRANT?!
ARE YOU ≶BZZT≶ IDIOTS?!
VAULT. KILL THEM!

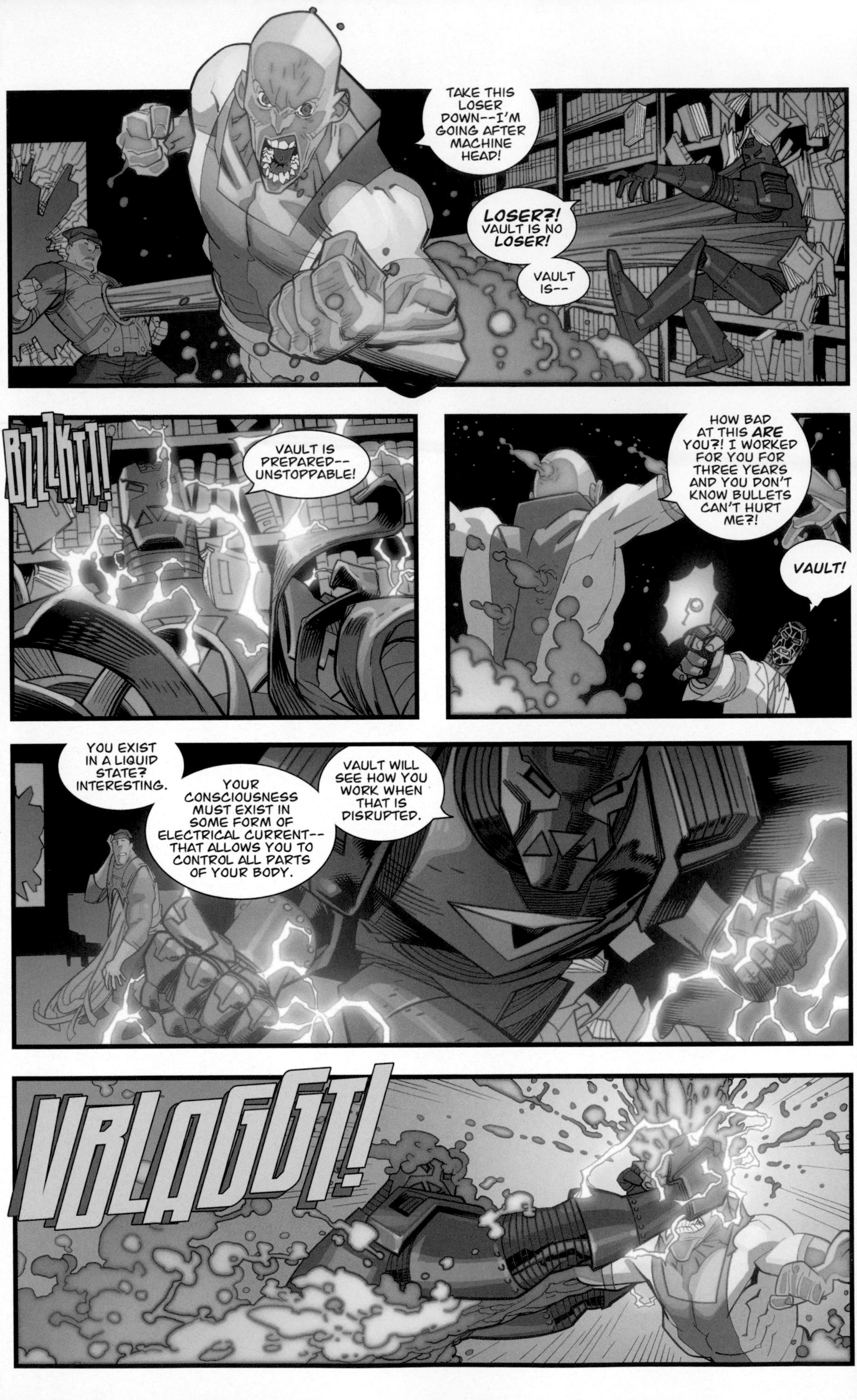
TAKE THIS LOSER DOWN--I'M GOING AFTER MACHINE HEAD!
LOSER?! VAULT IS NO LOSER!
VAULT IS--
BZZZKTT!
VAULT IS PREPARED-- UNSTOPPABLE!
HOW BAD AT THIS ARE YOU?! I WORKED FOR YOU FOR THREE YEARS AND YOU DON'T KNOW BULLETS CAN'T HURT ME?!
VAULT!
YOU EXIST IN A LIQUID STATE? INTERESTING.
YOUR CONSCIOUSNESS MUST EXIST IN SOME FORM OF ELECTRICAL CURRENT-- THAT ALLOWS YOU TO CONTROL ALL PARTS OF YOUR BODY.
VAULT WILL SEE HOW YOU WORK WHEN THAT IS DISRUPTED.
VBLAGGT!

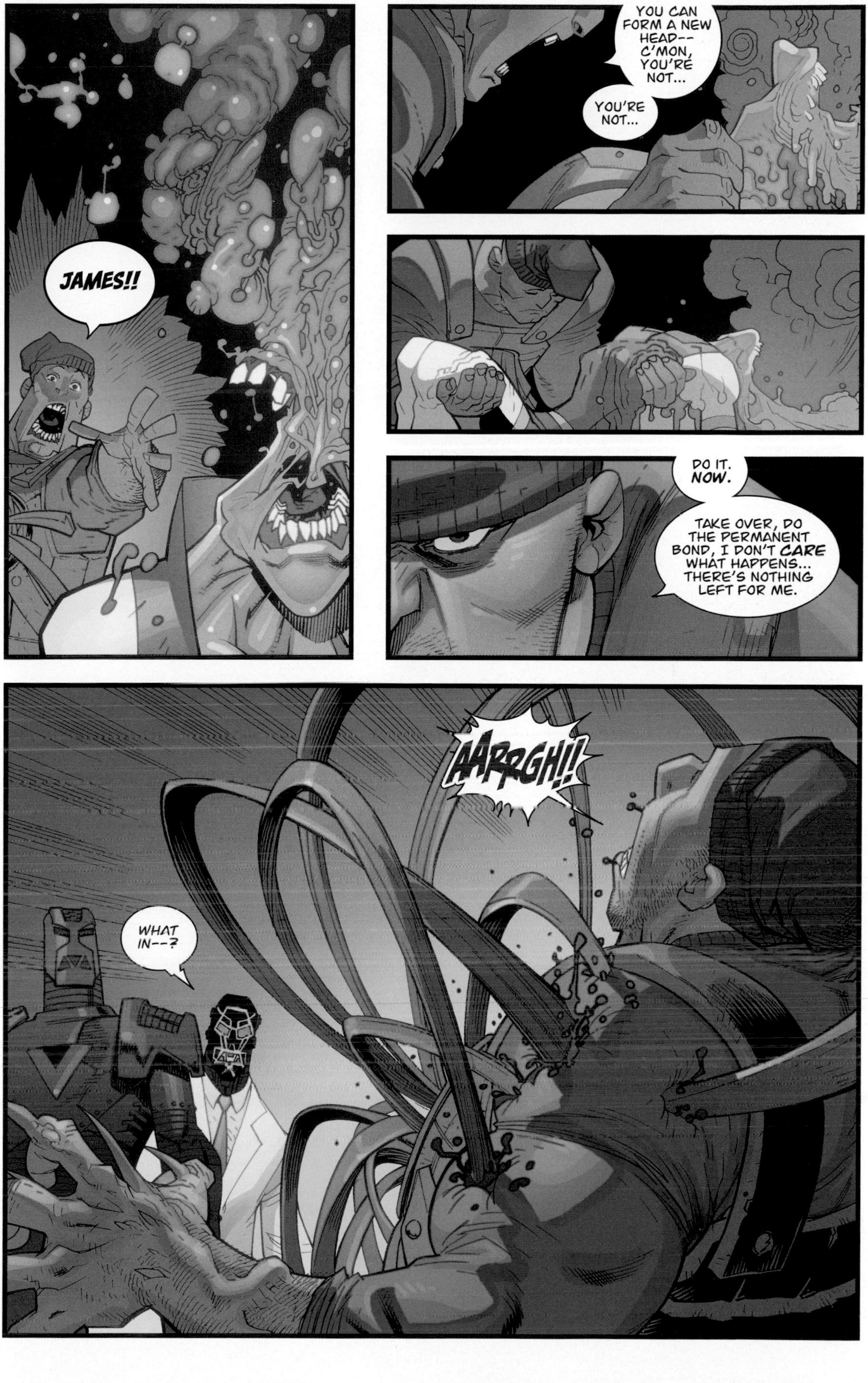
JAMES!!
YOU CAN FORM A NEW HEAD-- C'MON, YOU'RE NOT...
YOU'RE NOT...
DO IT. NOW.
TAKE OVER, DO THE PERMANENT BOND, I DON'T CARE WHAT HAPPENS... THERE'S NOTHING LEFT FOR ME.
AARRGH!!
WHAT IN--?

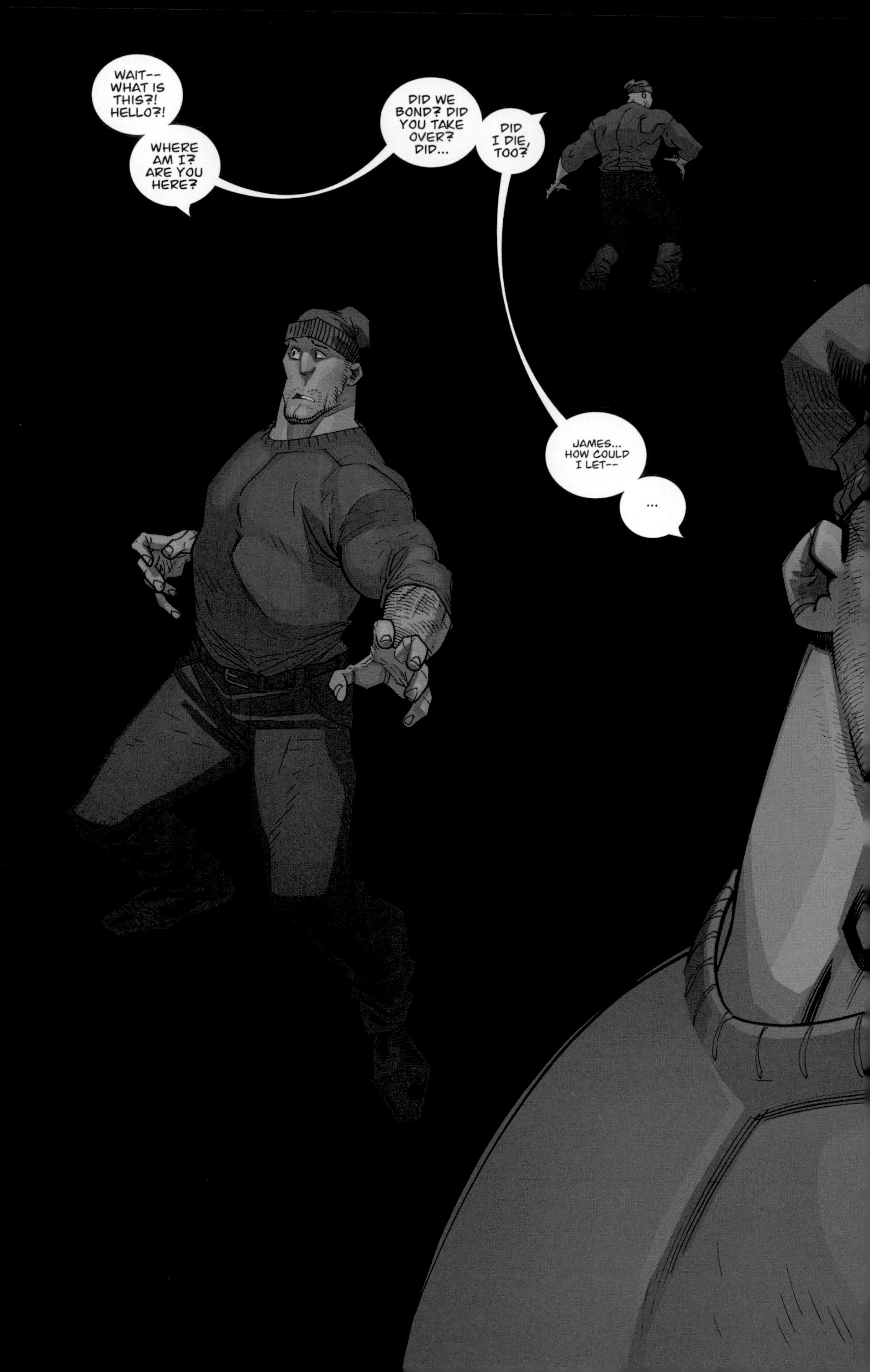
WAIT--
WHAT IS
THIS?!
HELLO?!
WHERE
AM I?
ARE YOU
HERE?
DID WE
BOND? DID
YOU TAKE
OVER?
DID...
DID
I DIE,
TOO?
JAMES...
HOW COULD
I LET--
...

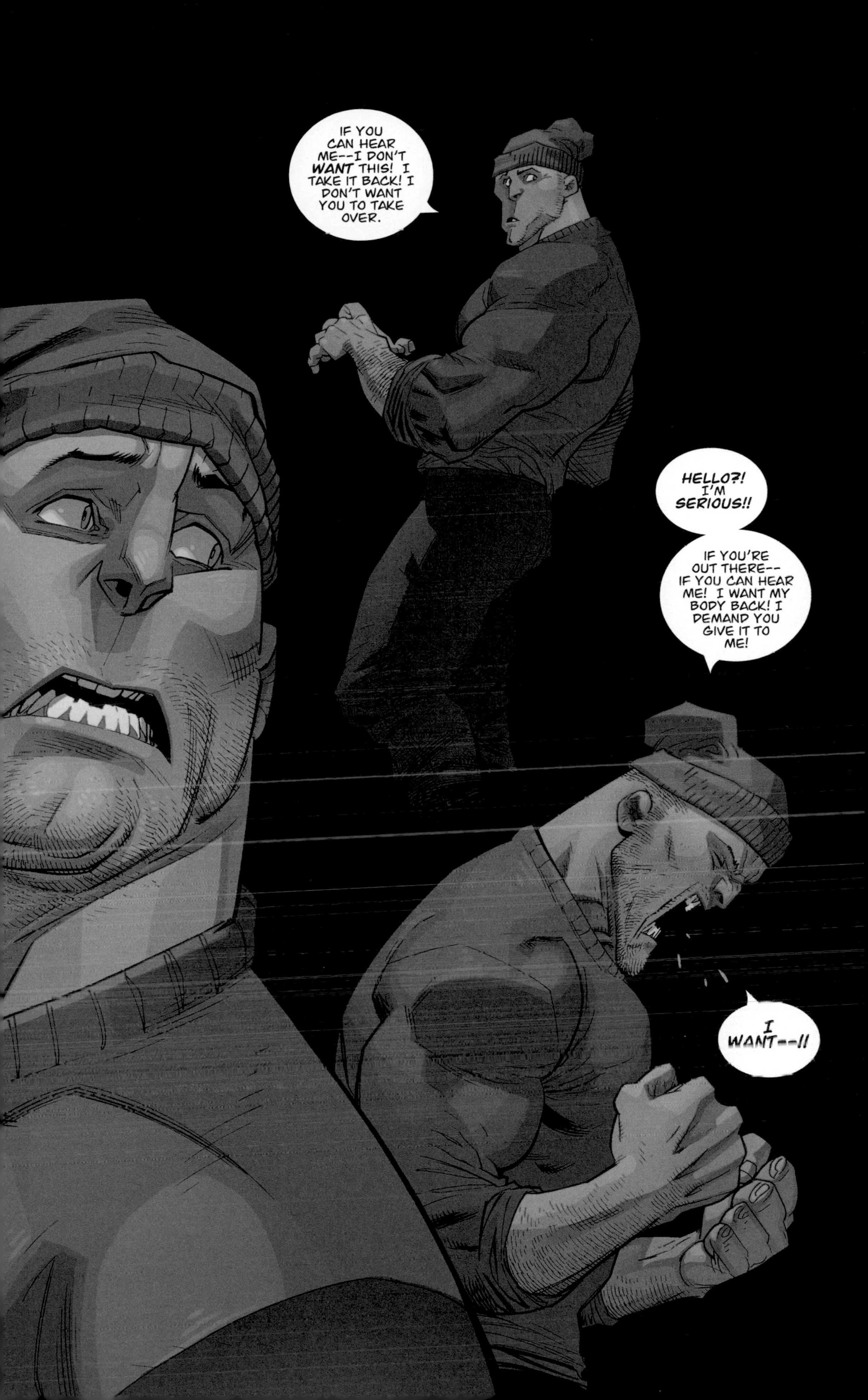
IF YOU CAN HEAR ME--I DON'T *WANT* THIS! I TAKE IT BACK! I DON'T WANT YOU TO TAKE OVER.
HELLO?! I'M SERIOUS!!
IF YOU'RE OUT THERE--IF YOU CAN HEAR ME! I WANT MY BODY BACK! I DEMAND YOU GIVE IT TO ME!
I WANT--!!

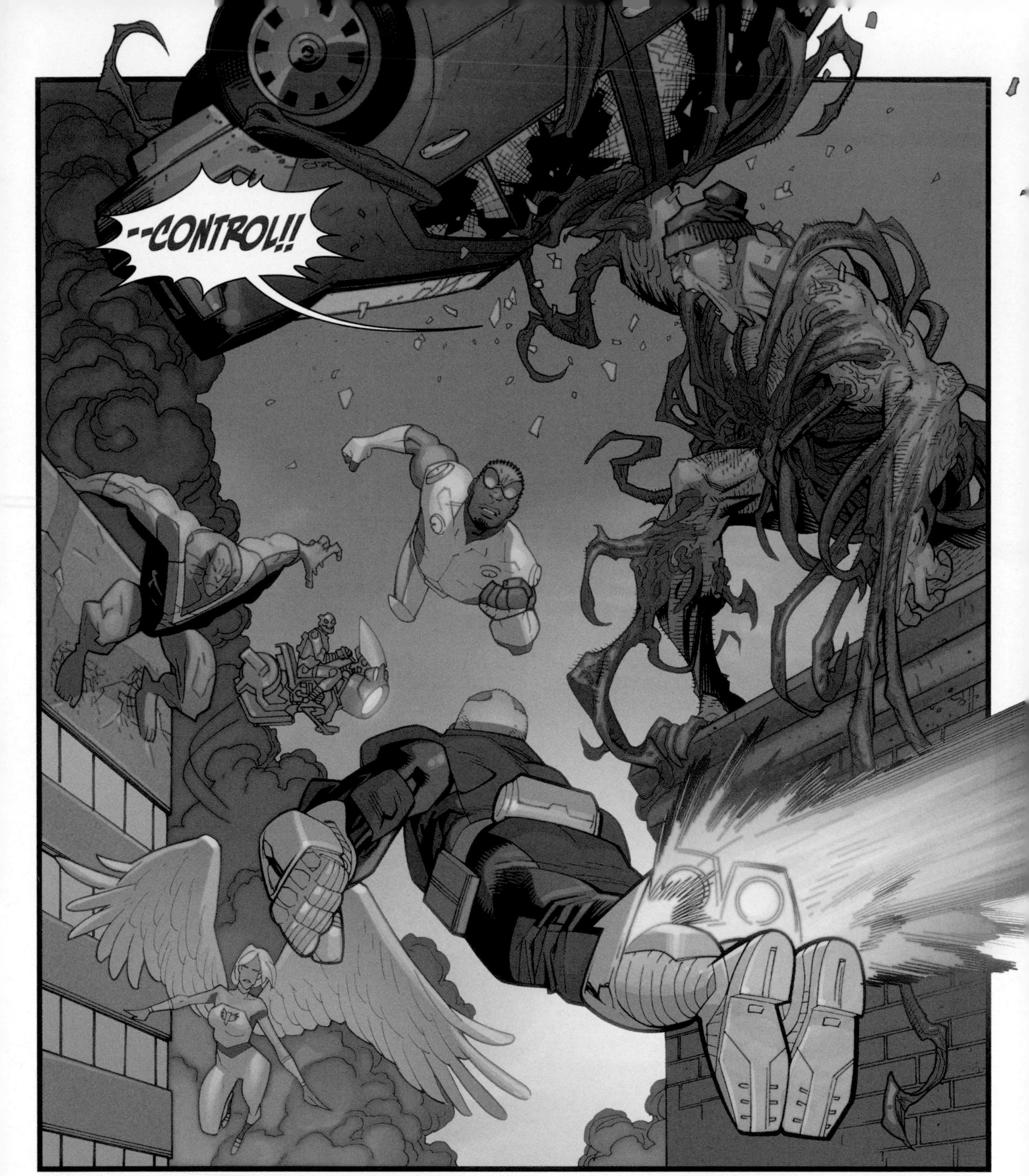
--CONTROL!!

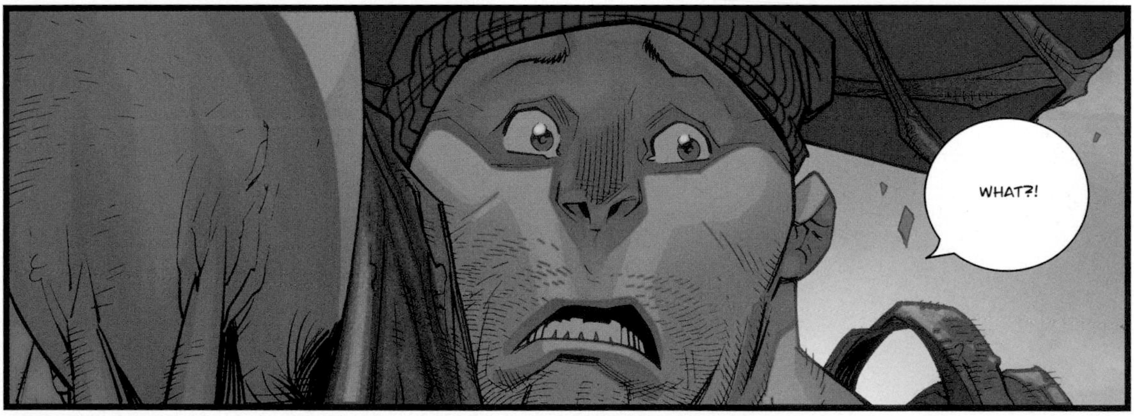
WHAT?!

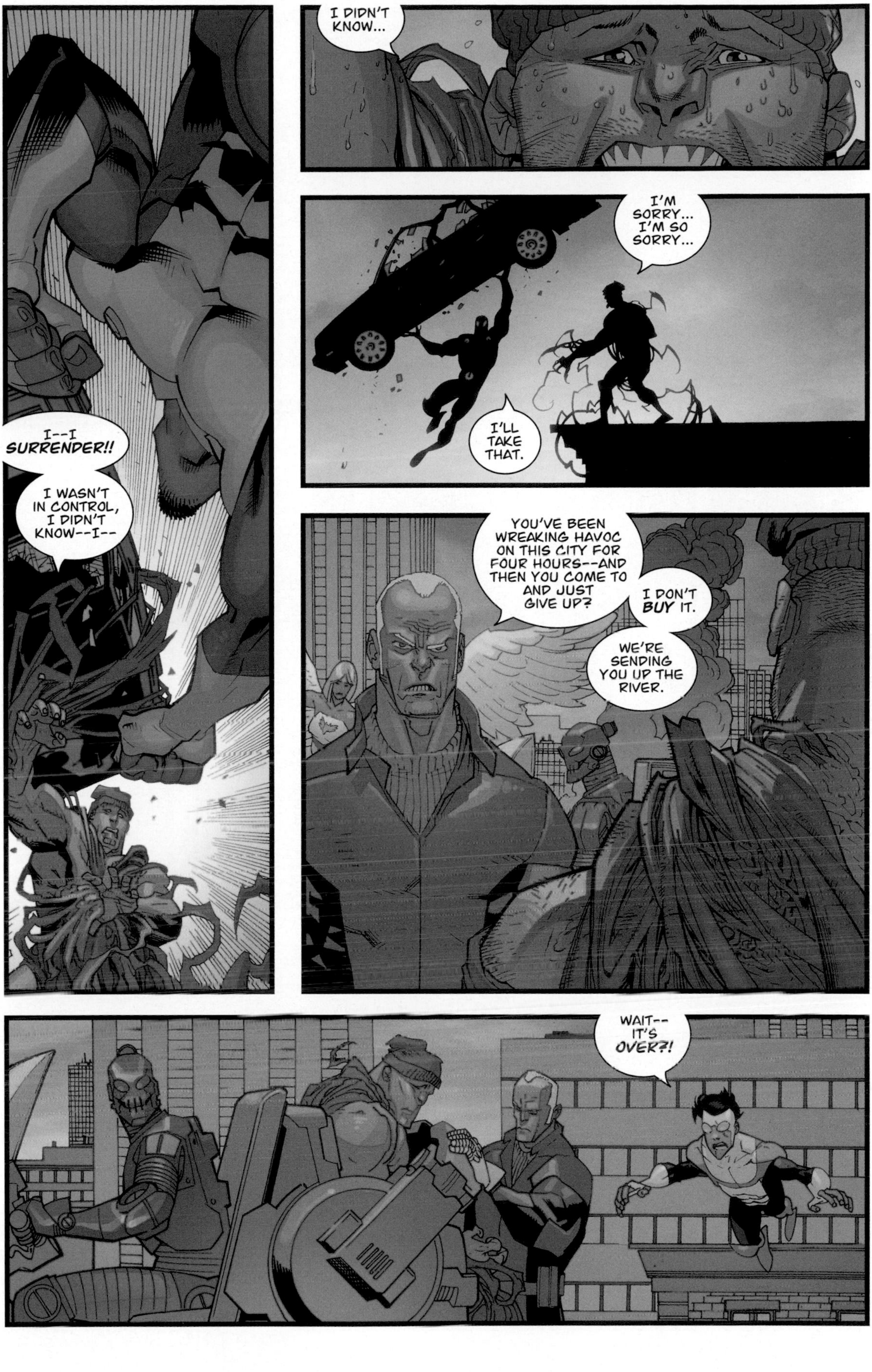
I--I SURRENDER!!
I WASN'T IN CONTROL, I DIDN'T KNOW--I--
I DIDN'T KNOW...
I'M SORRY... I'M SO SORRY...
I'LL TAKE THAT.
YOU'VE BEEN WREAKING HAVOC ON THIS CITY FOR FOUR HOURS--AND THEN YOU COME TO AND JUST GIVE UP?
I DON'T BUY IT.
WE'RE SENDING YOU UP THE RIVER.
WAIT-- IT'S OVER?!

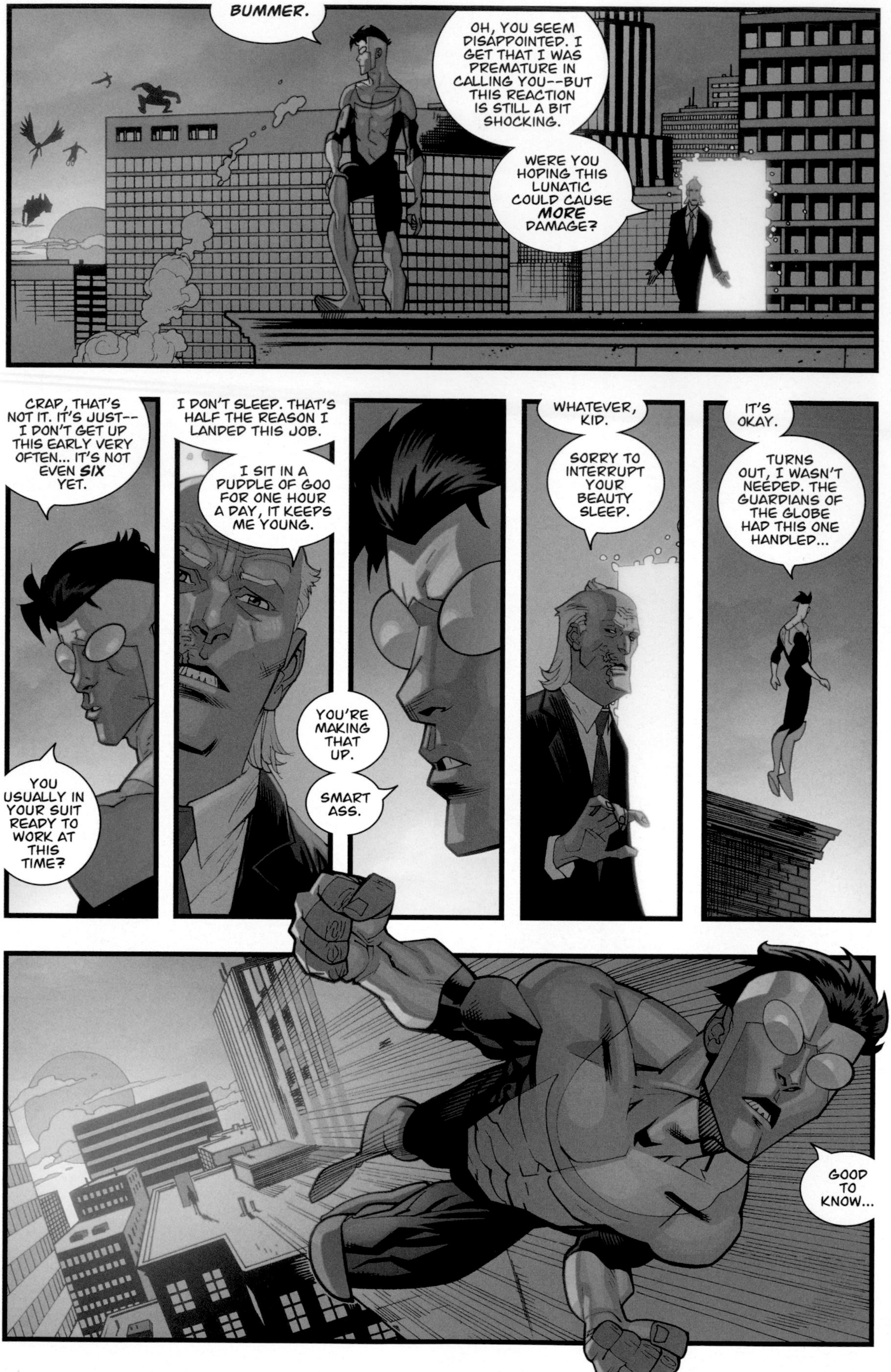
BUMMER.
OH, YOU SEEM DISAPPOINTED. I GET THAT I WAS PREMATURE IN CALLING YOU--BUT THIS REACTION IS STILL A BIT SHOCKING.
WERE YOU HOPING THIS LUNATIC COULD CAUSE MORE DAMAGE?
CRAP, THAT'S NOT IT. IT'S JUST-- I DON'T GET UP THIS EARLY VERY OFTEN... IT'S NOT EVEN SIX YET.
YOU USUALLY IN YOUR SUIT READY TO WORK AT THIS TIME?
I DON'T SLEEP. THAT'S HALF THE REASON I LANDED THIS JOB.
I SIT IN A PUDDLE OF GOO FOR ONE HOUR A DAY, IT KEEPS ME YOUNG.
YOU'RE MAKING THAT UP.
SMART ASS.
WHATEVER, KID.
SORRY TO INTERRUPT YOUR BEAUTY SLEEP.
IT'S OKAY.
TURNS OUT, I WASN'T NEEDED. THE GUARDIANS OF THE GLOBE HAD THIS ONE HANDLED...
GOOD TO KNOW...

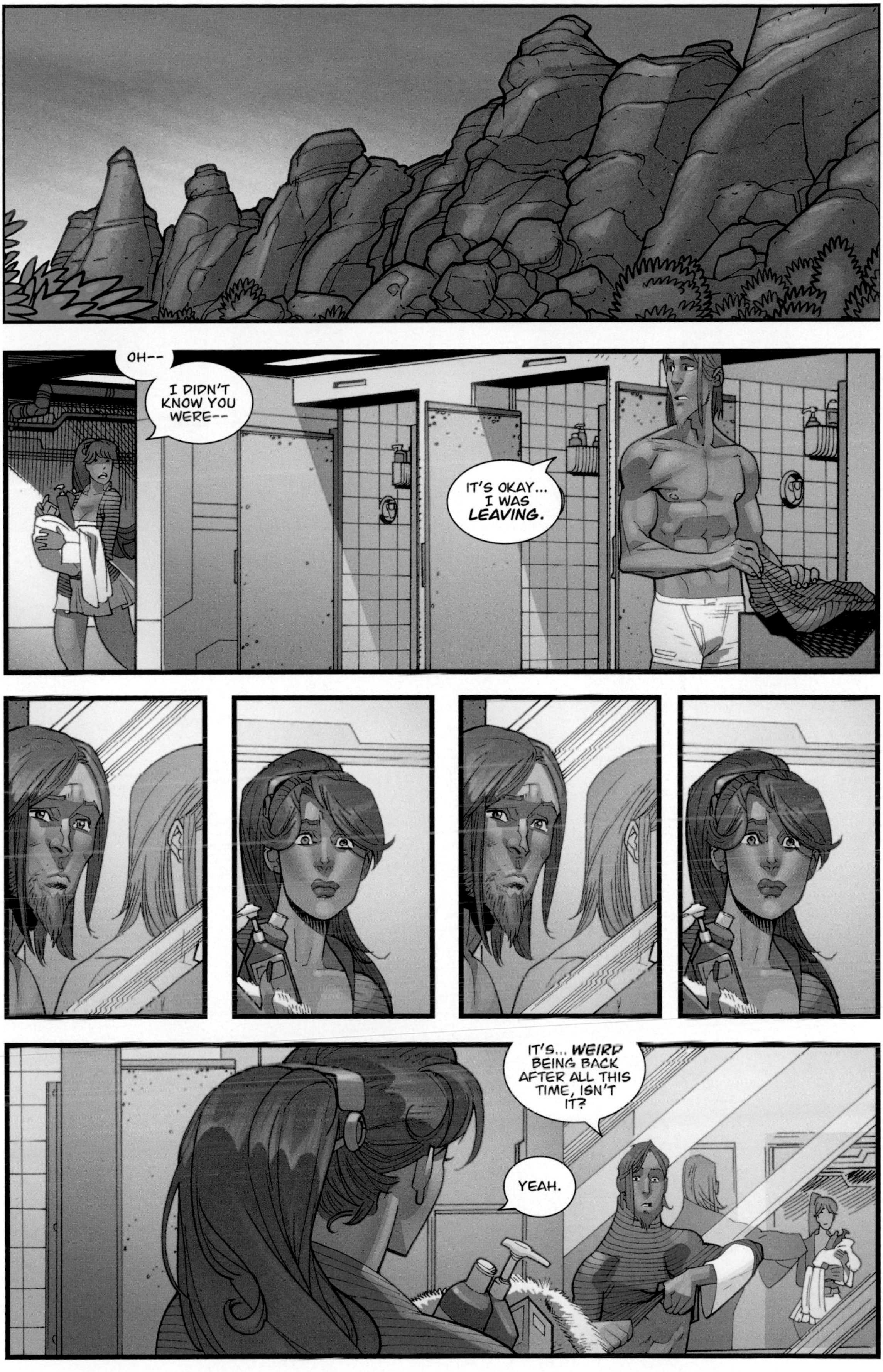
OH--
I DIDN'T KNOW YOU WERE--
IT'S OKAY... I WAS LEAVING.
IT'S... WEIRD BEING BACK AFTER ALL THIS TIME, ISN'T IT?
YEAH.

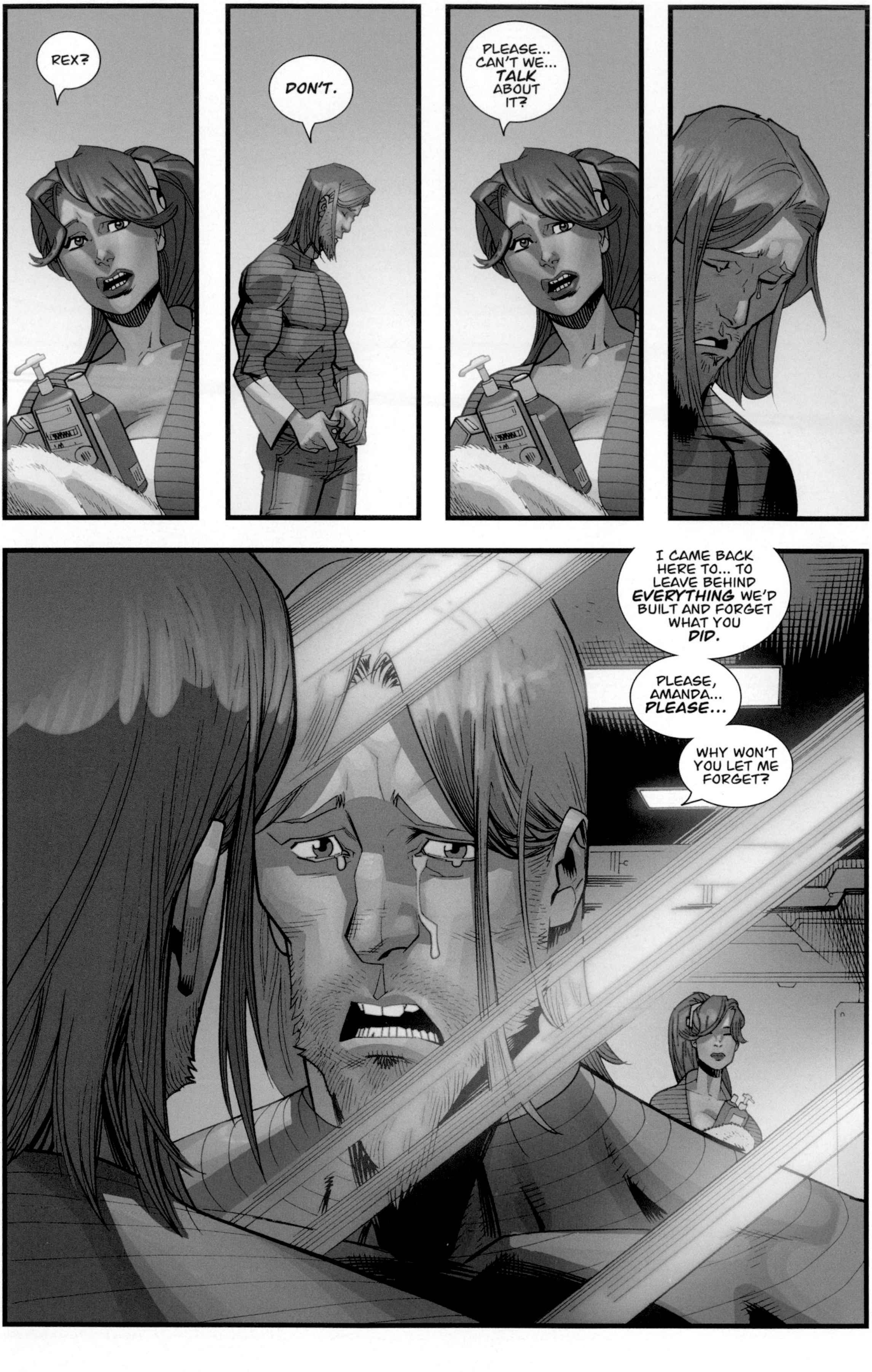
REX?
DON'T.
PLEASE... CAN'T WE... TALK ABOUT IT?
I CAME BACK HERE TO... TO LEAVE BEHIND EVERYTHING WE'D BUILT AND FORGET WHAT YOU DID.
PLEASE, AMANDA... PLEASE...
WHY WON'T YOU LET ME FORGET?

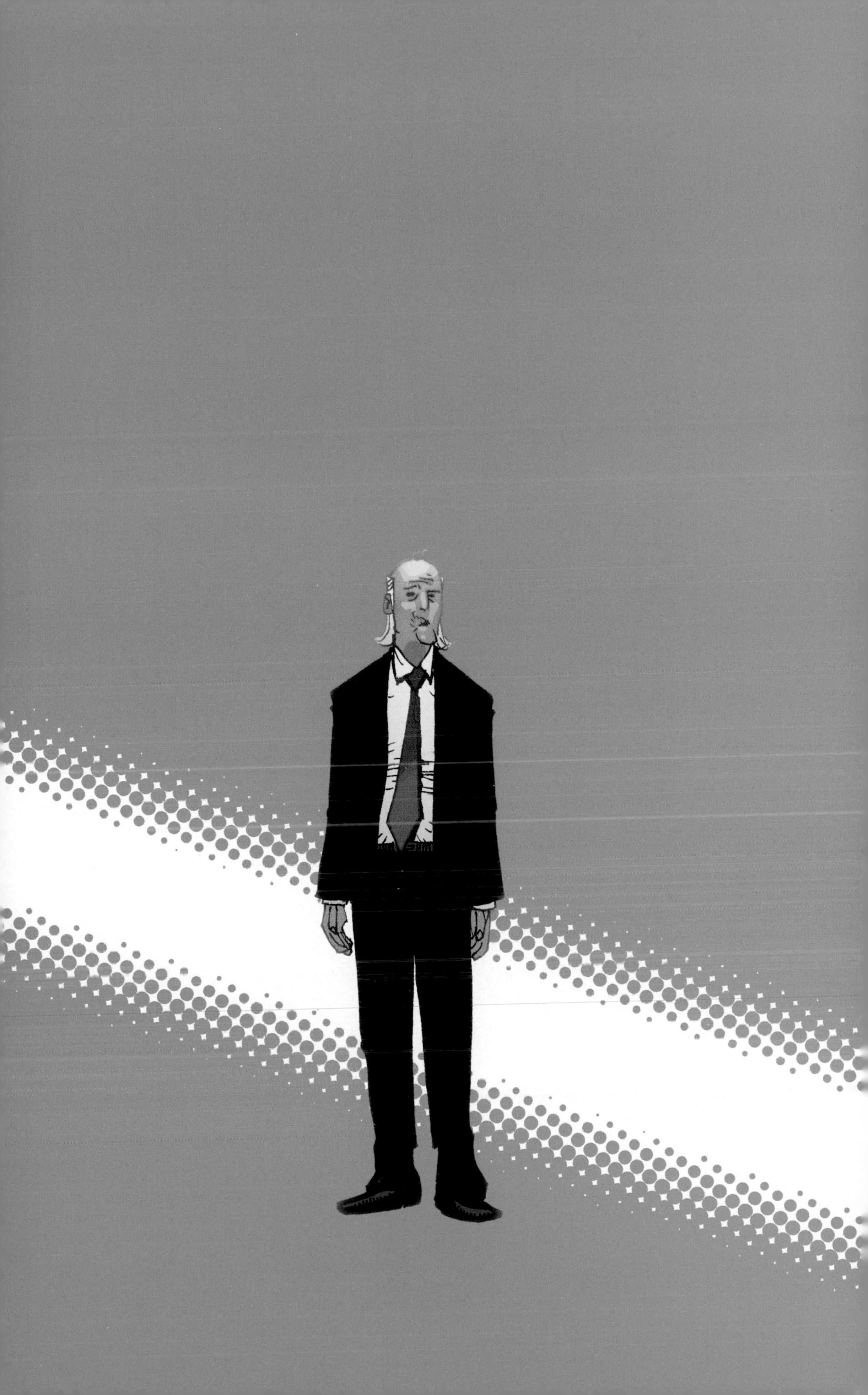

CHAPTER SIX

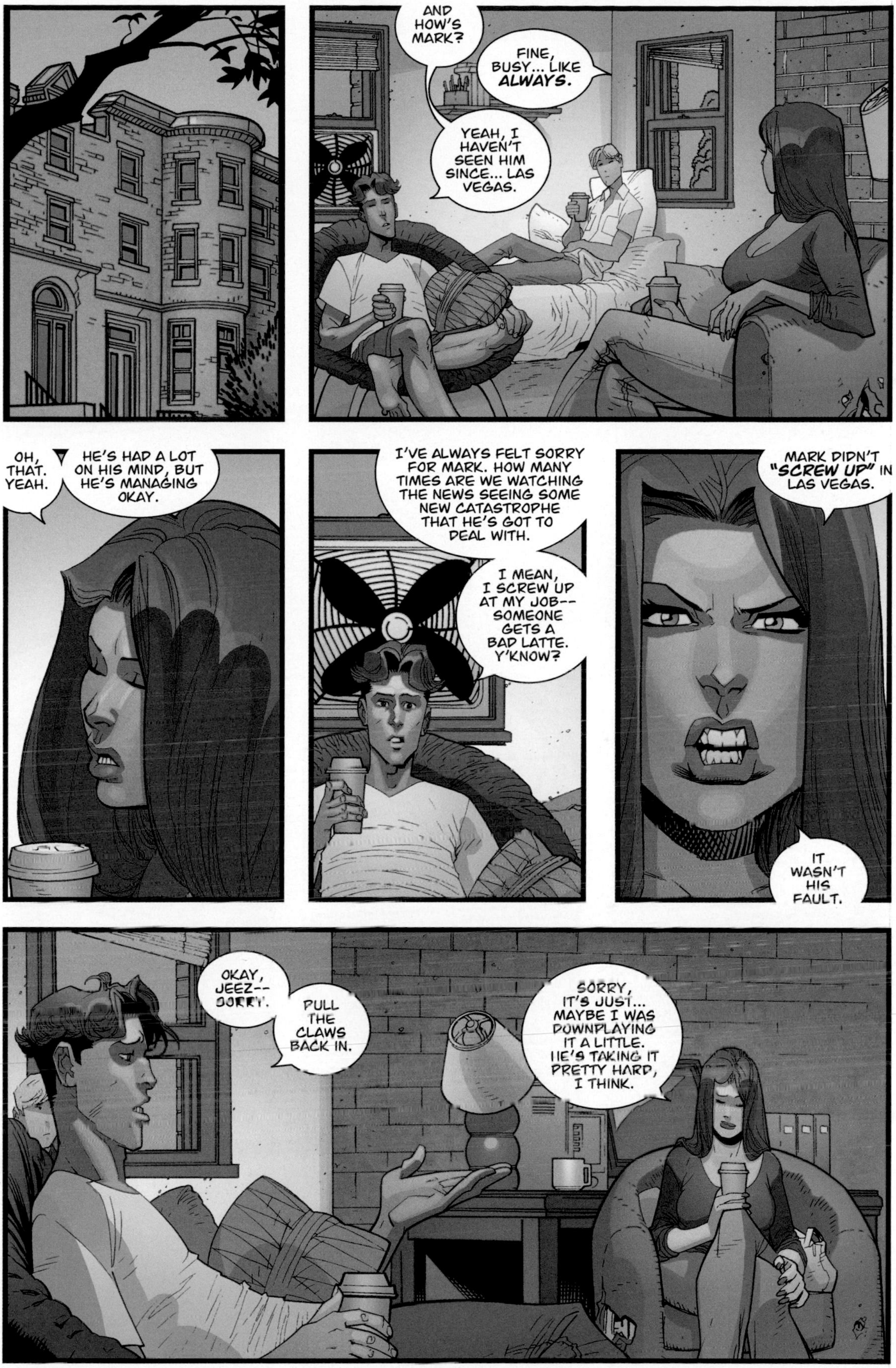
AND HOW'S MARK?
FINE, BUSY... LIKE ALWAYS.
YEAH, I HAVEN'T SEEN HIM SINCE... LAS VEGAS.
OH, THAT. YEAH.
HE'S HAD A LOT ON HIS MIND, BUT HE'S MANAGING OKAY.
I'VE ALWAYS FELT SORRY FOR MARK. HOW MANY TIMES ARE WE WATCHING THE NEWS SEEING SOME NEW CATASTROPHE THAT HE'S GOT TO DEAL WITH.
I MEAN, I SCREW UP AT MY JOB-- SOMEONE GETS A BAD LATTE. Y'KNOW?
MARK DIDN'T "SCREW UP" IN LAS VEGAS.
IT WASN'T HIS FAULT.
OKAY, JEEZ-- SORRY.
PULL THE CLAWS BACK IN.
SORRY, IT'S JUST... MAYBE I WAS DOWNPLAYING IT A LITTLE. HE'S TAKING IT PRETTY HARD, I THINK.

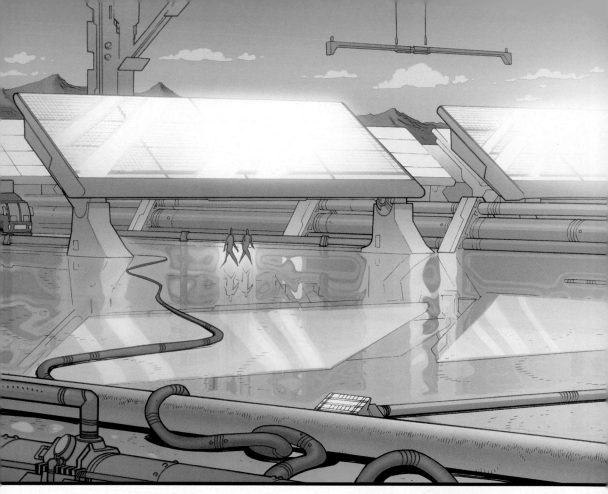

YES. THERE AREN'T ENOUGH RESOURCES TO REBUILD-- WE'RE INCAPABLE OF STARTING THIS CITY OVER FROM SCRATCH.

ALSO, SOME PEOPLE IN THE GOVERNMENT FEEL IT WOULD BE DISRESPECTFUL.

SO YOU'RE GOING TO FOLLOW THAT MANIAC'S PLAN AND COVER THE AREA WITH SOLAR PANELS?

YEAH, IT'S AMAZING! YOU CAN THANK THIS GUY HERE FOR MAKING IT ALL WORK.

OH, I BARELY DID ANYTHING.

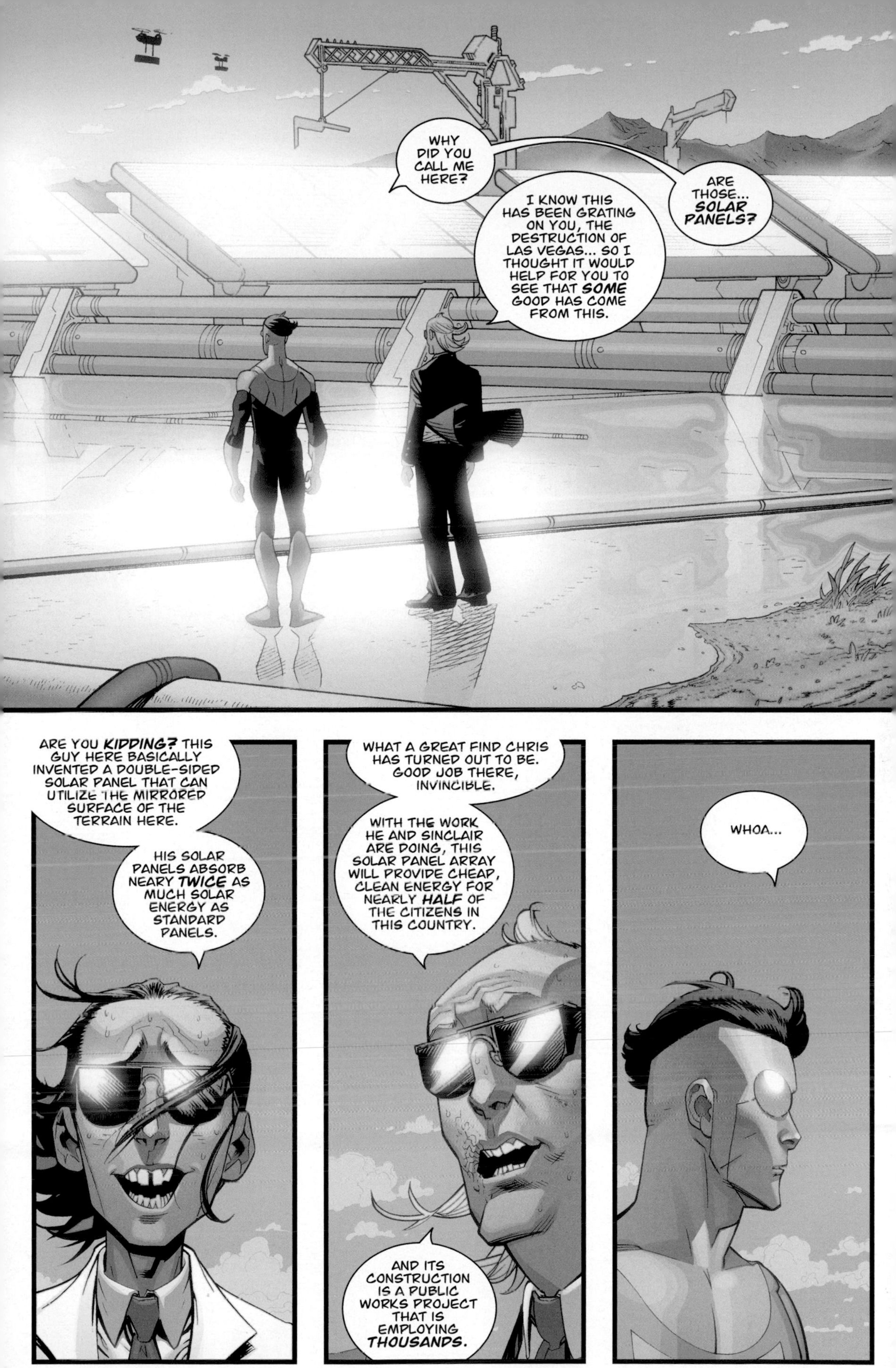
WHY DID YOU CALL ME HERE?
I KNOW THIS HAS BEEN GRATING ON YOU, THE DESTRUCTION OF LAS VEGAS... SO I THOUGHT IT WOULD HELP FOR YOU TO SEE THAT SOME GOOD HAS COME FROM THIS.
ARE THOSE... SOLAR PANELS?
ARE YOU KIDDING? THIS GUY HERE BASICALLY INVENTED A DOUBLE-SIDED SOLAR PANEL THAT CAN UTILIZE THE MIRRORED SURFACE OF THE TERRAIN HERE.
HIS SOLAR PANELS ABSORB NEARY TWICE AS MUCH SOLAR ENERGY AS STANDARD PANELS.
WHAT A GREAT FIND CHRIS HAS TURNED OUT TO BE. GOOD JOB THERE, INVINCIBLE.
WITH THE WORK HE AND SINCLAIR ARE DOING, THIS SOLAR PANEL ARRAY WILL PROVIDE CHEAP, CLEAN ENERGY FOR NEARLY HALF OF THE CITIZENS IN THIS COUNTRY.
AND ITS CONSTRUCTION IS A PUBLIC WORKS PROJECT THAT IS EMPLOYING THOUSANDS.
WHOA...

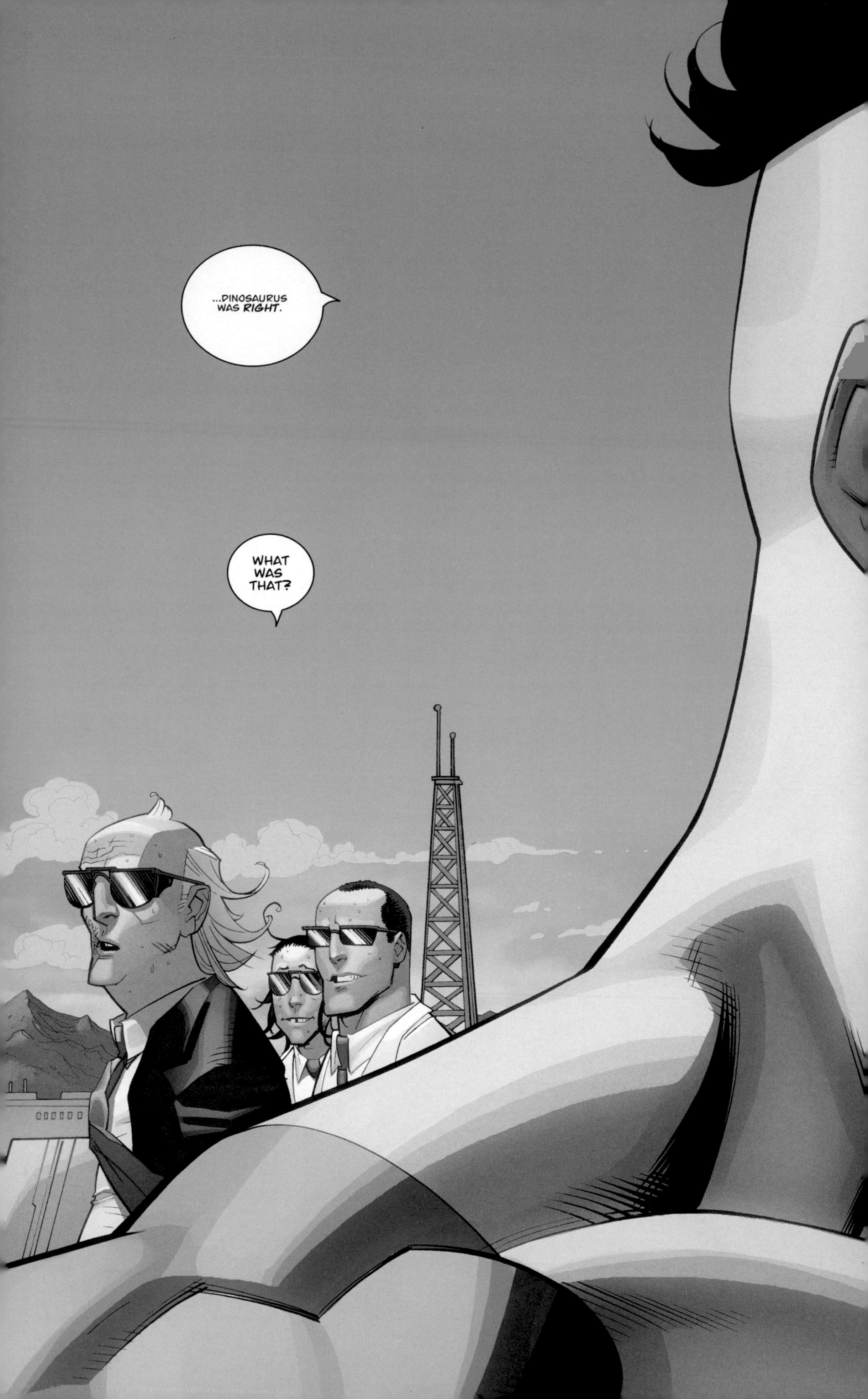
...DINOSAURUS WAS RIGHT.
WHAT WAS THAT?

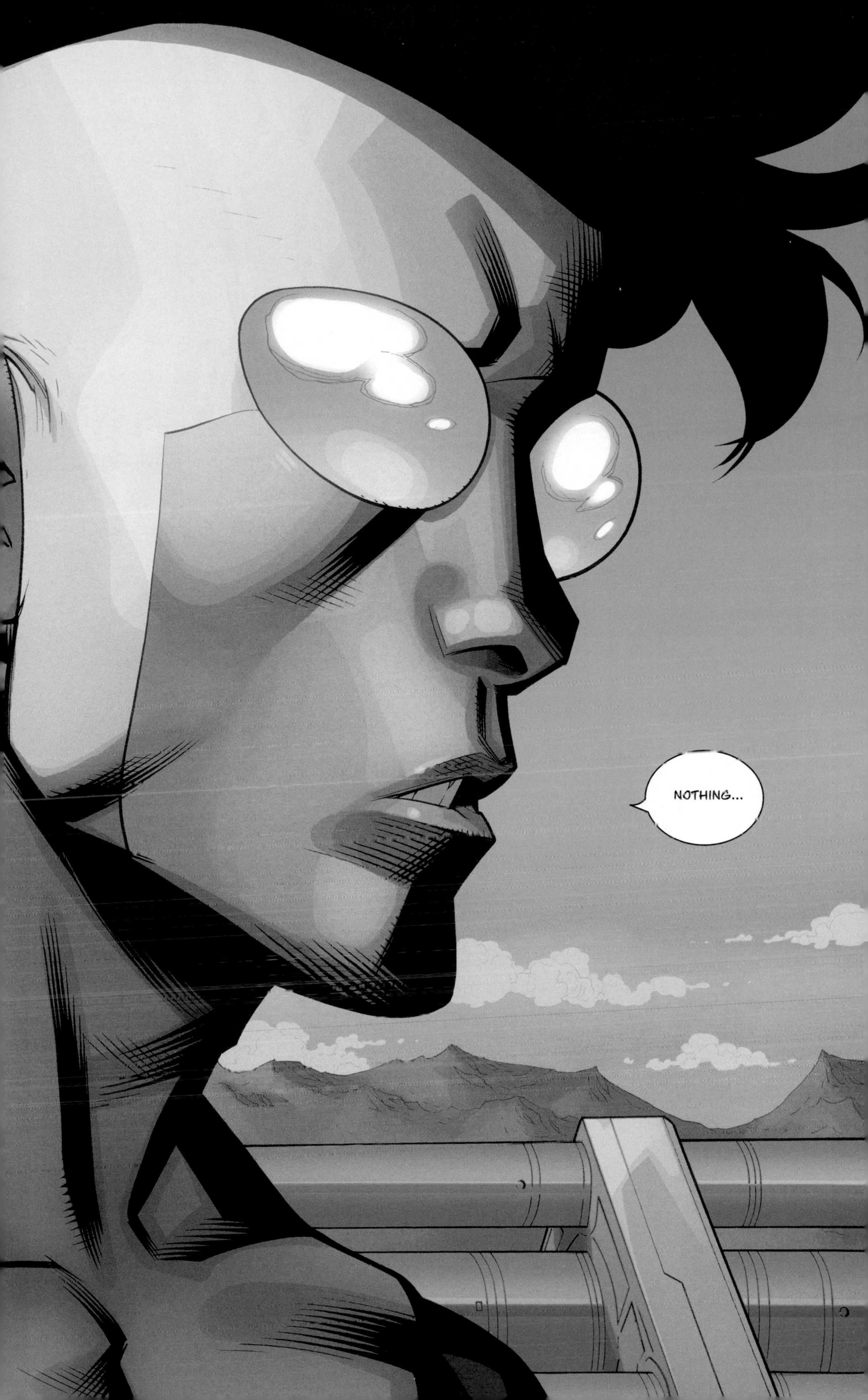
NOTHING...

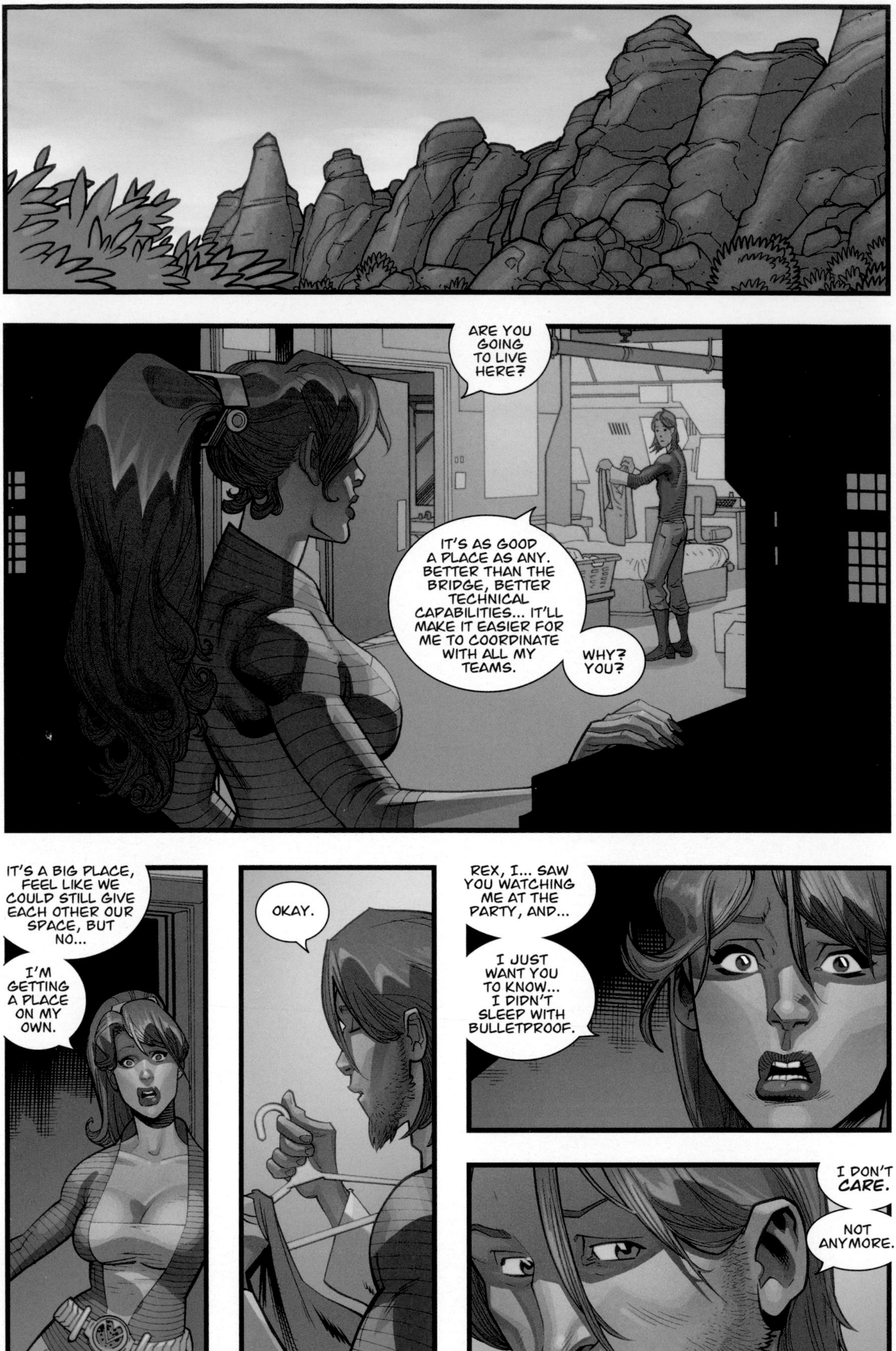
ARE YOU GOING TO LIVE HERE?
IT'S AS GOOD A PLACE AS ANY. BETTER THAN THE BRIDGE, BETTER TECHNICAL CAPABILITIES... IT'LL MAKE IT EASIER FOR ME TO COORDINATE WITH ALL MY TEAMS.
WHY? YOU?
IT'S A BIG PLACE, FEEL LIKE WE COULD STILL GIVE EACH OTHER OUR SPACE, BUT NO...
I'M GETTING A PLACE ON MY OWN.
OKAY.
REX, I... SAW YOU WATCHING ME AT THE PARTY, AND...
I JUST WANT YOU TO KNOW... I DIDN'T SLEEP WITH BULLETPROOF.
I DON'T CARE.
NOT ANYMORE.

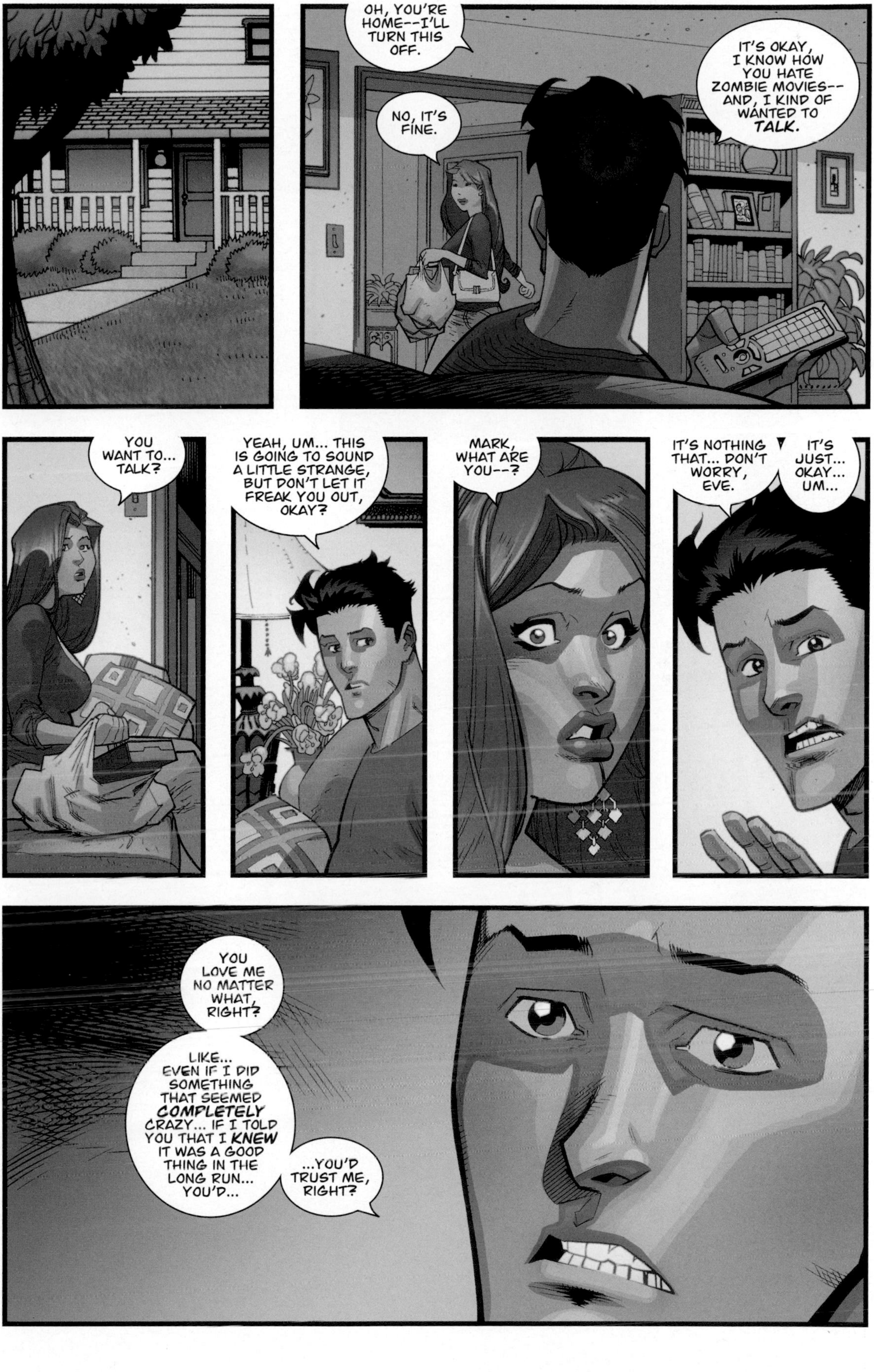
OH, YOU'RE HOME--I'LL TURN THIS OFF.
NO, IT'S FINE.
IT'S OKAY, I KNOW HOW YOU HATE ZOMBIE MOVIES--AND, I KIND OF WANTED TO TALK.
YOU WANT TO... TALK?
YEAH, UM... THIS IS GOING TO SOUND A LITTLE STRANGE, BUT DON'T LET IT FREAK YOU OUT, OKAY?
MARK, WHAT ARE YOU--?
IT'S NOTHING THAT... DON'T WORRY, EVE.
IT'S JUST... OKAY... UM...
YOU LOVE ME NO MATTER WHAT, RIGHT?
LIKE... EVEN IF I DID SOMETHING THAT SEEMED COMPLETELY CRAZY... IF I TOLD YOU THAT I KNEW IT WAS A GOOD THING IN THE LONG RUN... YOU'D...
...YOU'D TRUST ME, RIGHT?

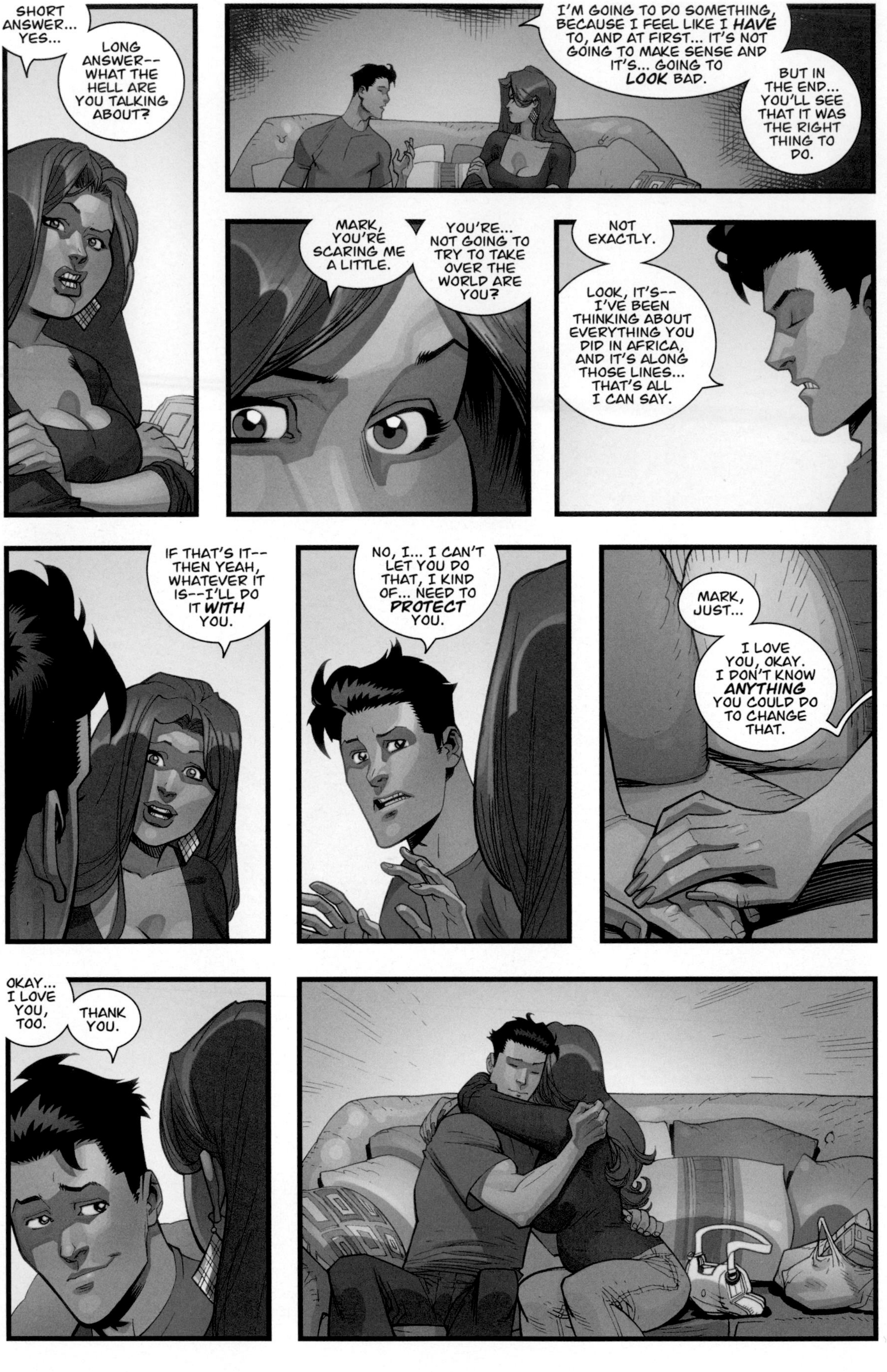
SHORT ANSWER... YES...
LONG ANSWER--WHAT THE HELL ARE YOU TALKING ABOUT?
I'M GOING TO DO SOMETHING, BECAUSE I FEEL LIKE I **HAVE** TO, AND AT FIRST... IT'S NOT GOING TO MAKE SENSE AND IT'S... GOING TO **LOOK** BAD.
BUT IN THE END... YOU'LL SEE THAT IT WAS THE RIGHT THING TO DO.
MARK, YOU'RE SCARING ME A LITTLE.
YOU'RE... NOT GOING TO TRY TO TAKE OVER THE WORLD ARE YOU?
NOT EXACTLY.
LOOK, IT'S--I'VE BEEN THINKING ABOUT EVERYTHING YOU DID IN AFRICA, AND IT'S ALONG THOSE LINES... THAT'S ALL I CAN SAY.
IF THAT'S IT--THEN WHATEVER YEAH, WHATEVER IT IS--I'LL DO IT **WITH** YOU.
NO, I... I CAN'T LET YOU DO THAT, I KIND OF... NEED TO **PROTECT** YOU.
MARK, JUST...
I LOVE YOU, OKAY. I DON'T KNOW **ANYTHING** YOU COULD DO TO CHANGE THAT.
OKAY... I LOVE YOU, TOO.
THANK YOU.

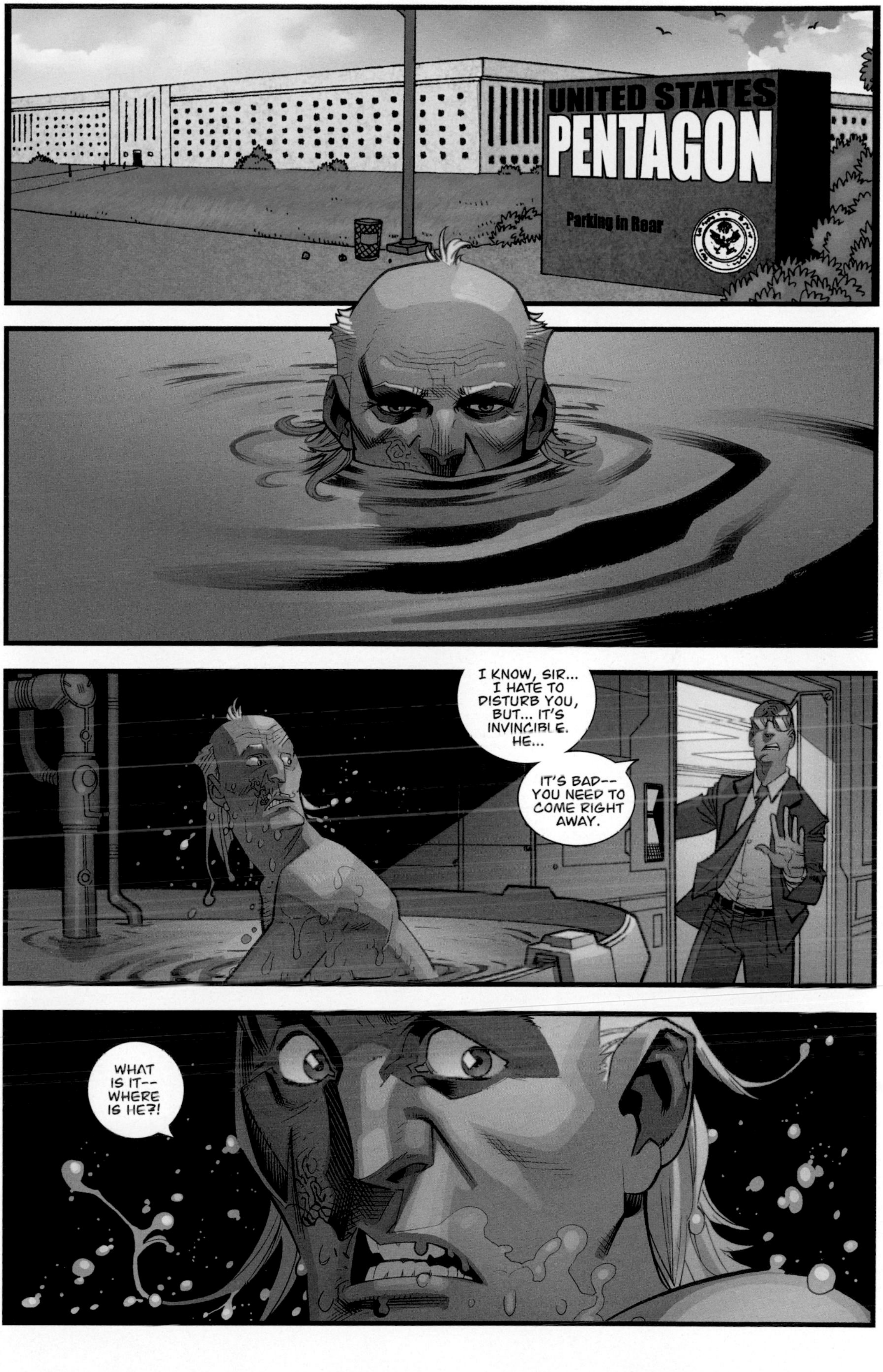
UNITED STATES
PENTAGON
Parking in Rear
I KNOW, SIR... I HATE TO DISTURB YOU, BUT... IT'S INVINCIBLE. HE...
IT'S BAD-- YOU NEED TO COME RIGHT AWAY.
WHAT IS IT-- WHERE IS HE?!

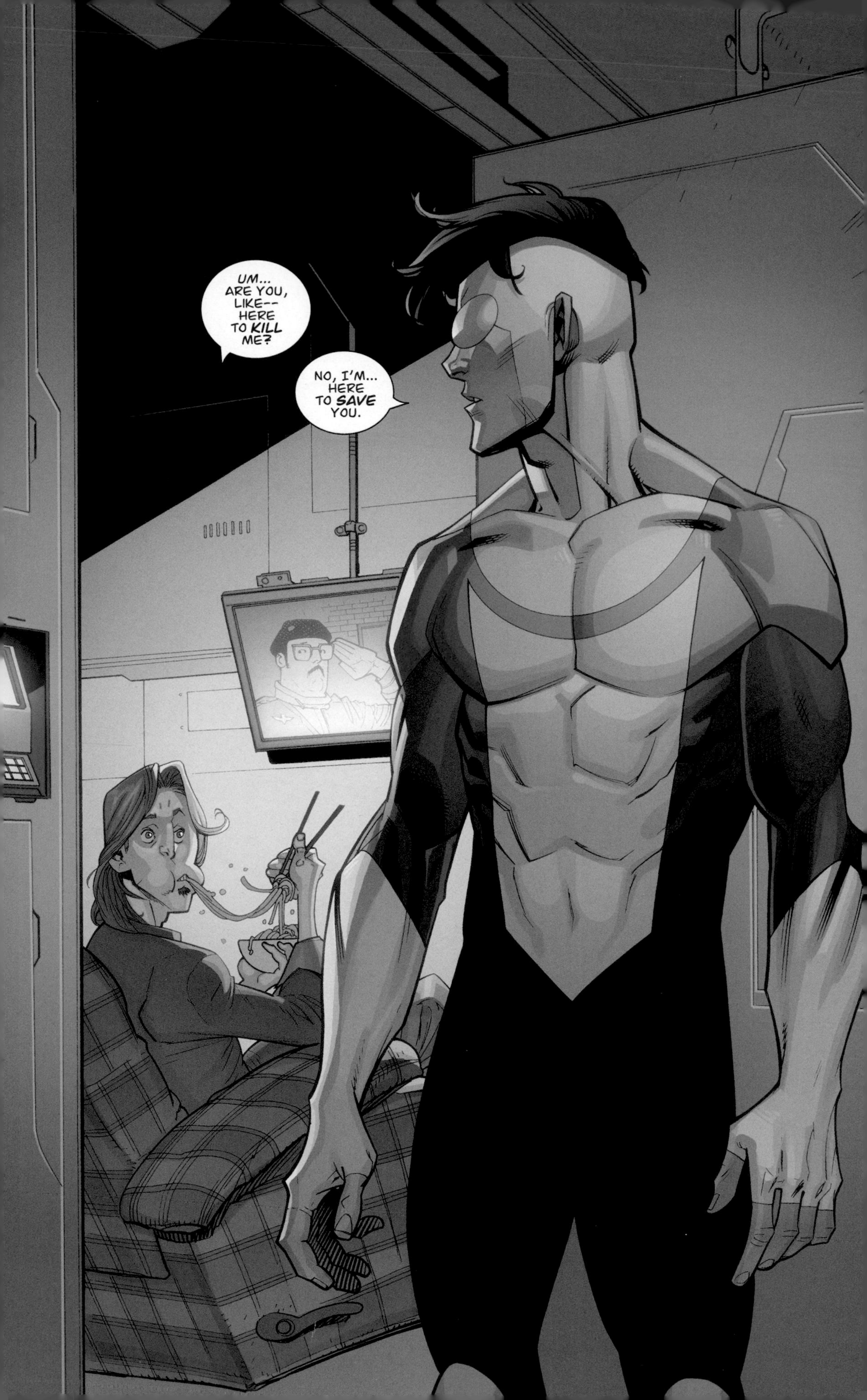
UM... ARE YOU, LIKE-- HERE TO KILL ME?
NO, I'M... HERE TO SAVE YOU.

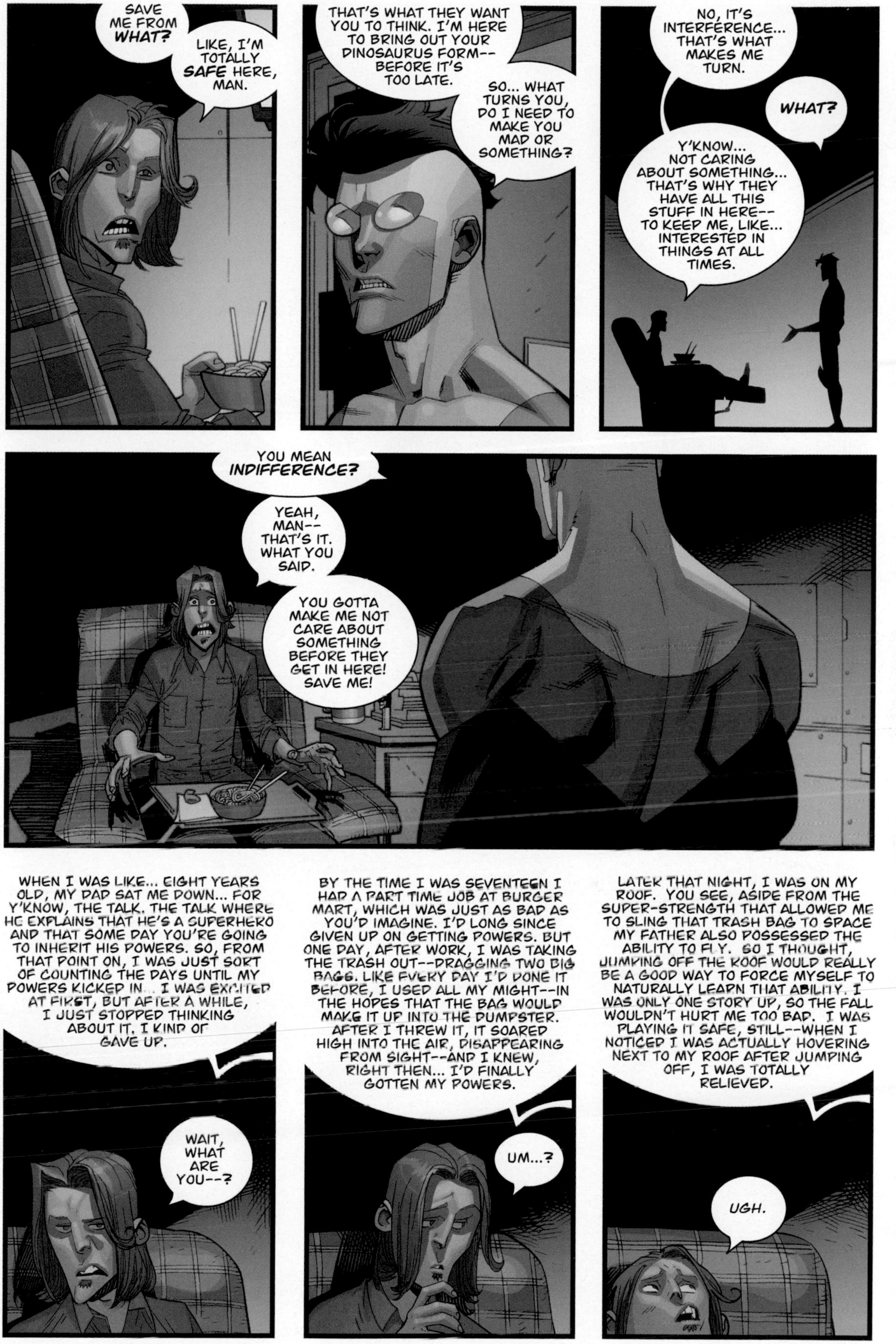
SAVE ME FROM WHAT?
LIKE, I'M TOTALLY SAFE HERE, MAN.
THAT'S WHAT THEY WANT YOU TO THINK. I'M HERE TO BRING OUT YOUR DINOSAURUS FORM--BEFORE IT'S TOO LATE.
SO... WHAT TURNS YOU, DO I NEED TO MAKE YOU MAD OR SOMETHING?
NO, IT'S INTERFERENCE... THAT'S WHAT MAKES ME TURN.
WHAT?
Y'KNOW... NOT CARING ABOUT SOMETHING... THAT'S WHY THEY HAVE ALL THIS STUFF IN HERE--TO KEEP ME, LIKE... INTERESTED IN THINGS AT ALL TIMES.
YOU MEAN INDIFFERENCE?
YEAH, MAN--THAT'S IT. WHAT YOU SAID.
YOU GOTTA MAKE ME NOT CARE ABOUT SOMETHING BEFORE THEY GET IN HERE! SAVE ME!
WHEN I WAS LIKE... EIGHT YEARS OLD, MY DAD SAT ME DOWN... FOR Y'KNOW, THE TALK. THE TALK WHERE HE EXPLAINS THAT HE'S A SUPERHERO AND THAT SOME DAY YOU'RE GOING TO INHERIT HIS POWERS. SO, FROM THAT POINT ON, I WAS JUST SORT OF COUNTING THE DAYS UNTIL MY POWERS KICKED IN... I WAS EXCITED AT FIRST, BUT AFTER A WHILE, I JUST STOPPED THINKING ABOUT IT. I KIND OF GAVE UP.
WAIT, WHAT ARE YOU--?
BY THE TIME I WAS SEVENTEEN I HAD A PART TIME JOB AT BURGER MART, WHICH WAS JUST AS BAD AS YOU'D IMAGINE. I'D LONG SINCE GIVEN UP ON GETTING POWERS. BUT ONE DAY, AFTER WORK, I WAS TAKING THE TRASH OUT--DRAGGING TWO BIG BAGS. LIKE EVERY DAY I'D DONE IT BEFORE, I USED ALL MY MIGHT--IN THE HOPES THAT THE BAG WOULD MAKE IT UP INTO THE DUMPSTER. AFTER I THREW IT, IT SOARED HIGH INTO THE AIR, DISAPPEARING FROM SIGHT--AND I KNEW, RIGHT THEN... I'D FINALLY GOTTEN MY POWERS.
UM...?
LATER THAT NIGHT, I WAS ON MY ROOF. YOU SEE, ASIDE FROM THE SUPER-STRENGTH THAT ALLOWED ME TO SLING THAT TRASH BAG TO SPACE MY FATHER ALSO POSSESSED THE ABILITY TO FLY. SO I THOUGHT, JUMPING OFF THE ROOF WOULD REALLY BE A GOOD WAY TO FORCE MYSELF TO NATURALLY LEARN THAT ABILITY. I WAS ONLY ONE STORY UP, SO THE FALL WOULDN'T HURT ME TOO BAD. I WAS PLAYING IT SAFE, STILL--WHEN I NOTICED I WAS ACTUALLY HOVERING NEXT TO MY ROOF AFTER JUMPING OFF, I WAS TOTALLY RELIEVED.
UGH.

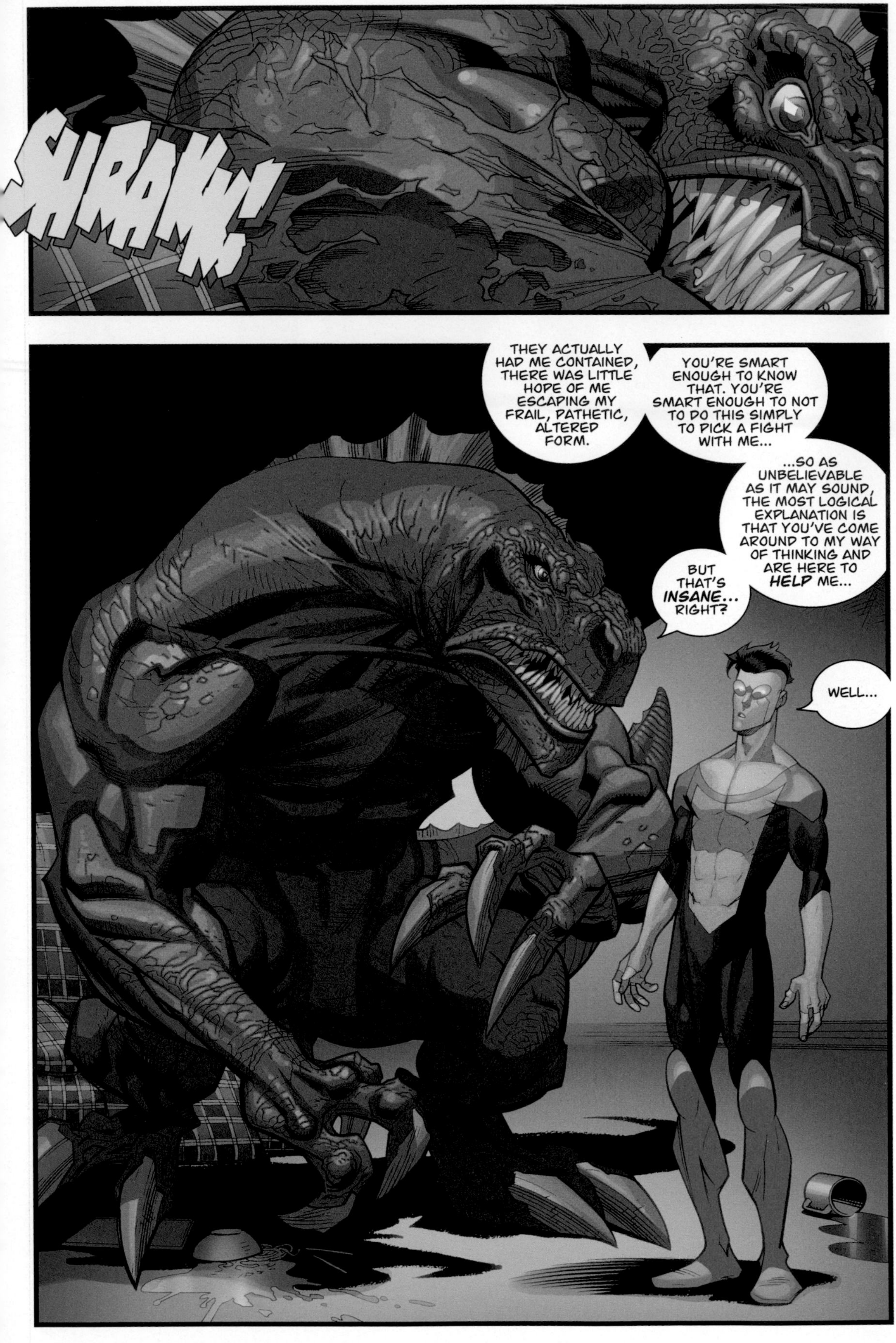
SHRAKK!
THEY ACTUALLY HAD ME CONTAINED, THERE WAS LITTLE HOPE OF ME ESCAPING MY FRAIL, PATHETIC, ALTERED FORM.
YOU'RE SMART ENOUGH TO KNOW THAT. YOU'RE SMART ENOUGH TO NOT TO DO THIS SIMPLY TO PICK A FIGHT WITH ME...
...SO AS UNBELIEVABLE AS IT MAY SOUND, THE MOST LOGICAL EXPLANATION IS THAT YOU'VE COME AROUND TO MY WAY OF THINKING AND ARE HERE TO HELP ME...
BUT THAT'S INSANE... RIGHT?
WELL...

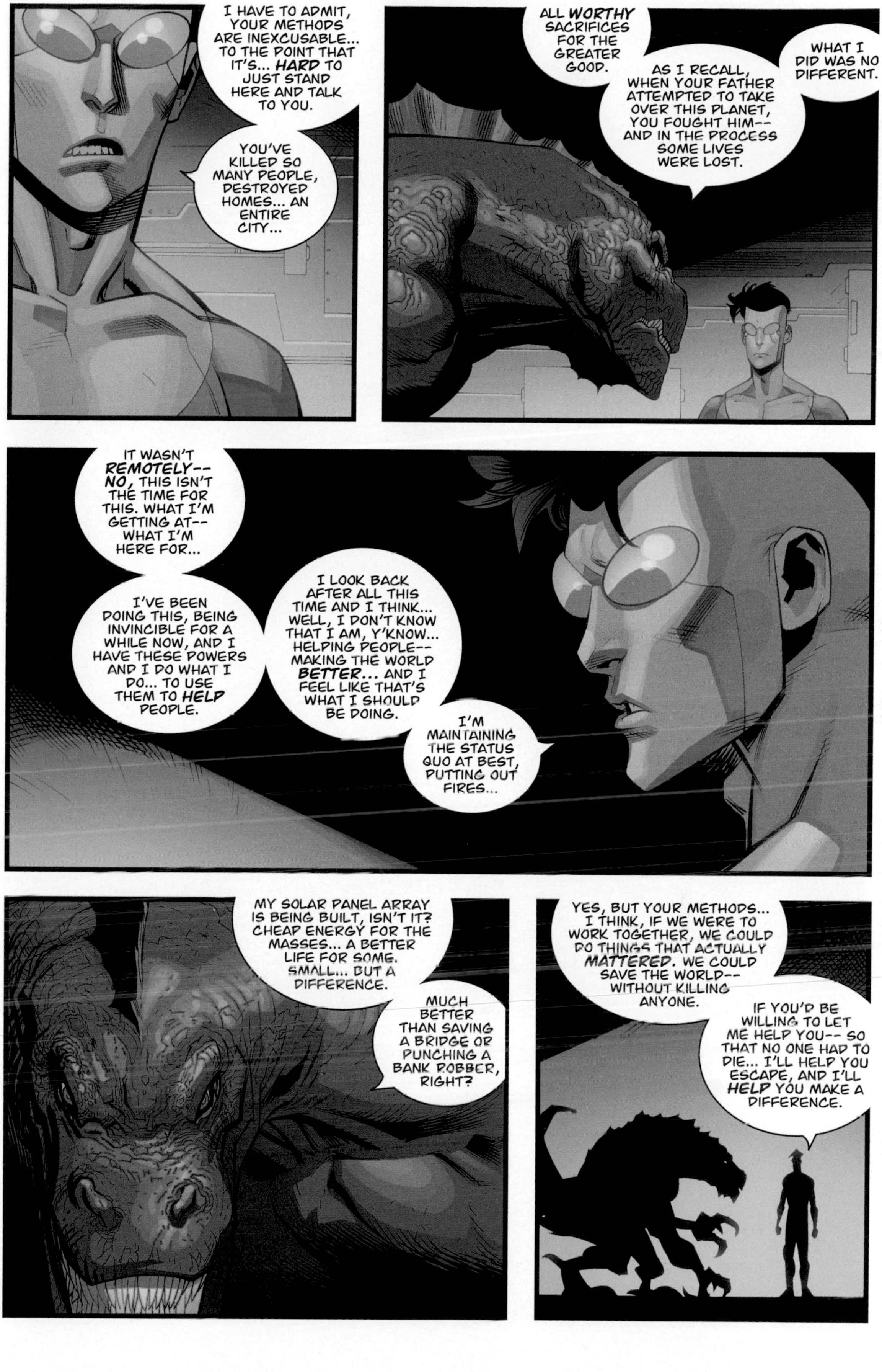
I HAVE TO ADMIT, YOUR METHODS ARE INEXCUSABLE... TO THE POINT THAT IT'S... HARD TO JUST STAND HERE AND TALK TO YOU.
YOU'VE KILLED SO MANY PEOPLE, DESTROYED HOMES... AN ENTIRE CITY...
ALL WORTHY SACRIFICES FOR THE GREATER GOOD.
AS I RECALL, WHEN YOUR FATHER ATTEMPTED TO TAKE OVER THIS PLANET, YOU FOUGHT HIM-- AND IN THE PROCESS SOME LIVES WERE LOST.
WHAT I DID WAS NO DIFFERENT.
IT WASN'T REMOTELY-- NO, THIS ISN'T THE TIME FOR THIS. WHAT I'M GETTING AT-- WHAT I'M HERE FOR...
I'VE BEEN DOING THIS, BEING INVINCIBLE FOR A WHILE NOW, AND I HAVE THESE POWERS AND I DO WHAT I DO... TO USE THEM TO HELP PEOPLE.
I LOOK BACK AFTER ALL THIS TIME AND I THINK... WELL, I DON'T KNOW THAT I AM, Y'KNOW... HELPING PEOPLE-- MAKING THE WORLD BETTER... AND I FEEL LIKE THAT'S WHAT I SHOULD BE DOING.
I'M MAINTAINING THE STATUS QUO AT BEST, PUTTING OUT FIRES...
MY SOLAR PANEL ARRAY IS BEING BUILT, ISN'T IT? CHEAP ENERGY FOR THE MASSES... A BETTER LIFE FOR SOME. SMALL... BUT A DIFFERENCE.
MUCH BETTER THAN SAVING A BRIDGE OR PUNCHING A BANK ROBBER, RIGHT?
YES, BUT YOUR METHODS... I THINK, IF WE WERE TO WORK TOGETHER, WE COULD DO THINGS THAT ACTUALLY MATTERED. WE COULD SAVE THE WORLD-- WITHOUT KILLING ANYONE.
IF YOU'D BE WILLING TO LET ME HELP YOU-- SO THAT NO ONE HAD TO DIE... I'LL HELP YOU ESCAPE, AND I'LL HELP YOU MAKE A DIFFERENCE.

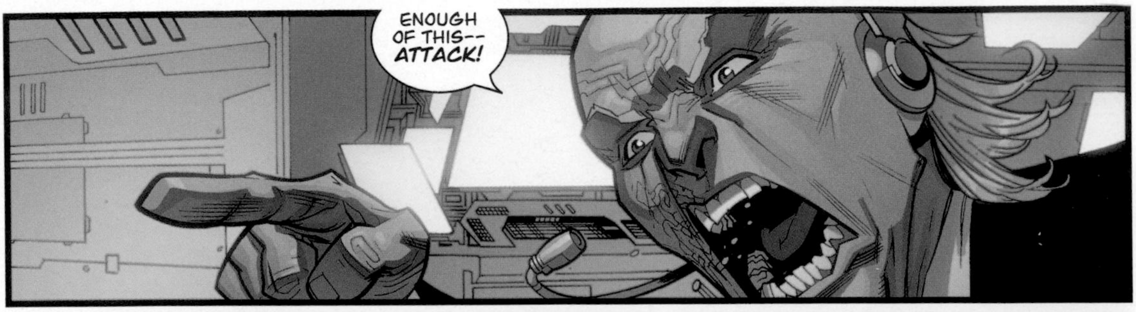
ENOUGH OF THIS-- ATTACK!
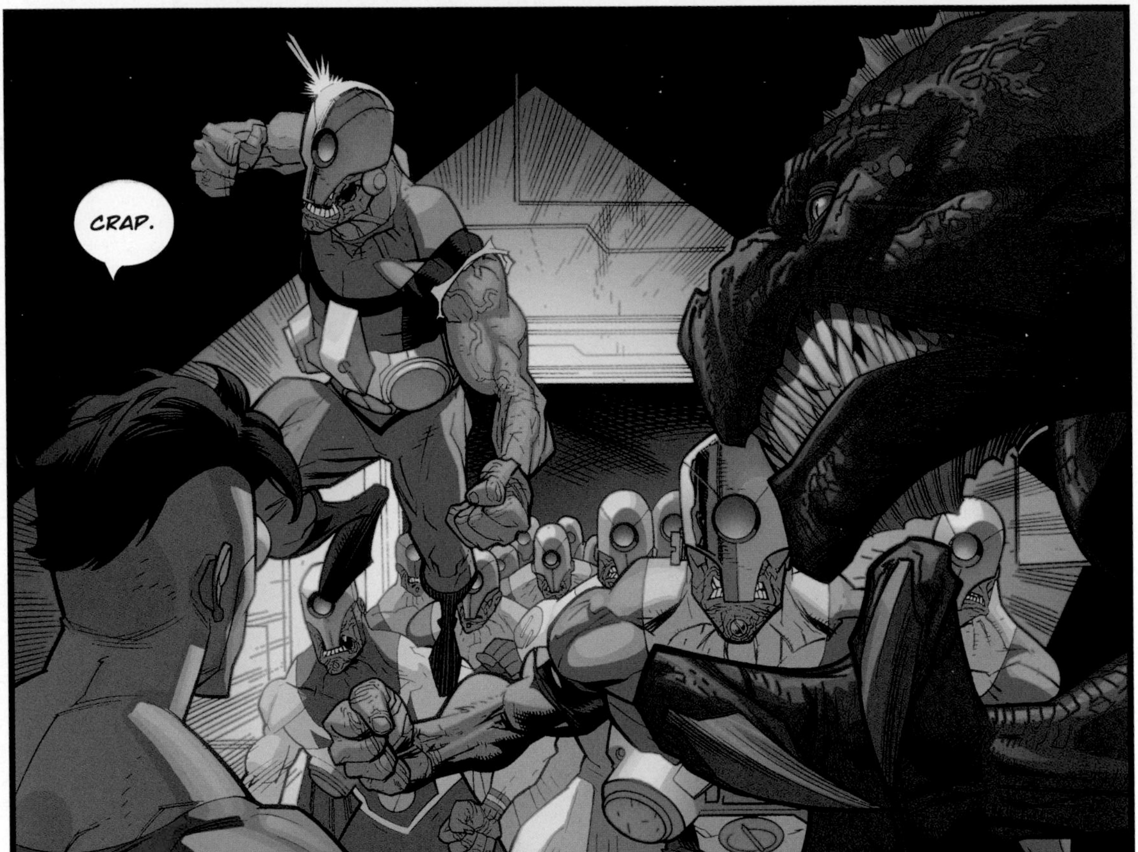
CRAP.
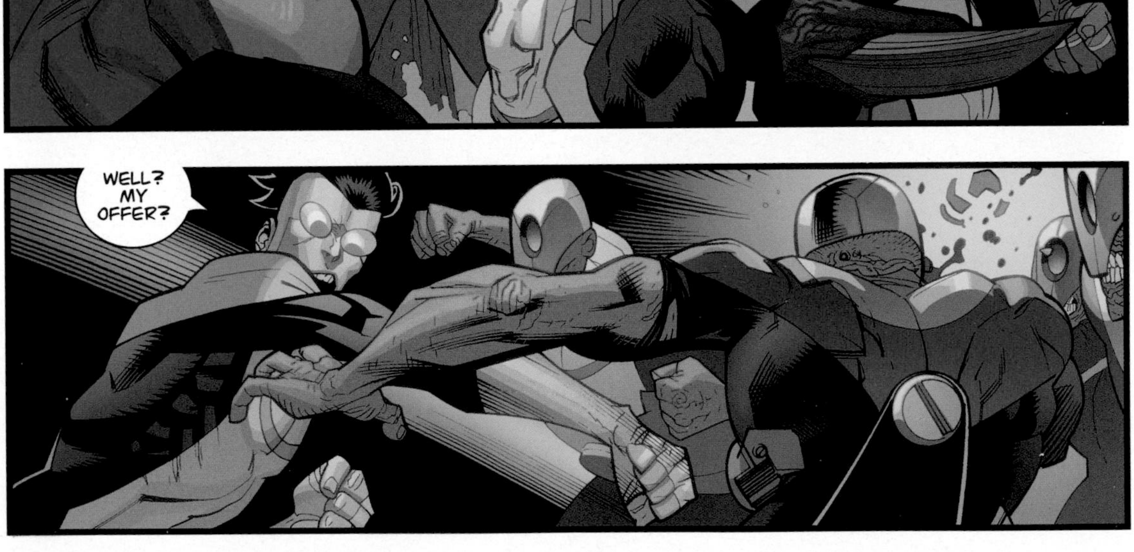
WELL? MY OFFER?

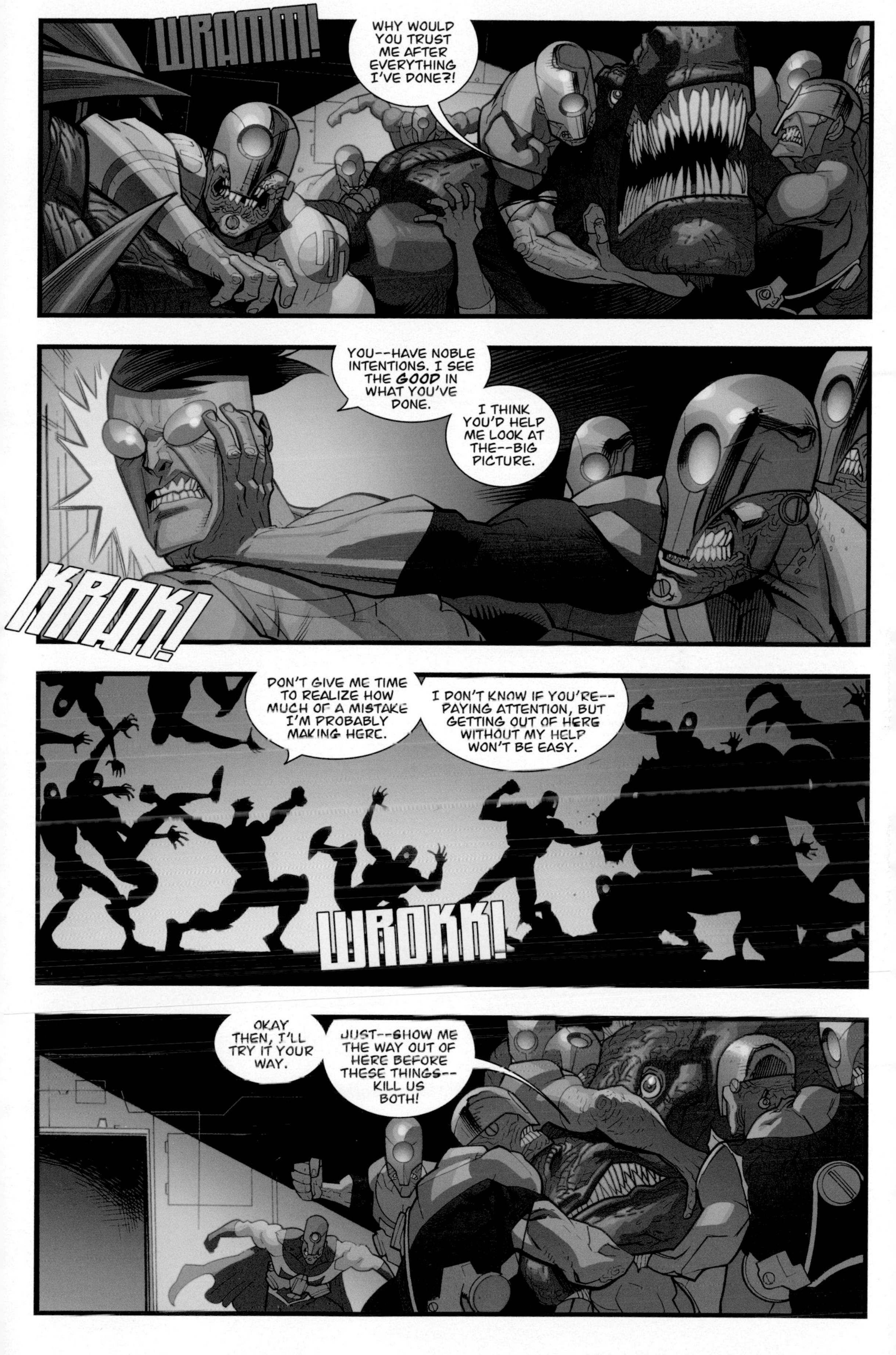
WRAMM!
WHY WOULD YOU TRUST ME AFTER EVERYTHING I'VE DONE?!
YOU--HAVE NOBLE INTENTIONS. I SEE THE GOOD IN WHAT YOU'VE DONE.
I THINK YOU'D HELP ME LOOK AT THE--BIG PICTURE.
KRAK!
DON'T GIVE ME TIME TO REALIZE HOW MUCH OF A MISTAKE I'M PROBABLY MAKING HERE.
I DON'T KNOW IF YOU'RE--PAYING ATTENTION, BUT GETTING OUT OF HERE WITHOUT MY HELP WON'T BE EASY.
WROKK!
OKAY THEN, I'LL TRY IT YOUR WAY.
JUST--SHOW ME THE WAY OUT OF HERE BEFORE THESE THINGS--KILL US BOTH!

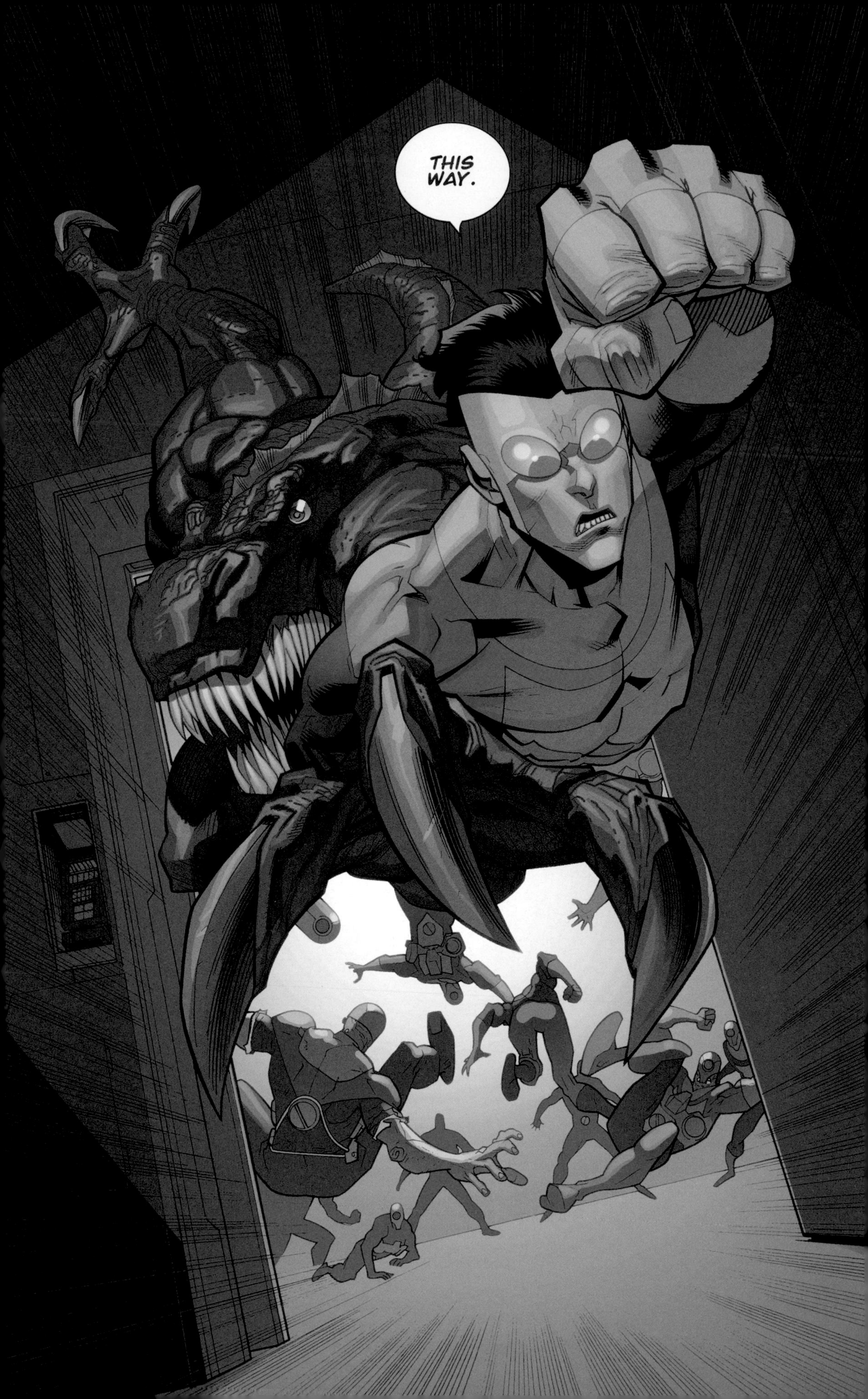
THIS WAY.

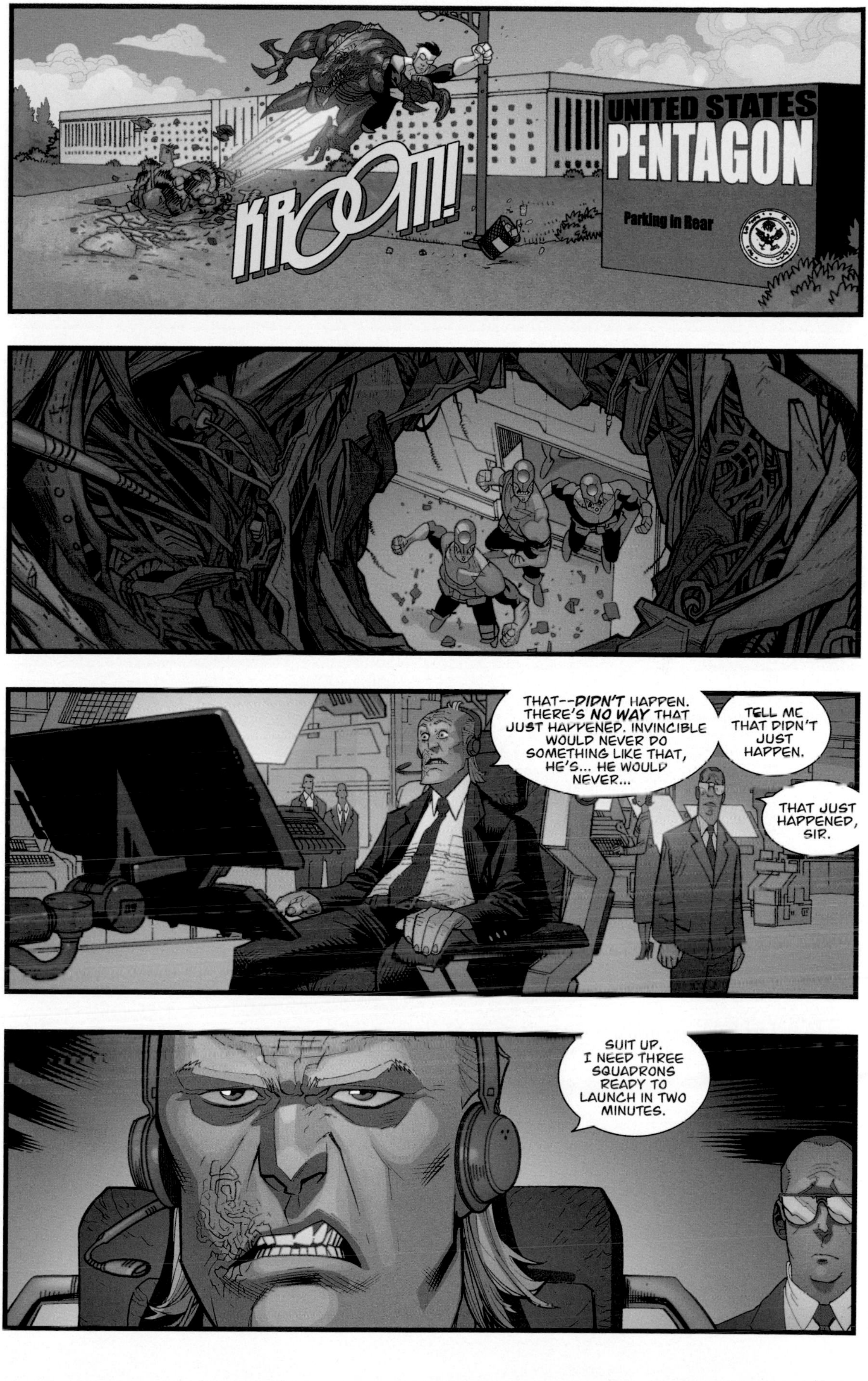
UNITED STATES
PENTAGON
Parking in Rear
KROOM!
THAT--DIDN'T HAPPEN. THERE'S NO WAY THAT JUST HAPPENED. INVINCIBLE WOULD NEVER DO SOMETHING LIKE THAT, HE'S... HE WOULD NEVER...
TELL ME THAT DIDN'T JUST HAPPEN.
THAT JUST HAPPENED, SIR.
SUIT UP. I NEED THREE SQUADRONS READY TO LAUNCH IN TWO MINUTES.

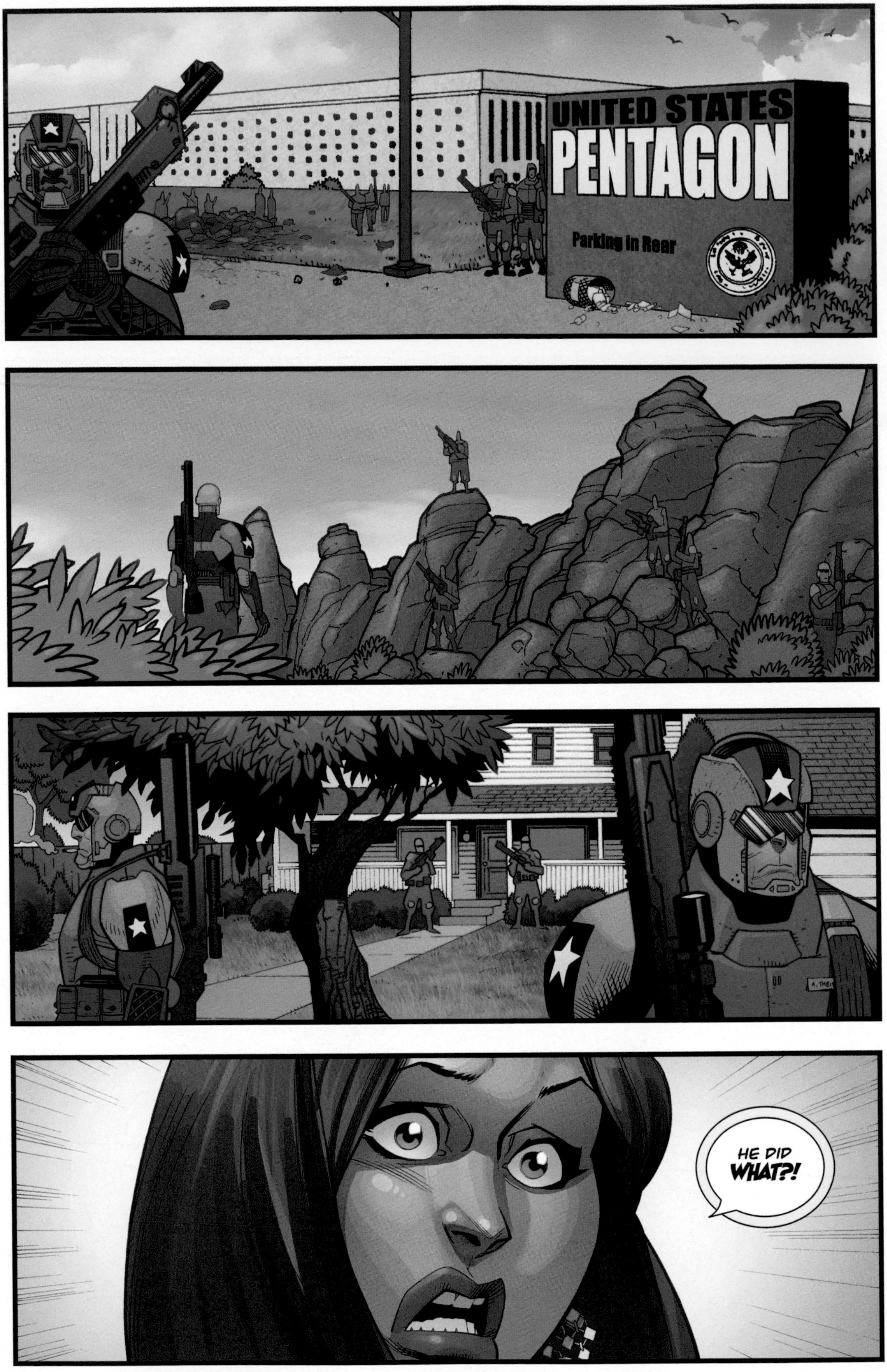
UNITED STATES
PENTAGON
Parking in Rear
HE DID WHAT?!

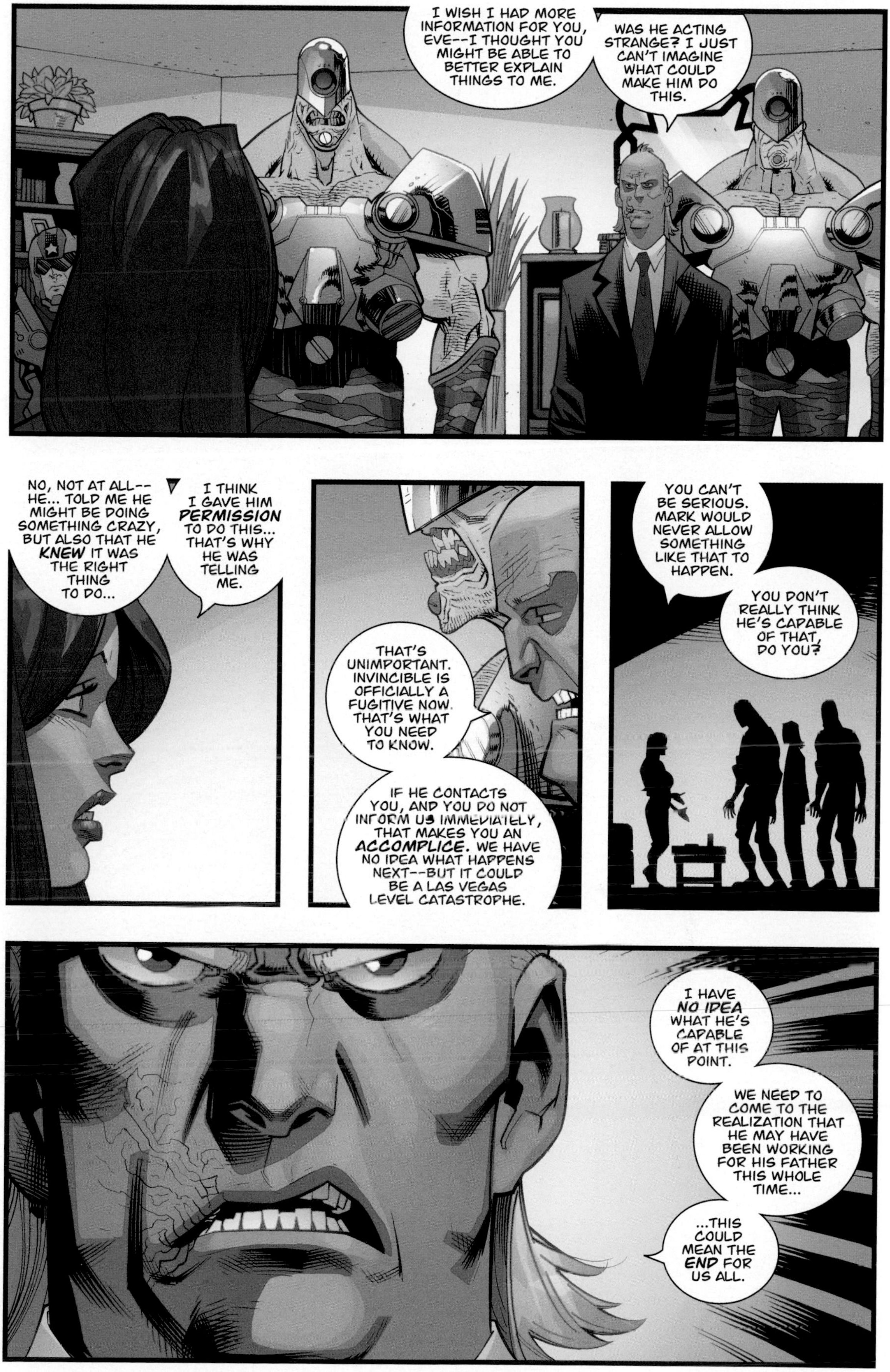
I WISH I HAD MORE INFORMATION FOR YOU, EVE--I THOUGHT YOU MIGHT BE ABLE TO BETTER EXPLAIN THINGS TO ME.
WAS HE ACTING STRANGE? I JUST CAN'T IMAGINE WHAT COULD MAKE HIM DO THIS.
NO, NOT AT ALL-- HE... TOLD ME HE MIGHT BE DOING SOMETHING CRAZY, BUT ALSO THAT HE KNEW IT WAS THE RIGHT THING TO DO...
I THINK I GAVE HIM PERMISSION TO DO THIS... THAT'S WHY HE WAS TELLING ME.
THAT'S UNIMPORTANT. INVINCIBLE IS OFFICIALLY A FUGITIVE NOW. THAT'S WHAT YOU NEED TO KNOW.
IF HE CONTACTS YOU, AND YOU DO NOT INFORM US IMMEDIATELY, THAT MAKES YOU AN ACCOMPLICE. WE HAVE NO IDEA WHAT HAPPENS NEXT--BUT IT COULD BE A LAS VEGAS LEVEL CATASTROPHE.
YOU CAN'T BE SERIOUS. MARK WOULD NEVER ALLOW SOMETHING LIKE THAT TO HAPPEN.
YOU DON'T REALLY THINK HE'S CAPABLE OF THAT, DO YOU?
I HAVE NO IDEA WHAT HE'S CAPABLE OF AT THIS POINT.
WE NEED TO COME TO THE REALIZATION THAT HE MAY HAVE BEEN WORKING FOR HIS FATHER THIS WHOLE TIME...
...THIS COULD MEAN THE END FOR US ALL.

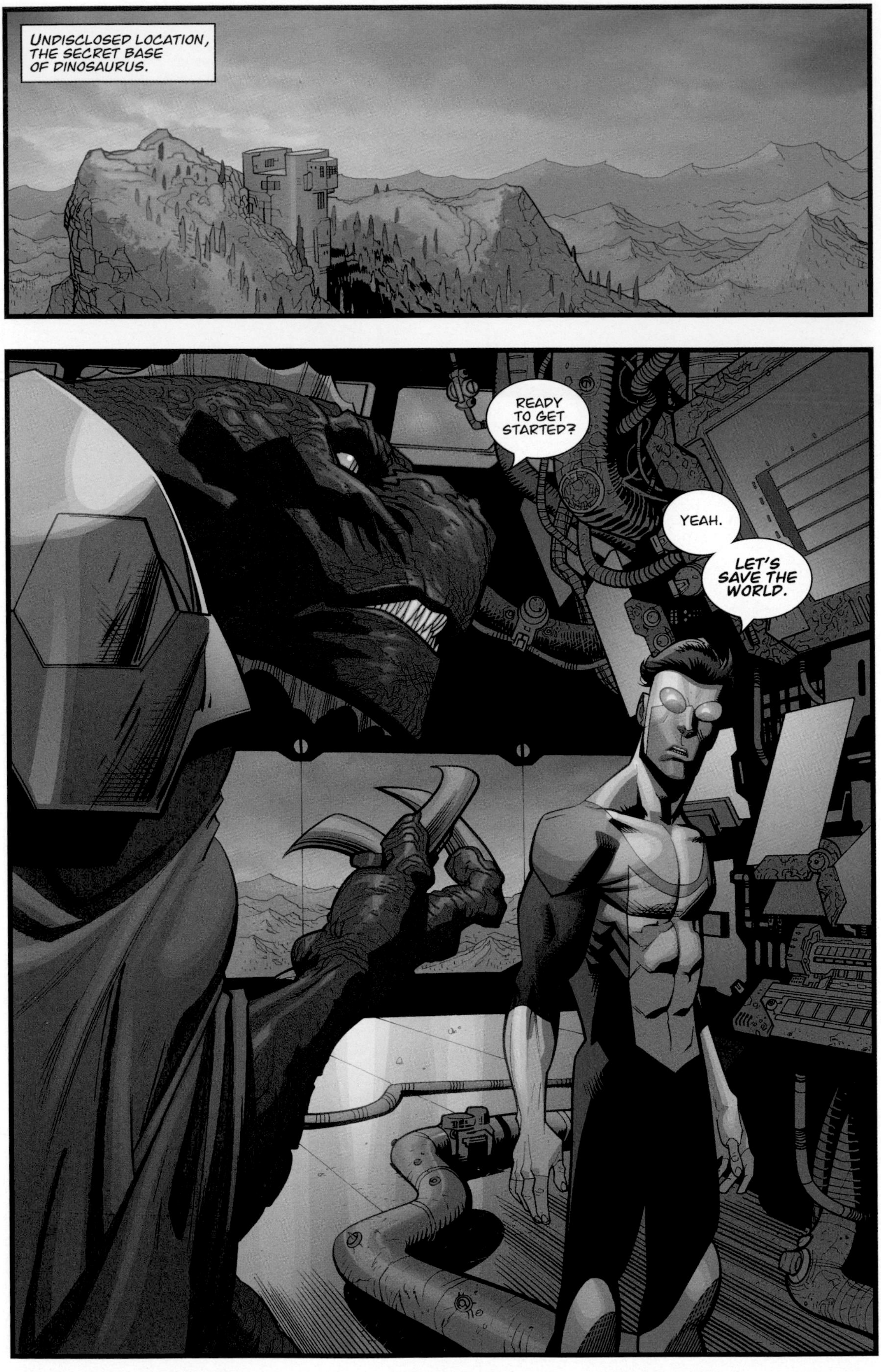
UNDISCLOSED LOCATION, THE SECRET BASE OF DINOSAURUS.
READY TO GET STARTED?
YEAH.
LET'S SAVE THE WORLD.

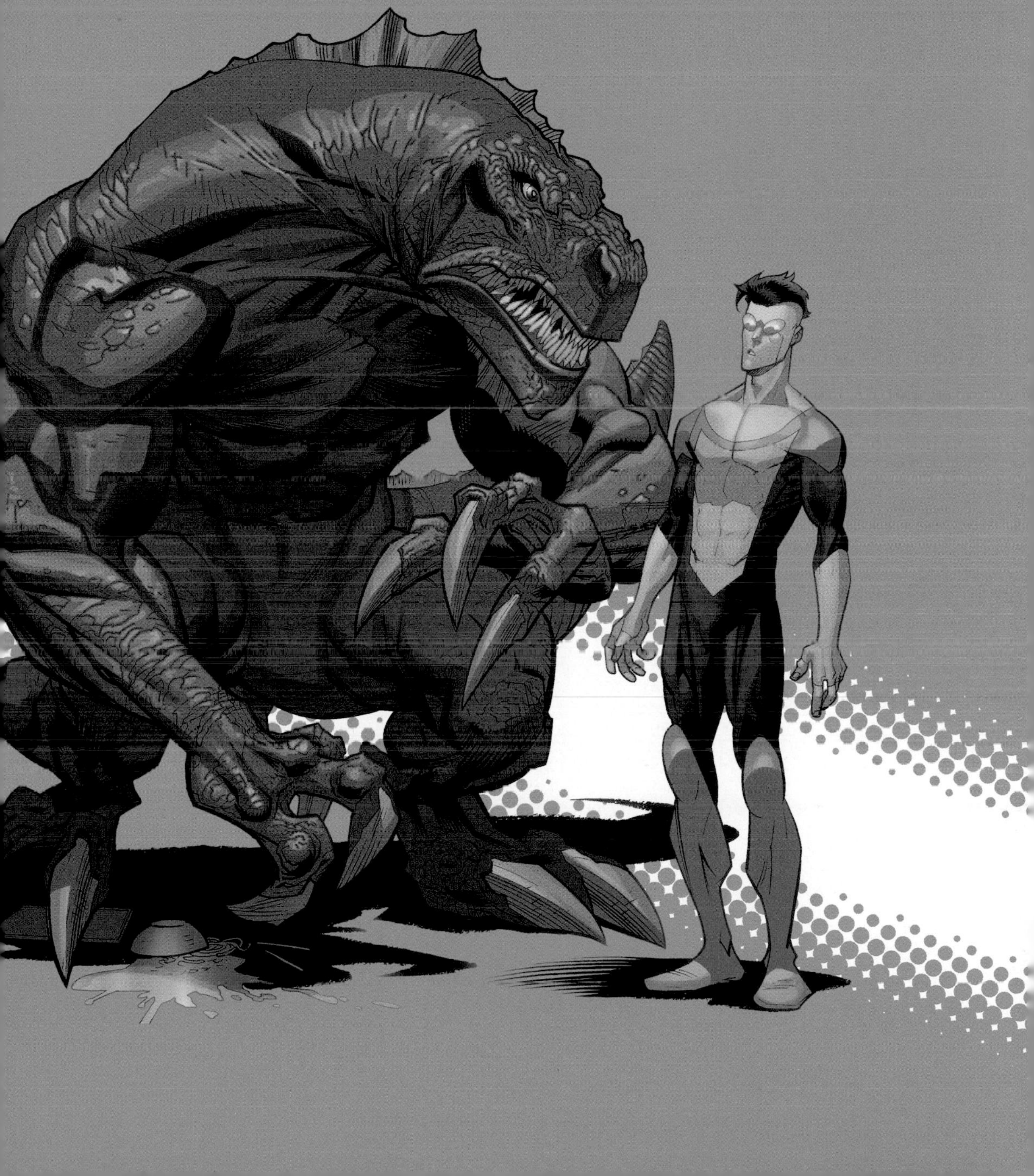

SKETCHBOOK

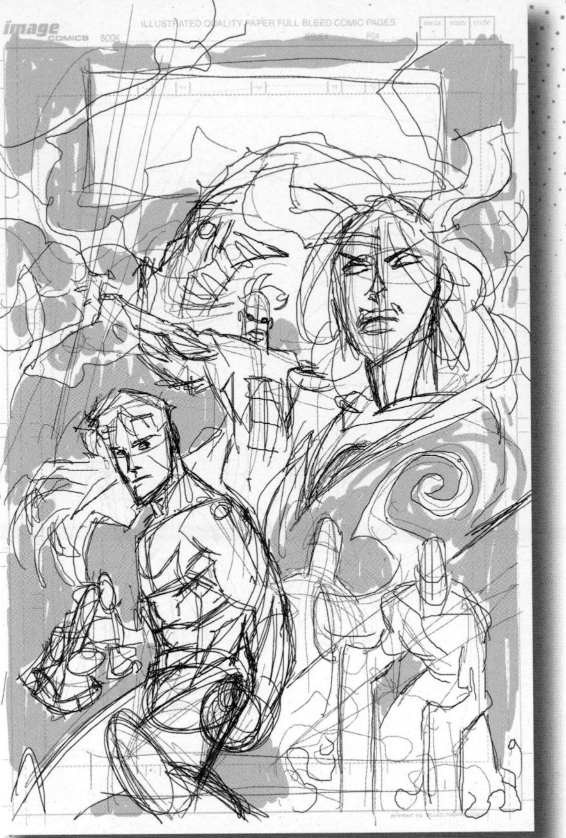

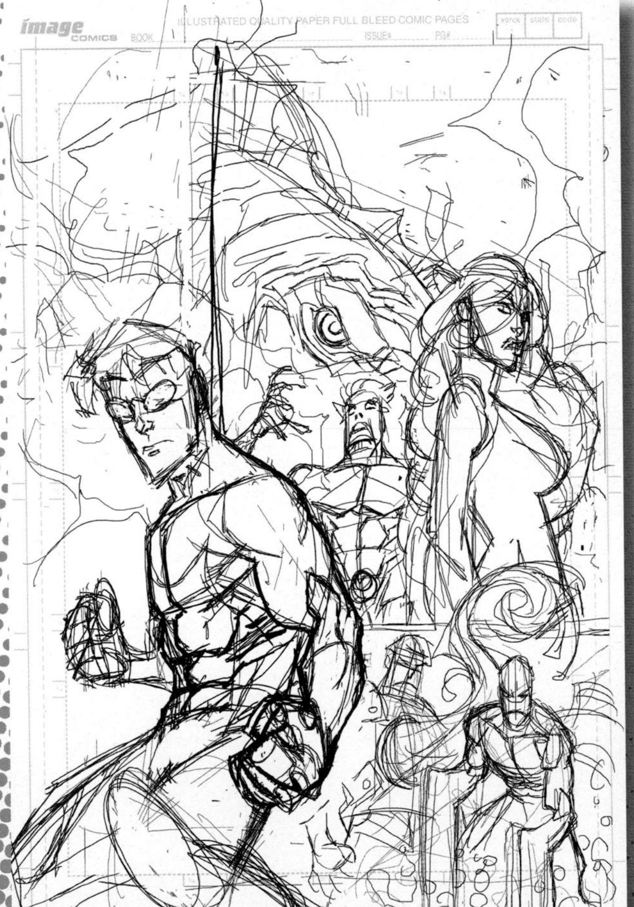

ROBERT KIRKMAN: I can't believe after fifteen volumes Ryan is still able to take our trade paperback cover motif and make it look cool and fresh and new. Great job all around. This was a fun batch of issues to do, setting up some reoccurring villains in the series while taking Mark down a possibly strange path. Love this cover!

RYAN OTTLEY: Hey there! Welcome! So here we are fifteen trade paperbacks in and I'm still loving this book. This first drawing you see here is a digital layout done on a Cintiq. I do a lot of digital layouts these days, you'll soon see why. This first one is a collage type layout, Robert likes the covers for these to be similar in ways, these TPBs all have some kind of panel arrangement, so Robert asked if I could incorporate those in somehow. That's what is amazing about doing layouts digitally, instead of re-drawing the whole thing I just moved things around, added some panels, and enlarged some figures. I then change the lines to a very light blue and print it off. I use that as a guide to do my finished pencils and inks the traditional way.

I didn't scan the pencils. I'm dumb. But here are the inks on the next page. Would've liked Dinosaurus to look a little cooler here. Ah well, live and learn.

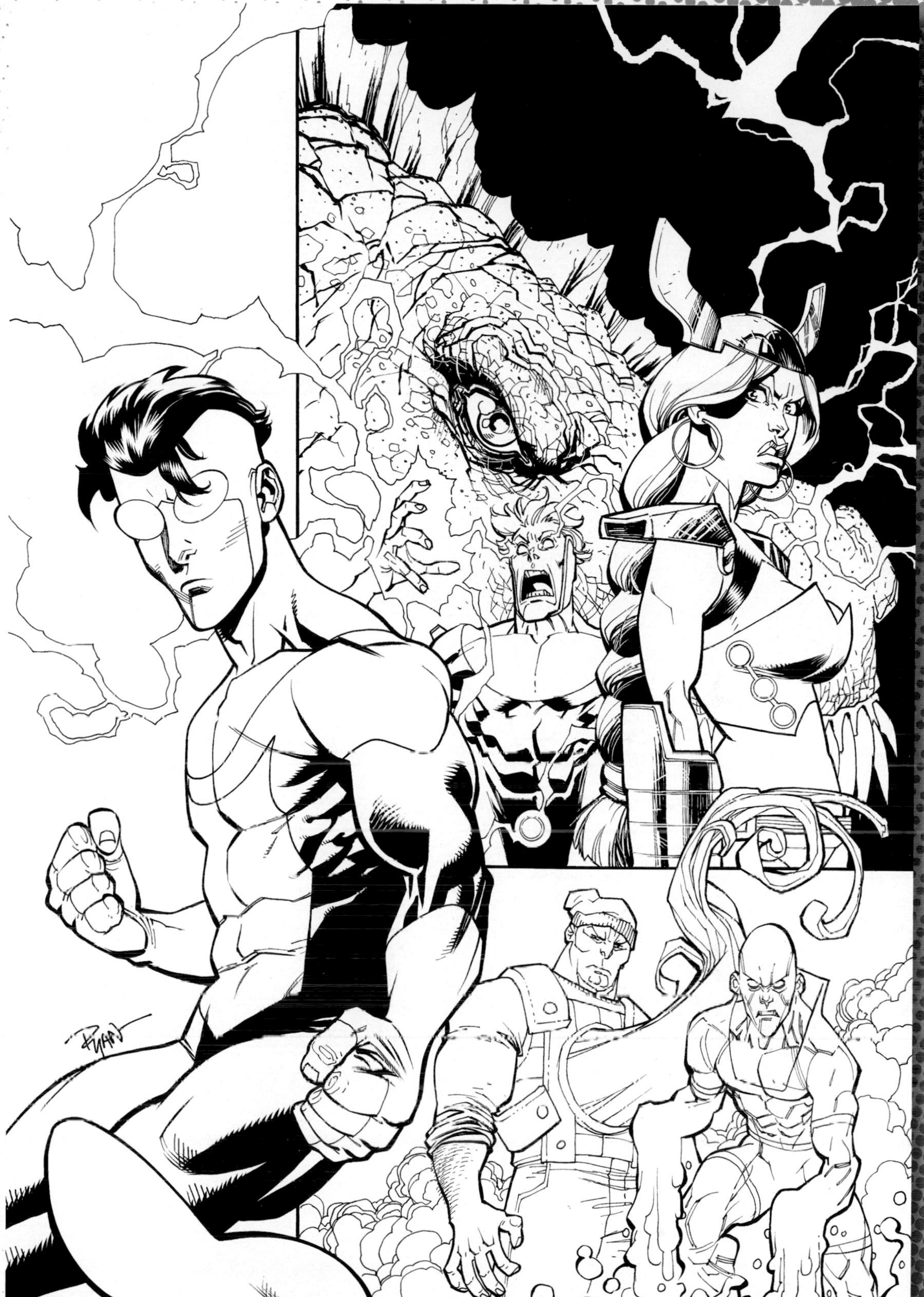

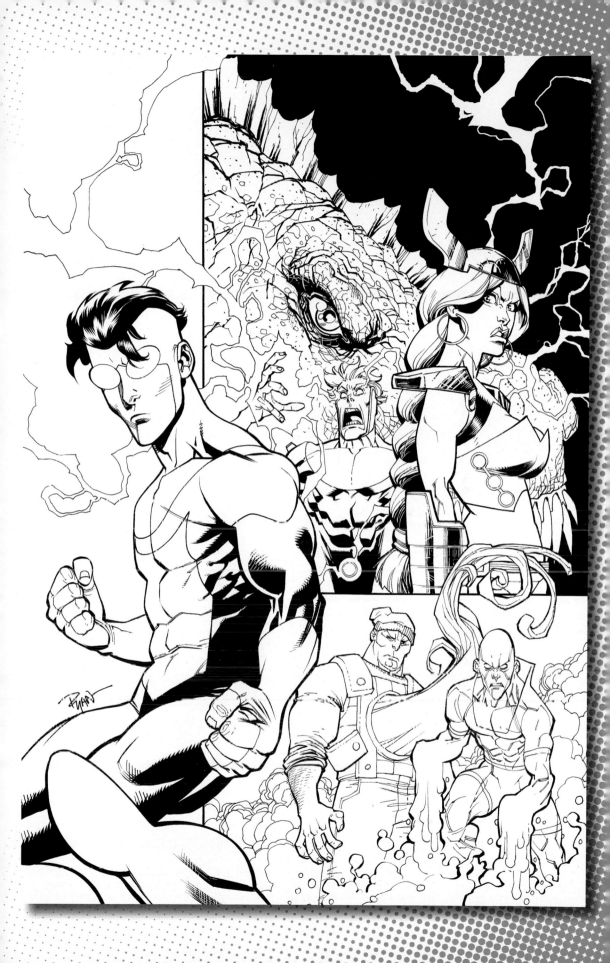

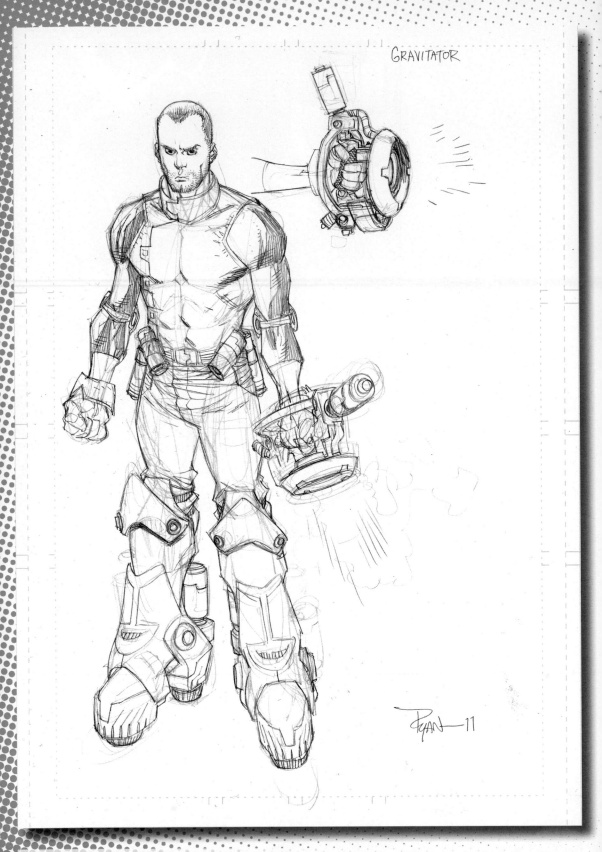

GRAVITATOR

Ryan—11

KIRKMAN: Ah, Gravitator... I love this guy. It was important to me, because this guy's story was somewhat goofy to begin with, that he not appear silly at all. Ryan is a pretty awesome character designer (this is boring, I just keep complimenting him, sorry). I dig the gun a lot. I just pretty much described the guns that Grifter used to use in the WildC.A.T.S. cartoon... and Ryan came up with something way cooler!

OTTLEY: Good ol' gravy tator. Always fun playing around with designs.

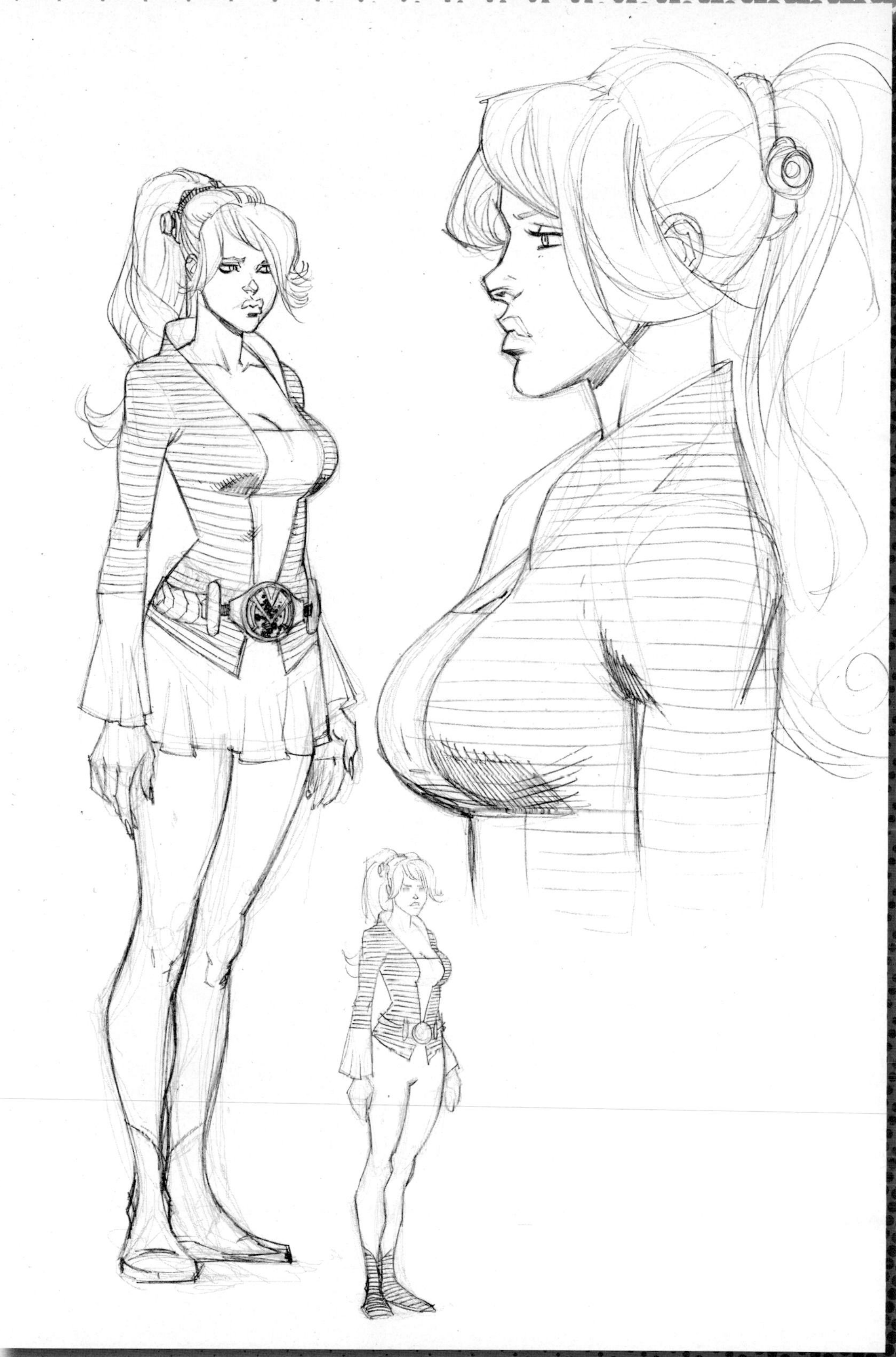

KIRKMAN: Monster Girl's new look. I wanted to reflect her time in the Flaxan dimension, that's why both her and Robot wear their sweet alien clothes all the time now--but also make her a bit sexy now that she's grown up, and look cool. Ryan does a great job again.

OTTLEY: Another design, glad she's back in the book. Monster Girl is the best. I drew a shot there with pants on her just in case Robert didn't like the skirt. He liked the skirt.

KIRKMAN: Here's a cool couple of covers. I especially love the cover for 79. It's a couple of couples watching a couple kids play. You don't see a lot of that on the covers of super-hero comics. And Ryan made it look great! And there's a Science Dog toy!

OTTLEY: I penciled this cover pretty tight because I was thinking about asking an inker to do their thing on it. I ran out of time so I just ended up inking it myself. I remember Robert asked me to draw Dinosaurus in a wrecked Las Vegas casino or something. Yeah, I kinda skimped on the background. I remember Robert said, "I asked for a destroyed Vegas and you give me a burning log cabin?!" Whoops. I have failed you Robert.

The cover to 81 was especially frustrating. I wanted to play around with different inking techniques here. I'm glad I saved my layout scan because my first go at inking this was terribly ruined. I had to print out a new layout and start all over. I'm really happy with how it turned out. The dry brush clouds is something I'd like to do again. Fun stuff, folks!

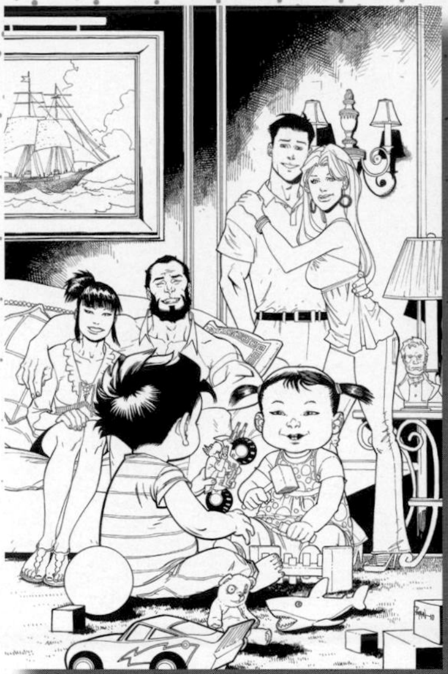

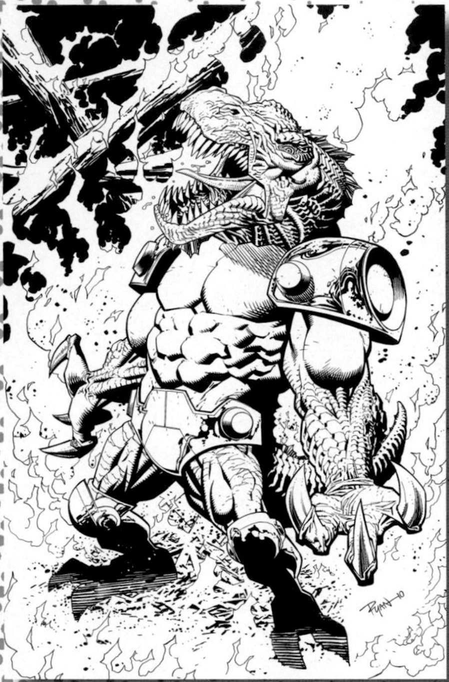

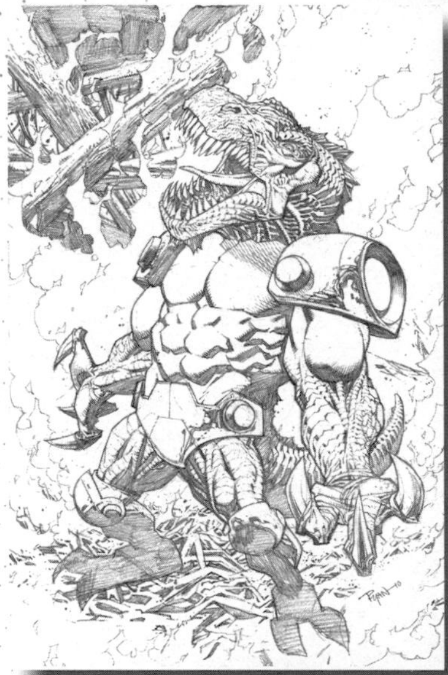

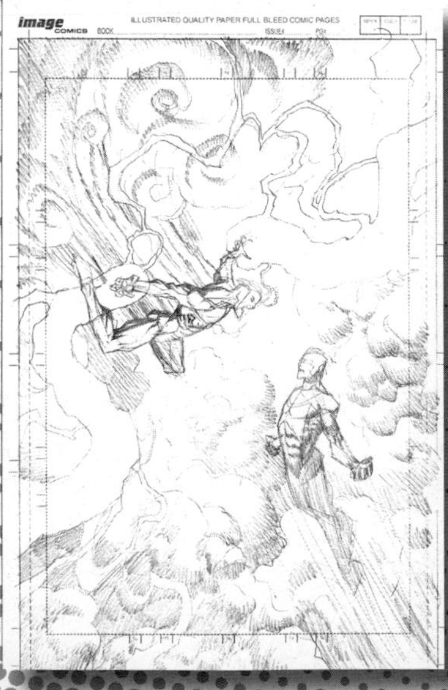
image
COMICS
ILLUSTRATED QUALITY PAPER FULL BLEED COMIC PAGES

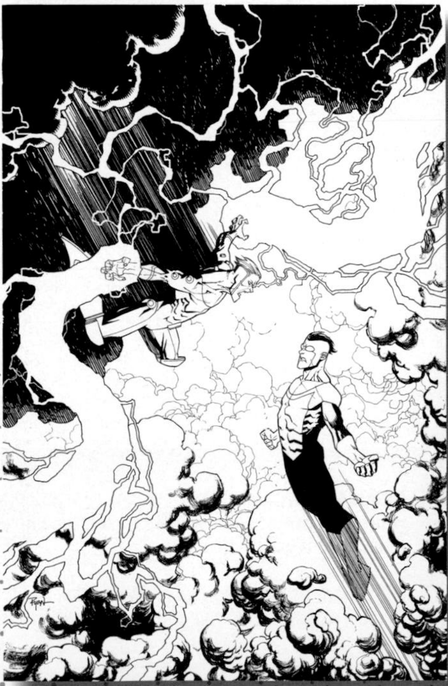

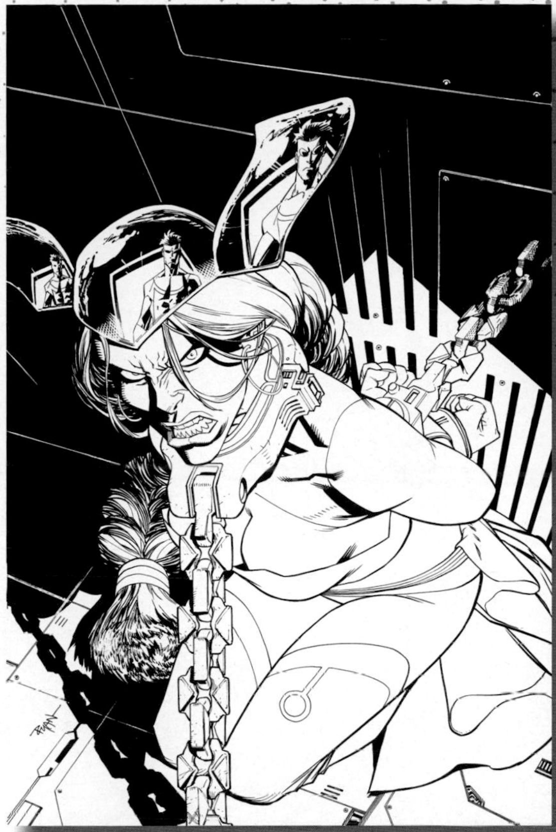
RYAN

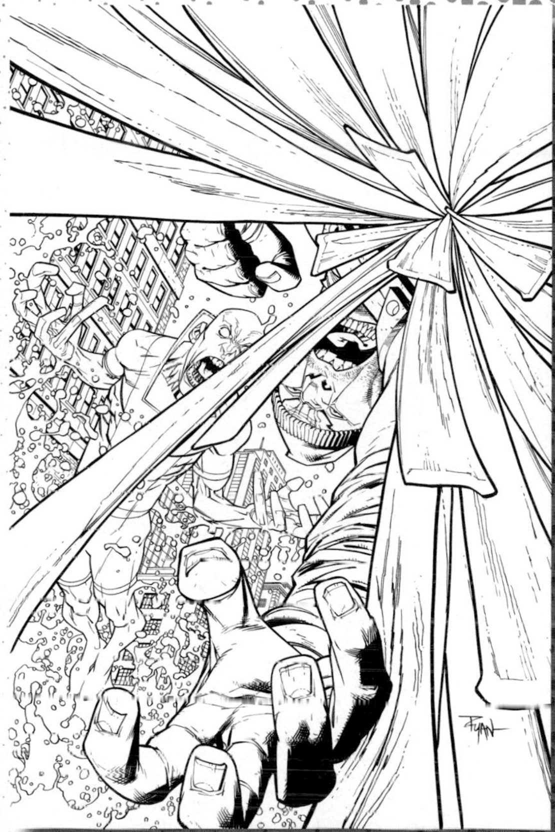
RYAN

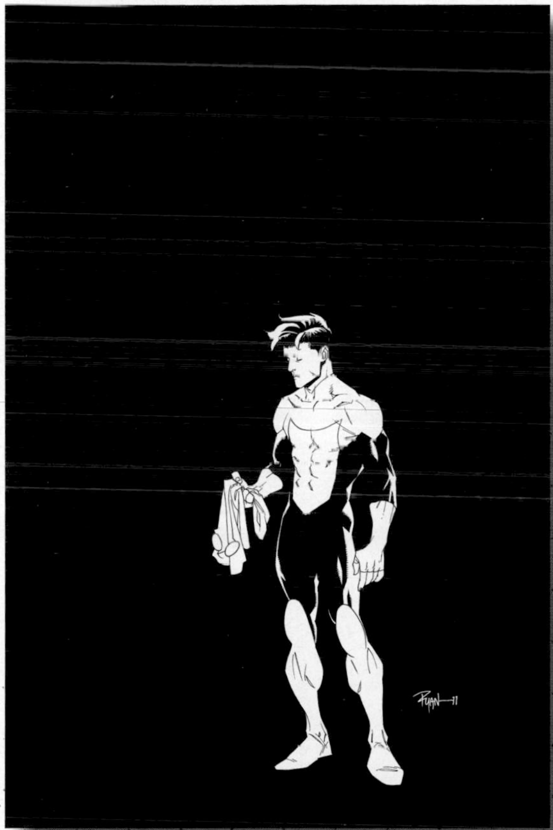
RYAN '11

KIRKMAN: Here's some more cool covers. Ryan, tell the boys and girls some inside info on these fine gems!

OTTLEY: What the, didn't I do thumbnail sketches of these covers Robert?! I know I did! BAH! I've failed again. They're probably in a drawer under a stack of papers somewhere. Sigh. Don't fire me.

Oh and 84, easiest cover ever!

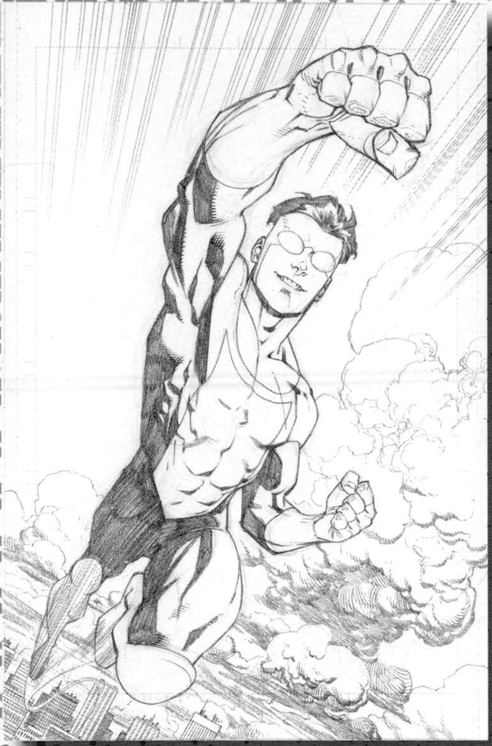

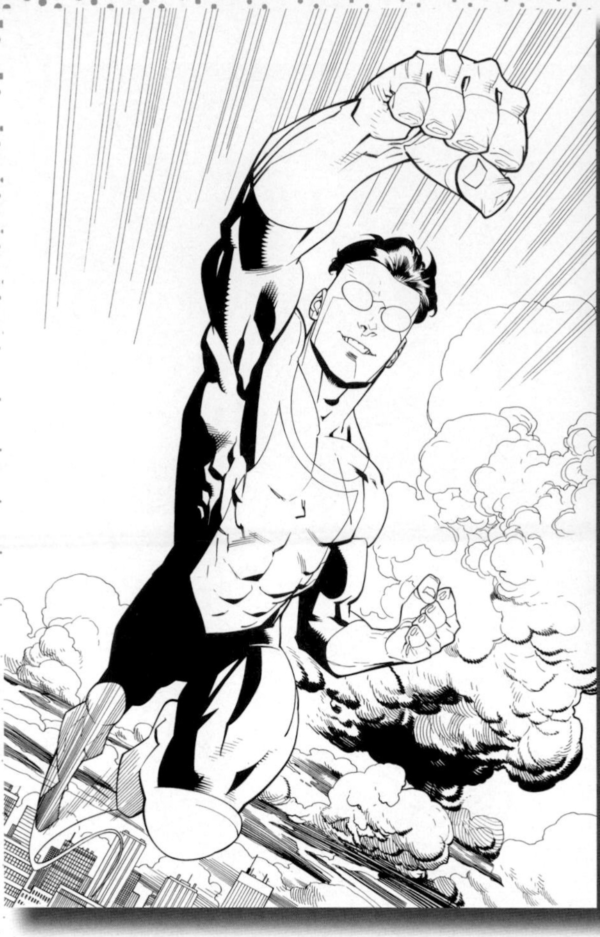

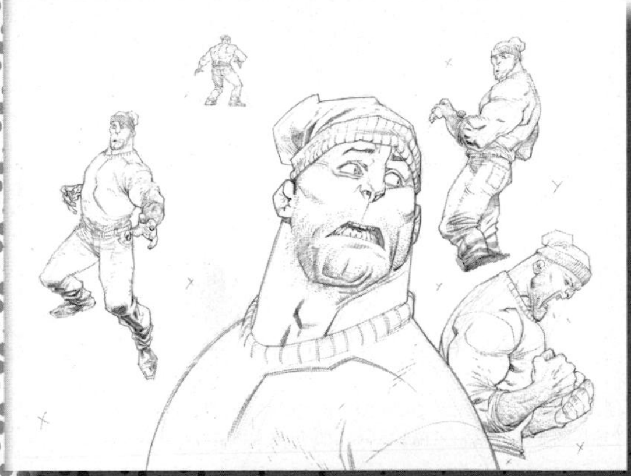

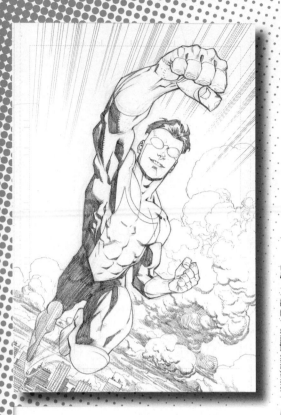

KIRKMAN: Some interior pages. Ryan--what's the story here?

OTTLEY: I really enjoy drawing faces like Tether Tyrant's. I always pictured him like an ex boxer, cauliflower ears, Kind of swollen around eyes and upper cheeks. Tough as nails. And his goofy rough face with stubble. Always a blast to draw. Sadly no one has ever asked for a Tether Tyrant sketch at a convention. Ah well, the bubble gum strands were a bit lame though. I like the new look for sure!

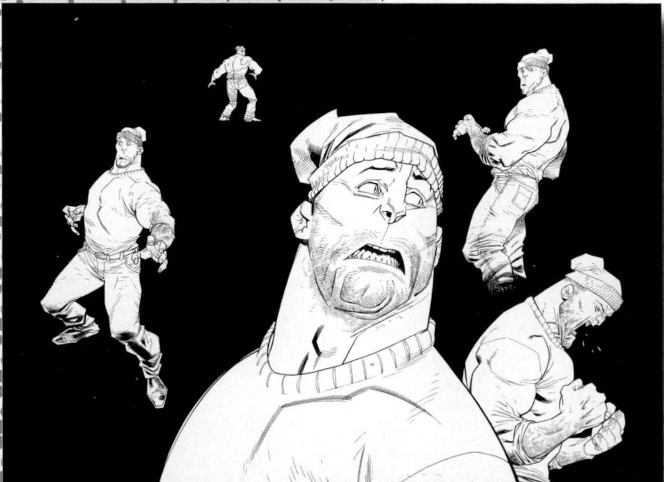

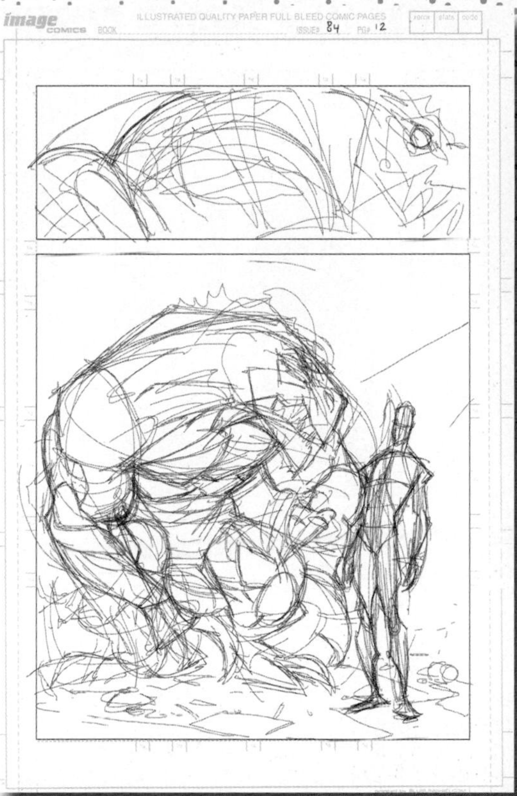

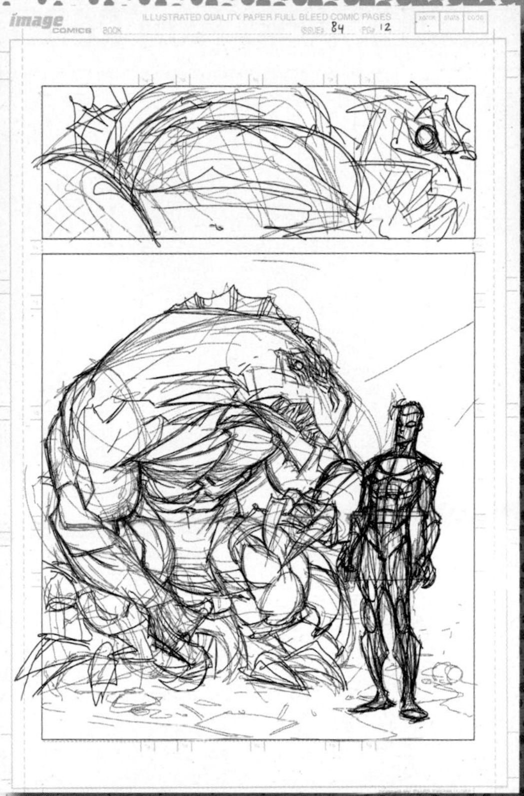

KIRKMAN: Another great page from Ryan Ottley. Two questions: 1. Does it get old being so awesome all the time. And 2. How cool is Dinosaurus? I mean really?

OTTLEY: 1. No. 2. Way.

Here Is more of the digital process. First one is a quick layout, second I tighten things up a little, defining chapes. Just enough info to give myself so I when I print this off I can just start penciling. Then I send it off to Cliff for inks! Woo comics!

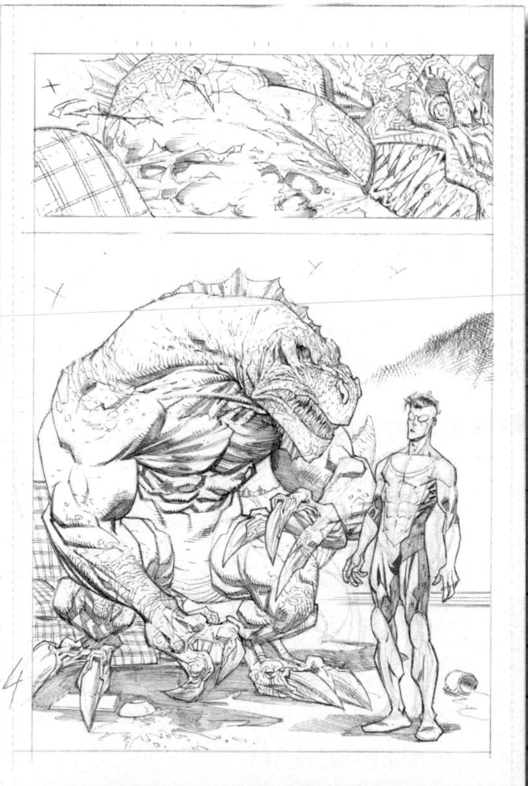

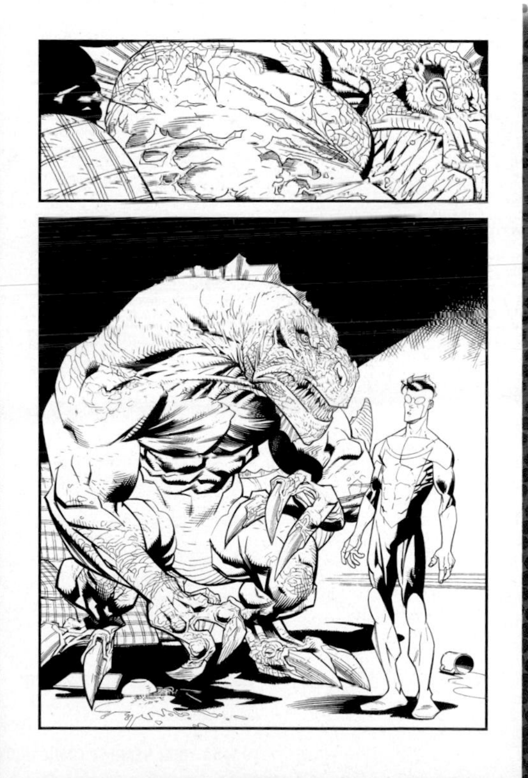

MORE GREAT BOOKS FROM ROBERT KIRKMAN & IMAGE COMICS!

PULLO McFARLANE GLAPION
AUNT
2
ROBERT KIRKMAN THE ROB LIEFELD
INFINITE
VOLUME ONE
KIRKMAN • OTTLEY • RATHBURN • RAUCH
INVINCIBLE
VOLUME FIFTEEN
GET SMART
ROBERT KIRKMAN CHARLIE ADLARD CLIFF RATHBURN
THE WALKING DEAD
WE FIND OURSELVES

THE ASTOUNDING WOLF-MAN

VOL. 1 TP
ISBN: 978-1-58240-862-0
$14.99
VOL. 2 TP
ISBN: 978-1-60706-007-9
$14.99
VOL. 3 TP
ISBN: 978-1-60706-111-3
$16.99
VOL. 4 TP
ISBN: 978-1-60706-249-3
$16.99

BATTLE POPE

VOL. 1: GENESIS TP
ISBN: 978-1-58240-572-8
$14.99
VOL. 2: MAYHEM TP
ISBN: 978-1-58240-529-2
$12.99
VOL. 3: PILLOW TALK TP
ISBN: 978-1-58240-677-0
$12.99
VOL. 4: WRATH OF GOD TP
ISBN: 978-1-58240-751-7
$9.99

BRIT

VOL. 1: OLD SOLDIER TP
ISBN: 978-1-58240-678-7
$14.99
VOL. 2: AWOL
ISBN: 978-1-58240-864-4
$14.99
VOL. 3: FUBAR
ISBN: 978-1-60706-061-1
$16.99

CAPES

VOL. 1: PUNCHING THE CLOCK TP
ISBN: 978-1-58240-756-2
$17.99

HAUNT

VOL. 1 TP
ISBN: 978-1-60706-154-0
$9.99
VOL. 2 TP
ISBN: 978-1-60706-229-5
$16.99

THE INFINITE

VOL. 1 TP
ISBN: 978-1-60706-475-6
$9.99

INVINCIBLE

VOL. 1: FAMILY MATTERS TP
ISBN: 978-1-58240-711-1
$12.99
VOL. 2: EIGHT IS ENOUGH TP
ISBN: 978-1-58240-347-2
$12.99
VOL. 3: PERFECT STRANGERS TP
ISBN: 978-1-58240-793-7
$12.99
VOL. 4: HEAD OF THE CLASS TP
ISBN: 978-1-58240-440-2
$14.95
VOL. 5: THE FACTS OF LIFE TP
ISBN: 978-1-58240-554-4
$14.99
VOL. 6: A DIFFERENT WORLD TP
ISBN: 978-1-58240-579-7
$14.99
VOL. 7: THREE'S COMPANY TP
ISBN: 978-1-58240-656-5
$14.99
VOL. 8: MY FAVORITE MARTIAN TP
ISBN: 978-1-58240-683-1
$14.99
VOL. 9: OUT OF THIS WORLD TP
ISBN: 978-1-58240-827-9
$14.99
VOL. 10: WHO'S THE BOSS TP
ISBN: 978-1-60706-013-0
$16.99
VOL. 11: HAPPY DAYS TP
ISBN: 978-1-60706-062-8
$16.99
VOL. 12: STILL STANDING TP
ISBN: 978-1-60706-166-3
$16.99
VOL. 13: GROWING PAINS TP
ISBN: 978-1-60706-251-6
$16.99
VOL. 14: THE VILTRUMITE WAR TP
ISBN: 978-1-60706-367-4
$19.99
VOL. 15: GET SMART TP
ISBN: 978-1-60706-498-5
$16.99
ULTIMATE COLLECTION, VOL. 1 HC
ISBN 978-1-58240-500-1
$34.95
ULTIMATE COLLECTION, VOL. 2 HC
ISBN: 978-1-58240-594-0
$34.99
ULTIMATE COLLECTION, VOL. 3 HC
ISBN: 978-1-58240-763-0
$34.99
ULTIMATE COLLECTION, VOL. 4 HC
ISBN: 978-1-58240-989-4
$34.99
ULTIMATE COLLECTION, VOL. 5 HC
ISBN: 978-1-60706-116-8
$34.99
ULTIMATE COLLECTION, VOL. 6 HC
ISBN: 978-1-60706-360-5
$34.99
THE OFFICIAL HANDBOOK OF THE INVINCIBLE UNIVERSE TP
ISBN: 978-1-58240-831-6
$12.99
INVINCIBLE PRESENTS, VOL. 1: ATOM EVE & REX SPLODE TP
ISBN: 978-1-60706-255-4
$14.99
THE COMPLETE INVINCIBLE LIBRARY, VOL. 2 HC
ISBN: 978-1-60706-112-0
$125.00
THE COMPLETE INVINCIBLE LIBRARY, VOL. 3 HC
ISBN: 978-1-60706-421-3
$125.00
INVINCIBLE COMPENDIUM VOL. 1
ISBN: 978-1-60706-411-4
$64.99

THE WALKING DEAD

VOL. 1: DAYS GONE BYE TP
ISBN: 978-1-58240-672-5
$9.99
VOL. 2: MILES BEHIND US TP
ISBN: 978-1-58240-775-3
$14.99
VOL. 3: SAFETY BEHIND BARS TP
ISBN: 978-1-58240-805-7
$14.99
VOL. 4: THE HEART'S DESIRE TP
ISBN: 978-1-58240-530-8
$14.99
VOL. 5: THE BEST DEFENSE TP
ISBN: 978-1-58240-612-1
$14.99
VOL. 6: THIS SORROWFUL LIFE TP
ISBN: 978-1-58240-684-8
$14.99
VOL. 7: THE CALM BEFORE TP
ISBN: 978-1-58240-828-6
$14.99
VOL. 8: MADE TO SUFFER TP
ISBN: 978-1-58240-883-5
$14.99
VOL. 9: HERE WE REMAIN TP
ISBN: 978-1-60706-022-2
$14.99
VOL. 10: WHAT WE BECOME TP
ISBN: 978-1-60706-075-8
$14.99
VOL. 11: FEAR THE HUNTERS TP
ISBN: 978-1-60706-181-6
$14.99
VOL. 12: LIFE AMONG THEM TP
ISBN: 978-1-60706-254-7
$14.99
VOL. 13: TOO FAR GONE TP
ISBN: 978-1-60706-329-2
$14.99
VOL. 14: NO WAY OUT TP
ISBN: 978-1-60706-392-6
$14.99
VOL. 15: WE FIND OURSELVES TP
ISBN: 978-1-60706-392-6
$14.99
BOOK ONE HC
ISBN: 978-1-58240-619-0
$34.99
BOOK TWO HC
ISBN: 978-1-58240-698-5
$34.99
BOOK THREE HC
ISBN: 978-1-58240-825-5
$34.99
BOOK FOUR HC
ISBN: 978-1-60706-000-0
$34.99
BOOK FIVE HC
ISBN: 978-1-60706-171-7
$34.99
BOOK SIX HC
ISBN: 978-1-60706-327-8
$34.99
BOOK SEVEN HC
ISBN: 978-1-60706-439-8
$34.99
DELUXE HARDCOVER, VOL. 1
ISBN: 978-1-58240-619-0
$100.00
DELUXE HARDCOVER, VOL. 2
ISBN: 978-1-60706-029-7
$100.00
DELUXE HARDCOVER, VOL. 3
ISBN: 978-1-60706-330-8
$100.00
THE WALKING DEAD: THE COVERS, VOL. 1 HC
ISBN: 978-1-60706-002-4
$24.99
THE WALKING DEAD SURVIVORS' GUIDE
ISBN: 978-1-60706-458-9
$12.99

REAPER

GRAPHIC NOVEL
ISBN: 978-1-58240-354-2
$6.95

SUPER DINOSAUR

VOL. 1
ISBN: 978-1-60706-420-6
$9.99
DELUXE COLORING BOOK
ISBN: 978-1-60706-481-7
$4.99

SUPERPATRIOT

AMERICA'S FIGHTING FORCE
ISBN: 978-1-58240-355-1
$14.99

TALES OF THE REALM

HARDCOVER
ISBN: 978-1-58240-426-0
$34.95
TRADE PAPERBACK
ISBN: 978-1-58240-394-6
$14.95

TECH JACKET

VOL. 1: THE BOY FROM EARTH TP
ISBN: 978-1-58240-771-5
$14.99

TO FIND YOUR NEAREST COMIC BOOK STORE, CALL: 1-888-COMIC-BOOK

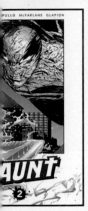

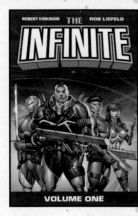

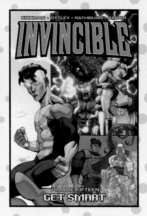

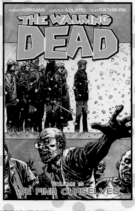

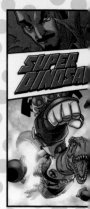